Also by
AMI McKAY

The Birth House
The Virgin Cure

THE
WITCHES
OF
NEW
YORK

AMI McKAY

First published in Great Britain in 2016
by Orion Books,
an imprint of The Orion Publishing Group Ltd
Carmelite House, 50 Victoria Embankment
London EC4Y 0DZ

An Hachette UK Company

1 3 5 7 9 10 8 6 4 2

A CIP catalogue record for this book
is available from the British Library.

Interior images: (feathers) © mart, (raven with key and roses) © Eisfrei,
(paper background) © design36, (phases of the moon) © Magnia,
all Shutterstock.com
Teapot, art nouveau woman, moth, raven, Egyptian advertisement taken from
3800 Early Advertising Cuts © Dover Book
Flourishes of various styles, floral borders, flowers taken from
Graphic Ornaments © The Pepin Press

ISBN (Trade Paperback) 978 1 4091 4351 2

Printed and bound by CPI Group (UK) Ltd, Crydon, CR0 4YY

www.orionbooks.co.uk

For Mary Ayer Parker
who was hanged at Gallows Hill,
September 22, 1692

A rebel! How glorious the name sounds when applied to a woman.

Oh, rebellious woman, to you the world looks in hope.

Upon you has fallen the glorious task of bringing liberty to the earth and all the inhabitants thereof.

MATILDA JOSLYN GAGE

Resist much, obey little.

WALT WHITMAN

THE
WITCHES
OF
NEW
YORK

September 4, 1880.

New Moon.

City of Wonders.

IN THE DUSKY haze of evening a ruddy-cheeked newsboy strode along Fifth Avenue proclaiming the future. "The great Egyptian obelisk is about to land on our shores! The Brooklyn Bridge set to become the Eighth Wonder of the World! Broadway soon to glow with electric light!" In his wake, a crippled man shuffled, spouting prophecies of his own. "God's judgement is upon us! The end of the world is nigh!"

New York had become a city of astonishments. Wonders and marvels came so frequent and fast, a day without spectacle was cause for concern.

Men involved themselves with the business of making miracles. Men in starched collars and suits, men in wool caps and dirty boots. From courtrooms to boardrooms to the newsrooms of Park Row; from dockyards to scaffolds to Mr. Roebling's Great Bridge—every man to a one had a head full of schemes: to erect a monument to genius, to become a wizard of invention, to discover the unknown. They set their sights on greatness while setting their watches to the drop of the Western Union Time Ball. Their dreams no longer came to them via stardust and angel's wings, but by tug, train and telegraph. Sleep lost all meaning now that Time was in man's grasp.

In the building beneath the tower that held the time ball, a mindful order of women sat—side by side, row on row, storey upon storey, one hundred young ladies in all, working round the clock to translate the wishes of men to dots and dashes. Transfixed by the steady *click-clack* of their task, the ghost of Mr. Samuel Morse hovered near. He'd tried to get to Heaven on numerous occasions, but could never seem to find his way past the tangled canopy of telegraph lines that criss-crossed the skies above Manhattan. What he needed was an angel, or better yet, a witch. Someone to translate the knocks and rappings of his soul, to convey all the things he'd left unsaid. Where could one be found? Were there any left?

In a halo of lamplight near the Western Union Building, a prostitute leaned her aching back against the bricks. Lips rouged, eyes rimmed with charcoal, she was waiting for a man. Puffing on a cigarette she'd begged off a stranger, she blew a steady stream of smoke rings in the air. At the edge of her sight, a shadowy figure in the shape of a fine-dressed gentleman appeared—five feet off the ground, coattails flapping in the breeze. Rubbing her eyes, the girl shook her head, thinking she'd had too much to drink. She swore, hand to God, she'd get off the booze one day, not now, of course, maybe in the spring.

As the ghost dissolved from her view, the girl flicked the stub of her cigarette to the ground and crushed it with the heel of her boot. Hand in her pocket she reached for a trinket she'd been given by her last john. "A lucky rabbit's foot," he'd said, "blessed by a bona fide witch." "Liar," the girl had complained when he'd offered her the charm along with half of what he was supposed to pay. "No, no, no," the john had insisted. "I tell you, she was *real* . . . a real witch with a very fine ass." With that, the girl had grabbed the trinket and sent the john on his way. Something was better than nothing. She needed all the help she could get.

Stroking the soft fur of the rabbit's foot, the girl thought of all she lacked. She was tired, she needed sleep, but she wanted more booze. When she glanced at the spot where she'd snuffed out the butt, there was a shiny new dime in its place. Picking the coin off the ground, she wondered if maybe the john had been right after all. Maybe the damn foot was lucky. Maybe the witch was real. Maybe her luck had changed because the john had dipped his willy in a witch and then dipped it in her, leaving behind some strange magic. There were worse things she could catch, she guessed.

In the shadow of the Great Bridge, a young widow knelt to plead with the river. Just after supper she'd spied something terrible in the soapy murk of her dishwater, a vision she'd seen once before, and she'd just as soon forget. Each time she closed her eyes, it came to her again—a man's face, bloated and blue, gasping for air. The last time she'd seen it, it'd been her husband's. This time it was a stranger's.

"I understand," the woman said to the river, touching the surface of the water with a finger. "I know how it feels to be slighted." She also understood that the river required payment from those who wished to cross it. Blood, flesh and bone were what it liked best. The widow didn't have much of anything to give as an offering—a few pennies, a splash of whiskey, the cheerful tune of an ancient song—but she hoped that if she were gentle, persuasive and kind, the river might change its mind. Was it witchcraft she was plying? She didn't care so long as it worked. Something had to be done. Something was better than nothing.

In the cellar of a modest house on the edge of the Tenderloin, a weary housekeeper lit a candle and said a prayer. Taper in one hand, glass jar in the other, she poured wax around the edge of the jar's lid to seal it shut. The jar—filled with stale urine, old needles, shards of mirror, brass buttons, bent nails and thirteen drops of blood from her left thumb—was what her wise grandmother had called a "witch's bottle." While others might call it humbug, the housekeeper saw the jar and its contents as her last hope to dispel the strange darkness that'd settled in her midst. What else could explain all that'd happened since the master of the house had passed? For weeks she'd been plagued by what she thought was a ghost or, perhaps, a demon, lurking in her room, stealing her sight, shaking her bed, night after night. What did it want? Where had it come from? Why wouldn't it leave her alone? Prayers, hymns and a desperate stint of almsgiving hadn't driven it away. She feared the terrible thing wouldn't rest until it saw her dead. Had she been cursed? Something had to be done. As her grandmother would say, *Wo gibt es Hexen, gibt es Geister.* Where there are witches there are ghosts.

In a quiet corner of a cozy teashop just shy of Madison Square Park, a magnificent raven sat on a perch, preening its feathers. As the bird tugged and fussed at its wing, three women conversed around a nearby table—one, a lady of considerable wealth, the others a pair of witches, keepers of the bird and the shop.

"Can you help?" the lady inquired, worry catching in her throat. "I'm at my wit's end. Something must be done."

One witch answered with a confident, "Of course."

The other humbly replied, "Leave it with us."

The raven cast an indifferent eye upon them. He'd witnessed this sort of thing before—the woman, unable to manage her affairs, needed a witch (or two) to make things right. That was all fine and good, but he was more interested in a faint sound coming from overhead, an enchanting jangle akin to when prisms on a chandelier touch. But how could that be when there was no chandelier to be found in the shop? He was certain unexpected magic was afoot.

Tea was poured, complaints and concerns heard, sympathy given. Crystal ball and grimoire consulted. Palms and tea leaves read. How pleased the bird was when he noticed the tray of teacakes in the centre of the table had barely been touched. How pleased the lady was when the witches presented her with a small package tied with red string.

The lady was sure she felt something move within the parcel. A tiny tremor of mystical vibration, perhaps? A sign of things to come? She'd heard rumours from a friend of a friend that these women could work miracles. She prayed it was true. She wanted to believe. Lowering her voice, she said, "You swear this thing has been touched by witchcraft?"

One of the women gave a polite nod and said, "Of course, my dear, of course."

The other replied with a smile and a shrug. "Call it what you like."

The raven simply cocked its head. It was all he could do not to laugh.

By Knot of One.

THIRTY-SIX MILES UP the Hudson as the crow flies, a young woman stood atop the widow's walk of a grand house in Stony Point. To the east lay the silhouettes of ships' masts and church towers beneath the first stars of night. The girl was looking for signs of change—in the skies, in the weather, in her heart.

"Starry. Crisp. Clear," she pencilled in a small notebook. Licking the tip of her finger, she raised it above her head to check the direction of the wind. *Nothing unusual*, she thought. *Nothing unusual ever happens here.* "NW wind," she wrote beside her other observations. "No sign of rain."

Bright and bored at seventeen, Beatrice Dunn longed for her life to take an extraordinary turn. She had no reason to think such a thing would ever happen—still, she hoped, she prayed, she wished.

She knew, from reading yellowed copies of *Scientific American* and *The Old Farmer's Almanac*, that the slightest shift in chemistry, in temperature, in the atmosphere, in the stars, could bring about tremendous transformation. An avalanche begins with a sound or a misplaced step. Gunpowder explodes with the tiniest of sparks. One flaw in a steam boiler can lead to catastrophe. Lightning can be conjured inside a jar. From time to time Beatrice made lightning of her own by scuffing her feet on the rug in her room and touching her finger to one of her iron bedposts. A sharp charge of static would run through her hand as her nightgown clung to her skin, and the tiny hairs along the back of her neck rose to attention. Occasionally the taste of metal fizzled in her mouth. It was a childish act, she supposed, but it thrilled her nonetheless. If only she could find a spark to set the tinder of her days ablaze.

She'd read in the *New York Herald* that great changes were set to sweep the world in the coming days.

Strange, malefic times (whatever cynical people may say to the contrary) are soon to begin, due to the presence of an immense planetary influence not seen on the Earth for two thousand years. The vitality of every living thing will be subjected to extraordinary pressures. Surely miracles and mayhem will arise in its wake.

To prepare for whatever might come her way, Beatrice had begun keeping track of things that couldn't be explained. Charting every instance of the miraculous that appeared in the news, she faithfully logged them in her notebook as she did the weather, noting the hour of their occurrence, as well as the phase of the moon. She aimed to measure the rate of the inexplicable, the temperature of strange.

According to her records thus far, instances of unnatural phenomena had risen substantially in the last month. Most notably within the city of New York.

AUGUST 1—*Woman Has Premonitions of Death.*
AUGUST 5—*Doppelgänger Seen on Delancey Street.*
AUGUST 10—*Girl Thrives Without Food or Drink.*
AUGUST 15—*Ghosts Haunt the Fifth Avenue Hotel.*
AUGUST 20—*Accusations of Witchcraft Abound.*

To Beatrice, such accounts were deliciously compelling—not only for the fantastic stories they held, but for the many questions they raised.

What is the weight of a soul? Where does it go when we die?
Are there such things as ghosts?
Can they speak to the living?
What of spirits, demons, fairies and angels?
Can dreams hold portents, visions, foretellings?
Are witches real?
Does magic exist?

Night after night, kitchen shears in hand, she'd sit at her desk clipping squares and columns of newsprint to pin to the walls of her room. Printed matter from *Vennor's Almanac*, *Scientific American*, *The Ladies' Companion*, *Frank Leslie's Illustrated Newspaper*, *New York Saturday Journal*, *The Fireside Library* and *Madam Morrow's Strange Tales of Gotham* soon crept across the rose-patterned wallpaper, replacing blossoms and stems with headlines, illustrations and odd bits of news.

Even the advertisements intrigued her. *Find God! Find your match! Find your fortune in the west! Become an expert in calligraphy, telegraphy, engraving, pottery, telepathy, mesmerism, clairvoyance, embroidery, pianoforte, violin. Charm lessons, five cents! Discover the ancient art of getting what you wish!* The back pages of every newspaper were peppered with the calling cards of mediums, clairvoyants, seers and mind readers, boasting the ability to converse with spirits, predict the future, find lost treasures, conjure true love. *Madam Morrow the Astonisher. Miss Fortuna the Lucky. Mrs. Seymour. Madame Prewster. Miss Adelaide Thom.* Was it possible for one city to contain so many mystics? Beatrice was counting the days until she could discover the truth for herself. Twelve days, thirteen sleeps.

RESPECTABLE LADY SEEKS DEPENDABLE SHOP GIRL.

Must be well versed in sums, etiquette, tea making and the language of flowers.
Room and Board provided.
Candidates will be considered on one day ONLY
September 17, 1880   One to five o'clock

TEA AND SYMPATHY.

933 Broadway, New York, New York.
Those averse to magic need not apply.

Beatrice had spied the notice while combing through the latest issue of *Harper's Weekly*. As soon as she'd seen it, she'd felt it was meant for her. Even though she guessed there'd be other girls who'd feel much the same, she couldn't imagine that any of them were half as qualified as she was. Had they read *Flowers and Flower-lore* by Reverend H. Friend, cover to cover? Did they have an aunt who was as staunch about the proper preparation of tea as her aunt Lydia? She doubted it, especially when it came to the latter. Her proficiency with sums was excellent, her appetite for wonder insatiable. She'd need to brush up on her etiquette, but she could do that quite easily with a quick re-reading of *How to Behave*.

If she didn't get the job, then she'd simply march down Third Avenue to the Cooper Union and enroll in their women's course on telegraphy. She'd already committed Mr. Morse's code to memory by practicing the longs and shorts of it on the end of a ruler she'd rigged with elastic to the edge of her desk. If her quest to become a telegrapher failed, then she'd return to her aunt's house in Stony Point, the place she'd called home for the last seven years, and resign herself to a safe, secure and predictable life.

Was she nervous?

-.-- . ... (Yes.)

Was she frightened?

-. --- (No.)

She'd travelled to New York first as a child, holding fast to her mother's hand and then, after her parents' passing, once a year in the spring with Aunt Lydia by her side. This time, however, there'd be no frantic rush to find the perfect hat, no fretting over fumes from the train aggravating her aunt's lungs, no worry about getting there and back in a day. This time she was going alone, and she was going to stay. Although she cared for her aunt and would miss her dearly, she relished the thought of being someplace Lydia wasn't.

Their relationship had been brought about by a vigorous strain of smallpox that'd swept through Albany in the summer of 1873. Beatrice, just shy of her tenth birthday, was the only person in her house to survive. Not long after her parents had died, the court had appointed her mother's sister, Lydia Floss, to serve as Beatrice's guardian "until such time as Miss Dunn is legally wed, or turns nineteen." With quiet composure, Lydia had collected Beatrice's belongings, then whisked the girl away to the Floss family homestead in Stony Point. "Nothing here but blue skies, green pastures and hard-working folk," Lydia had told the girl. "I can't remember the last time someone fell ill or came to any harm." They'd lived there, just the two of them, in a house so large that even their shadows occasionally got lost.

Beatrice was given proper clothes to wear, healthful food to eat, a roof over her head. Aunt Lydia, the beneficiary of her family's estate, and a spinster by choice, had always shown Beatrice a great deal of interest and respect, and, when occasion called for it (on birthdays, at Christmastime, on the anniversary of her parents' deaths), an appropriate amount of affection. Lydia had raised Beatrice in the way she wished she had been raised, by teaching the girl to pick up books because of a love of learning (rather than a desire for praise), to do good deeds because of an enduring belief in kindness (rather than a fear of God's wrath). While the other girls in Stony Point were braiding one another's hair and spreading schoolyard gossip, Beatrice had preferred to sit by the fire (or in summer, under a willow tree in the back garden), reading and making figures between her fingers with a loop of string— cat's whiskers, cup-and-saucer, owl's eyes, the witch's broom. When girls her age began pairing off with young men at dances and church socials, Lydia had encouraged Beatrice to look beyond the altar by handing her tracts from teacher's colleges and nursing schools, with words of encouragement scrawled in the margins.

Fortune favours the prepared mind.

Beauty seeks attention. Intelligence commands it.

As an ardent follower of Miss Susan B. Anthony, Lydia believed the only path to a woman's betterment was through making her own way. If that path led Beatrice away from Stony Point, then so be it.

With that in mind, Beatrice had told Lydia of her plans over her aunt's favourite breakfast (poached eggs, rosehip tea and toast with blackberry jam). Much to the girl's surprise, Lydia hadn't balked in the slightest. She hadn't lectured her about the dangers of the city, or warned her about seducers and swindlers lurking around every corner. If Beatrice hadn't known better, she might've thought Lydia was happy to see her go. In the end, her aunt had given her blessing in the best way she knew how. "According to Miss Anthony," she'd said, "'the girl who is able to earn her own living and pay her own way should be as happy as anybody on earth.' There's no match for the sweetness independence brings. Nothing would make me happier than to see you succeed."

Staring at the sky, Beatrice thought, *Thirteen sleeps before my departure. How lucky am I?* "Luck," of course, according to her aunt, "is what happens when preparation and opportunity collide." What then of magic, Beatrice wondered, of destiny, of kismet?

She'd recently read an account of a strange charm being found by a farmhand in the rafters of a run-down cottage outside of Tarrytown where a witch was supposed to have lived. It'd been fashioned from the simplest of things—a length of string, a few ratty feathers and six stray hairs (probably from the witch's head). Nine knots had been tied along it, to secure the feathers and hair. When a farmer's wife from the next house over had been asked by a newspaper reporter if she'd ever seen the likes of such a thing before, she'd eagerly replied, "Yes, indeed I have! 'Tis a witch's ladder, for healin' the sick, protectin' loved ones, cursin' yer enemies or gettin' what you wish. It contains some of the strongest magic there is. Once the spell's complete, its magic will be stored in the charm forever. So long as the ladder remains whole, so too will the magic. There's a rhyme that goes along with it, to help the spell set. Would ye like to hear it?"

Taking three black feathers, a length of string and six strands of red hair from her own head, Beatrice began tying knots to secure her wish, reciting the farmwoman's verse as she went.

By knot of one, my spell's begun.
By knot of two, it will come true.
By knot of three, so may it be.
By knot of four, this power I store.
By knot of five, my spell is alive.
By knot of six, the spell I fix.
By knot of seven, the future I'll leaven.
By knot of eight, my will be fate.
By knot of nine, what's done is mine!

She hoped the farmer's wife was right. She hoped the magic would prove true. She wanted to believe—in miracles, in fate and in witches too.

Twelve days. (Thirteen sleeps.)

Those averse to magic need not apply.

September 17, 1880.

Full Moon.

The time between first and second sleep is neither slumber nor waking. Too much dark and your mind will stay at rest, too much light and your dreams will surely flee. Use this time wisely—for writing spells, summoning spirits, and most importantly, remembering your dreams. Queens have been crowned, schemes hatched, fortunes gained, demons defeated, lovers found—all from visions born in the stillness of the night. In dreams, our souls are given the eyes of Fate. **Dreams must be encouraged by all possible means.**

—*From the grimoire of Eleanor St. Clair*

Between Sleeps.

ELEANOR ST. CLAIR was fast asleep—a pair of silver scissors tucked under her pillow, a sprig of lavender tied to the post of her bed. The scissors were for protection against curses and other dark magic; the lavender, to foster sweet dreams. As the clock in the shop below her moved through its hourly dance, gears clicking, pendulum ticking, hammer poised to strike, Eleanor stirred, but didn't wake. The clock, as if it meant to take pity on the tired woman, slowed to a stop just shy of two. Adelaide Thom, Eleanor's partner and friend, had forgotten to wind it again.

Moonlight shone in the windows of the building where Eleanor slept. Nestled between Markowitz's Bakery and the ticket office for the Erie Railroad, the unassuming storefront was easy to miss. The awning was faded, its crank frozen with rust. The door was in need of a fresh coat of paint. The sign above it, a simple placard with modest letters painted in cerulean, read: ST. CLAIR AND THOM, TEA AND SYMPATHY. EST. 1879. To most passersby, the place was neither remarkable nor inviting. To a select society of ladies who spoke the right words and asked the right questions, it was a place of whispered confessions and secret cures—a refuge run by women they could trust.

The crippled awning and peeling paint were of no consequence to Eleanor, who saw no need to attract undue attention from zealots, skeptics or the law. Assisting women through their difficulties carried certain risks. A young female doctor from the Women's Infirmary had been thrown in the Tombs by Anthony Comstock and his Society for the Suppression of Vice for fashioning pessaries from bits of sea sponge and silk floss (Distribution of Contraceptive Devices). A bookseller, who'd sold copies of *Fruits of Philosophy: The Private Companion of Young Married People* from behind his counter, had met a similar fate (Distribution of Obscene Literature). The abortionist Madame Restell, considered by some to be a saviour, by others a sinful hag, had slit her own throat to avoid two years of hard labour. Apothecaries no longer carried French safes or "preventative powders" for fear that Comstock would shutter their shops.

Women who found themselves in trouble were left to their own devices, or worse yet, to quackery. Mail-order medicines under the guise of vegetable compounds, regulating elixirs and an assortment of pills (renovating, periodical, Catholic and lunar) promised to "restore female regularity, remove weakness of the stomach, dissolve unwanted uterine growths." While clever language allowed their makers to avoid the long arm of Comstock, the packages in which their remedies were delivered could easily be intercepted and destroyed. Even when the item arrived safely and was used accordingly, there was no assurance a product would make good on its boasts. "Desperate times make for desperate women," Adelaide had quipped. "And desperate women with rich husbands mean more money for us."

But Eleanor hadn't gone into business with Adelaide for the money. In her eyes, their venture was more about duty than due. While Adelaide had been born a creature of the city, Eleanor had been born in a humble cottage on the banks of the Bronx River. Her mother, Madame Delphine St. Clair, was a keeper of spells, a *gardien de sorts*, so Eleanor had spent her childhood learning to embrace the traditions of her ancestors: growing herbs, keeping bees and mixing potions. She'd come from a long line of wise women that stretched back to the shores of Normandy and to the woman after whom she'd been named—who, in her mother's words, "had been twice a queen as well as a witch." Eleanor's mother had also taught her to carefully guard her gifts. "Always needed, ever hunted," was her motto—spoken each day before rising, written in the margins of her grimoire, carved into the wood of her daughter's cradle beneath the family crest. She told Eleanor, "A shepherdess sees to the care and feeding of her flock, a seamstress sees to the cut of a lady's dress. Witches see to things best sorted by magic—sorrows of the heart, troubles of the mind, regrets of the flesh. This is what we do. That is who you are."

Delphine had left Paris for New York in the spring of 1848 after yet another revolution had rocked France. Newly pregnant and alone, she'd settled in the cottage on the edge of her brother's farm and waited for her husband (and her baby) to arrive. Eleanor was born late that December, but Madame St. Clair never saw her husband again. Her brother had kept her and her new baby fed by sharing any surplus he had from the farm, and she'd provided the rest of whatever she needed for herself and Eleanor by offering her services to the women of the surrounding countryside, dubbing her little home "l'Hermitage."

Once a month, she'd bundle Eleanor in blankets and paddle a little rowboat down the river to deliver bottles and jars of her concoctions to a handful of apothecaries in the city. Over the years Eleanor became as much apprentice as daughter, happy to learn all she could about tinctures, elixirs and the traditions of the "cunning folk."

For a time, she'd abandoned those ways, choosing to leave home and study at the Women's Medical College in Manhattan, but when her mother had taken ill not quite a year into her studies, Eleanor had returned to l'Hermitage to care for her in her dying days. In the two years since Madame St. Clair's passing, Eleanor hadn't once considered going back to school. What she'd learned of modern medicine had only made it clear to her that the lessons her mother had taught her were the ones she held most dear. Honey infused with saffron, cinnamon and horny goat weed makes an effective aphrodisiac. A tonic of valerian, mugwort and poppy heads promises deep sleep and sweet dreams. A pastille containing liquorice, skullcap and chasteberry tames an aggressive lover's lust. A mix of rose petals, lavender, lemon balm and hawthorn berries soothes a broken heart. Red clover, oatstraw, nettle and red raspberry ready a woman's womb for child bearing. Tea brewed from tansy keeps a woman's blood on course. Tansy failing, there are other herbs that can bring things around: black cohosh, milkweed, pennyroyal, oarweed, Queen Anne's lace. Or, as her mother liked to sing, "Parsley, sage, rosemary and thyme . . ." Whenever Eleanor was concocting a batch of this or that, Adelaide preferred to sing a different sort of tune: "Buds, berries, leaves and roots . . . keep a girl healthy, wealthy and loose!"

Eleanor could only wish her task was as simple as that. For every woman who sidled up to the shop counter wishing to have her heart mended, her beauty increased, her lover made true, her courses stayed or started, there was a host of enchantments, incantations and charms for Eleanor to keep in mind. "Of all the creatures under Heaven," her mother used to say, "women are, by far, the most perplexing. It stands to reason that the path to solving their troubles is just as convoluted. Travel it with care, my dear. No matter a lady's concerns or burdens, be they heavy as a millstone or light as a feather, every word she speaks must be heard, every tear she sheds considered."

Over the years, Eleanor kept track of the lessons she'd learned by recording them in a large leather-bound book she'd been given by her mother, a grimoire grown so thick, the binding was split. The first time she'd brought the thing out in Adelaide's presence, her friend had cringed at the sight of it.

"It won't bite," Eleanor had teased, caressing the book's cover. "Cross my heart, hope to die."

Sheepishly, Adelaide had replied, "I've seen it, it's seen me, that should be enough."

Adelaide was young yet, twenty-one to Eleanor's thirty-two, and she'd already suffered more than her share of sorrow. Still, the young woman's quick wit, sense of style, head for business and keen intuition made her the ideal partner—the perfect complement to Eleanor's unkempt braids, stained apothecary's apron and brilliantly cluttered mind. Eleanor's only quibble with the girl was that she hadn't yet accepted the truth of who she was—a seer filled with untold promise, a wise-woman in the making. If only Adelaide would stop hiding behind the ratty deck of fortune-telling cards she kept in her pocket, and embrace the gifts that so clearly had been passed on to her in her blood. In all her life, Eleanor had never met anyone who could peer so thoroughly into the minds and hearts of others as Adelaide could, yet remain so oblivious to the truth in her own.

"Don't be so hasty to dismiss true magic," Eleanor had advised after Adelaide had recoiled from her grimoire. "Your gifts are stronger than you think."

"Stop plying me with your hocus-pocus," Adelaide had said. "I'm not like you, and my mother was most certainly not like yours. I'm just a girl from the wrong side of Chrystie Street, born to a slum-house mystic who lived on petty schemes and poppy juice. The only thing my mother ever gave me was reason to doubt her."

"You shouldn't speak ill of the dead."

"She never spoke well of me, unless you count the night she sold me away."

"Don't talk like that . . ."

"Fine," Adelaide had said. "I wouldn't want to give you the morbs."

"Honestly, Adelaide, you should take these things seriously."

"Oh, but I do," Adelaide had said, giving the grimoire a sideways look.

"I could teach you how to use it," Eleanor had offered. "I'm sure you'd be a quick study."

Adelaide had flatly refused. "Women come to me when they wish to hear what they already know. They come to you when they want a miracle. I'll stick with turning cards, if it's all the same to you. It's easier that way."

"Someday what's easy might not be enough," Eleanor had warned.

With a smile and a shrug Adelaide had replied, "When that day comes, you'll be the first to know."

They bickered sometimes but they were fast friends; two strong-willed women who refused to conform to society's expectations. Just after New Year's 1879, Eleanor had received a letter from a former medical school colleague. *I thought this might be of interest to you,* the last line of her note had read. Attached was an advertisement for a private nurse's position in the city. Thinking a change might do her good, she'd shuttered her mother's cottage and headed for the city with a bag full of tinctures and her pet raven. Adelaide Thom would prove to be the most exasperating patient she'd ever cared for, and, next to her raven, her most loyal friend.

Resting on a bamboo perch near the head of Eleanor's bed, the witch's pet raven ruffled his feathers and peered into the darkness. Squinting at his mistress, the bird wondered when she might wake. He recalled a time in the not so distant past when she'd wake in the middle of each night without fail to light a candle, sit by his side and tell him her dreams. The bird remembered every last one of her visions, no matter how odd or insignificant they'd seemed. How long had it been since she'd last risen in the night? Was she ill? Had she been cursed? Or perhaps, the raven wondered, had man's misguided ambition made the city around them shine too bright? How distracting the sparkle of their false lights was at night, their world barely fit for anything, most especially dreaming.

He'd been opposed to leaving the countryside, but it hadn't been his choice to make. He'd promised her mother that he'd stay by Eleanor's side, no matter what. The great sorceress was dead, so the promise was no longer negotiable. He often wondered if Eleanor, too, missed the mossy banks of the river, the sound of frog song in the evening, the sweet buzzy chorus of cicadas rising and falling in the dark.

He tried to rouse her by tapping at the gold band that rested around his leg, an ancient ring that bore the inscription, "Alle my trvst." *Tap, tap, tap,* he rapped persistently. *Tap, tap, tap.*

Pulling her pillow over her head, Eleanor gave the bird a gentle scolding. "Perdu!" she grumbled. "Let me sleep!"

Perdu, from the French, meaning stray or lost, generally reserved for things such as dogs, husbands and hope. If the bird ever had another name, he couldn't remember what it was.

"Wake up," he chortled, soft and low. "Wake up, wake up, wake up . . ."

Eleanor did not obey.

Poor thing, thought the bird. *How tired she must be. The world is too much with her.*

The raven was not alone in his concern.

As Perdu sat and wished for the company of his mistress,

two shadowy beings stood at the foot of her bed. They, however, wished for Eleanor to remain asleep.

At first blush, the strange creatures might've been mistaken for a pair of guardian angels. Made from equal parts memory, mischief, goodwill and longing, they belonged to an ancient order of Fay who involved themselves exclusively with the fashioning of dreams. Eleanor, who'd never seen one face to face, had been taught to refer to them collectively as the Dearlies, a name her mother had assigned to them in hopes that her daughter might take kindly to the peculiar creatures and their work.

"Is that truly what they're called?" Eleanor had asked, when she was nose-high to her mother's hip.

"No," Madame St. Clair had answered, "but they must keep their true name a secret from the dreamers they assist. A person may read or write the name, but if they speak it, they'll never dream again."

Flitting to Eleanor's side, one Dearly took hold of the edge of her blanket with its nimble fingers. Then stealing under her covers, it laid its head on her chest.

"What are you doing?" the second Dearly asked, following close behind.

"Hush!" the first Dearly scolded. "I'm measuring the space between her heartbeats."

"Why for?"

"To calculate her willingness, to see when the time is right."

"To give her the dream?" the second Dearly inquired. To this point in his life (short by Dearly standards, yet biblical by mankind's), he'd only been allowed to tend to the dreams of dogs. He'd been terribly good at it, though, earning himself the name Twitch, on account of his ability to inspire a great deal of tail thumping, whimpering and muffled yelps in the canines under his care.

"Yes, of course, to give her the dream," the first Dearly replied. "We've only got one chance to get it right." This Dearly was called Bright, due to her vast intelligence, and because whenever demons were about, she glowed with a vibrant blue light.

Plucking a whorl of lavender from the stems tied to Eleanor's bed, Twitch went about the business of preparing the air so the woman's dream might take. Chewing on the flower's buds until his breath was laced with their scent, he readied himself to send the aroma through a tiny clay pipe pointed in Eleanor's direction.

"Move closer," Bright instructed with an impatient wave of her hand. "She hasn't got the nose of a Chien de Saint-Hubert." Always aware that a person's surroundings are what prepare the mind for dreaming, Bright used every trick she held in her practical, sturdy rucksack of a brain to assist her in her work—from casting bits of spider's silk on Eleanor's eyelashes to clipping the wings off a fly that buzzed too near. Just as a master mason takes great pains in constructing a wondrous cathedral, so too did Bright take the utmost care in crafting Eleanor St. Clair's dream. She checked the loft of Eleanor's pillow and cooled its surface by fanning it with her wings, determined that this night, above all others, her charge's sleep would be held together with flying buttresses of stone, rather than wattle and daub.

"How will we know if it's worked?" Twitch interrupted, now sitting cross-legged atop a bedpost, puffing away on his pipe.

"We won't," Bright answered, shaking her head, "not until we do."

"In a second, in a minute, in an hour, in the morning?"

"Not until we do."

"All will be well," Twitch announced, in an effort to bolster his wavering confidence. "This will be good, my friend, you'll see."

"You shouldn't say such things," Bright said with a sigh. "And don't count yourself my friend just yet. A wise Dearly never speaks of success."

Rolling his eyes, Twitch teeter-tottered his head. "What's the harm, I say. It's never hurt me yet."

"There are other forces at work besides ours," Bright warned. "Don't forget that."

Like Perdu, Bright had been with Eleanor since the day she was born, and she, too, was worried that something had come between the wise-woman and her dreams. What else could explain Eleanor being stuck in her sleep, night after night? Bright figured the trouble might have been caused by the grief that still lingered in Eleanor's heart over a love affair that'd gone wrong, not to mention the overall harried nature of her life. Recently she'd started talking in her sleep, sighing over holding too many secrets and mumbling complaints against the landlord. Whatever the cause of Eleanor's distress, Bright was determined to carry on as best she could. If only she could speak to Eleanor directly, she'd tell her that she was truly sorry for her troubles. Grief, regret and demons were among the most difficult problems to banish, as they had a terrible tendency to hover between a dreamer and her Dearlies. Madame St. Clair had always blamed such troubles on the Devil, claiming, "Satan never sleeps. He stays awake so he can order his demons to mix more straw into the wheat." Bright didn't know much about the Devil, and believed him to be more invented than real, but she understood quite a lot about demons. They were evil, occasionally smart and always happy to interfere with people's dreams.

"Will she remember the dream when she wakes?" Twitch asked.

"If we've done it right," Bright replied.

"Do you think she'll tell the bird?"

"Perhaps."

"Is that good?"

"Yes."

"Will it do what needs to be done?"

"Dreams aren't bound by wants or needs. Dreams do as they please."

The vision Bright tucked inside Eleanor's mind was simple, elegant and brief. Meaning to transport the woman far from her cares, Bright conjured a hill in the dark of night, surrounded by an ancient landscape that Eleanor had never seen, yet knew in her blood. At the top of the hill a great bonfire burned, built from an enormous scaffold of twisted sticks and branches. Its flames climbed high into the night sky, hissing and crackling, and sending up sparks. Overhead the moon looked helplessly on as moths dove and spun and sizzled to their deaths.

Perdu was there, too, perched in a craggy yew tree, just steps from the fire. Spreading his wings and opening his beak, he let out a surly *caw*. The glow of the fire shone in his eyes, and smoke curled from his tongue.

Before long, a young woman entered the dream, approaching from the shadows. Circling the fire, she sang a tune under her breath, much like a child who wished to banish her fears.

May you rise with the sun, ready to make hay.
May the rains come at night to wash your cares away.

May you sleep with the angels sittin' on your bed.
May you be an hour in Heaven a' fore the Devil
knows you're dead.

Bending low, she crouched in front of the fire, her pale skin and copper-coloured hair illuminated by its flickering light. With a curious sense of calm she reached out her hand and plucked an ember from the centre of the flames. Cradling it in her palm, she turned and held it out to Eleanor.

"You must help her," Bright whispered in Eleanor's ear, mimicking her mother's voice. "Two is good, but three is better. She is the first of many."

Before Eleanor could act, the girl was consumed in a tumult of flames. When the fire threatened to devour Eleanor as well, Perdu flew from the tree and covered her eyes with his wings. With that, the vision was gone.

"Is it done?" Twitch asked, hovering over Bright's shoulder.

"Yes," Bright answered, "it's done."

Twitch snuck behind Perdu, steadied himself on the raven's tail and yanked hard on one of the raven's feathers. "Ready or not, it's begun!"

Flapping and spitting, Perdu let out a loud squawk.

Eleanor woke with a start. In her confusion she thought she smelled smoke, but soon realized a gust of wind had whistled down the chimney pipe, kicking up a sudden whirl of cold ashes in the room's iron stove. Sitting up, she struck a match, lit a candle and tried to hold on to what was left of her dream. To her dismay, all that remained was the sensation of feathers brushing against her cheek, a fleeting glimpse of the girl's face, and the overwhelming sense that no matter how hard she tried, she'd always be too late to save her.

"Douce?" Perdu said with a gentle coo. *Douce*, his name for her, from the French meaning soft, gentle and sweet (generally reserved for things such as melodies, candies, animals, cakes and sometimes little girls).

Eleanor beckoned to the bird and said, "Come here, old friend."

Perdu cooed again, and hopped to her side.

Tenderly stroking the tiny feathers that graced the top of the raven's head, she asked the bird a question she'd often asked her mother in her youth. "How old is Perdu?"

"Older than you," the bird replied with a throaty chuckle.

Her mother had sworn a thousand times over that it was Perdu who'd taught Eleanor to speak. "He's older and wiser than you and me and all our mothers." Eleanor had never imagined her mother's words could be true, even though she'd always wished them to be.

"Was that you?" she asked her pet. "In my dream?"

Perdu gave a solemn nod.

"Did you see the girl clearly?"

He nodded again.

"Don't forget her," Eleanor said. "Remember the girl."

Cocking his head, Perdu repeated her instruction. "Remember the girl."

As Eleanor returned Perdu to his perch, the Dearlies looked on from behind a coal scuttle, waiting for their chance to leave.

"You should apologize to Perdu," Bright said, wagging her finger at Twitch. "Tell him you meant no foul."

Twitch gave her a confused scowl. "Why should I?" he asked. "He's just a harmless bird."

"He's not harmless," Bright warned, her cheeks turning blue. "And he's no bird."

SHE KNOWS ALL, SEES ALL, TELLS ALL!

ZULA MOTH

Mind Reader.
Seeress.
Matchless Beauty.

PAST. PRESENT. FUTURE.

Come see her foretell the fate of those
who dare to inquire!

Exclusive to Dink's Palace of Illusions,
Houston and Bowery—New York, New York.

The Girl Who Knows.

ADELAIDE THOM BEGAN the day by readying herself to read the minds of others. Dressed in an elegant day suit of blue watered-silk (bustle high, waist cinched, lace cuffs buttoned around her wrists), she seated herself at a small dressing table near the window in her room. She recited no incantations, cast no summoning spell. The only rituals the young seer performed were pinching colour into her cheeks, tugging a comb through her hair, patting rouge onto her lips.

Gone were the trappings of her days as a sideshow sweetheart on the Bowery—the wild, unruly Circassian curls, the fine embroidered robes from "the Orient," her image and the moniker ZULA MOTH printed on countless posters and cartes-de-visite. *Easy come, easy go*, she thought as she stared at a faded photograph pinned above her looking glass. *I'll never see that girl again.*

Her work at the Palace of Illusions had been a clever deception, invented by the theatre's owner, Mr. Thaddeus Dink. Each night before Adelaide would come out on stage, the impresario had rapped his cane on the boards and exclaimed, "From the depths of a squalid slave market in the dark heart of Constantinople comes a girl so alluring, so mysterious, you'll wonder if she's real. I implore you, dear friends, to pinch yourselves—you're not dreaming. Once she's in your presence, who knows what might occur!"

Adelaide's enormous halo of curls had been achieved by washing her hair with stale beer. The costumes she'd worn had been fashioned by a seamstress who'd dressed wax figures at the dime museum next door—General Washington crossing the Delaware, President Lincoln at his moment of death, Bloody Mary seated on her throne, Joan of Arc tied to the stake. Even Adelaide's stage name was only half hers—and that half had questionable origins as well, supposedly whispered to her father by a mythical pear tree that'd once stood at the corner of Thirteenth and Third. *Call the child Moth*, the twisted tree had said to him, its branches bending low, leaves brushing against his ear. The tree was long gone, as was her father, so she couldn't query either of them. Had she ever believed the tale to be real? Yes, when she was little (and sometimes still, whenever a rare south wind rustled through the leaves of the locust trees in Madison Square Park). Whether the tale was true or not didn't matter much anymore. Adelaide was simply glad to have one pleasant childhood memory to call her own.

By the age of thirteen she'd been sold three times over—first, by her mother as a lady's maid, then by a brothel madam as a child whore, then by Mr. Dink as a Circassian Beauty—all in the space of a year.

She'd fought hard to make her way from the run-down tenement where she'd been born to the rooms of a well-appointed suite on Gramercy Park, but her struggles hadn't ended there. On New Year's Day 1879, her life had taken a devastating and tragic turn, leading her to move house and change her name again. She'd chosen *Adelaide*, because she'd thought it to be a more respectable form of "Ada" (the name her mother had wanted to give her at birth), and *Thom*, because she'd wanted a name that would remind her of who she'd been without giving herself away.

Surveying her reflection in the mirror she said her name aloud as if it were an invocation to a prayer. "Adelaide Thom," she whispered, savouring the sound of it as it tumbled off her tongue.

Miss Adelaide Thom

MIND READER. SEERESS. WITCH.

Daily consultations at St. Clair & Thom — Tea & Sympathy
Evenings by appointment

Adelaide next rehearsed her smile. Eye soft, lips together. Yes, that looks best. Something that'd once come so naturally now required effort. Putting her hand to her face, she traced the taut, wormy borders of her misfortune, a sinewy web of scars that ran from nose to ear, brow to chin, down the left side of her face. Where her left eye had been was a hollowed wink, a gruesome puckered dimple. With the tip of her finger she gave her cheek a gentle nudge in an attempt to return it to its proper shape. This was to remind herself of how she wished to appear—less crooked, more sincere.

"Half past eight and all is well!" Eleanor's voice echoed up the stairs. This was her not-so-subtle way of letting Adelaide know she was about to open the shop. On this particular morning, however, the cheerful greeting was swiftly followed by the din of shattering crockery.

"*Merde*!" she heard Eleanor exclaim, followed by the sound of a stomping foot.

"Everything all right?" Adelaide called.

"No worries," Eleanor replied. "I'm fine. All's well."

With that, Perdu let out a shrill whistle. "Top off the pot!" he cried. "Top off the pot!"

"Quiet, you insufferable heap of feathers!" Eleanor scolded. "This is your fault, for not letting me sleep."

The bird gave a penitent coo.

Adelaide stayed put listening as Eleanor took up her broom and swept the remains of a broken teapot into a metal dustpan. With each rattle and scrape, the left side of Adelaide's mouth quivered, eventually finding its way into an uncontrollable frown. Would the day ever come when she'd no longer be unnerved by the sound of something shattering? Even when a clumsy child dropped her penny-lick on the pavers, or a young rough tossed an empty bottle to the gutter, she could not curb her reaction. Worst of all were the times when the sound occurred only in her mind. Holding her breath, she waited for the memories that came along with the sound to pass, knowing they wouldn't leave until she'd relived them.

She'd been standing on the sidewalk in front of her house on Gramercy Park, waiting for a hansom cab. Normally, she would've waited inside until the driver called at the door, but she'd been invited to a New Year's soiree at Delmonico's and she didn't want to be late. Pulling her wrap around her shoulders, she'd bowed her head against the brisk wind. She hadn't noticed the young woman in the hooded cloak coming at her, clutching a bottle.

"Fucking witch!" the woman had cried, throwing vitriol in Adelaide's face.

In the next instant Adelaide felt the acid burning her flesh, she heard the bottle breaking. The last thing she remembered was the woman's figure slipping out of sight.

If she believed in God, then she might've also believed that what happened was punishment for her sins. How many transgressions had she committed in her short life? God only knew. Lusting, thieving, lying—she'd done more than a bit of each. Or maybe what she'd been punished for was living an unconventional life. She was a New York woman through and through, rather than a lady. She did as she pleased, went where she wanted. She laughed immoderately, adored the music of Offenbach and shunned the Women's Christian Temperance Union. She rode by herself on streetcars and elevated trains. She went to the theatre, the opera house, the concert hall—alone. She took strolls through the fashionable (and unfashionable) parts of town, unattended. She'd had her share of rivals, but she'd done her best to ignore them—sideshow performers who'd resented the fact that she'd been "made" a freak (and a beautiful one at that) rather than born one, soothsayers and skeptics who'd tried (and failed) to uncover the secrets of her trade, jealous wives who'd resented her failure to share their addiction to domesticity.

Thank heavens her attacker had been caught and promptly shuttled off to Blackwell's Island. The cruel madwoman turned out to be someone she knew, but barely—a magician's assistant who'd briefly been part of the sideshow and then was cut loose. Adelaide couldn't say what she'd done to incur the girl's wrath. She couldn't remember ever getting in her way.

If not for the kind soul who'd promptly come to her aid— washing her face with snow, helping her to her feet, getting her swiftly and safely to Bellevue and into a surgeon's hands— who knows what might've been her fate? She'd been told that as she lay on the table of the operating theatre, a wondrous, inexplicable thing had occurred. After the morphia, ether and iodine, after the skillful plucking of her eye and the careful stitching of what little eyelid remained, after the tidying of the remaining flesh of her cheek, she'd died on the table. Evidently the shock of it all had done her in, and the surgeon, finding no pulse, had instructed his assistant to note the time. No sooner had the young man reached into his pocket to retrieve his watch than Adelaide had gasped and jerked back to life, caus- ing the doctors assembled around her to startle and scratch their heads. She'd laughed when she'd first learned of it, rel- ished the thought of their puzzled faces. How perfect that she should give her greatest performance on such a stage, with her blood weeping into the sawdust strewn about the floor.

Flowers and well wishes arrived in the days after the inci- dent, first at the hospital and then at Adelaide's home as she lay sequestered in her bed. Her dearest, oldest friend, Dr. Sadie Fonda-Hetherington, came all the way from Ocean Grove to see to her every need. But as soon as Adelaide had been able to dress herself and make a cup of tea, she'd turned to her friend and said, "It's time for you to leave."

"Come stay with me," Sadie had urged. "James and I will take good care of you. There's plenty of room to spare."

"Heavens no," Adelaide had replied. "I'll frighten your children out of their wits."

"Are you sure?" Sadie had asked, shaking her head. "I've no doubt you can look after yourself, but won't you be lonely?"

"Pity doesn't sit well with me. It causes too much commotion. It makes me a nervous wreck. There's only so much mending I can do in the company of friends."

Within a week of Sadie's departure, a knock came at the door, and Adelaide had answered it to discover a woman standing on her stoop with a leather gripsack full of tinctures in one hand, and a birdcage with a sulking raven in the other.

"I'm Eleanor St. Clair. I'm here in response to the ad in the *Evening Star*," she had announced.

"What ad?" Adelaide had asked.

"This one," Eleanor had replied, handing over a feathery bit of newsprint.

PRIVATE NURSE DESIRED.

**Knowledge of wound care,
nervous ailments and the
pharmacopoeia required.**

Reply to: PO Box 314 Ocean Grove, New Jersey

Room and board provided.

"I didn't place this," Adelaide had said, returning the paper to its owner.

"No," Eleanor had replied, brushing past Adelaide and into the house's foyer, "but the woman who did said you'd say precisely that. She also said that I should tell you, 'There's no sense arguing, the deed is done.'"

It'd never occurred to Adelaide to flee the city after the destruction of her beauty. Even if she had, New York would've refused to let her go. She felt now, more than ever, that the city wasn't done with her, or she with it. If there ever was a place where one could start again, it was Manhattan. Move a block, and your enemies become your friends. Move ten blocks and you might never see anyone you knew again. She'd gained a new costume, as it were, complete with a mask that could never be removed, and she'd soon learned there were advantages to that sort of thing as well as to calling herself a witch. In their gawking and their pity, people made themselves quite vulnerable. She saw more clearly now with one eye than she ever had with two—people's desires, fears, hopes, dreams and sins were laid bare before her, plain as day. With that in mind she'd come up with the notion of opening the teashop. Eleanor had resisted the plan at first, but after some persuading she'd finally agreed to it. "You'll be the Tea," Adelaide had said, "I'll be the Sympathy." They'd started their venture the previous autumn selling tea, potions, advice and fortunes to the women who shopped on Ladies' Mile.

She could hear Eleanor still shuffling about downstairs, muttering under her breath. Adelaide couldn't tell if it was in response to Perdu, or just a symptom of being over-worked. More and more she'd noticed that Eleanor was exhausted at the end of the day—that her shoulders slumped and her eyes looked tired. Seeing her that way had made her wonder what she would have done without Eleanor. She owed so much to the woman and their friendship. That's why she'd decided to take a page from Dr. Sadie and placed an ad of her own for a shop assistant in *Harper's Weekly*, the *Evening Star* and the *New York Times*. As Eleanor went about her morning ritual of sprinkling salt and tea leaves across the threshold to keep the ghosts at bay, Adelaide hoped that what she'd done might serve as a bit of magic to help lighten Eleanor's load.

Placing her hat on her head, she tilted the brim slightly forward and to the left. *Less crooked, more sincere.* Gingerly draping the hat's scalloped veil in front of her face, she took a deep breath and set her mind on the task ahead. The pro-spective shop girls would be arriving just after noon. How many? God only knew. Surely one of them would suit. She'd know the right one when she saw her, she was sure of that. Someone with spark. Someone they could trust. Someone to help Eleanor in her work, without being a pest.

Just as she was about to make her way downstairs, the familiar scent of cherry liqueur filled the room. Pungent and sweet, it was a scent that Adelaide had always associated with her mother. This sort of thing had happened from time to time since the attack (coming out of the blue, like the mysterious sounds she heard in her head), but it'd never been this strong or seemed so close, and it'd never occurred in the shop. Perhaps Eleanor's magic couldn't keep the ghosts away after all.

"Is that you, Mama?" Adelaide asked, not really expecting an answer. "If it's you, give me a sign."

As quickly as the scent had come, it vanished.

Go on with you then, Adelaide thought. *You won't like what I have to say.* In death, as in life, Adelaide's mother was largely absent. Whenever Adelaide had tried to address her spirit—out of grief, out of anger, out of curiosity, out of desperation—she'd never gotten so much as a boo from the other side. All she wanted from her was the answer to one question: *Did you ever regret selling me away?* Once, in her frustration she'd asked Eleanor if she'd be willing to help her contact her mother's ghost, but Eleanor had firmly replied, "I can't help you with that."

"You can't, or you *won't?*"

"Those who can properly converse with the dead are rare. Anyone who dares to dabble in such matters without proper knowledge is dreadfully misguided. The laws that govern the dead are not the same as ours."

"Have you tried? I'm sure you could do it."

"That's not how it works."

"How do you know?"

"I just do."

After that, Adelaide had chosen to pursue the matter on her own. She'd read many articles, attended countless lectures, even sought out mediums she'd read of in the paper in hopes that she might find at least one of them to be real. She hadn't been home last night to wind the clock because she'd gone to Washington Square to visit Mrs. Seymour, a woman who reportedly acted as a conduit for spirit. But when she'd gotten there, the woman's husband had said she was gone. "Good riddance, too!" he'd roared. "I was about to ship her off to the lunatic asylum on Blackwell's Island." Disappointed, Adelaide had put off going home, choosing instead to wander the city in pursuit of other, more pleasurable, spirits.

"Will you be coming down anytime soon?" Eleanor called up the stairs. "Your tea is getting cold."

"Be right there," Adelaide replied.

Opening the top drawer of her dressing table, Adelaide brought out a delicate, heart-shaped bottle. Where it once had contained a generous dose of fine French brandy, it now held the glistening, floating orb of her left eye. Putting her lips to the glass, she kissed it and made a wish, "May the right girl appear, today."

"Careful what you wish for," her mother's ghost chirped from behind the eye in its watery little chamber, silent to Adelaide's ears.

THE GREAT OBELISK

The Egyptian monument commonly known as "Cleopatra's Needle" is due to make landfall in Manhattan today. In anticipation of the next leg of the three-thousand-year-old obelisk's journey, it was moved yesterday evening up the Hudson to a dockyard at Ninety-Sixth Street via a pair of sturdy pontoons. Although the Needle, a seven-storey, two-hundred-ton piece of granite, arrived from Alexandria aboard the SS *Dessoug* in late July, the obelisk was left in the ship's hold at the dock at Staten Island until such time as the tide might conspire to carry it ashore.

CLEOPATRA'S GUARD

Even while the obelisk was settled in the ship's hold, eager curiosity seekers came in great numbers to see it. Unable to delay their enthusiasm, the visitors balanced upon a series of planks supported on dinghies in order to board the vessel. Upon reaching their destination, the visitors were greeted by a solemn-faced, smartly dressed watchman holding a lighted candle who led them into the dark region of the ship where the obelisk lay. "What a strange fellow!" one visitor remarked. "He never spoke a word the entire time I was aboard the ship." Rumour has it the watchman was first spotted standing among the ruins when archeologists unearthed the Needle's pedestal and insisted on accompanying the obelisk all the way to

New York. Some say he's not a man at all but rather a mystical *jinni* sent to guard the monument who will vanish when it no longer requires his protection.

A True Survivor

The obelisk has survived many hardships and journeys through the ages—the storming of Heliopolis, an arduous trip down the Nile, an earthquake at Alexandria, and last but not least, a perilous voyage across the Atlantic. Still, there are naysayers who question whether Cleopatra's Needle will ever reach its final resting place in Central Park. If and when it does, will anyone pay it any mind "way up there" on Greywacke Knoll, among the shantytowns and the sparse constellation of mansions that surround the park? Commodore Henry Honeychurch Gorringe, the man in charge of moving the Needle, says they will. So, too, do the multitudes of Freemasons that populate this country, including Mr. William Vanderbilt, who paid a pretty sum to fund the Needle's trip. No doubt these men are especially enamoured with the object, as they believe certain markings found upon it hold great symbolic ties to their order.

The Obelisk Speaks

What significance, if any, does the obelisk hold for the rest of us? What secrets are hidden in the many hieroglyphs carved into the Needle's faces? An expert in translations has confided to the *Daily Messenger* that he believes the glyphs foretell the future of America. Whatever meaning the ancient markings hold, the obelisk has certainly got New Yorkers under its spell.

Beatrice Dunn Takes Flight.

"ONE TICKET FOR the nine-thirty train to New York, please."

"Sorry, miss, the last passenger train left at half past seven."

"The last train for the day? How can that be? Don't they usually run every two hours?"

"They do, but not today. There's an interruption on the tracks."

"What sort of interruption?"

"Don't know."

"Are you sure there won't be any more trains?"

"Well, miss, all I've heard from the head office is that our passenger service is disrupted until further notice. For all I know that could mean today, tomorrow or next week. You can wait here if you like, but I can't make any promises."

Picking up her bag, Beatrice turned from the station agent and looked for a bench where she could sit to sort her thoughts. For weeks she'd had the day mapped out, down to the minute. Was this roadblock a sign that she should turn back? Reaching inside her pocket, she felt for the witch's ladder she'd fashioned from her hair, feathers, string and wishes. Shaking her head over the faith she'd put in the crude little charm, she wadded it up and tucked it deep inside her bag. *Serves me right for believing I could perform even the simplest bit of magic*, she thought. Still, until now, everything had gone right.

8:00–8:40 Breakfast with Aunt Lydia. Oatmeal with stewed apples, tea with honey and milk. Lydia had insisted on it. "Such hearty fare will keep you sated and help to deter motion sickness on the train." Their conversation had been cordial and kind—not too anxious on Beatrice's part, not too sentimental on Lydia's.

"Will you be coming to visit me in the city?" Beatrice had asked, more out of obligation than desire. She knew that Lydia didn't like to travel, that she'd made the annual trip to New York solely on her account, that the speed of the train caused her to fret and that the fumes aggravated her lungs (the faintest hint of smoke in the air could set her wheezing). Still, Beatrice had thought she should extend an invitation to let her aunt know that she'd be missed. "Perhaps you could travel by steamboat instead of train," she'd suggested. "It might do you good to take in the fresh air along the river."

"I've got all the fresh air I need right here," Lydia had countered. "If it's all the same to you, I'd rather stay put. I'm sure you'll get back to Stony Point for holidays."

"Of course I will," Beatrice had assured her. "And I'll write each and every day with all the details of my adventures."

Saying this had made Beatrice feel incredibly guilty, for she knew she'd just told her aunt a terrible lie. There might well be things she'd see or do or say while she was away that she wouldn't wish to share with Lydia. It wasn't that she didn't love and trust her aunt, it was just that she'd reached the point where she believed she should keep certain things private if she was ever truly going to belong to herself. "Those adventures of yours had better be plenty grand," Lydia had teased, bringing a handkerchief to the corner of her eye. Her words had been in jest, but the tears were real.

"Oh they will be," Beatrice had said, kissing her finger and crossing her heart. "I promise." And then she, too, required the aid of a handkerchief. Although she knew Lydia would be fine on her own, she still worried about her. Over the years certain women in Stony Point had been awfully pointed in their opinions about the way Lydia had chosen to raise her. In recent days they'd been quick to play Cassandra, predicting all manner of misfortunes for Beatrice—seduction, illness, injury and so on—all stemming from Lydia's liberal attitudes and her consent to letting her niece go. Beatrice couldn't wait to prove them wrong.

8:40–8:45 Goodbyes. "I'm not one for lengthy farewells," Lydia had announced as she stood next to Beatrice on the wide front porch. Slipping her hand in her pocket, she'd pulled out a lovely silver brooch and pinned it to the collar of Beatrice's coat.

"What's this?" Beatrice had asked, turning the edge of her lapel so she could examine the trinket—a beautiful striped feather encased in a delicate oval of glass.

"It's a wren's feather," Lydia had answered, "for protection and luck. Your father gave it to your mother on the occasion of your birth, but she thought it so precious, she rarely wore it. She gave it to me before she died and asked that I give it to you on a special occasion—such as your wedding or the birth of your first child."

"Maybe we should wait until then," Beatrice had said. "Maybe you should hang onto it for me a little while longer?"

"No," Lydia had responded. "Today's the day."

Fearing she might cry, Beatrice bowed her head and turned

away, thinking helplessly that even proper goodbyes were hard. Lydia had taken great pains to keep her away from her parents in their last days, and although Beatrice no longer harboured any hard feelings towards her aunt over the matter, losing the chance to say goodbye to them had left a mark on Beatrice's heart. Within that mark, dark and deep, lay Beatrice's biggest fear—that one day, when the balance of the life she'd lived with her parents inevitably tipped in favour of her life without them, all her memories of their time together, precious and irreplaceable, would be lost. "Thank you," she'd whispered to Lydia as she'd given the woman's hand a gentle squeeze. "I'll cherish it, always."

8:45–9:00 Stagecoach to Stony Point Station. The stage had been on time, the ride uneventful. Beatrice hadn't brought any trunks to stow and they'd made no stops for other passengers. Lydia had kindly offered to send along anything she might need from home once she was settled, and with that in mind Beatrice had packed only an extra dress (blue calico with velvet trim), a dressing gown, a pair of felt slippers, a cotton chemise, three hair ribbons (red, yellow and blue), a hair brush, a light shawl, an assortment of unmentionables, five handkerchiefs (two lace, three cotton), needles and thread, a bar of lavender soap, a tin of pins, pen and ink, pencils and paper, her book of observations, and the latest issue of *Madam Morrow's Strange Tales of Gotham* for reading on the train. She'd tucked everything neatly inside a sturdy carpetbag that Lydia had given her.

In preparation for the day's travel, Beatrice had pulled her hair into a long braid, and donned a practical dress of dark green broadcloth. Along with black patent leather boots, a light plaid ulsterette and her favourite straw hat, she'd felt her ensemble accentuated her youth without seeming too naïve. The last thing she'd wanted was to appear fresh off the boat. She'd read enough of Madam Morrow's tales to know what happens to girls like that.

As an extra precaution, she'd sewn most of the money she'd saved for the trip into the hem of her petticoat. It wasn't much—enough for a couple nights lodging, and a ticket back to Stony Point—but she couldn't afford to lose it. When the stage had reached the station, she'd carefully handed over what she owed the driver, including a modest tip, and then proceeded to the ticket booth with plenty of time to spare, or so she'd thought.

Sitting on the bench now, she considered her next step. Should she wait for a train that might never come? Should she call it a day and go home? If only she'd come to the station earlier! She'd barely slept all night and had been ready to leave by sunrise. Still, she'd wanted to give Lydia a last morning together. She'd figured that by taking the 9:30 train she'd still be able to get to the teashop before the appointed hour and maybe even be the first in line. How many applicants could there be? She had no idea. All she knew was that the closer she was to the front of the line, the sooner the shopkeeper's search could end, and the sooner her life in the city would start.

"Perhaps we could take the steamboat?" a gentleman's voice suggested. "There's one that leaves at noon from Grassy Point."

Beatrice turned to find that he wasn't speaking to her, but to a woman dressed in a red silk dress whose bonnet was adorned with a matching spray of ostrich feathers.

"I guess it will have to do," the lady sighed, the plumes on her bonnet trembling.

Figuring the steamboat might have to do for her as well, Beatrice rose to follow them.

As they made their way off the platform, a train whistle sounded in the distance. Stopping short, Beatrice waited for it to sound again. The next time the whistle blew it was somewhat closer, and when she looked down the tracks she could see a train approaching the station. Rushing to the ticket window, she rapped on the counter to get the station agent's attention. "What's that train?" she demanded.

"The New York Central."

"When's it set to leave?"

"Ten a.m., but it's freight only."

"Why's it running when the passenger trains aren't?"

"Milk, hay and potatoes don't give a fig if they're on time."

Smoke belching from its engine, the train pulled into the station with a string of boxcars hitched behind it.

Beatrice picked up her bag and turned to leave, walking past groups of farmhands loading heavy cans of milk and barrels of apples. Just as she was about to exit the station, she recognized a young man who was hefting sacks of potatoes, one after another into the dark hold of a boxcar. It was Joseph Wheeler, the eldest son of the owner of one of the largest farms in Stony Point. She and Joseph had gone to school together and their families had held adjacent pews at the Stony Point Presbyterian Church. Beatrice watched as the young man loaded the last of his sacks into the car, then hopped up and stowed a sturdy handcart. When he didn't reappear, she realized he meant to go along for the ride.

"Joe!" Beatrice called. "Joseph Wheeler!" she tried again, feeling like a fool. As she hurried towards the car, she prayed she hadn't been mistaken, that it truly was Joseph she'd seen.

"Beatrice Dunn?" Joseph said when she arrived at the car's door. "What on earth brings you here?"

"I'm going to the city, or at least I was."

As he wiped his brow with his handkerchief, Joseph asked, "Miss your train?"

"Not exactly. The station agent says my train's not running. I couldn't even get a ticket."

"That's a shame," he said with a shrug. "Guess I'll get there before you." He always did like to tease.

"You and your potatoes," Beatrice said.

Joseph let out a laugh.

"Think I might join you and your russets?" Beatrice ventured to ask.

"Oh, I don't know," Joseph replied, actually scuffing the toe of his boot on the boxcar's dusty floor.

Beatrice didn't know what else to say.

"I wouldn't mind the company, of course," Joseph said at last, grinning at her. "You're welcome to come along, but I have to warn you—you're in for a pretty bumpy ride."

The train's whistle sounded a sharp toot, announcing its departure.

"I don't care about a few bumps," Beatrice said, holding out her bag. "Mind taking this for me?"

"Happy to," Joseph replied, pulling the carpetbag into the hold. Then offering his hand to Beatrice, he exclaimed, "All aboard!"

She spent much of the journey perched atop a heap of burlap sacks that Joseph had arranged for her. "It's this," he'd said, "or get that pretty-looking getup of yours covered in god-knows-what."

"Thanks," she'd said, blushing. "How thoughtful of you."

She was glad when Joseph turned his back to sit in the open doorway of the car, legs dangling over the edge.

When they were younger, he'd often leaned forward on the edge of the church pew behind Beatrice to flick the frayed end of a goose feather at the back of her neck. Time and again she'd ignored his pestering, guessing he was only doing it to get her in trouble. Once, when they were older, he'd asked her if he could walk her home from school, but she'd thought the invitation was another one of his pranks. She'd replied by snorting out an awkward laugh, which Joseph had promptly taken as a "no." *All the girls like Joseph Wheeler*, she'd thought. *What would he want with me?* When he'd made the same request the following week, this time loud enough so every girl within ten feet could hear, Beatrice had turned tail and run, hot tears of embarrassment streaking down her face, chased by the titters of the other girls and the disbelief in their jealous eyes.

Carefully shifting on her sacks, Beatrice turned the collar of her coat up and held it around her neck to shield herself from the raw nip of wind coming through the car's door. She found herself longing for warmth and solid ground under her feet. Determined not to succumb to regret, she stared past Joseph in the open door, and became transfixed by the ever-changing view. Moss-green pastureland skirted the tracks as they rolled past, and beyond that, she could see the Hudson River. Haystacks dotted the land, and a lone dairy cow made its way along a winding path to the water. Had the gentle beast managed to break through the barnyard fence? One could hope. One could pray. One could wish.

Closing her eyes, Beatrice remembered a farm she used to visit with her parents when she was a child. Why they'd gone there she couldn't remember, but she did recall the farmer's wife allowing her to feed the chickens, and milk their favourite cow. How pleasant it'd felt to rest her head against the velvety warmth of the Holstein's flank as she went about the steady grasp and tug of emptying its udders. What she wouldn't give to be back there again, to feel her mother's gentle hand on her shoulder, to hear the farmer's wife sing in time with her work.

> *May you rise with the sun, ready to make hay.*
> *May the rains come at night to wash your cares*
>   *away.*
> *May you sleep with the angels sittin' on your bed.*
> *May you be an hour in Heaven a' fore the Devil*
>   *knows you're dead.*

She guessed they'd been travelling for well past an hour. How much longer would it take to get to New York? By passenger train the trip usually took a little over two hours. Was it the same for freight? By the way her belly was rumbling, Beatrice guessed it must be getting close to noon. *Click-clack, click-clack, click-clack.* Fingering the coins in her pocket, she wondered if she should offer to pay Joseph for her passage. She hadn't had to buy a ticket at the station, so she had more than enough to share.

Holding out a quarter, she called to him over the noise of the train. "Here," she said, "this is for you."

"Why for?" Joseph asked, getting up and coming to sit by Beatrice's side.

"For letting me come along with you and your potatoes."

The young man waved the offer away. "There's no need for that. I'm happy for the company." Then taking an apple and a knife from his knapsack, he sliced a wedge from the ripe red fruit and offered it to Beatrice.

Grateful, she took the slice and bit into its crisp, sweet flesh. Now he was next to her she couldn't help feeling that she needed to fill the space between them with whatever thoughts came into her head. Mouth half full, she nervously sputtered, "Did you know the trains in the city are elevated? Three storeys off the ground. Every three minutes a string of train cars atop one of those tracks rattles from one end of the city to the other. For a nickel you can ride from Battery Park to the Harlem River. Of course there's noise and smoke and showers of hot cinders that get spewed to the streets below, and there's always a risk of falling from the platform, or getting pushed by the crowds, but five cents is a small price to pay for turning hours to minutes, don't you think?"

Joseph smiled at her, then pointed to the sacks of potatoes piled all around them. "Me and the russets go to the city most every week, you know."

"Right," Beatrice said, feeling stupid. "Of course. I'm sorry. I should've known."

How ridiculous it was for her to think that she could understand all that was worth knowing about a place simply from reading newspapers and guidebooks, and from a yearly jaunt with Aunt Lydia to the tamest parts of the city. Had she ever stayed in New York overnight? If she had, she couldn't remember it. But it was too late to turn back now. All she could do was try her best not to look as uncomfortable and scared as she felt. "Shouldn't be long now," Joseph said, checking his watch. "Know where you're goin' when we get there?"

Beatrice said, "Madison Square Park, or thereabouts."

"Nice spot," Joseph replied. "Be sure to visit Lady Liberty's torch while you're there. Even without the rest of her attached, it's truly something else."

"You've seen it?"

Beatrice had begged Lydia many times over to take her to the park to see it, but her aunt had insisted they wait until the statue was whole and in place on Bedloe's Island.

"Just last week. Even climbed to the top to have a look around. You get a great view of the Fifth Avenue Hotel from up there."

"Have you been to the hotel as well?" Beatrice asked, now thinking that anything might be possible when it came to Joseph Wheeler.

"Yes," he said, "but only in the lobby. To tell you the truth, the place is far too fussy for my taste. All that velvet and crystal and marble makes me anxious."

The thought of Joseph standing amongst the hotel's elite clientele made Beatrice smile. "Do you stay over in the city on these trips?"

"Sometimes. I've got cousins who run a saloon near the Bowery. I stay with them on occasion."

"The Bowery," Beatrice repeated. She'd read of it in *Madam Morrow's Strange Tales of Gotham*, which had described the street as having pits dug into the floors of every beer hall for cock fights and rat-catching matches, and prostitutes plying their trade on every corner. Biting her lip, she said, "Sounds nice."

Joseph shrugged. "It's not, but they're good people and it's a place to rest my head." Pitching his apple core out the door, Joseph turned so he could meet Beatrice's eyes.

"What is it?" she asked, wiping her face with a handkerchief, hoping to brush away the smudge of dirt she imagined must be there.

"Nothing," Joseph said, his cheeks turning pink.

"Joseph, be honest. I've an important appointment ahead. I can't afford to look shabby."

"Your face is fine," Joseph said.

"What is it then?"

Sunlight shone through the slats of the boxcar and across his face. "I always figured you'd go away someday," he said. "To New York, or out west, or maybe London or Paris."

"Whatever made you think that?"

"Because you aren't like any of the other girls in Stony Point."

Just then the train's wheels began to squeal on the tracks, and they came to a stop.

"Are we there?" Beatrice asked.

Sticking his head out the door and looking both ways, Joseph answered, "We're close, but we're not at the station."

They could both hear a great commotion building outside as a man shouted, "Stand back! Everyone, stand back!"

"Come on," Joseph said, "let's go see what all the fuss is about."

"Are you sure it's safe?"

Joseph took her hand in his, helping her up. "We'll find out."

Climbing out of the car, they picked their way down a steep rocky grade to a scrubby patch of grass. A crowd had gathered around the engine, which had stopped just shy of a curious contraption that'd been laid over the tracks. Made from massive wood beams that supported a set of iron rails with cannonballs for bearings, it held an enormous wooden box at one end and a bright red steam engine at the other. A sturdy chain attached the engine to the box, presumably to haul the box across the tracks. Beatrice recognized the odd shape at once. "That's Cleopatra's Needle," she whispered to Joseph. "It has to be." Glancing around she saw that, indeed, they were stopped next to the dockyard on the Hudson where the pontoons were moored after carrying the Needle up the river.

One by one the other farmhands who'd been riding along with their goods got off the train to join them, and they all moved to get a better view.

"Clear the area!" a red-faced man began to shout. His was the same voice that earlier had instructed the crowd to stand back.

Beatrice couldn't see past the sack-coated men who now surrounded her, their hats cocked to the backs of their heads, their weathered hands on their hips. When one of the men spat to the side without thinking, his spittle landed on the toe of her boot. He stared at Beatrice and grinned.

Dragging her boot across a clump of grass, she thought, *Welcome to city life.*

"Why are we standing around looking at a box?" the rude man groused.

"'Cause Vanderbilt paid for it," the man next to him answered.

"How much?"

"A hundred thousand smackers."

"You lie."

"I don't."

"You do! You told me there'd be something to see—that there's just a box."

Beatrice and Joseph found their way past the men to a less crowded spot where the sound of the steam engine drowned out the men's chatter. The grind of the chain winding on its spool along with the growling churn of cannonballs tumbling in their channels caused the ground to shake as the obelisk inched forward. Soon the terrible sound of metal scraping against metal squealed through the air. Holding her hands over her ears, Beatrice looked on as a man standing atop the obelisk waved a white flag and signalled for the engine to be brought to a stop.

A chorus of whoops and hollers erupted from the contraption's crew to celebrate the safe delivery of the Needle across the tracks.

Atop the roof of a warehouse nearby, two men were observing the proceedings. One was a photographer hired by Mr. Vanderbilt to document this important moment in the obelisk's journey. The other was Gideon Palsham, a master architect who had a great interest in ancient stone structures and anything said to have been touched by magic. While the photographer stood hunched behind his camera, cloaked in a heavy black cloth, Palsham caught sight of Beatrice. He watched the girl intently, never taking his eyes off her. She was the only female in the crowd, the only one of her kind. As the photographer drew the cover over his lens, the train's whistle sounded, calling its passengers back.

Beatrice held fast to Joseph's arm. Who could've imagined that she'd arrive in New York at the same time as this magnificent wonder? Perhaps there was magic in the world after all. Everything she'd read about the obelisk had pointed to it being an object of untold mystical powers.

Tugging at Joseph's sleeve, she hoped she might convince him to stop so she could get a better look at the obelisk.

Although it was dressed in wood planking and laid on its side, she couldn't help but feel that she should pause to honour it. "Joseph, wait," she said. "I'll just be a moment."

Looking up to make sure he'd heard her, she discovered that the sleeve she'd gotten a grip on wasn't his: a stranger now stood in his place. Flustered and confused she pulled away from the gentleman. "I'm so sorry," she said. "I thought you were someone else."

"It's quite all right," he said, turning to protect her from the jostling crowd. "I'd like to help you, if I might."

His skin was the colour of nutmeg, and his face was lined with wrinkles as if he'd spent most of his life turned towards the sun. He wore no hat, but his greying hair was neatly combed and his beard came to a jaunty point. Dressed in pinstriped trousers and a double-breasted waistcoat, he held his jacket over his arm. The sleeves of his linen shirt were loosely rolled to his elbows, but the blue silk ascot he wore around his neck was properly tied and fixed with a silver pin in the shape of a scarab. When he smiled, a gold-capped tooth glinted in the corner of his grin and his dark eyes shone with steadfastness. Although Beatrice hadn't any reason to trust him, she was certain he didn't mean her harm.

"Thank you," Beatrice found herself saying as the crowd continued to push on around them.

"This way," the gentleman said, leading her to a platform of wooden skids, directly beside the obelisk. "Just until those barbarians pass."

From where she stood, Beatrice could see a team of men going about the business of dismantling the portion of the contraption that still obstructed the tracks. They were making quick work of it, and she was sure the train's conductor wouldn't waste any time once the tracks were clear. "I should be getting back on the train," she said.

"Have you come a long way?"

"Not nearly as far as the obelisk," Beatrice answered him with a smile.

Patting the side of the box the man said, "It has been a long journey."

"Have you travelled with it the entire way?" Beatrice asked.

"I have indeed," he replied with a solemn nod. Pointing to a brass handle on the side of the box, he asked, "Would you like to see it?"

Glancing back at the train, Beatrice shook her head. "I'd love to, but I really must go."

"I won't let them leave without you. I promise." Gently sliding the wooden panel to the left, he revealed a space just large enough for Beatrice to peer through. "Go on," he urged. "It misses being seen."

Beatrice stuck her head inside the box. The space was filled with the smell of damp stone, reminding her of the smooth rocks she'd collected along the Hudson as a child. Standing on tiptoe, she shifted slightly to one side to allow a bit of sunlight to pass into the box. All at once she could see the rosy, mottled surface of the obelisk; the graceful curve of a glyph was within her reach. She traced it with her fingers. The stone was cool and damp, and when she held her palm against it, she could feel a low, steady pulse. Was it the obelisk? Was it the train's engine preparing to depart? Or was it just her heart, racing with excitement? Giddy with wonder, she let out a soft laugh, which to her surprise echoed quite freely inside the dark space. It carried on long after it should have, fading into an eerie, undulating whisper. Closing her

eyes, Beatrice leaned forward and said, "Hello?" half thinking if she waited long enough, she might receive an answer.

"Beatrice!" a voice shouted behind her. "Beatrice Dunn!"

Withdrawing her head, Beatrice turned to see Joseph
approaching, wringing his cap in his hands. "Come away from
there, we'll miss the train!"

The gentleman who'd opened the box for her was gone.

Not waiting for Joseph to reach her, Beatrice climbed
down from the platform on her own. Misjudging the distance, she stumbled and tripped on the hem of her skirts, and
landed in a heap on the ground. Her world went sideways,
then black. The last thing she heard was the sound of coins
tumbling out of her petticoat, cheerily ringing as they lost
themselves among the planks and stones.

The Known World is filled with mystical messages. Signs, portents and foretellings come in many guises—smoke on the wind, sparks from a fire, ripples on the water, lines in the sand. If you wish to master magic, pay attention. If you wish to master love, do the same.

—From the grimoire of Eleanor St. Clair

Shop Talk (and Secrets).

Eleanor lit the wick on a small kerosene stove and watched the flame flicker and bloom in the heater's isinglass window. Filling a copper kettle, she placed it on the stove's iron rest, and waited for the water to boil—and for the three women who were standing at her counter to make up their minds.

"I quite like the hibiscus," the youngest woman remarked. "Doesn't it smell divine?"

"Orange pekoe is my favourite," said the woman on her right.

"You must try the Darjeeling," urged the woman to her left.

Each of them had paid a recent visit to the shop, albeit alone and for very different reasons. Mrs. Orange Pekoe had been in search of a tonic to help her sleep, Madame Darjeeling had requested an elixir to foster desire, and Lady Hibiscus had required a tincture of Queen Anne's lace to clear the womb and restore peace of mind. This pretty young woman had also been responsible for Eleanor's broken heart. For a few blissful weeks in the spring they'd carried on an affair, quietly hidden from the rest of the world, even Adelaide. All through the month of May it'd been flesh against flesh—honey sucked off fingers and breasts, silk sashes wrapped around wrists, feathers plucked from bonnets for tickling thighs and ribs. "This must remain a secret," Lady Hibiscus had insisted, "just between us two." She was promised to a gentleman of great social prominence and had no intention of breaking their engagement. Eleanor thought she could stay levelheaded, but being dismissed by the young woman had hurt more than she'd imagined. Once the wedding was over and done, the girl's affection had turned to calculated indifference. Still, she insisted on coming into the shop for this and that, never giving so much as a nod to her former place in Eleanor's life. *If that's what she wants,* Eleanor had vowed to herself, *so be it.*

As the trio took turns sniffing at open tea tins, Eleanor covered her mouth to stifle a yawn. Her sleep had been fitful and brief, especially after her dream, and before she'd known it the sun had risen and it was time to drag her tired body out of bed.

There'd been books to balance, and remedies to concoct, linens to press and honey pots to fill. There'd been blessings to recite, spells to consider, and a pleasant exchange with Mr. Markowitz's son, a bright-natured boy named Isaac, who'd come to the door bearing a basket of baked goods to sell. Feeling generous, Eleanor had chosen to buy the whole lot—three glazed lemon tarts, one loaf of scalded rye, and an assortment of teacakes, fritters and biscuits (honey, apple and buttermilk).

Despite her exhaustion, Eleanor quite liked waking when most of the city's inhabitants (including Adelaide) were still half asleep, and the only sounds on the sidewalk were the yappy bickering of newsboys and the cheerful swell of the milkman's voice singing a ditty as his wagon rolled by. This morning she'd even taken a few moments to sit on the roof amidst the maze of potted herbs that surrounded her two small beehives and collect her thoughts.

Everything in the humble potager had had its beginnings in her mother's garden, from lemon balm to lavender, from mugwort to mint. As the sun hit the rooftop, a few keen bees had straggled forth from their hives. Soon, Eleanor thought, all her golden beauties would be taking to the air to nuzzle among the late summer blooms of Madison Square—the last of the daylilies that surrounded the fountain in the park, the bright asters and pot marigolds that graced every flower box on Fifth Avenue, the hardy roses that climbed the trellises of the grand houses on Marble Row. Soon, their sisters would commence their preparations for autumn's chill by capping their stores for winter and ridding themselves of anything that got in their way—failed eggs, lost wings, and every last one of their brothers, whose usefulness had come to an end. Crouching near a hive, Eleanor had listened in on the glorious steady hum of their work. This, and the heady scent of their honey, never failed to make her worries disappear.

Carrying this sense of contentment in her heart, she'd gone about her daily tasks with ease until the teapot had crashed to the floor. Oddly enough, she hadn't been standing anywhere near the pot when it fell. Only the lid had survived, sitting safe and untouched in the centre of the counter. Perdu's startled cries of "Top off the pot!" had caused her mother's voice to sound in her head. *Top off the pot means a stranger's coming to call.*

Madame St. Clair had always put great faith in the happenstances that occurred while making, serving and drinking tea: *two spoons placed on the same saucer mean a wedding will soon follow; two women pouring from the same pot means one will soon carry a child; tea spilled from the spout of a carried pot means a secret will soon be revealed; tea stirred while in the pot will surely stir up a quarrel.*

Sometimes Eleanor wondered if her mother's sayings mattered anymore. The world was changing at an alarming pace and the city right along with it. Perhaps all these changes called for a new sort of magic, one divined not from teacups and spoons, but from the *rickety-tick* of the elevated trains as they roared past, or the flickering haloes cast by the street lamps that stood outside her window. Something strange was in the air, she was sure of it, but she couldn't put her finger on exactly what it was. How was she supposed to understand what the city was trying to tell her when she couldn't properly remember her dreams? Closing her eyes, she tried once more to catch a glimpse of her most recent vision, but she only felt off-balance and dizzy, as if she were about to fall from a great height. Had some dark spectre come into the shop without her knowing? A ghost, a ghoul, a demon, the Devil in disguise? She'd always been so careful to keep the place protected and safe. "Mother, help me," she'd whispered. Then, *"Mère, aide-moi."*

"I can't decide," Madame Darjeeling said shaking her head.

"Neither can I," Mrs. Orange Pekoe seconded.

"Nor can I," said Lady Hibiscus.

Can't you? Eleanor thought. She really wanted to hate the girl but couldn't. She watched as the young woman nervously turned her wedding ring around her finger. Was something bothering her? Was something wrong? "Why don't I brew a pot of each so you can sample them all?" she suggested. "My treat."

"That would be lovely," said Madame Darjeeling.

"Simply splendid," remarked Mrs. Orange Pekoe.

"If it's not any trouble," Lady Hibiscus added.

As Eleanor set the tea to steep, a single honeybee clung fast to a fold in her sleeve. Perdu, watching intently from his perch, spotted the bee before his mistress. Flapping his wings, he bobbed his head and exclaimed, "Treat, treat, treat!"

Mrs. Orange Pekoe's eyes went wide with disbelief. "Was that the bird?" she asked.

Lady Hibiscus smiled and nodded. "I've heard him speak before."

"What a clever trick!" exclaimed Madame Darjeeling.

Holding a bit of teacake in the palm of her hand, Eleanor offered it to Perdu. "What's gotten into you?" she whispered. "You're acting like a spoiled brat."

The bird refused to take the sweet.

Eleanor ignored her pet's antics and resumed the work of preparing the tea. "Why don't you ladies take a seat? I'll only be a minute."

Perdu hopped to the counter and took hold of her sleeve with his beak. He knew what he wanted, even if she didn't.

The bee, enticed by a pitcher of honey Eleanor had placed on the counter, crawled out of hiding, and moved towards her hand.

"Well hello, m'dear," Eleanor said, spotting the object of Perdu's desire.

"Treat!" Perdu demanded again.

"She's not for you," Eleanor scolded, moving out of his reach.

Had it been a drone, she might well have handed the doomed creature over to the raven to gobble up, but this bee was no drone. She was a healthy female, meant to be rushing from flower to flower in the last days of harvest. Knowing the ruckus the little darling would cause if she happened to get tangled in Madame Darjeeling's curls, Eleanor poured a single drop of honey onto a saucer, gently transferred the bee alongside it, and covered them both with an empty, upturned cup. For a moment, the bee bumped and buzzed against the porcelain in protest, but as soon as Eleanor bent near the cup and whispered, "Patience, my dear, you'll soon be free," she stopped.

Perdu returned to his perch to sulk.

Amidst a collection of Moroccan lanterns, tasselled pillows and tufted furniture, Adelaide Thom was sitting in the back corner of the shop, taking advantage of a brief lull in her morning. She'd been holding court since half past nine, turning cards and entertaining questions from a steady stream of clients.

Miss Edith Jones. A dear, bright girl, always on time. She came in blushing, fidgeting, heart aflutter. Crossed her legs at the ankles, once, twice, three times over. So keen to fall in love.

Her question: *Is he the one?*

Her cards: Courtship. Jealousy. Disappointment.

Adelaide's answer: *He thinks he is, but his mother does not.*

The mother of the "he" in question was Mrs. Marietta Stevens—socialite, widow, owner of the Fifth Avenue Hotel. She'd visited Adelaide the previous day for her own consultation, during which she'd heartily complained of Miss Jones's pursuit of her son and repeatedly asked if she might eventually find success in breaking up the pair. All signs had pointed to yes. (*What a pity*, Adelaide had thought. *Edith is such a lovely girl.*)

Mrs. Violet Pritchett. Newlywed. Face aglow. Dress hugging her figure. Downed two cups of peppermint tea in quick succession. Complained of shoes feeling tight, and of stiff, swollen fingers.

Her question: *When shall I get with child?*

Her cards: Fortune. Plenty. Home.

Adelaide's answer: *Congratulations, my dear, you already are.*

Mrs. Rose Blanchard. Nervous. Quiet. Eyes downcast. Every time she moved, the right cuff of her dress shifted, revealing a ring of dark bruises on her wrist.

Her question: *When will it end?*

Her cards: Deceit. Ruin. Death.

Adelaide's answer: *Not until you leave him, or he's dead.*

Mrs. Blanchard's response: *It's easier to kill a man than to divorce him, I'd guess.*

Adelaide thought that she'd like to kill the woman's husband herself, if she could get away with it. Perhaps she could pose as a housemaid and slip the powder of some noxious root from Eleanor's cupboard into his coffee. Until she could think of a better plan, poor Mrs. Blanchard would have to go it alone.

Checking her watch Adelaide saw it was five past noon. The prospective shop girls would be arriving in less than an hour. She knew that she should inform Eleanor since her partner hated surprises, even when they were good.

Shuffling her cards, Adelaide posed a question of her own, in hopes the answer might direct her to do what she wished, rather than what she should.

Miss Adelaide Thom. Hopeful. Confident. Impeccably dressed. Holds her impatience in check with the steady tap of her left foot.

Her question: *What will Eleanor think of me if I don't tell her?*

Her cards: Falsehood. Treachery. The Judge.

Her answer: *Nothing good.*

Picking up the cards, Adelaide shuffled them back into the deck as quickly as she could. As with her sitters, they had served to remind her of what she'd already supposed. She didn't need them to discern the truth, but having them near certainly didn't hurt. By turns, they gave her courage to say what needed to be said, or admonished her to stay quiet when she might've been inclined to speak too freely. Frayed and worn at the edges, they'd come from another era, each card holding a simple, crude illustration skirted by a word or two of description written by a shaky hand in English, German, Italian and French. The reverse of each card had been decorated with a curious symbol, a flaming heart entwined in the grip of two snakes. When Eleanor had first seen the cards, she'd asked all sorts of questions. *Where did they come from? Has anyone blessed them? Are they enchanted? If so, by what order of magic?* All Adelaide could say was that they'd been left for her long ago at the ticket booth of Mr. Dink's sideshow with a note that had simply read, "From an admirer." Since the loss of her eye, she'd been especially grateful to have them, as they gave her sitters something to gaze upon other than her face. (Not a day went by without someone trying to get a better look at what sat beneath her veil.) Slipping the cards inside her pocket, she checked her watch again—twenty after twelve. *Time's a wastin', Adelaide. Tick-tock. Tick-tock. Tick-tock.*

Approaching Eleanor, she sweetly said, "Sorry, I forgot to wind the clock."

"I would've done it myself," Eleanor replied, "but I couldn't find the key."

"You couldn't?" Adelaide asked. "That's strange. I left it where I always do, inside your favourite teapot."

"The pot is no more."

With a nod, Adelaide said, "So that was the crash I heard. I'm sorry for that too."

"Did you leave it out on the counter?"

"The clock key?"

"No, the teapot."

"Why would I? What are you getting at?"

"You were out so late . . . Where were you, by the way?"

"Here and there. No place special."

"I see."

"I wasn't drunk, and I didn't touch your teapot."

"I didn't say that—"

"You didn't have to."

"It's just you look a little worse for wear."

"I do?"

"Only in the way that I can see. No one else can tell."

Staring at her reflection in the mirror behind the counter, Adelaide turned first to the right and then to the left. As she leaned forward to get a better look, she felt a sharp, nagging twinge of pain. Over time, she'd come to accept her scars, but she often wondered if she'd ever get used to the pain. If only she had some way of predicting when it was coming, and how long it would last. It'd been a week since her last bout and she'd even begun to hope that perhaps she might be rid of it at last. If it had to persist, why couldn't it be of some use? Why couldn't it warn her of impending danger or of the presence of insufferable company, at the very least? "Give it time," Eleanor had advised. "It may prove useful yet." One could hope. One could pray. One could wish.

"Cup of tea?" Eleanor asked, staring at Adelaide with concern.

"Thank you, yes."

"Willow bark?"

"That would be good."

Eleanor could always tell when the pain was with her. As she turned to her herbs, Adelaide took a deep breath. *It's now or never*, she thought. "There's something I've been meaning to tell you."

"What's that?" Eleanor asked.

"Promise you won't get angry?"

Eleanor sighed. "It *was* you who misplaced the pot, wasn't it? Honestly, Adelaide, I wouldn't be half so displeased if you'd just confessed it from the start."

Just then the bells above the door jangled, announcing the arrival of another customer. Perdu glanced up from his perch, and then resumed his sulking over the loss of the bee. The three ladies sitting in the window seat turned to stare, taking a brief nosy pause before continuing their discussion of the impending resurgence of the bustle.

When Adelaide turned and spied the woman standing in

the doorway, she abandoned her conversation with Eleanor.

"Mrs. Dashley," she said, advancing on her with open arms.

"Miss Thom!" Judith Dashley replied, enthusiastically kissing the air on either side of Adelaide's cheeks. Lace parasol in hand, pearls at her bosom, she was a perfect specimen of a Fifth Avenue *Femme*, a true New York Lady.

She was also Adelaide's best customer, coming to the shop for tea and divinations every day of the week except Sundays throughout the season. This was her first visit since she'd gotten back to town after her summer in the country, and Adelaide had high hopes that they'd resume their previous schedule. If the lady wished to consult the cards on a regular basis, who was she to say no?

"I trust your holiday agreed with you," Adelaide said. "You look radiant."

"You flatter me," Judith replied with a blush.

"I only speak the truth," Adelaide said. "It's my gift as well as my curse."

"Trust me, my dear, it's the city that's put a spring in my step. That, and getting away from the damnable scenic riverfront at Tarrytown. The place was simply crawling with catch-penny girls come by steamboat from the city hoping to land themselves a rich lad. Oh, to be young and free and taut and firm, and to have more life ahead, than not!" Jutting out her chin ever so slightly, she forced a small pucker of crepey wrinkles to disappear from her neck.

"I'm sure when they caught sight of you, they were sick with envy."

"I'm sure they didn't give me a second thought."

"You underestimate the impression that earned beauty can make."

"Whether or not, I'm thrilled to be in your company. Alden returned two weeks ago, so I was stuck playing whist with a tiresome circle of Tarrytown hens. The cottage was starting to feel more like a barnyard than a retreat."

"You must be glad to be back on Marble Row."

"I'm back, yes, but not exactly at home. The house is being refurbished and won't be finished until the New Year. Alden and I are staying in a suite at the Fifth Avenue Hotel for the duration. Some say the hotel's decor is passé, but I don't mind it one bit. Call me old-fashioned, but I feel it fits the history of the place." Lowering her voice she gleefully added, "You know, they say it's haunted . . ."

"Do they really?" Adelaide replied, knowing full well the hotel's reputation for ghosts.

"That they do."

"Care to sit?" Adelaide suggested.

"Oh, yes please," Judith replied.

Leading Judith to her secluded corner in the back of the room, Adelaide said, "Make yourself comfortable. I'll fetch the tea. I can't wait to hear about the socialites and spectres you've encountered at the hotel so far."

Aside from liking Judith's money, Adelaide had grown quite fond of the woman herself. They'd met at a psychic demonstration featuring a medium who called herself Mrs. Saunders and her spirit guide, Little Moon. As Mrs. Saunders had prattled on, eyes rolling back in her head (supposedly possessed by her guide), Adelaide had noticed that the woman seated next to her in the darkened theatre was holding back tears. In an attempt to comfort her, Adelaide had leaned close and whispered, "None of this is real."

The stricken woman had whispered back, "Don't you believe?"

"In ghosts, yes. In this dog-and-pony show, no."

"Have you ever seen a ghost?"

"Possibly, yes. Have you?"

"Once, I think. It was the spirit of my dear son, Billy, staring up at me from the bottom of a silver fruit bowl. He died when he was only seven."

Placing her hand on the woman's arm, Adelaide had said, "I'm sorry for your loss."

"Have you lost someone too? Is that why you're here?"

"My mother, when I was just a girl."

"Oh, heavens, that's awful," the woman had remarked, putting her hand to her mouth.

Adelaide hadn't been sure if the woman was reacting to her loss or the scars on her face. Still, she'd handed the woman her calling card and said, "Perhaps we'll meet again someday."

The next morning Judith Dashley had come to the tea-shop and requested a meeting with Adelaide. "I think I need a little respite from chasing the dead," she'd said. "I'd like to turn my attention to the business of living. Can you give me any advice on how to do that?"

"What shall it be today?" Adelaide asked as she poured tea into Judith's cup. "Your usual consultation?"

Judith stirred in a splash of milk. "Actually," she said, biting her lip, "I'm here to give you some news."

"Colour me curious."

Leaning forward, Judith said, "I've someone who wishes to meet you."

"Any friend of yours is a friend of mine. Tell her to come to the shop and to mention your name. I'll be sure to put her at the top of my list."

Lowering her eyes, Judith shook her head and said, "I can't."

"Whyever not?" Adelaide asked.

Blushing, Judith answered, "Because it's not a she, but a he."

Now it all made sense. Judith's hemming and hawing, her schoolgirl blush. Whoever he was, Judith Dashley was smitten with him. Had she been unfaithful to her husband? No, not yet. She showed no signs of that—none of the excuse-laden talk that accompanies guilt, or the all-too-upright posture of infidelity. With a teasing laugh Adelaide asked, "He's quite handsome, yes?"

Eyes darting to the side, Judith measured the memory of him from shoes to hat. "Oh, yes."

"And tall, too," Adelaide pressed, "and not of your family."

"Why do I bother thinking anything could come as a surprise to you!" Judith exclaimed. "What a gift you have. I wish I could do that."

"Careful what you wish," Adelaide said with a smile. "Now why don't you tell me why this mystery man wishes to meet me, or do I have to guess that as well? You know I don't suffer salesmen, preachers or politicians, so if he's one of those, you needn't bother."

"He's a doctor," Judith said, "and highly regarded."

Resisting the urge to touch her scars, Adelaide asked, "What kind of doctor?" Handsome or not, she'd been poked and prodded and examined enough.

"He's an 'alienist,'" Judith explained, "a doctor of the mind. He's keenly interested in studying the way women think and something he calls 'intuitive inclination.' Alden's been a long-time acquaintance of his father's, but I only met him when we dined together last night. He's been away in Paris, furthering his studies, but he recently came back to the city to settle his father's estate. Alden's asked him to speak at the annual conference of the Fraternal Order of the Unknown Philosophers. Isn't that exciting?"

"Just," Adelaide said.

"When I told him of your gifts, he begged me to arrange a meeting as soon as possible. He's such a charming fellow, I simply couldn't say no. Will you meet with him?"

"Only if you tell me his name," Adelaide replied.

"Oh yes, I suppose I should do that. It's Dr. Quinn Brody."

"Shall we try for tomorrow morning, then, say half past ten, at the hotel?"

"Half past ten it is," Judith replied with a smile. Raising her teacup she added, "Here's to intuitive inclination."

Shortly after Judith's departure, the three ladies in the window seat also took their leave. As Eleanor cleared their table, she discovered that each of them had tucked a calling card, on which they'd written a note, beneath their saucers.

Mrs. Orange Pekoe's card read, "More of the same, please, sent to this address."

Madame Darjeeling's card simply said, "Success!"

Lady Hibiscus's note was more pressing. "I must speak with you soon, in private."

Eleanor upended her former lover's cup on its saucer and turned it three times. Righting it, she peered into the bowl to inspect the leaves. Her mother would never have done such a thing without the tea drinker's consent, but in light of their past and the urgent tone of the young woman's note, Eleanor felt she was in the right. Eyes half closed, she gazed at the shape of the leaves until they formed a series of images in her mind. First an apple, then a snake, then a broken quill. *An affair of the heart gone wrong. A couple divided.* Running out the door, Eleanor stared down the street in the direction Lady Hibiscus had turned, hoping the woman might still be nearby. Sadly, she was out of sight.

As she turned to go back inside, she saw that a long line of young women had formed outside the shop.

The girl at the head of the line stepped forward and asked, "Excuse me, ma'am, is it time?"

"Time for what?" Eleanor replied.

"For considerin' a new girl to work in your shop?"

"Whatever gave you that idea? You must have the wrong address."

Pointing to the sign above the door the girl asked, "Ain't this St. Clair and Thom's teashop?"

"It is, but we're not looking to hire anyone."

The girl stepped forward to press a square of newsprint into Eleanor's hand. "The paper said you is . . ."

Without even a look at the paper, Eleanor said, "I'm sorry, but it's a mistake." Staring pointedly at the ever-growing queue, she gave the girl a curt nod and said, "Pass it on."

Back inside the shop, Eleanor locked the door and turned the sign in the window to Closed. "Adelaide," she said, folding her arms across her chest, "what was it you wanted to tell me?"

As Adelaide came towards her, struggling to find the right words, Perdu threw back his feathered head and squawked, "Top off the pot! Top off the pot!"

Adelaide laughed.

Eleanor did not.

Adelaide looked out the window in time to see the last of the prospective shop girls disperse. Hand on the doorknob, she thought she might chase after them so the day wouldn't be a complete bust.

"Don't," Eleanor said, eyes narrowed.

Adelaide threw up her hands. "I was only trying to help."

"You were only thinking of yourself."

"How is hiring an assistant for *you*, thinking of myself?"

Eleanor was tired, fragile, fed up, and worried about what she'd seen in the cup. "You act on every whim that pops into your head without thinking of the consequences. Did it ever occur to you that I might like a say in the matter?"

Adelaide bit her lip. She couldn't recall ever seeing her friend react quite like this.

Eleanor pressed on. "I'm sure it didn't because it never does."

"What's that supposed to mean?"

"Just look around this place," Eleanor said, gesturing towards Adelaide's corner. As of late her taste in decor had begun to spill over into the rest of the shop—a gilded mirror here, a pair of velvet curtains there. "It's starting to look more like a bordello than a teashop."

The remark stung, but Adelaide didn't take the bait. She sensed that Eleanor's words, though pointed and somewhat true, were hiding a deeper anger, she hoped meant for someone else. Arguing with her would only make matters worse. Shrugging into a wrap, she announced, "I'm going out."

"Of course you are," Eleanor muttered, fetching her grip-sack from behind the counter. Then, as Adelaide went through the door, she said, "I hope you have your key, because I'm going out as well. I can't say when I'll be back."

The two witches went their separate ways—Adelaide storming off towards the park, Eleanor marching, with grip-sack in hand, to search for Lady Hibiscus.

Knocks and Rappings.

BEATRICE ARRIVED AT Tea and Sympathy to find the shades drawn and the door locked. Twisting the bell, she waited for someone to answer. When no one came, she gave three loud raps on the window. She was late, she knew, but it was only two o'clock. Why was the shop closed? Had the owners already found their girl and called it a day? Just as she was about to walk away, she heard a sound on the other side of the door. "Hello?" she called. "Is anyone there?"

When no one responded, she began to wonder if perhaps she'd been hearing things. The spill she'd taken at the dockyard had left her terribly unsettled, and she hadn't felt right since. A small, aching bump had formed where she'd hit her head and she could only recall bits and pieces of how she'd gotten back to the train. Had Joseph led her safely across the tracks or had he scooped her up and carried her? In any event, he'd been incredibly kind, arranging the burlap bags in a comfortable nest, offering her a drink from a flask he'd squirrelled away in his knapsack. Of course he'd forgotten to tell her that the flask contained whiskey, and she'd wound up spitting half the stuff out. Still, the shock of the alcohol burning down her throat had caused her to sit upright and see straight, so in that sense it'd done the trick.

As soon as they'd arrived at the station, Joseph had placed a pile of silver coins in the hand of a carriage driver and instructed the man to deliver Beatrice to her destination. Helping her inside the carriage he'd asked, "Are you sure you'll be all right?"

"Yes, of course," she'd lied. "I'm perfectly fine, I swear it. Thanks for all your help, and best of luck with your russets."

Now her head was throbbing as she stood outside the shop. The sounds of the city seemed to echo around her—voices crowding in her ears from all directions, strangely more within than without. She felt as if she'd been run over by a train rather than riding on one. She'd so wanted to make a good first impression, and now she was late, and so unwell. Not ready to give up just yet, she rang the bell again.

A loud thump sounded on the other side of the door, followed by silence.

Leaning to peer through the keyhole, Beatrice discovered an eye staring back at her. It was dark and shiny and definitely not human.

"Hello," she called again, unsure as to whether or not she wanted an answer.

"Who's there?" a voice responded, soft and sweet.

Before Beatrice could reply, the lock clicked, the knob turned, and the door opened wide. No one was there to greet her. Choosing curiosity over fear, she entered the shop.

The place was dimly lit, yet welcoming and warm. The scents of tea, dried herbs and honey filled the air. It reminded her of the chapel of the Stony Point Presbyterian Church on

Christmas Eve, all close with beeswax candles, cedar boughs and age-old mysteries. To her great relief, the cacophony that'd been ringing in her ears was suddenly silenced.

"Hello?" she quietly called, hoping to find a friendly face at last.

"Hello," a voice, eerily like her own, replied from overhead.

Looking up, Beatrice discovered a large raven perched atop the open door. "Heavens!" she exclaimed, dropping her bag to the floor.

Flapping to Beatrice's feet, Perdu hopped in a wide circle around the girl then waddled towards her bag to peck and pull at its clasp.

Amazed by the creature's antics, Beatrice bent down to the bird and asked, "Was it you who let me in?"

With a hearty *caw*, Perdu vigorously nodded.

Beatrice laughed, feeling as if she were Alice, gone through the looking glass.

In the back of the room someone seconded her laughter.

"Who's there?" Beatrice asked, taken by surprise.

No sooner had the girl posed the question than the shop's door slammed shut, and the air in the room turned cold.

Perdu lit on the counter and began to hiss. The feathers around his neck puffed into a menacing mane.

Beatrice wasn't sure if she should stay or run.

"Care to have your palm read?" a voice asked from the shadows. "Your future revealed?"

Slowly walking towards the voice, Beatrice came upon a beautiful woman seated at a small, round table. Silver hoops dangling from her ears, silk scarf tied around her head, bangles clanging on her wrists, she looked every bit like the woman whose image graced the back covers of *Madam Morrow's*

Strange Tales of Gotham, a woman who Beatrice had always assumed was Madam Morrow herself.

"I've come to inquire about the position that was advertised in the paper," Beatrice replied. "Are you the shop's owner?"

Silver hoops swinging as she shook her head, the woman said, "No one's here."

"Perhaps I'll come back another time," Beatrice faltered.

"Come, sit!" the woman ordered. "Give me your hand."

Those averse to magic need not apply.

Remembering the words that had appeared at the bottom of the newspaper notice, Beatrice wondered if the fortune teller's invitation might be some sort of test. Seating herself across from the woman she extended her hand.

As the Gypsy turned Beatrice's hand palm up, her own fingers turned pale and withered and her face went blue with death. When the Gypsy opened her mouth, no words came out, just the stink of dank river water, fishy and thick with rot. Gasping, the woman began to choke as if she had something caught in her throat. Before Beatrice could move to help her, the fortune teller stuck her crooked finger between her teeth to retrieve the thing that was causing her distress. With a violent tug and a terrible retch, she brought up a long length of old fishing net tangled with seaweed and oyster shells.

Beatrice hid her face in her hands and made a wish, *Let this be a dream. Let this all be a terrible dream.*

When she opened her eyes the Gypsy had vanished. Sighing with relief, Beatrice tried to stand, but found she was trapped in her seat. Her wish might have caused the woman to disappear, but it hadn't set her free. Her own dress was now dark and heavy and wet—water dripping from her sleeves and skirts, and pooling on the floor at her feet. From the murky puddles a nest of eels emerged, slithering around her ankles. Struggling to escape, she let out a terrible scream and fainted.

Eleanor returned to the shop to find the girl lying in a heap on the floor, and Perdu pacing frantically beside her. Racing to her side, she listened for her breathing, wrapped her fingers around her wrist. "Hello, miss?" she said in her ear. "Please wake up."

Fanning the air in front of the girl's face, she implored again, "Miss . . . wake up."

Perdu stayed close, tilting his head with concern.

Taking a phial of smelling salts from a chatelaine at her waist, Eleanor removed the lid and waved it under Beatrice's nose.

With a terrible grimace, Beatrice opened her eyes.

"Are you all right?" Eleanor asked. The girl had a bump on her head that looked angry and fresh, but at least it wasn't bleeding.

"I think so," Beatrice answered, trying to make sense of her surroundings.

Eleanor helped her to her feet and then to a nearby couch. "I'll get you some water," she said, "or would you prefer tea?"

"Tea," she answered, then remembering her manners, she added, "please."

As Eleanor busied herself behind the counter, Beatrice struggled to collect her thoughts. Was the woman who'd just offered her tea the same woman who'd offered to read her palm? Surely not. Unless, of course, her brain had taken her on some bizarre flight of fancy. Perhaps the bump on her head was worse than she'd thought.

"Here you are," Eleanor said, handing Beatrice a cup. "This should help."

"Thank you," Beatrice said, inhaling the tea's sweet scent.

"Chamomile, lemon balm, lavender and St. John's wort," Eleanor said. "To soothe your nerves."

Closing her eyes, Beatrice took a sip.

Eleanor asked, "When was your last meal?" The poor thing really did seem unwell.

"Breakfast," Beatrice answered, "although I did have a bite or two of apple on the train."

Fetching a plate of teacakes, Eleanor placed it in front of her.

"Thank you," Beatrice said, pinching a small, sticky sweet between her fingers. "They look delicious."

Eleanor smiled as Beatrice gobbled down the cake. Now that the girl was awake and alert, she began to wonder where she'd appeared from. Likely she was just a straggler, a late-comer from the horde of young women she'd turned away outside the shop. But that didn't explain how she'd gotten inside the place—Eleanor was sure she'd locked the door—or why she'd found the young woman in a dead faint on the floor. Weirdly, the girl seemed familiar to her, yet she couldn't place her face. "How exactly did you get in here?" she asked at last.

Beatrice nervously cleared her throat. "The door was open," she stammered. "Well, it was locked at first, but then it was open." Sheepishly pointing to Perdu, she added, "I know this might sound impossible, but I think the bird let me in."

Eleanor looked at Perdu for confirmation.

Puffing out his chest, Perdu gave Eleanor a defiant stare.

Eleanor wondered if she should be interrogating him, not the girl.

At least I didn't imagine the bird, Beatrice thought. *At least he's really here. I saw him before, I see him now. That's a good sign.* "I'm very sorry for causing such a fuss," she said to Eleanor. "As I said to the woman when I first came in, I was hoping to apply for a position in the shop."

"What woman?" Eleanor asked with a scowl. Had Adelaide enlisted this girl?

"There was a woman sitting at a table in the back when I arrived," Beatrice said, "at least I think there was." The table where the Gypsy had sat was no longer there.

"What did she look like?" Eleanor asked, thinking her suspicions were about to be confirmed.

"She was a fortune teller," Beatrice replied.

"In a blue silk dress with a matching hat and veil?"

"No, not at all like that," Beatrice said. "She was a Gypsy, with scarves and bangles and big silver hoops in her ears. She seemed friendly enough at first, but then she changed, or perhaps I was just falling ill, but I swear it looked to me as if she turned into a ghost."

Eleanor bit her lip, knowing exactly who and what she'd seen.

Pacing up and down the length of the counter Perdu squawked, "Top off the pot! Top off the pot!"

"Perdu!" Eleanor scolded. "Hush!"

Sulking, the raven settled down next to Beatrice's bag and again began to peck at its clasp.

Hands trembling, cup rattling in its saucer, Beatrice set her tea aside. She wasn't sure if she was suffering from exhaustion or fear. Perhaps both. "Please don't think me mad," she said, wringing her hands. "I believe I might have train brain, or railway spine, or whatever they call it. The passenger train wasn't running from Stony Point, so I rode the freight train instead. Then we stopped and I fell and by the time I got here, my mind was a complete mess. After that I began hearing things, and quite possibly seeing things too. I don't know what's come over me. I usually travel quite well."

Reaching for Beatrice's cup, Eleanor filled it to the rim. "Here," she said, "have more tea, Miss—"

"Dunn," Beatrice said, realizing she hadn't given the woman her name. "But you can call me Beatrice."

"I'm Eleanor St. Clair, half of St. Clair and Thom."

"Thank you for your kindness, Miss St. Clair," Beatrice said reaching again for her cup.

Eleanor nodded. "You said you fell?" she asked. "Care to tell me about it?" She couldn't help but feel there was more to this than a bumpy train ride or a knock on the head. She didn't think the young woman had it in her to lie, so her talk of ghosts was quite concerning. *First the teapot, now this? What was next?*

"Yes. I fell when the train got stopped outside the city so the great obelisk could pass."

"Cleopatra's Needle? That must've been quite something."

Beatrice nodded. "I got off the train so I could see them move it across the tracks."

"And that's when you fell?"

"No," Beatrice answered. "I fell after it got moved. Right after I touched it."

"I see," Eleanor said, gooseflesh blooming up the length of her arms. She'd heard rumours that the obelisk was imbued with ancient magic. As she continued to regard Beatrice, Perdu finally managed to open the girl's bag. Fishing out a long, knotted string from inside it, he hopped to Eleanor's side and dropped the thing in her lap. "Remember the girl," he softly cooed. "Remember the girl."

"Where did you get this?" Eleanor said, examining the hair and feathers that were tied along the length of it. She recognized it at once for what it was.

"I made it," Beatrice confessed with a nervous chuckle. "It's nothing, really, just a childish plaything."

"I wouldn't say that." As Eleanor turned the string between her fingers, the fiery strands of Beatrice's hair that'd been twisted into the charm glinted in the sun. Eleanor smelled smoke, tasted ash on the tip of her tongue. *Remember the girl.*

Blushing, Beatrice insisted, "Truly, it's only a silly charm. They call it a witch's ladder, or some such thing."

"I know what it is," Eleanor replied, her breath catching as she recognized Beatrice for who she was.

"I only wanted to make a wish come true," Beatrice whispered, embarrassed and ashamed.

With a smile Eleanor placed the charm in Beatrice's hands. "I think it worked."

A Moth Seeks the Light.

NOT WANTING TO go back to the teashop while it was still light—she'd had enough of Eleanor for one day—Adelaide had taken a train to the Fulton Ferry and made her way to Vinegar Hill. As the ferry cut across the East River, passing alongside the Great (yet unfinished) Bridge, Adelaide had stared at the magnificent structure, amazed at the way the labourers skittered like spiders along the network of steel suspension wires attached to the bridge's main cables. Oh to be so fearless! The last time she'd visited the bridge, they'd barely begun the work of winding the wire cables. She'd stood on the banks of the river that day, still whole and even happy, her hand tucked in the arm of a man who'd insisted upon reciting poetry to her. He was a good person, lovely in every way, which is why she'd cut him loose. She hoped that he'd found happiness, and that he hadn't used up all his poetry on her. Love had never been in her cards.

Just as on the night she'd met Judith Dashley, today

Adelaide was on a search for a true medium. She'd visited countless sideshows, dime museums, lecture halls, theatres and séances only to be met with disappointment. Vinegar Hill was a departure from the usual places she looked, but once she'd read the newspaper notice, she couldn't resist the chance to seek out Mr. Beadle and his witch. Just in case.

Standing across the street from the Beadle house, Adelaide wondered if she should bother knocking on the door. *Perhaps he isn't home*, she thought. From the outside, it didn't look much like a place a witch or her affiliated ghosts might dwell. The storey-and-a-half cottage was modest, and recently whitewashed. At the end of a side street off a side street, the house was older by far than the many brick buildings that crowded it. As Adelaide walked up the steps to the door, she hoped that Mr. Beadle would be as welcoming as his home appeared. "Here goes nothing," she said taking hold of the door's knocker and giving it a loud rap.

A few moments later, an elderly man in a wool sack-coat answered the door. He stared at Adelaide with bloodshot eyes.

"Mr. Beadle?" she asked.

"I'm he," the man replied, squinting in an effort to see past her veil. "Why do you ask?"

"I'd like to speak with you about the notice you placed in the *Times*."

Mr. Beadle wiped his nose with a limp handkerchief and came closer to his visitor. Taking a deep sniff as though to breathe in the scent of Adelaide's perfume, he fixed his gaze on her décolletage. He smiled a queasy-making smile, and said, "Lilac parfum's my favourite."

Adelaide took a step back. "Are you receiving visitors?"

"I can be seen," he answered.

"Thank you," Adelaide said, "I won't take too much of your time."

Mr. Beadle turned and led Adelaide down a long, narrow hallway. As she followed him, she wondered if he really did have a witch, or if he'd simply placed the ad in order to bring strangers into his lonely little life. In her experience, people who had no one to care for but themselves were either mad, sad or guilty of some unspeakable crime. Her hatpin was quite sharp and could be used to pierce the papery skin of his neck if need be. She'd use the ivory-handled stiletto she kept tucked in a leather sheath on her right boot only as a last resort.

"Here we are," Mr. Beadle said, opening the door to a small parlour.

Its trappings were as sparse as the hairs on Mr. Beadle's head. A single tin candlestick, a stub of tallow listing in its well, sat on a table between two windows. A rocking chair had been placed to one side of the table, and a small three-legged stool to the other. In the corner, a pot-belly stove was ticking with heat, a kettle humming on its top, spitting drops of water. Mr. Beadle pulled the windows' faded paper shades halfway down against the late afternoon sun. Without offering Adelaide a seat, he settled himself in an armchair close to the stove. "So," he said, rubbing his hands together then holding them out to the heat, "you've come to inquire about my witch, have you?"

"Yes," Adelaide answered, choosing the rocking chair. The room had suddenly taken on the smell of scorched wool, and she hoped that Mr. Beadle wasn't about to go up in flames.

"Tell me, miss," Mr. Beadle said, "have you ever been bewitched?"

"Not to my knowledge."

Taking a pipe and a pouch of tobacco from his pocket, Mr. Beadle went about the tuck, tamp and puff of preparing a smoke. "Well," he said, when the stem was clenched between his teeth, "it's a very hard thing to suffer. This witch of mine, she got me good. She has me right hexed. Some days I can barely speak nor eat. Every time I put my head down to sleep, I wonder if I'll wake. I haven't worked a lick in weeks."

"How do you make your living?" Adelaide asked, unable to imagine that there was any work he was fit enough to do.

"I'm a carpenter," Mr. Beadle said. "A coffin maker as of late. I expect to get back to it soon, God willing."

From the way the man's pipe was shaking in his hand, Adelaide doubted that Mr. Beadle could hold a hammer, let alone swing one. "How did you come to encounter this witch?"

"How does anyone come to know a witch?" Mr. Beadle replied, shaking his head. "It's not like I went looking for one. Only a fool would do that."

"Yes," Adelaide said. "Only a fool. So she came to you, unbidden?"

"No, no, no," Mr. Beadle replied. "A witch can't enter your house unless you invite her in, and that there was my mistake. My wife passed on several months ago, God bless her soul, and I needed someone to do the things she done—cooking, cleaning, fetching things—so I asked around, looking for a maid. Not long after, a young woman came to my door, fresh-faced and sweet, staring at me with the prettiest blue eyes you ever did see." Taking a puff on his pipe he added, "That's important, so don't forget."

"What's that?" Adelaide asked, wishing Mr. Beadle's witch might show up and put an end to the man's prattling.

"Her pretty blue eyes," Mr. Beadle replied. "The prettiest shade of blue."

"So you said."

"That girl and I," Mr. Beadle went on, "we talked a good spell, and in the end, I agreed to let her live here in exchange for her service. There's nine rooms and that's plenty to spare, so she moved in and took the big room upstairs. She also asked if she might use the cellar from time to time for this and that, and I didn't see any harm in it. I never had reason to go down there, so why should I care? She said she'd been married to a sailor, but shortly after they were wed, he'd taken a job on that godforsaken bridge and fallen to his death. With her husband gone she'd had to fend for herself. She had no one in the city and no means to get back home to her family in Scotland. She was a Scotch lass, you see. That's important too."

"So she was Scotch," Adelaide said, tapping her foot in time with the ticking of the stove.

After a hacking cough, Mr. Beadle carried on with his tale. "The first strange thing I noticed was the noises. Her room was directly over mine and every night I heard great rackets up there—voices, wails and whispers, along with footsteps that thudded across the floorboards as if someone was being chased around and around and around. One morning when she was out, I went and tried the door so I could see what she'd been up to, but the door was locked. When I looked through the keyhole, I saw she'd traced a great circle on the floor in a white powder what looked like chalk. In the very centre of the circle was a little black book and next to it, a long, twisted stick. Seeing that was too much for me! Witches use circles to commune with demons and ghosts, you know, and I'm certain that was her intent." Eyes wide, Mr. Beadle added, "I always knew there was witches in the world, but I never thought I'd have one in my house!"

Adelaide guessed it wasn't the first time he'd looked through that keyhole. "Did you confront her with what you'd found?"

"Of course I did!" Mr. Beadle exclaimed. "And no sooner had I put it to her, than she said to me, says she, 'Mr. Beadle, I didn't do it.' 'You did,' says I, holding my ground. 'I saw it with my own two eyes.' 'Mr. Beadle,' says she, 'I didn't. I'll get my Bible and swear to it.' Then I says to her, says I, 'If you swore to it on a thousand Bibles I wouldn't believe you.' After that she started crying and talking gibberish about how she'd heard a voice calling to her from the river. The next time she looked at me, I saw that one of her eyes was turning black. If you've ever seen a witch, you'll know that they always have one black eye. No matter what colour their eyes was before, when they get to be witches, one eye goes black. That's when I knew it wouldn't be long before she'd be trying to take one of my good eyes from me." Pointing at Adelaide's face he asked, "Is that what happened to you? Did a witch get your eye?"

"Not quite," Adelaide replied. If only she had her bottled treasure with her to show Mr. Beadle. Imagine what he'd have to say about that.

"Count yourself lucky," Mr. Beadle said with a nod. "This witch tried all she could to do me in. She thought I'd believed her, but the next time she went out to do the shopping, I figured I'd better check the cellar. So I went in very careful, walking on tiptoe, clear to the back of the chimbley. It was there I found a bundle of rags, tied around a bunch of bones, no doubt belonging to a black cat. There was a bigger bundle beside it, so I opened that one, too, and found it was a pair of men's pantaloons. They was covered with a fine white powder, just like you'd find on a person that's bewitched. I got some of the stuff on me by accident and everywhere it touched my skin it made little spots like pinheads with little circles around them. They itched like crazy when the sun went down. They nearly drove me mad."

"I can imagine," Adelaide said, guessing it was more likely that Mr. Beadle had a nest of bed bugs in his mattress than a witch in his house.

Scratching at his wrist, Mr. Beadle added, "And that wasn't all I discovered down there."

"No?" Adelaide asked.

"Just yesterday I found a little bunch of black hair all wadded up and half buried in the cellar floor. It looked as if it was a piece cut off of the witch's own plait. No sooner had I brought it up and laid it on the table, than it began to wiggle around, rising in the air before my eyes! It frightened me so much that I threw it in the fire. If I hadn't done it, I don't think I'd be alive now. I've heard tell that's the way witches work with hair. To bewitch a person they'll take a bunch of their own hair and bury it, and as soon as it rots, the person dies. But I burned that hair, so it can't rot. Thanks be to heaven, I'm still alive."

"Thanks be," Adelaide said. She thought this man was ridiculous, but her mother had believed in a similar sort of magic. "Never let a stranger get hold of your hair," she'd warned young Moth. "Powerful magic can be done against you by the person who has it." Every night she'd collected the hair from their brushes along with any stray hairs she found on the floor. She kept the hair tucked inside a cloth bag she used as a pincushion, and when the bag got full, she'd cast the hair into the fire while reciting a prayer. Then she'd tell her daughter once again the tale of poor Mrs. Deery, who'd had her hair stolen by an angry sister and then given away to a bird. "The bird wove it into its nest, round and round, back and forth, between sticks and spider webs, causing Mrs. Deery to go mad. The woman walked the streets of the city, afraid of everyone and everything, turning about in circles until she ran right into a delivery wagon and her brains got smashed to bits." The lady who'd bought Adelaide from her mother had cut off her braid with one terrible snip of her scissors, though eventually Adelaide had gone free and the woman had gotten what she deserved. "So where is your witch now?" Adelaide asked, half expecting Mr. Beadle to say she'd flown away on a broomstick.

"A gentleman came three days ago to take her."

"What kind of gentleman?"

"A reverend," Mr. Beadle answered. "He said it's his speciality to look after such business. When I told him I was certain there'd be trouble in it for him, he said not to worry. Then he asked for me to direct him to the witch so he could take care of the rest. It was going on half past ten, so I told him that I guessed she was down at her usual spot by the river. She went there most every day to mark the time and place of her husband's passing. Before the reverend left, I gathered up the girl's things, including what I found in the cellar, and gave it all over to him. He said the only way to be rid of her and her magic was to leave no trace of her in the house. I haven't heard from either of them since."

"What do you suppose he did with her?" Adelaide couldn't help but imagine the worst.

"I don't really care now that my problem's solved," Mr. Beadle answered. "Maybe he'll put the screws to her, or dunk her in the river. I think a witch is worse than a murderer, don't you? A murderer kills you all at once and it's over, but a witch kills you by inches. I think witches ought to be killed themselves. They used to kill them in this country and I hear they still kill them over in Scotland. Send her back, I say."

"Did the gentleman happen to give you his name?"

"I was so pleased to get rid of the girl, I didn't ask. He was well spoken and finely dressed. When I offered to pay him for his services, he refused to accept one penny. I told him he was either a saint or gone mad. I'm sure he'd make a killing if he charged for this sort of thing. They say they got rid of all the witches long ago, but I say they're wrong. Witches are like rats. Where there's one, there's a hundred."

Rising from her chair, Adelaide moved to take her leave. "Thank you for your time, Mr. Beadle. I hope no other witches ever cross your path." *For their sake, not yours*, she thought.

"Thank you kindly, miss," Mr. Beadle said, puffing on his pipe. "You wouldn't happen to know of any girls who might be looking for a housekeeping position, would you? A God-fearing American-born girl, of course."

"I'm afraid I don't," Adelaide said, shaking her head.

Mr. Beadle didn't get up to see her out, so she showed herself to the door. Pausing at the threshold, she spat on it to place a curse on Mr. Beadle's head. She'd seen her mother give such curses to anyone who'd done her wrong. "That," Adelaide said, "is for the blue-eyed maid. Wherever she may be."

Beware the Lure *of* WITCHCRAFT!

Do not let yourselves be fooled by those who say that witches are a thing of the past. WITCHCRAFT is alive and well in America, thanks to a NEW order of WITCHES who are eager to pull the unwitting, the curious and the weak into their web of deceit. These are worrisome times, dear friends. Do not let the renewed workings of the DEVIL take away what our forefathers fought so hard to secure.

Sly in her approach, the NEW WITCH targets men and women alike. Whether dressed in the garb of the "Old Country" or in the fashion of everyday women, she is EVIL in disguise. GENTLEMEN, do not let yourselves be enchanted by her flattering words! By the time you realize the destructive nature of your association, it will be too late! LADIES, do not be tempted to admire these foul creatures, for YOU are her most valued prey! It is a witch's greatest triumph to lure God's daughters away from family, hearth and home.

HOW does she do it? By touting intelligence over righteousness, books of black magic over the Bible, superstition over faith, fashion over modesty, politics over prayer. Crafty in her dealings, she takes on many forms— the healer, the fortune teller, the academic, the suffragist, the spiritualist—all in an effort to lead others astray. TRUE women of GOD do not trouble themselves with such matters. TRUE women of GOD know and obey HIS laws.

 TIMOTHY 2:11 **But I suffer not a woman to teach nor to usurp authority over the man, but to be in silence.**

The WITCHES that plague our city must be rebuked and cast out!

COME to **The Church of the Good Shepherd** to hear HIS word. LEARN of Satan's ways so we might prove victorious over him. SHARE your knowledge of EVIL DOERS so we may bring them into the LIGHT. Do not be afraid. The power of the LORD is on our side.

All are welcome who seek the light. —Rev. Francis Townsend

Mr. Beadle's Witch.

Lena McLeod had been locked in a cold dark cellar for three days. She'd barely had any food to eat except for a hunk of stale bread she'd been given the first night. It'd been so salty she hadn't been able to keep it down. After gagging it up she'd begged her captor for water. "Please," she'd cried, "take pity on me. My thirst is terribly strong."

"Salt is the bane of witches," Reverend Townsend had said, seeming to take pleasure in her pain. "God will soothe your thirst if you repent of your sins."

Lena had not known what to say to that, and was too afraid to speak.

The next day he'd come at her with questions and accusations, threatening to hit her with a thick wooden rod he liked to smack against the palm of his hand. It was carved with primitive markings—circles, crosses, daisy wheels and double Vs—much like those that'd been scratched into the willow tree that stood outside the stone wall of the churchyard in Lena's village in Scotland. Her great-great-grandmother Mrs. Davina Hale had been hanged there, found guilty of witchcraft long before Lena was born.

"State your name," Reverend Townsend had said, prodding her with the rod.

Breath stuttering, Lena answered, "Mrs. Lena McLeod."

"Do you know where you are, Mrs. McLeod?"

"In a house of God?"

"And do you know why you're here?"

"I've done nothing wrong," she insisted. "Please let me go."

"I'm afraid I can't do that," the Reverend replied.

"I'll do whatever you want," Lena pleaded.

Leaning close, the Reverend whispered in her ear, "I'll keep that in mind." As he straightened up he asked, "Is your husband living, Mrs. McLeod?"

"No sir, he's dead."

"How long ago did he die?"

"One year ago this December."

"And how did he come to pass?"

"He fell from the Great Bridge."

"And you had nothing to do with it? You did nothing to cause it?"

"No, nothing," Lena answered honestly, yet feeling sick with guilt. Not a day had gone by since Johnny's death that she hadn't blamed herself for it. She should've believed the signs when she first saw them and not let him walk out the door. There'd been talk in her family of other women having similar visions, that Davina's gifts had been passed down through her blood, but Lena's mother, a God-fearing woman, had told her it was best not to pay any attention to such tales. The foretelling had seemed so strong . . . but, still, she'd been afraid that if she told Johnny what she'd seen, he'd think she'd gone mad. (For a time, she'd thought maybe she had.) She'd seen his face in the washbasin the morning of his death, staring up at her through the soap flakes, then rising to the surface, gasping for air. But she'd let him go to the bridge. Then she'd grown frantic and decided to warn him. She'd been ready to climb the wobbly footbridge made of planks and wire that stretched to the top of the caissons, but the foreman hadn't let her pass.

Instead she'd knelt at the water's edge. "What if I gave you my life for his?" she'd asked the River in her desperation.

"That's not how it works," the River had answered. "The choice is made."

Within the hour, Johnny was dead.

"And you came to live with the good Mr. Beadle sometime after that?" the Reverend asked.

"I did," Lena answered.

Cradling her chin in his hand, the Reverend tipped her face so her eyes met his and said, "And you seduced him into taking you on."

"I did not!" Lena cried.

"But you had no means to support yourself and no place to go." Taking a little chapbook from his pocket the preacher laid it in Lena's lap. The title on the cover read, *Madam Morrow's Book of Potions, Hexes and Spells.* "Is this yours?" he asked.

"Yes."

"So you don't deny it?"

"No sir," she said.

"What was the purpose of your having it?"

"A woman at the market offered it to me after my husband died. She said there was a spell in there for talking to the dead. I was mad with grief, so I took it. I was curious and desperate. I wanted to be sure he was all right."

"And what of the things Mr. Beadle found in his cellar?"

"I was only trying to scare him a little. He was awfully mean to me."

The Reverend hadn't stopped heaping abuse upon her since then. No matter how hard she begged, he hadn't relented. He'd said it was God's will for him to test her and if she came through clean he'd let her go. He'd taken her clothes and burned them. He'd cut her hair and burned it too. He'd collected her urine for God knows what purpose. He'd pricked her arms, her thighs, her breasts and every freckle she had with a hot needle. He'd asked her to recite the Lord's Prayer, but when she'd done so in her native tongue, he'd beaten her with the rod and told her "those are the Devil's words."

She was never sure when he was going to torment her. She could hear his footsteps overhead, pacing, at all hours of the day and night. She was free to move about the room but there was no escape. The furnishings were sparse, the floor was dirt, the walls stone and the door always locked.

To pass the time she sat and looked at a single small window, high on the back wall. It was bricked over on the outside, braced by thick bars sunk deep into the stone on the inside. For a short while each day, a scant beam of light shone through a crack between the bricks. This morning, while she lay on her straw mattress, the light had heralded a vision that floated and danced before her eyes. She was hanging by a noose from the willow tree, her body swinging next to Davina's.

Shrugging out of her cotton shift, she tore it into long, ragged strips. She sang the Lord's Prayer as she braided the strands together, even laughed as her sadness turned to elation.

Ar n–Athair a tha air nèamh,
Gu naomhaichear d'ainm.

Standing on a rickety stool, she tied one end of the rope to one of the bars in the window.

Thigeadh do rìoghachd.
Dèanar do thoil air an talamh,
mar a nìthear air nèamh.

She fashioned the other end into a hangman's knot and slipped it over her head.

Tabhair dhuinn an-diugh ar n-aran làitheil.
Agus maith dhuinn ar fiachan,
amhail a mhaitheas sinne dar luchd-fiach.
Agus na leig ann am buaireadh sinn;
ach saor sinn o olc:

Stepping off the stool she let God do the rest.

oir is leatsa an rìoghachd,
agus an cumhachd,
agus a' glòir,
gu sìorraidh. Amen

Reverend Townsend found her body not long after, limp with death, her flesh still warm. Hand lingering on her calf, he was disappointed, then relieved, then deliciously satisfied.

There was immense beauty in the demise of evil. Falling to his knees he uttered a prayer of thanksgiving.

Before he'd finished, before he'd even begun to consider what he might do to get rid of the young woman's body, two strangers entered the room from the cellar doorway. Like a pair of funeral mutes, wearing long frock coats and wide-brimmed hats, the men moved with an air of quiet, unshakable purpose.

Startled, Reverend Townsend feared he was caught. "She did herself in," he stammered. "There was nothing I could do."

One of the men approached him and placed a steady hand on his shoulder. "Go to your bedchamber," he ordered. "Fast and pray until first light."

Pointing to the open door the other man said, "Leave us now. All will be well."

September 17, 1880, Evening.
St. Clair and Thom,
Tea and Sympathy,
933 Broadway,
New York, New York

Dear Aunt Lydia,
I am well. I am safe.
Please send my winter coat, my second pair of
shoes, my other day dress, and my Sunday best to
the above address at your earliest convenience.
As you may have guessed, the position is mine!
More soon, when I am properly settled.

With affection,
Beatrice.

Messages From Abroad.

ELEANOR SAT IN the window of the teashop that night, waiting for Adelaide to return. Feet propped on a low wooden stool, she nursed a cup of blackberry tea and wondered where the day had gone. So much had happened, yet it felt as though the day had passed in a blink. She hated days that ended with more questions than answers.

Beatrice had retired upstairs, and Eleanor hoped the girl would soon be nodding off to sleep with Perdu on his perch at her side. Seeing the toll the day had taken on the girl, Eleanor had offered up her own bed for the night. They'd make a cozy place for her in the garret tomorrow. Besides, Eleanor had so much on her mind, she wasn't sure she could sleep. Her head was still swimming with the day's events—her argument with Adelaide (which she was sorry for now), the strange circumstances of Beatrice's arrival, and the unsolved puzzle as to what was troubling Lady Hibiscus (she never had caught up with her old lover). If she did need some shuteye, she could always curl up on the couch, or lie down next to Adelaide for a spell. That was, if Adelaide ever decided to come home. She could use her friend's advice in sizing up their new girl.

"You say you're from Stony Point?" she'd asked Beatrice over dinner.

"Yes, Miss St. Clair," Beatrice had answered. She was so polite, so sweet!

"Please, call me Eleanor."

"Yes, ma'am . . . I mean, Eleanor."

"Stony Point is on the Hudson, up past Sleepy Hollow?"

"Yes," the girl had answered. "Just across the river from Verplanck."

Eleanor wondered if Stony Point, like Sleepy Hollow, was a place of covered bridges, haunted burial grounds and headless horsemen. Had Beatrice really spotted a ghost in the shop or had she brought it with her? She'd come to the city with so little in hand, had she really planned to win the job and stay here? And what of the witch's ladder Perdu had found in her bag? Well done, dear bird. His nose for magic was as keen as ever.

The charm was far more than the simple plaything Beatrice had made it out to be. Did the girl truly not know what she'd done? How could she not see the perfection in her handiwork, feel the magic bound in every knot? Was the girl being fully honest? Had she run away from someone, or from some terrible deed? "And no one's missing you?" she'd asked, hoping to get to the bottom of the matter.

"My aunt Lydia, I suppose," Beatrice had answered. "But I'm here with her blessing, if that's what you're wondering."

"Yes," Eleanor had said with a laugh, "I suppose it is." What would Adelaide do faced with such a situation? *Confess a little, learn a lot.* "I come from an out-of-the-way place as well," Eleanor had confided. "I know how tempting it can be to leave the past behind."

"Where was that?" Beatrice had asked.

"On the Bronx River," Eleanor had replied.

"Was it anywhere near Fordham Village?" Beatrice asked. "I hear it's lovely there."

"No," Eleanor had said, shaking her head. "It's far too small to have a name. There isn't even a road leading to it. You can only get there by water."

"Sounds idyllic," Beatrice had said with a smile.

"It was," Eleanor replied.

Taking another sip of tea, Eleanor wondered how her mother's cottage was faring. Her uncle had promised to keep an eye on it, but she guessed he was too busy with farm and family to give it much attention. She hoped it hadn't gotten terribly overgrown or broken down. She hadn't been there since early spring when she'd gone to collect fiddleheads from the forest. She'd like to see the place again, someday soon, perhaps—to pick apples from the craggy trees that surrounded the garden, to collect hips from the wild roses that grew along the hedgerows, to raid the cellar for a bottle or two of elderberry wine.

In the last days of her life, Madame St. Clair had ordered Eleanor to sit by her side so she might confess all her secrets. In those sad, beautiful, drawn-out hours, Eleanor had sat quietly with pen in hand as her mother recited a number of stories she'd often told her in her youth. The lively tales of peasants and princes, witches and queens, came to life again in her mother's ailing voice—her advice peppered with laughter, her warnings accompanied by tears. The last story she'd recited was "The Princess Who Wished to Be a Witch," an eerie tale filled with magic and wonder and a raven who bore a striking resemblance to her dear Perdu.

The Princess Who Wished to Be a Witch

Long ago, a beautiful princess named Odoline wanted to become a witch. Her mother, the Queen, had died when she was born and aside from the Queen's jewels and robes, all Odoline had left of the woman were the precious books she'd collected in her library. Whenever she grew tired of listening to her five quarrelsome brothers bicker (which was quite often), she'd steal away to the library to sit and read and ponder.

Among the volumes were a handful of books devoted to tales about sorceresses, seers and witches. As a young girl, Odoline's nurse had told her that the women in the tales were her kin, connected to her by her mother's blood. When Odoline had asked her father, the King, if what her nurse had said was true, he'd laughed and said, "Those are nothing but fairy tales, dear daughter." Sure enough the stories were populated by fairies (and trolls and ghosts and demons, too), but Odoline found more truth in the pages of those books than in her daily life. It wasn't long before she was able to read the magic that lived between the stories' lines.

When the time came for her to choose a suitor, her father called forth the brightest and strongest princes and knights of the land. One after another Odoline rejected them, sometimes dancing only one dance at a ball or watching one jousting match, so she could return to her studies in the library.

The King, at his wit's end, sought the counsel of a sage, hoping he might have a solution to the problem. After a brief conversation with Odoline (where she barely looked at him over the top of a book), the sage had returned to the King. "Leave it with me," he said, "I'll take care of it."

Not long after, a handsome young prince named Sev came to the castle and presented a gift to Odoline—a book of tattered parchment, bound in chains and fixed with a heart-shaped lock. "'Tis a book of spells," he said, "the most powerful known to man. I give it to you along with the key, but you must promise never to open it."

Sev, of course, was the sage in disguise, and he'd hatched a terrible plan. He knew that the princess had witchery in her blood and desired to become a great sorceress. Seeing her powers as a threat to his own, he sought to deny them to her. The book was indeed as powerful as he claimed, but he was willing to part with it to secure his place in the kingdom. He'd charmed the book to tempt the princess so the minute she gave in to its powers, she'd feel the wrath of its curse. The book contained spells of all sorts—including precise instructions on how to summon demons. Those who understand magic know that demons have their uses, but only when tempered by the company of angels. The book contained the names of forty angels. The number of demons it named was forty-one.

Odoline did indeed choose Sev for her suitor. In return for his gift she gave him a gold ring inscribed with the words, "All my trust." The book sat for one hundred days unopened on her desk while the pair danced and sang and made love in the corridors and gardens of the castle. The key to the lock on the chains that bound the book was tied safely on a scarlet ribbon around Odoline's neck.

When the day of her wedding arrived, Odoline snuck away from her attendants to sit alone in her library. She wished to find a verse to read to her new husband on their wedding night. Spying the book of spells on the desk, she went to it. When she touched it, the chains around the book began to rattle, the lock began to shake. "Who is Sev to forbid *me* to open it?" she thought. "It belongs to me and I'll do with it as I see fit." Removing the key from around her neck, she opened the lock and shook the chains free from the book.

Instantly, a cloud of darkness swirled around the princess and a terrible howling sounded in the air. An enormous demon appeared before her, growling, snorting and gnashing his teeth.

"Heaven assist me!" Odoline cried, but no angel came to her aid.

The demon stared at Odoline with hungry yellow eyes, then opened its gaping, ragged mouth. "When the balance of good and evil is tipped towards hell, nothing can save you," it said.

Odoline was sure this wasn't true. She'd read about angels as well as demons and knew that each one had their strengths and weaknesses. "State your name," she demanded, knowing the demon would be compelled to answer by the witch's blood that flowed in her veins.

"Malphas," the demon hissed, foaming at the mouth.

It was a name that Odoline knew well. Malphas was the mighty prince of Hell with forty legions of demons under his command, second only to Satan. Malphas, builder of towers, strongholds and monuments. Malphas, destroyer of desires and dreams. Malphas was also known as "the giver," because when conjured by a witch, he was bound by her magic to spare her life and present her with a familiar. "Bring me a companion," Odoline said, making the sign of the horns with her fingers. "And then be gone."

The demon threw his head back and roared. "Because of you," he said, "all witches will suffer! They'll be forever cursed to hide their gifts from the light." Then he vanished from the room leaving behind the stench of sulphur and a heap of black feathers at Odoline's feet.

When Odoline bent to inspect what Malphas had given her, she discovered a handsome, bright-eyed raven with a gold ring around its leg.

That was the day Odoline declared herself a witch.
It was also the day the hunts began.

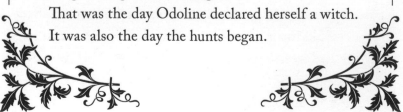

After Madame St. Clair had recited Odoline's tale one last time, she'd tugged at something around her neck. To Eleanor's surprise, it was a scarlet ribbon. She was sure she'd never noticed her mother wearing it in the past. "Take the key," her mother had whispered, "to remind you of our past. Demons may cross your path, but you have the power to beat them."

As Eleanor had dropped the ribbon around her own neck, her mother had struggled on, her words catching on every breath. "The time will soon come when witches won't be born, but made. The first will come to you. She'll need to learn. You must teach her."

"How will I know who she is?" Eleanor had asked, desperate to make sense of her mother's words.

"Perdu knows," her mother had answered. "He's always known."

Within hours of her mother's passing, two men had come to the door wearing the dark frowns and wide-brimmed hats of undertakers. "May we assist you in your time of sorrow?" they'd asked. Eleanor hadn't the faintest notion of how they'd gotten there, or how they'd found out about her mother's death. In her grief, she'd considered letting them in, thinking her mother might have summoned them without her knowing, but Perdu had kicked up a terrible fuss. Flying to the peak of the roof he'd cried out as if he were in agony. In an instant, a flock of ravens had appeared, darkening the sky overhead. In the midst of their cacophony, Eleanor had sworn she'd heard the words, "All my trust." She'd told the men, "Thank you for your offer, but there's nothing for you here."

She herself had dug a grave under a hawthorn tree and laid her mother to rest. Then she'd gone to the bees to tell them their mistress had died. Perdu had grieved alongside her as she'd wept among the hives, and followed at her heels as she'd cast spells of protection over every inch of the land and every corner of the house.

"Here's to you, Maman," Eleanor said, finishing her tea and holding her cup to the air. Then upending the cup on its saucer, she turned it three times round. If ever she needed the counsel of the leaves, it was now. When she turned the cup and saucer over again, she heard a loud clang. Setting the saucer aside, she discovered that the key her mother had given her was resting inside the teacup's bowl, its scarlet ribbon spilling over the rim.

"What witchery is this?" Eleanor whispered, staring at the key in disbelief. She hadn't worn the thing in ages, hadn't looked at it in months. She'd kept it hidden in her room, safe from any chance of losing it. Placing the key around her neck, she rushed to the counter to fetch a jar of salt. Spreading a thick line of grains in a wide circle around herself, she chanted a spell of protection.

Thrice around, the circle's bound.

Sink all evil to the ground.

O goddess good, of day and night,
Protect this place with all your might.
By the magic power of three,

Summon the angels to accompany me.
So may it be, so may it be, so may it be!

As Eleanor spoke the last words of the spell, Adelaide came through the door, wobbling to and fro and smelling of absinthe. Standing outside the circle, she shook her head. "I don't want to know."

"Quiet," Eleanor shushed her, reaching out to Adelaide, inviting her to cross the line.

Adelaide immediately saw the fear in Eleanor's eyes. "What's happened?"

Clutching Adelaide's hand, Eleanor answered, "I'm not sure."

As Beatrice slept, Twitch lay on her pillow, propped on his elbow, chin in hand. With a lovesick sigh he stared at the girl, then reached out to tuck a curl behind her ear. "You're beautiful," he whispered. "If only I could tell you to your face."

"Stop it," Bright scolded, cuffing Twitch on the back of his head. "You know it's against the rules. Besides, it won't do her any good. Flattery does nothing but cloud a girl's judgement."

"Humph," Twitch said, before resuming his adoration of Beatrice.

Although she wasn't about to admit it, Bright was enjoying watching the girl sleep as much as Twitch was. It was a relief not to have anything to do outside of observing the sweet-faced creature. Twitch was right, she was a beautiful thing—so full of new-found magic that Bright could taste it in the air. It was fresh, like morning dew on rose petals, delicious as the nectar in a honeysuckle blossom. Still, Bright wasn't about to encourage Twitch's silly notions. When it came to Beatrice Dunn, they couldn't afford to make mistakes. That's why they wouldn't be building her any dreams—not yet.

September 18, 1880.

Waning, gibbous moon.

A NOTE on WAYWARD GHOSTS.

Most witches needn't bother with ghosts. There's magic enough to be found among the living. Still, it's important to know how best to deal with stray spirits, if and when they should cross your path.

The likelihood of this happening is great. Spirits of a confused, uneasy nature often clamour after magic and those who practice it (especially newborn babes with witchery in their blood, and young, inexperienced witches). For the most part, they mean no harm. Do not confuse their activities with the work of various otherworldly folk—demons, goblins, imps, elementals, shadow beings, angels, fairies, nymphs, gnomes, elves and so on.
Most hauntings are brief affairs marked by the typical signs—strange shadows on the wall, odd reflections in mirrors, scents lingering in the room, draughts of cold air, bumps in the night. Should these signs persist or increase, they may indicate an infestation. Poltergeists are often the most troublesome of the lot. They can move objects with ease—within a room, about the house, and in rare cases, from one time or place to another. Should these things happen, be wary but not afraid. Do your best to allow the spirit to pass through, unchecked. It's likely they have important business to which they must attend, just as you have yours. . . . *continued*

If wayward ghosts insist upon disrupting your life or your dwelling place, look first to yourself for the reason why. Have you done something to encourage their presence? Did you leave your house or yourself unprotected? Have you moved a sacred object from its proper place? Did you bring a relic of unknown origins into your home? Has a person of questionable motives crossed your threshold in the recent past? Have you disturbed sacred ground, either knowingly or unwittingly? Have you undertaken mundane tasks during sacred hours? Did you trifle with magic to call upon the dead? (There are proper ways to go about this. Rules must be obeyed.)

Whenever possible, make amends without directly addressing the deceased. Endeavouring to make contact without taking proper precautions is a recipe for disaster. Such activities should only be carried out by experienced witches skilled in the art of necromancy.

—*From the grimoire of Eleanor St. Clair*

Mirror, Mirror on the Wall.

"WHERE'S PERDU?" ADELAIDE asked, hands on her hips. She'd come downstairs that morning and the bird hadn't announced her arrival. He always made a point of it, especially when she'd slept in: she swore the bird liked to stir up trouble.

"He's with Beatrice," Eleanor answered, pouring tea into a pair of cups—one for Adelaide, one for herself.

Adelaide pondered the name "Beatrice," but found she couldn't place it.

Placing a small pitcher of honey on the counter, Eleanor prompted, "Our new girl—"

"Oh yes, that's right," Adelaide said. "I almost forgot."

She'd been dreadfully tipsy when she'd come home for the night so the memory of her conversation with Eleanor was sketchy at best. Squinting against the sunlight that was streaming through the shop windows, she tried to think if there was anything important (other than the girl, of course) that she might've forgotten.

After her fruitless trip to see Mr. Beadle's witch, she'd stopped by the Fifth Avenue Hotel for a late supper. She'd hoped she might run into Judith Dashley ahead of their scheduled meeting with the mysterious Dr. Brody.

Although she hadn't had any luck spotting Judith, the soup du jour had been clam chowder, which she loved. The hotel kitchen served it beer-garden style, with brown bread and a side of baked beans drowned in syrupy molasses sauce. The dining room had bustled with the usual evening crowd— ladies gossiping after a long day of shopping, businessmen courting out-of-town clients, and politicos embroiled in a heated discussion about the best way to get their man into the White House. The election was less than two months away, and Senator Roscoe Conkling and his merry band of Republicans had set up shop at the hotel for the duration. He and two of his Conklingites were at the next table going back and forth about what would win more votes: promising to back the struggling economy with the gold standard, or reminding the public that theirs was the party that'd preserved the Union by winning the war.

Conkling stood firm on his views. "Men want to be assured that the money they make, however much or little that might be, is as good as gold."

The man to his left shook his head. "Times are tough for the average Joe. Best not get them thinking about money. Heaven knows Garfield's business record doesn't instill much confidence." The portly fellow had a line of beer foam clinging to his moustache.

"Hear, Hear!" the man to Conkling's right bellowed. "I say let's not make this about Garfield at all. Who cares about a farm boy from Ohio? The only way he's going to win is if we point the finger in the other direction. Blame the Dems for everything that's gone wrong—secession, the war, hard times . . . need I go on?" He was long-necked and gangly, the Jack Spratt to his foamy-faced companion.

Conkling looked as if he'd smelled something rotten. "Do you really think we can play the war card again? How long can we get away with waving the bloody shirt?"

"It worked for Hayes," the portly one replied.

"Barely," the gangly one sighed.

"Barely's good enough," Conkling said. "So long as you're the winner."

Adelaide didn't know much about Conkling's political leanings, and she didn't much care to, but she knew quite a lot about his reputation among women. The greying yet virile statesman had been known to go a round or two in the boxing ring as well as between the sheets with several of his colleagues' wives. The previous summer he'd been caught with his pants down while tending to Mrs. Kate Sprague at her summer home in Rhode Island. Her husband, the Governor of the Smallest State, had reportedly held a shotgun in his hand while showing Conkling the door.

After waving away the dessert cart, Adelaide had treated herself to a glass or three (or had it been four?) of absinthe. Each time the waiter dutifully poured her more, she'd squinted at the dose line and pronounced, "It looks a little short." Balancing a slotted silver spoon across the rim of her glass, she'd gotten on with the artful task of preparing her drink. First came a sugar cube, carefully set on top of the spoon. Then came a measure of cold, clear water, meted out in drips. When done correctly, it created a beautiful, cloudy mixture. To Adelaide the stuff looked as inviting as the tall, refreshing glasses of milk they served at the Central Park Dairy on hot summer days. *Here's to life's short play and all that*, she'd thought, as she'd raised her glass to her lips. *Here's to Anthony Comstock and all the fine ladies in the WCTU! Here's to the green fairy and to making mischief! Here's to the Fifth Avenue Hotel and its resident ghosts!* (Thinking back, there was a distinct possibility that she'd said those things out loud.)

As the anise-flavoured liquor had wriggled its way through her senses, she'd turned her attention from the obstreperous politicos to the hotel's owner, Mrs. Marietta Stevens, who was making her evening rounds through the dining room, stopping at every table to hand out compliments and gather whatever morsels of information her patrons cared to offer. Each time she'd said her goodnights and farewells, she'd ended the conversation by saying, "It's by my guests' happiness that I prevail." It was an effortless performance that Adelaide greatly admired.

Time and again the press had referred to the widowed Mrs. Stevens as "a woman of lowly beginnings," but Adelaide regarded her as a woman to be revered. What's more, she thought that if she hadn't married Mr. Paran Stevens, the famous hotelier, she would've made one hell of a mind reader. Marietta had the knack for knowing what people needed before they knew they needed it, and the forethought to commit a person's secrets to memory until such time as they might be of use. Adelaide prided herself on the fact that she and Marietta were more alike than different, and that a woman of such influence chose to come to her for advice. While she wasn't sure there was anything in particular she could do about the romance that'd blossomed between the widow's son and Edith Jones, she figured she should at least ask if there'd been any progress one way or another. When Marietta had reached her table, Adelaide had asked, "How goes the disenchantment of Miss Jones?"

"Slow," Marietta had replied, settling down next to Adelaide.

Adelaide wished she didn't have to choose sides in the matter. Edith Jones was a lovely young woman, keen and bright and observant. Adelaide was convinced that if no one got in her way she'd go quite far in life. "You said the girl has an active mind, no?"

"It never stops."

"Not to worry, then. She'll think herself out of her passion for your son, eventually. I say let the affair run its course."

"I suppose that's all I can do, for now," Marietta replied. "I've more pressing matters at hand."

"Anything I can help you with?"

Marietta had stared across the room, thoughts clearly

turning in her head. Fingers steepled, she'd finally looked at Adelaide and said, "Perhaps."

Waving to the waiter for another dose of absinthe, Adelaide leaned close to Marietta and said, "Go on."

"I hate to admit it," Marietta whispered, "but it's the ghosts."

Shaking her head, Adelaide said, "I thought you believed they weren't real."

"Let's just say they've been rather convincing as of late."

"How so?" Adelaide asked, intrigued by Marietta's words.

"Extinguishing gaslights in the corridors, knocking over chairs with abandon, showing their ghoulish faces to the help. The chambermaids are beside themselves and my poor housekeeper, Mrs. Fisher, can barely keep up with their wild tales and silly superstitions."

Adelaide gave a sympathetic nod. "Perhaps you should consider that such occurrences might be reason to rejoice. I've heard encounters with wayward spirits are all the rage among certain circles."

Marietta rolled her eyes. "Be that as it may, for every spook-loving Judy that thrills at the mention of ghosts, there's a shrinking violet who'll pack her bags and head somewhere else."

"Your ghosts may be less trouble than you think," Adelaide suggested. "You just need to persuade them to follow your command."

"The trouble is they're not on my payroll. I haven't any clout when it comes to making them behave. You wouldn't happen to know anyone who can reason with spirits, would you? I don't want some sideshow charlatan, mind you, but the genuine article."

The sideshow remark wounded Adelaide, but she'd let it slide since Marietta had no inkling of her past. "I might," she'd answered. Eleanor had never said she couldn't talk to ghosts. She'd only said she wouldn't.

"Well if you come across such a person, please send her straight to me. Imagine the business I'd pull in if I could get those sneaky little ghouls to do my bidding!"

After another round of absinthe, Adelaide had finally made her way back to the shop, her limbs numb and heavy, her head feeling as if it might float away on the cool autumn breeze. Aside from the brief moment of confusion she'd suffered when she'd first come through the door, it'd seemed a positive sign to find Eleanor off her nut and circled by a line of salt sprinkled on the floor. Perhaps she could talk to ghosts after all! Waiting for her chance to broach the subject, Adelaide had only half-listened as Eleanor went on about Perdu and a late train and some girl who'd fainted in the shop. When Eleanor had gotten to the part where she'd announced that she'd taken the girl on as hired help, all Adelaide had been able to think was that it didn't seem quite fair that she hadn't gotten any say in the decision, especially after it'd been her idea to put the notice in the paper in the first place.

Remembering she was still slightly sore over the matter, Adelaide glowered at Eleanor. "So where is this Beatrice now?"

Pointing to the ceiling, Eleanor whispered, "She's asleep."

"Asleep?" Adelaide exclaimed, hoping to make enough noise to rouse the girl. She didn't appreciate having to tiptoe around someone she'd never met.

"Hush," Eleanor scolded. "She won't be any good to me if she's under the weather. I told you of the state she was in . . . don't you remember?"

"Right, right," Adelaide said, not wanting their discussion to turn to the state *she'd* been in last night. Better that Beatrice be on the receiving end of Eleanor's bedside manner. A vague memory of Eleanor slipping into bed beside her sometime in the night led her to ask, "Were you up late?"

"Not too late." Eleanor clutched a key that was hanging around her neck then slipped it under the collar of her dress. Adelaide didn't think to make anything of it. Eleanor had any number of amulets she wore to assist her with her magic—a bone trinket carved in the shape of a hand, a locket containing the whiskers of a black cat. Adelaide had stopped keeping track of them all. "Let's hope Sleeping Beauty wakes up soon or I'm afraid you'll regret giving her your bed."

Eleanor shook her head. "Did anyone ever tell you that you talk in your sleep?"

"I do not," Adelaide replied.

"Yes, you do."

"Tell me then, what did I say? Anything good? Did any burning confessions fall from my lips?"

"Nothing worth repeating."

The ghost of Adelaide's mother looked on while the two women bickered. She remembered what it had been like to share a bed with her daughter, how the child's wiry little legs had kicked about under the thin covers, and how, yes indeed, she'd had a tendency to blather in her sleep. *I was "Mama" then*, she thought. *And you were my little "Moth." Who am I now? What have we become?*

She didn't like this business of Moth calling herself "Adelaide," which sounded snobbish to her ears. But who was she to judge? She hadn't held her child enough, she knew that now. She'd never been able to give the girl a decent life. She hadn't wanted to raise her with things that would make her weak—hugs, lullabies, kisses, hope, dreams, love—so she'd replaced comfort with disinterest and hard knocks. She'd only done what she'd thought was best. How could she have known that she wouldn't be able to protect her—not in life, not in death?

It haunted her still. That's why she was chasing after Adelaide. She wanted to tell her daughter everything she'd left unsaid, and more importantly, of the things she'd witnessed since she'd gone beyond the veil. If only she hadn't spent all her time with her daughter feeding her sorrow! She might've saved them both from so many terrible things. Now she was being punished for it, bound by chains of regret—for how she'd lived and how she'd died—sentenced to stand at her daughter's side during every bad thing that'd happened to the girl since. She'd watched helplessly on that terrible day when her dear girl had been attacked, her screams of warning unable to reach Adelaide's ears.

"Moth!" the spirit cried. "Do you hear me? Listen to me, Moth!"

Upstairs, the bottle in Adelaide's desk rolled from side to side.

Scowling, Adelaide waved her hand in the air. "Damn flies. Always buzzing in my ear."

The spirit gave up her pestering and hid between two teapots. *She'll hear me soon enough,* she thought. *That damned know-it-all fairy promised me as much.* The scheming pixie had brokered a deal with her, allowing her to slip through a crack unprotected by Eleanor's spells in exchange for her agreeing to do the fairy's bidding—break a teapot, move a key, show herself to the girl.

Oh, maybe it hadn't gone the way the fairy had instructed, but she was only having a bit of fun. She hadn't meant to scare the poor child. How was she to know she'd be so delicate? In the end she'd done as she was told. She'd enticed the girl to come into the shop and the girl had stayed. In the dark of night as the pixie had fluttered near the girl's bed, the cranky spirit had tipped her over, wing over ass, and asked, "Why can *she* see me when my own daughter can't?"

"She's special," the fairy had answered before turning her back.

Humph, the spirit thought. *We'll see about that.*

At ten o'clock, Beatrice came downstairs with Perdu hopping at her heels. "Good morning, Miss St. Clair," she said. "I hope I'm not too late."

"You're right on time," Eleanor said, pouring a cup of tea for her. Offering her a plate filled with sliced cheese and sugared pastries, she asked, "How are you faring this morning? I trust you had a good sleep?" Pulling a saucer of raw stew meat from behind the counter, she set it on the floor for Perdu.

The bird sank his clawed foot into the largest chunk to hold it steady. Tugging it into stringy bits with his beak, one by one he flipped each morsel into the air, then gobbled it down.

Adelaide stared at Beatrice over the rim of her teacup.

"I'm feeling much better, thank you," Beatrice replied. "It was awfully generous of you to lend me your bed." Then reaching for a piece of cheese she said, "I hope you'll see fit to put me to work today. Otherwise I'll feel awfully spoiled."

Adelaide smiled and said, "Perhaps Miss St. Clair's only fattening you up so she can boil you like a ham hock and eat you with a side of cabbage."

Beatrice let out a nervous laugh.

"Adelaide!" Eleanor scolded. "Behave yourself." Turning to Beatrice she said, "Beatrice Dunn, meet Adelaide Thom."

Grinning, Adelaide looked to Beatrice. Lifting her veil away from her face she said, "You know I'm teasing, don't you, dear?"

Beatrice's eyes went wide. "Yes, of course, Miss Thom," she stammered, offering Adelaide her hand. "It's nice to meet you."

Adelaide gave the girl's hand a firm squeeze. *We'll see about that*, she thought. "So lovely to meet you too, Beatrice."

Perdu chortled, then tapped at his plate. All that was left was a runny puddle of blood.

"Here," Eleanor said, setting a bowl of water in its place. "Drink up."

Dipping his beak, the raven slurped the liquid into his mouth, then tipped it down his throat.

Adelaide nicked a pastry from Beatrice's plate, tore a sizable chunk from it and stuck it in her mouth. Returning the remainder of the sweet, she said, "You don't mind, do you? I couldn't resist."

Beatrice gave Adelaide a kind smile. "Not at all," she said. "Help yourself to the rest of it if you like. I'm not really one for sweets. My aunt Lydia says they make the senses sluggish."

Licking the sugar off her fingers Adelaide said, "How sad."

Eleanor squinted at Adelaide. A warning-shot across the bow. Adelaide kept her sights fixed on Beatrice. "How old are you?" She reached for the wounded pastry. (*And why shouldn't she? The girl didn't want it.*)

"Seventeen, this past summer."

"Seventeen!" Adelaide exclaimed. "I can barely remember it."

"Ha!" Perdu squawked, with a violent shake of his head.

Eleanor smiled at her pet.

Ignoring the bird, Adelaide studied Beatrice—the sweet timbre of her voice, the casual confidence in her posture, the sincere interest in her dewy eyes. Eleanor hadn't bothered to mention she was a beauty. Save for the small scrape on her forehead (which the poor girl had tried to hide with one of her shiny curls), everything about her was measured and neat, near perfect. Even the bright blue ribbon tied at the end of her braid was crisp and clean. The girl's face was much the same—not a trace of ill will or disappointment was discernible on it. *And oh, what a searching gaze! She's waiting for me to like her. How frustratingly endearing! If she expects my approval today, she'll have to wait.* Spying the clock on the shelf behind the counter, Adelaide turned to Eleanor and said, "Oh my, look at the time. I must fly. I'm off to breakfast with Judith at the Fifth."

"When will you be back?" Eleanor asked, wiping the powdery trail of sugar Adelaide had left on the counter. "What am I to tell your sitters?"

"Tell them they should've made an appointment," Adelaide said with an indifferent shrug. Walking to her table in the back of the shop, she hung an elegantly lettered sign on her chair: THE SEER IS OUT.

"Wait," her mother's ghost called, flying out from her hiding spot. She desperately wanted to follow her daughter but was afraid to leave the shop in case she might not be able to get back in.

"Ta-ta," Adelaide said, as she headed out the door. Bells jangled in her wake.

"I don't think she likes me," Beatrice whispered to Eleanor.

"Give it time," Eleanor said. "She'll come around."

Clearing away the dishes, Beatrice glanced at the mirror behind the counter and caught sight of Adelaide's mother's ghost. She stifled a scream.

Silver hoops glinting in the looking glass, the Gypsy woman put her finger to her lips.

Flapping to the counter, Perdu stared sideways at the mirror. "Ta-ta," he squawked. "Ta-ta, ta-ta, ta-ta!"

"Ta-ta," the ghost whispered as she faded from sight.

A Preponderance of Marys.

THE FIFTH AVENUE HOTEL stood on a bed of bones—
lacy, worm-etched remains of the poor, finding their way to
dust. Skull by jaw by rib by spine, they were nestled as tight
as cordwood in a maze of pauper's pits that stretched out from
below the building, under the streets of Madison Square and
beneath the walkways of its pleasant, manicured park. Time
and progress had caused these unfortunate souls to be forgotten, but their restless echoes had lived on, rising up through
the cobblestones and pavers, acting as ghostly ether, provok-
ing fear and dark thoughts. This is what happens when the
dead don't get their due. This is what happens when the past
is ignored.

In the hotel's grand, marble-tiled lobby, the ghost of Mr.
Paran Stevens sat waiting for his wife, Marietta. The impatient
spirit's preferred seat was neither comfortable nor fancy, just
a well-worn spot at the end of the long wooden bench nearest
the Twenty-Third Street entrance. Above the doorway was a
large sign that read LADIES ONLY, marking it as a special
entrance for unaccompanied women who wished to be discreet on their visits here. It was a change Marietta had
insisted they make when they'd first taken over the lease, just
one of the many savvy schemes she'd hatched in the early days
of their May–December marriage. Back then, everything

Marietta had done had seemed (at least in Paran's eyes) to be
inspired by some greater, all-knowing force of fiscal intuition.
Who could've guessed that placing a single square of choco-
late on a patron's pillow would stir such feelings of goodwill?
Or that offering late supper to both the patrons and the public
would result in the dining hall being filled to the rafters every
night? Oh, what a terrific team they'd been! He'd never have
been half so successful if he hadn't married his darling wife.

The ladies of Mrs. Astor's 400 had relished making a scandal of their union—"She's a chiseller." "She's a grubber."
"She's a climber." "She's his daughter's age, for heaven's sake!"
In the end, his dear Marietta had risen above all the chatter,
proving herself equal to (in his eyes, better than) the lot. Best
of all, she'd forced New York society to accept her on her own
terms. No, she hadn't come from money or the upper crust;
and yes, her words sometimes could be cutting, hurtful and
rough, but anyone fortunate enough to find themselves in her
good graces knew the truth—there never was a truer friend
than his wife.

Paran had quietly expired in his own bed one bright April
day in 1872. For a short time, he'd haunted the parlour of their
home on Marble Row, but he'd soon grown tired of listening
to the laments and platitudes of those who came to pay their
respects. "How can we go on without him?" they'd cried.
"What a tragic loss," they'd said. The words were nothing but
hollow kindnesses, meant to fill the uncomfortable silences
of mourning—the daylight hours when the company of
others is inescapable, the days between death and burial, the
parade of firsts without the deceased marked by holidays,
anniversaries, birthdays and so on. He'd hovered near his
family for as long as he could stand it, hardly able to bear the

disparity between Marietta's sorrow and the brave face she put on for their two children. Each night, after she'd fallen asleep, he'd kissed her weary brow and blessed her dreams. Soon, he'd decamped to the hotel, feeling it was the best place for him to be.

Tapping a foot, Paran watched out the window, on the lookout for his wife. Forty-six was far too young for her to be a widow, to be draped head to toe in Henrietta cloth. Why did she insist on continuing to wear the dreadful uniform of mourning, day after day? He wished he could tell her, "Enough already." He also wished he knew when she was going to arrive! What day was it again? Spotting a gentleman with a copy of *Frank Leslie's Illustrated Newspaper*, Paran guessed it must be Saturday. He hated the way time moved on the other side—there was no sensible ebb and flow to it. Days dragged on at a snail's pace or flew past like a hawk diving after its prey. In a blink, a whole month could be gone and he'd be left wondering what he'd been doing while it'd passed. Eight years into it and he still hadn't mastered the best way to go about the business of being dead.

At least he'd figured out this—just as a child learns reading, writing and arithmetic, the dead had to tackle their three Rs as well: revenge, regret and reconciliation. Luckily, he'd lived his life in such a way that there was little revenge to exact, especially since the other two Rs kept him working round the clock. Currently he was involved with a task of the heart, getting Marietta to reconcile her differences with their dear son, Harry, over the matter of Miss Edith Jones. Time was of the essence. He'd seen the Reaper hovering over Harry, on account of a sickness settled in the boy's lungs that had no cure. The reprieve Harry had gotten this past summer from breathing the fresh air along the shores of Bar Harbor wasn't going to last. Was Marietta aware of their son's ill health? If she was, she wasn't letting it show. *Let him be happy, my dear*, Paran thought. *He isn't long for this world. Let him have at least a taste of what we once had!*

He'd been diligently trying to communicate with the living—getting up the nerve to pass through a body, rather than simply brushing near; knocking over progressively heavier objects, a hat, a wine glass, a coat rack—in hopes of getting through to Marietta. Last week he'd pestered a beggar woman who liked to feed birds in the park because he'd been told by another spirit that she'd been known (on rare occasion) to speak the words of the dead. The woman hadn't entered into a conversation with him, or even looked as if she'd known he was there, but he'd felt a great sense of accomplishment when she'd flapped her arms and yelled, "Paran Stevens is here!"

"Good morning, Mr. Stevens," a spirit said to him now as she passed by. (The same spirit who'd told him of the woman in the park.)

"Good morning, Mary," he replied, with a tip of his hat.

He'd been sitting in this same spot near the Ladies' Entrance eight months after he'd passed on the fateful cold December night when she'd met her death, horribly, in this very hotel. He watched the little spectre as she glided through walls and wafted past patrons on her way to scrub the marble steps of the hotel's grand staircase. He wondered why, in his ghostly form, he still bothered to wear a hat, and why the girl held fast to the handle of her bucket as it sloshed with the memory of hot, sudsy water. Why were they still here? Was this all there was to death? Had St. Peter become so choosy he wouldn't grant them entrance into Heaven? *That might be true for me*, Paran Stevens thought, *but surely not for this spectre and the ten other hard-working, kind-hearted girls who'd died with her in the fire.* They were the girls who'd scrubbed the hotel floors, the woodwork, the dishes, the laundry. None of them had done anything to deserve such a terrible lot.

They'd been young, hopeful immigrants, mostly of Irish descent, who'd never seemed bothered by the fact that their pretty, freckled cheeks were covered with smudges by day's end. He hadn't paid much attention to them while they'd been alive, something he regretted in his present state. They'd all known him by sight, addressed him by name, but he'd not taken the time to learn theirs. Whenever Marietta had scolded him for his lack of interest in the staff, he'd complained that there were too many Marys among the help, from the chambermaids to the scrubbing girls, from the cooks to the calligraphers. How was he supposed to remember who was who?

After the girls had died, though, he'd come across their spirits circled around the smouldering ashes of the fire. Hands clasped, they'd been reciting the rosary, calling for Mother Mary to bless them in their time of need. *Holy Mary, Mother of God, pray for us sinners, now and at the hour of our death.* In the years that'd passed since then, he'd tried asking them their names, but they'd always refused to answer. At first, he'd thought it might be a small punishment for his indifference to them when he'd been alive, but over time they'd kept refusing, all the while growing more alike than different in movement and appearance. Eventually he'd stopped asking.

Sometimes late at night he saw them floating about in the corridors, wailing like banshees as they made their way to the attic. They'd changed in the afterlife, their sweet natures now prone to turn spiteful and angry at the slightest provocation. Afraid of what they might become when there was no one among the living who remembered who they once had been, Paran Stevens prayed for them, fervently and often. "God bless the Marys," he whispered, before resuming his wait for his wife. "Keep them whole. Give them peace."

Mary Corday, Margaret Connor, Delia Cummings, Mary McCabe, Lizzie Moran, Margaret Campbell, Margaret Fagan, Mary Donnelly, Hannah Ward, Mary J. Heavey, Kate Cushing.

The hotel's head housekeeper, Mrs. Fisher, was conducting her Saturday morning inspection. She recited the scrubber girls' names twice a day—each morning after making the daily roll call, each night after calling for lights out. Once a week she visited Old St. Patrick's Cathedral on Mulberry Street to light candles in their memory. Her girls were never far from her thoughts, and always in her heart. How could she forget them or the terrible way they'd died?

By the time she'd been alerted to the fire, the entire west wing of the attic was engulfed in flames, the streams of water from the pumper wagons failing to staunch the raging blaze. She'd stood outside, tears freezing on her cheeks as a chorus of screams howled from above. Firemen, mere shadows on the roof, dragged hoses this way and that as a group of brave porters pulled as many girls as they could through broken windows and skylights. Carriages rushed from all directions to take in the sight—liveried vehicles with ladies and gents inside, as well as a string of wobbly hacks crowded with fast women and their gallants, half drunk with the night's dissipation. Pacing the ground floor of the hotel, Mrs. Fisher helped wherever she could—bringing hot tea to half-dressed ladies sitting on their trunks, shutting the door to the reading room so the laughter and cigar smoke of the business-men crowded inside wouldn't seep into the lobby. When the rescued maids began to scurry through the front door, she'd ushered them into a private parlour so she could count their heads. "Oh Mrs. Fisher," they'd cried, sobbing and shivering while wringing their hands. "It's a terrible calamity. The worst thing I ever saw!" Between curses and prayers, the trembling young things had taken turns recounting the horror they'd escaped and guessing what might've caused it.

"The fire shot right up the stairwell—we had no way out."

"Do you suppose someone dropped a candle on her way up to bed?"

"More likely Mary McConnell's lover dropped his lantern on his way back down."

"The windows were shut tight, the bars fixed fast to the frames. If the boys hadn't torn them out, we would've cooked in our beds."

"The gas jet in a laundry closet was missing its guard. It was only a matter of time before a pile of linens caught light."

"I hope they can get everyone out before it's too late."

"Where's Mary Katherine?"

"Where's Mary Margaret?"

"I'll bet Mary Grove forgot to turn down her lamp again."

"The smoke was black as pitch. We could barely find our way through it."

Nine girls had gotten trapped in the last two rooms on the corridor. Before the porters could reach their window, the timbers of the roof fell in, sealing their fate. The best anyone

could hope was that they were already dead when it happened. Six were found in a heap by the window. Two more
were huddled under a bed. One was in the middle of the
room, her knees bent in prayer, a crucifix in her hands. Two
others managed to escape through a skylight only to die at
Bellevue later that night. Half of the girls were burned beyond
recognition. There was only one staircase that led to their
quarters, with no other way out. Hadn't anyone ever thought
of what might happen if a fire broke out? The wall between
the men's and women's rooms was built like a fortress, and
solid bars covered the windows—they'd been put there by the
proprietors to protect the girls' honour. Instead they'd served
as a death sentence. *Isn't that always the way,* Mrs. Fisher had
thought, *man's fears causing him to do things that lead to far
greater sins.*

In the dark of the night, the coroner had asked Mrs. Fisher
to view the corpses, hoping she might tell him who was who.
At the time she'd been in such a state, she hadn't been able to
bring herself to do it, but when first light had come, she'd
made the daily roll call, noted which girls were missing, and
found her way to the morgue. The sight she'd seen when she'd
gotten to Bellevue was as alarming as the fire itself. The line
for those who wished to have a look at the dead snaked down
Twenty-Sixth Street and around the block. For every person
who thought they might've lost a dear one, a hundred more
were there to gawk. Visitors entered from the left and exited
to the right, slowly moving past the dead as if dancing a
strange, macabre reel. The girls' bodies were hideous to
behold—flesh burned off their faces and limbs, bones exposed
and charred black. When it was Mrs. Fisher's turn, she'd
covered her face with her handkerchief and held her breath,

not because of the stench, but because she was afraid the Reaper might be standing guard, waiting to choose who'd be next. Straight off she'd identified three of the girls—one by a ring on a finger, one by a cross around the neck, and one by what little remained of a face. The coroner had quickly drawn sheets over their bodies and set three wooden lids in place. Mrs. Fisher had never imagined she'd feel such relief in hearing a coffin nailed shut.

Nearly eight years on, the fearful, living maids who worked under her supervision would come to her in the middle of the night, scared and begging not to be sent back to their beds in the attic. "Oh Mrs. Fisher, don't make me go back there. One of the Marys is floatin' over my bed, ready to wrap her sooty fingers around my neck!" On any given night, a handful of frightened chambermaids or scrubber girls might smell smoke when there weren't any fires lit, see handprints on frosty windowpanes, or hear voices wailing in the stairwell.

Truth be told, Mrs. Fisher had had her fair share of run-ins with the spirits as well. She'd felt their presence wax and wane over time, their powers growing greater as daylight grew shorter and winter drew near. During the recent full moon they'd seemed especially restless, rattling the doors of her linen closet, and sending the pitcher next to her washbasin crashing to the floor. The mere thought of it raised the hairs on the back of her neck. She tried her best not to speak of these things to anyone, especially not the guests. She'd given the maids strict orders to follow suit. Still, from time to time, one or more of them would try to make contact with the ghosts, by asking them to blow out a candle or to play with a needle tied to the end of a string. Whenever she caught wind of such activities, the housekeeper would pull the guilty maids aside and say, "I don't want to hear of you doing that again. Never trouble trouble until trouble troubles you."

As Mr. Stevens' ghost resumed his watch for his wife, and Mrs. Fisher went about her business of checking for dirt and dust, a steady stream of guests came and went from the lobby. A parade of maids (some living, some dead) scurried down the corridors, arms laden with baskets of roses and fruit. A trio of men from Mr. Knox's hat shop appeared with tape measures in hand, ready to fit top hats and derbies (silk, felt or beaver) to the crowns of eager heads. A bevy of well-dressed ladies gathered in the main entryway, keen to begin their morning promenade through Madison Square Park. A boisterous throng of gentlemen poured into the reading room, their brows waggling with speculation and wagers concerning bears, bulls and horses—new and old, lame or dark. They'd embraced Friday night with open eyes, ears, arms, legs, thighs, lips, tongues, mouths. They'd seen the sights. They'd eaten rich food. They'd met interesting strangers. They'd drunk too much. They'd witnessed a theft, a threat, a pursuit, a fight. When Saturday morning came, they'd woken up (with or without companionship), unaware that the hotel was filled with ghosts.

The Amazing Dr. Brody.

DR. QUINN BRODY copied the items from the morning edition of the *Times Gazette* into a small leather-bound journal. Clean-shaven and bespectacled, he sported a Newmarket coat because he didn't wish to bother with the numerous buttons of a double-breasted Albert. Holding the journal steady against a tottery table in the corner of the gentlemen's reading room of the Fifth Avenue Hotel, he whispered to himself as he wrote, his one hand made of wood, the other of flesh. It'd been seventeen years since he'd lost his right hand and forearm in the war, yet he still wasn't quite comfortable writing with his left. He could've saved himself time and effort by tearing the notice from the paper and shoving it in his pocket, but the newspaper didn't belong to him, so he felt he had no right to it. Even though he'd already paid the room's attendant for two cups of coffee, he wasn't a paying guest.

Most men wouldn't have given a second thought to committing the trivial crime of ripping a small article from the paper. In fact most men wouldn't have thought it a crime at all, but they weren't Quinn Brody. The middle-aged doctor was far from being without sin, but he liked (no, he needed) to feel that the things he did and said and thought served to subtract from the overall chaos of the world. There was enough nonsense to go around these days without him adding to it. Besides, who wanted to open the morning paper and find a hole torn out of its middle?

His fellow alienists liked to explain men's foibles, rants and rages as "occasional surges of masculinity." Nothing was wrong, per se, nothing a bit of cattle roping, rough-riding and hunting out West couldn't fix. If those prescribed activities couldn't be arranged, then just about any strenuous activity would do. The male mind was, after all, resilient, bold, daring, quick, meant to be taxed. It was built to be elastic and forgiving, especially during the most difficult of times, in the most trying places—from the examination halls of Yale and Harvard, to the battlefields of Gettysburg and Antietam. Still, if Quinn Brody had learned anything during the War Between the States, it was that men's minds, even those of the strongest, brightest and most even-tempered, could come unhinged when faced with unspeakable horrors. A few of the soldiers he'd known had gotten past their tribulations, but many had remained irreparably damaged by what they'd experienced, their hearts and minds changed forever. Still others, unable to put their demons to rest, had—by rope, pistol, knife or poison—taken their own lives.

With the loss of his arm in that war, Brody had been forced to grapple with demons of his own—memories, hallucinations, nightmares. Lying in the Stump Hospital day after day, he'd sworn he could feel a variety of strange sensations in the limb that was no longer there—the pain of his wound, the curling of his fingers, the touch of a gentle hand. One morning during rounds, the famed neurologist Dr. Silas Weir Mitchell had diagnosed him with "phantom limb," a common ailment among soldiers who'd lived through an amputation. What the doctor hadn't mentioned was whether there was a cure for the condition or how long it might last. His only advice had been, "Don't let it make you less of a man."

Mitchell's words had served as little comfort to Brody, who until then had served admirably as an assistant surgeon in New York's Fighting 69th. One minute he'd been tightening a tourniquet around the leg of a wounded soldier in preparation for amputation, and the next he'd been reeling from a deep nick in his arm caused by the head surgeon's overreaching scalpel. Three days later, when gangrene set in, the surgeon had amputated Brody's limb too. Everything that'd come after had led him to his current occupation.

Although he'd lost the ability to slice and saw and cut, he'd gained an intense fascination for deciphering the human mind. Like the mountains and canyons of the Wild West, the lobes and folds of the brain provided vast spans of uncharted territory to explore. What wondrous secrets the mind held within it! What curious, inexplicable tasks it could perform! Closing his eyes, he put his own brain to the test, contemplating the limb he'd lost. In an instant he was overwhelmed with the feeling that his arm had been restored, so solid and perfect, he was sure he could reach out and grasp anything he wanted—a ripe red apple, a tankard of beer, a beautiful woman's breast. It was maddening and miraculous all at once. How could something that had disappeared so long ago still persist?

"Hallo there, Brody!" a gentleman's voice boomed, breaking the doctor's reverie. "Old friend, is that you?" Dressed in a brown checkered suit, the man limped towards the doctor's table, aided by a silver-handled walking stick: Bartholomew Andersen, formerly Private Bart Andersen of the 20th New York Infantry. The two men had spent several months together at the Stump, in adjacent iron cots amidst the rows that stretched down the length of the recovery ward. Andersen had saved a dozen of his fellow soldiers from certain death at Fredericksburg, then taken a Minie ball to the left shin. The men had all lived, but Andersen's leg hadn't stood a chance.

Brody replied, "Andersen, my good man. You look to be in fine fettle." For obvious reasons, he did not offer the hearty handshake and clap on the back customary between veterans.

Andersen exclaimed, "I knew it was you!" Pulling up a chair he added, "How goes the fight, St. Nick?"

Andersen had made a point of assigning ridiculous yet apt monikers to every man he'd encountered at the Stump. He had branded a young soldier from Cincinnati who'd been fitted with a glass eye, Buckeye Jones, and Brody, St. Nick. How long had it been since they'd last seen each other? More than a decade, Brody guessed. He'd lost everyone he loved since then—his wife, his mother, his brother, and most recently, his father. Not wishing to recount past miseries, he only replied, "I can't complain."

"Good, good," Andersen said with a smile. "So what brings you to the Fifth on this fine morning, business or pleasure?"

"Business," Brody answered, figuring "pleasure" would lead to more questions. "And you?"

Tugging a large gold watch from his pocket, Andersen made a show of checking the time. "Business, like you."

"Your business is clearly more profitable than mine," Brody teased, responding to Andersen's obvious cue.

"Can't complain," Andersen said, flashing a toothy grin. Polishing his watch on his lapel, he asked, "Are you living in the city, or just passing through?"

Brody wasn't quite sure what to say to that. He'd returned to New York at the start of the summer after being away in Paris, and found his father was gravely ill. Much of that season had been spent in a daze, the hours alternately racing or crawling past as he tried his best to help the frail man navigate the passage from this life to the next. There'd been hands to hold, sheets to change, names to remember. Then letters to write, arrangements to be made and promises to keep. The funeral had been a lovely affair (as far as those things go), attended by two hundred upstanding citizens from New York and beyond, chief among them the members of the Fraternal Order of the Unknown Philosophers.

The dozen or so members of the group had been of great comfort to Brody, congregating every Wednesday evening in his father's optician's shop to carry on with the work of the order—the pursuit of the unknown. Brody had closed the shop to business, but had left the sign hanging over the door: MR. TOBIAS BRODY, OPTICIAN. IMPORTER AND MAKER OF PHILOSOPHICAL INSTRUMENTS, SINCE 1834. He hadn't given much thought as to what he was going to do with the place, or whether or not he was going to stay. The Philosophers were so happily consumed with planning their upcoming symposium; he hadn't had the heart to turn them away. He'd actually grown quite fond of them these past few weeks, especially Mr. Alden Dashley, a man who wasn't afraid to admit he didn't know everything about everything. Brody had been surrounded by arrogance (intellectual and otherwise) while in Paris and he'd almost forgotten what it was like to move among forthright peers and good friends.

"I'm living here," Brody finally answered, thinking it might be time he made up his mind to stay.

"Same here," Andersen said, nodding. "I've got a little place over on Twenty-Sixth. How about we team up tonight, for old times' sake? We can play some Faro, take in a boxing match, paint the town red. I hear there's a house in the Tenderloin with girls who cater to stumpies. You keen to pay it a visit? Excepting the gambling, I'll happily foot the bill. It's been a good week."

Shaking his head, Brody replied, "I'm sorry, but I've got other plans." He'd been looking forward to spending a quiet evening in front of the fire—browsing through old issues of *Scientific American* and reading a novel he'd picked up at Brentano's Books called *Dr. Heidenhoff's Process*, about a doctor who develops a mechanical method of eradicating painful memories from his subjects' brains.

Andersen persisted. "Send your regrets and come out with me instead. I promise it'll prove more entertaining than whatever you've got planned." Leaning forward on his elbows he lowered his voice and said, "How about I take you out to Blackwell's Island to dance with the lady lunatics."

Brody stared at Andersen. "Surely you jest."

"Not in the least," Andersen replied, raising an eyebrow. "The place boasts several inmates who are young and fair and not too far out of their heads. It's Manhattan's best-kept secret. Whole parties of gents take a ferry out there on Saturday nights to have a waltz or two and tour the asylum. The musicians that play for the dances are some of the finest in the city, on par with the little orchestra that plays at Delmonico's."

"Sounds like quite the outing," Brody said, attempting to hide his disgust.

"Remember the nurse who used to look after us at the Stump?" Andersen asked.

"Nurse Fitch," Brody said, the haggard woman's face looming in his mind. Most of the men had been terribly unkind to her, so foul he'd wondered why she hadn't poisoned their pabulum.

"Fitch the Bitch!" Andersen said with a laugh. "Hand to God, one of the loonies at the asylum is the spitting image of her. You gotta see it to believe it."

"Perhaps another time," Brody offered.

Handing Brody his card, Andersen said, "God, it's great to see you. Let's get together soon, eh St. Nick?"

"Soon," Brody replied, tucking the card away. Rising from his seat he gave Andersen a polite bow. "Be well," he said as he headed for the door.

Andersen bellowed after him, "You too, you old stumpy!"

In the lobby, Brody stopped to check his watch—twenty after ten. His breakfast with Alden's wife and her interesting friend, Miss Thom, was almost upon him. He'd hoped to have time to conduct a brief experiment of psychical research before their arrival. "Damn Andersen," he mumbled under his breath. How could one person talk so much without saying anything of interest? *Never mind all that now*, he thought. He needed to make the most of the minutes he still had.

Taking a small brass compass from his pocket, he held the instrument in the palm of his hand. Walking towards the Ladies' Entrance, he kept his eyes fixed on the compass's needle. Judith Dashley had told him that every time she got to the end of that corridor, she felt as if she was surrounded by beings she couldn't see: "The air grows cold, even when the door's shut, and I get gooseflesh up and down my arms." Surprisingly, she hadn't seemed the least bit troubled by it. On the contrary, she'd been downright giddy when she'd explained that she suspected the beings were the ghosts said to inhabit the hotel.

Like her, Brody was intensely interested in what remained after someone (or something) had been lost. If a phantom of his arm remained after his limb was taken, it stood to reason that a shadowy figure of a whole person might be left behind after death. If he could sense his missing arm, then why wasn't it possible for Mrs. Dashley to sense the presence of beings who'd passed? Sensing the spirits of the dead wasn't enough to prove they existed, of course, but surely such sensations shouldn't be dismissed. What was needed was measurable evidence. He liked Alden's wife well enough, but she wasn't, by any stretch of the imagination, well versed in the scientific method or, for that matter, true mediumship.

Dr. Brody paused at the end of the corridor. No sooner

had he stopped than the needle on his compass began to spin with wild abandon, moving so erratically he thought the instrument might break. Oh, ho! This was better than he'd hoped! He'd guessed that if there were any ghosts near, the compass would register an electromagnetic disturbance, but he'd never imagined the sign would be so blatant. Smiling broadly, the doctor stared at the whirling needle and whispered, "Would you look at that!"

Mr. Stevens' ghost flew to the doctor's side and peered over his shoulder.

The spirits of three scrubber girls raced down the corridor towards them pursuing a smaller, younger ghost—that of a little boy. He was new to the hotel, but not to the afterlife. "Master Dashley!" they sang in unison. "Get back here you little imp! If you don't do as we say, we'll put you in the dumbwaiter and send you through the wash!"

Scampering like a scared rabbit, Billy Dashley's spirit slipped between Dr. Brody's legs and ran towards his mother who was coming down the corridor from the main staircase.

Judith Dashley felt a chill rush up her spine. "Dr. Brody," she said, pulling her shawl around her shoulders. "Weren't we supposed to meet in the dining hall?"

Quickly stowing his compass, Dr. Brody said, "You're quite right, Mrs. Dashley. I hope I haven't kept you waiting."

Placing her hand on the doctor's arm, she whispered, "You can't fool me. I saw what you were up to."

"You did?" Brody answered. He couldn't recall discussing his theory of ghostly energies and electromagnetic forces with her the other night at dinner. In fact he was positive they hadn't. Was she as much of a mind reader as she claimed her friend to be?

"Of course I did," she replied with a wink. "You were hoping to catch a glimpse of Miss Thom upon her arrival. I knew I shouldn't have pointed her out to you through the teashop window. It doesn't seem fair that you can recognize her when she knows next to nothing about you."

"It seems perfectly fair to me," Brody teased. "How else am I to believe in her abilities as a seer? I put my trust in you, Mrs. Dashley. I hope you haven't deceived me."

Cheeks turning pink, Judith stammered, "I assure you, I haven't!"

"And I can assure you that I wasn't attempting to ambush poor Miss Thom. If you must know, I was hoping to cross paths with a ghost."

Judith's eyes lit up. "So you believe what I told you about my encounters here?"

"I believe you felt something, yes."

"Am I to take it that you believe in ghosts?"

"I neither believe nor disbelieve, but I hope to settle the matter for myself very soon. I envy your confidence when it comes to detecting spirits."

"You shouldn't," she said, shaking her head. "While it might be fashionable for a lady to attend a public lecture on the afterlife, or participate in a séance from time to time, claiming to have seen a ghost yourself does not go down well in polite circles. I confess I'm rather envious of you and Alden and the rest of the Philosophers. You men of science, you *possibilitists*, as my dear husband would say, can engage yourselves in the pursuit of the unknown around the clock and no one bats an eye. If a woman of social standing dares to speak of what can be felt but not seen, or unwittingly mutters to herself under her breath, why, it's off to the doctor to have her head examined! I suppose by confessing my experiences to you I've given you my trust, dear doctor. I hope you're the man I think you to be."

"What sort of man is that?" Dr. Brody asked.

"A man who believes women."

Quinn Brody had certainly encountered plenty of men who didn't, Dr. Mitchell being foremost among them. After the war, he'd studied with Mitchell at the Infirmary for Nervous Diseases, and as a result he'd quickly discovered the full measure of the man. In nearly every case that involved a female patient, he'd witnessed Mitchell chastising them (often quite severely) for "thinking, day-dreaming and fretting, too readily and too much." He'd diagnosed every woman who had a stray feeling, craving, desire, wish, interest, worry, affection, inkling, suspicion, knowing, predilection or ability, with nervous exhaustion. In an attempt to cure these "poor creatures" he'd ordered them to be shuttered away at home, or committed to an asylum. There was no strenuous activity prescribed, no adventure-filled trips to the West—only bed rest and boredom leading to loneliness and desperation.

When Brody had tried to discuss the matter, the cranky neurologist had insisted, "They've got no one to blame but themselves. They've taxed their minds into a state of nervous exhaustion. Someone needs to tell them enough is enough. Women's minds are weak and fragile, invariably prone to shock, disorder, delusion and hysteria." Finding Mitchell's methodology woefully lacking, Brody had chosen to go to Paris in search of more progressive thought. He'd had no idea that once he got there, he'd discover something far worse.

As the chimes in the lobby announced the half hour, Judith said, "Miss Thom will be here any minute. Shall we head to the dining hall and wait for her there?"

"After you," Dr. Brody replied.

Adelaide arrived ten minutes late, wearing a scarlet promenade dress trimmed with jet buttons, swirling soutache, and a fluted silk flounce elegantly circling the hem of her skirt. Her matching veiled bonnet was topped with a cluster of crepe roses, and a single black ostrich plume poised like a jaunty question mark atop her head. Her tardiness had been calculated so she might catch sight of Dr. Brody before they met face to face. Pausing behind a potted palm inside the dining hall entrance, she scanned the room for Judith.

She spotted her friend at a secluded corner table a few yards away, giving her full attention to a gentleman Adelaide assumed was the doctor. Taking a long look at him, she decided that perhaps he did warrant the blushing Judith had done when she'd mentioned his name in the shop. His dark hair was swept to the side and slightly unkempt, yet his face was freshly shaven. This said to Adelaide that although he wasn't one to fuss over his looks, he liked the feel of hot towels on his neck and the scrape of the barber's blade against his chin. Looking on in some amazement, she watched as Judith gestured enthusiastically (no doubt telling the poor man every last detail of the ongoing renovations at Marble Row) while Dr. Brody nodded and smiled, and barely spoke. How refreshing it was to see a man sit contentedly, free from the urge to dominate the conversation. Each time he took a drink from his cup, his movements were thoughtful, refined, exact.

Before she could appraise him any further, she caught Judith glancing impatiently towards the door. *Better get moving*, Adelaide thought, straightening her skirts. There was a fine line between running late and being rude, and when it came to Judith Dashley, it was best not to cross it.

Gliding past three Boston ferns, a cluttered teacart and a handful of waiters, Adelaide approached the table with a friendly smile. "Good morning," she said.

"My dear Adelaide!" Judith turned in her seat, the wires of her bustle softly creaking in protest. "So lovely to see you at last." (Judith's way of saying, "You're late, but you're forgiven.")

Dr. Brody had risen from his chair and was waiting to be introduced.

Adelaide stared at him, biting her lip.

Commanding. Proper. Shoulders back. A military man.

Eyes, blue. Long lashes. Faded handkerchief, monogrammed.

Nose freckled, shoes dusty. He likes a good walk.

Crow's feet. Dimple in the chin (the Devil is within).

"Miss Adelaide Thom," Judith announced, "allow me to introduce Dr. Quinn Brody."

"A pleasure to meet you, Dr. Brody," Adelaide said, ready to extend her hand in greeting should the gentleman offer his.

"The pleasure is mine," Brody replied, keeping his hand at his side.

Adelaide drew her hand back as if she were a cat with an injured paw. *How stupid am I?* she thought. *Why didn't I notice the slight tick in his right shoulder, the stiff false fingers at his cuff? Why didn't Judith share this important detail instead of leaving it as a surprise?* Flushed with embarrassment, she stumbled slightly as a waiter offered her the chair next to Brody's. "Thank you," she said, relieved to take her seat. It wasn't the doctor's lack of an arm that had unsettled her, it was being caught unawares. She was the one who was supposed to take people by surprise. She was supposed to have, as it were, the upper hand.

The waiter stood at attention, pressed towel draped over his arm.

"Are we ready to order?" Judith asked, breaking the awkward silence.

Brody handed Adelaide the menu card. "I've already made up my mind," he said.

Adelaide gave the card a cursory glance. "Shirred eggs, and tea, please," she said, before passing the card to Judith.

Judith handed it to the waiter. "Just toast and tea for me."

"I'll have the shirred eggs as well," Brody said, "and another cup of coffee."

Adelaide lifted the dark swath of her lace veil and pinned it to the top of her hat. *No need to hide*, she thought. *Let's see what other secrets Judith may or may not have kept.*

There was no moment of shock when Brody looked at her face, no revulsion, no wide-eyed stare, no uncomfortable downward gaze. Only a warm, kindly smile, as if he were seeing an old friend.

Adelaide knew this had to mean that Judith had somehow arranged for the doctor to catch sight of her before their meeting. Perplexed, she wondered, *Dear Judith, what are you playing at?*

Judith was watching her with smug satisfaction. Giving her friend a sideways glance, Adelaide got a sly, encouraging wink in return. *Ah ha!* she thought. Judith means to make a match. All that blushing, all that talk about the handsome Dr. Brody wasn't meant to be a confession, but an enticement.

How many times had Judith boasted of her talent for match-making—describing in great detail the joy she'd felt in swapping place cards at this or that soirée in order to kindle the flames of desire? Adelaide had never dreamed she'd be on the receiving end of one of Judith's romantic schemes. What nerve! Step right up and see the one-armed man converse with the one-eyed girl! *Well Mrs. Dashley, if it's a show you want, you're about to get one.*

"Would you like me to pour your tea for you?" the waiter asked, returning to the table with breakfast.

"Yes," Judith answered with a polite nod.

"No," Adelaide said, shaking her head. Staring at Judith she added, "I can help myself."

Judith frowned and spooned a generous helping of orange marmalade on her toast.

Dr. Brody stirred sugar into his coffee, one lump at a time. Turning to Adelaide, he gamely said, "Mrs. Dashley tells me you're a mind reader by profession. A seer of sorts."

"I am," Adelaide answered.

"Fascinating," Brody said, taking a sip. "I'm curious to know, what exactly does that entail?"

"A little of this, a little of that."

Judith wiped a few stray crumbs from the corner of her mouth. "Come now, Adelaide, that's not much of an answer."

Adelaide pierced the quivering yolk of one of her eggs with her fork. "It wasn't much of a question."

Judith forced a laugh. "Why be so coy? Dr. Brody won't give your secrets away."

"He can do whatever he likes with my secrets. I'll happily tell them to him right now." Staring at Brody she said, "One: I don't play tricks. Two: I don't entertain skeptics."

At that, Judith dropped her cup, spilling tea down the front of her dress. "Oh dear!" she exclaimed, dabbing at her skirt with her napkin. "If I don't see to this right away, the stains will never come out. You'll excuse me, won't you?"

"I'll come with you," Adelaide offered.

"No, no," Judith protested. "You stay and enjoy your breakfast. It wouldn't be right to abandon the good doctor."

Looking puzzled, Brody said, "If you both must go, I'll be fine alone—"

"Nonsense," Judith said, standing. "Adelaide will stay. I insist."

Dr. Brody stood, as per good manners.

Adelaide stood, too, wishing she could give Judith a piece of her mind. "We'll catch up later, then? Perhaps at the shop?"

"Yes," Judith answered, "at the shop." Then moving close to Adelaide she gave her a kiss on the cheek. In a soft whisper she said, "Stop making everything so difficult. He's really a lovely man."

Pulling away from her friend, Adelaide said, "Good day to you, Judith."

After Judith had made her farewells, Adelaide and the doctor sat down and ate their eggs in silence.

Once Adelaide had thought things through, she realized that Brody had been as much in the dark as she as to Judith's scheme. Furthermore, it had been quite a long time since she'd shared a meal with a polite and handsome man. Before the attack, she'd had no trouble making small talk with any gentleman she met; in fact, she'd prided herself in being a flirt. That part of her now felt distant and foreign, but she supposed she could make an attempt at being interesting, at least. There was nothing left to do then but be herself. Saying the first thing that came to mind, she asked, "Did you keep it?"

"Hmm?" Dr. Brody asked, looking around as if there was something he might've missed.

"Your arm?" Adelaide said. "Did you keep it? Maybe give it a proper burial?" She wanted to see how far she could take things before the gentleman flinched. "I once met a man who paid to have the bones of his left leg extracted after his limb was taken. He keeps them on display in his house."

"Interesting," Dr. Brody replied. "But no, I lost it in the war. It was too . . . well never mind what it was. Suffice to say, there wasn't much left to keep."

Adelaide poured herself another cup of tea. Maybe this wouldn't be a complete wash after all. "As you may have gathered, I'm not squeamish," she said, pointing to her scars.

"Ah, well then," Brody replied. "I'll put the same question to you. Did you keep it?"

Laughing, Adelaide answered, "Yes. It resides in a lovely little bottle beside my bed."

Dr. Brody laughed, too, then held up his cup to show the waiter he wanted more coffee. Turning back to Adelaide he said, "I'd like you to know that I'm not a skeptic."

"What are you then, Dr. Brody?"

"A man of science."

"Aren't they the same?"

He shook his head. "A skeptic is only interested in being right. I'm only interested in finding truth."

"Even if there's a chance your theories are wrong?"

"Especially then, because it means I might be on my way to discovering something new."

All Adelaide could think was that the doctor's eyes were a beautiful shade of blue. (And, if she wasn't mistaken, there was a shade of interest in them, too, keen and real and the slightest bit improper.) Maybe Judith's matchmaking powers were greater than she'd guessed. There was only one way to find out. "Scientists occupy themselves with theories, tests and demonstrations, do they not?" she asked.

"Largely, yes."

"Then why bother discussing my occupation when I can treat you to a demonstration."

"Here?"

"Why not?" Adelaide said. "I'm willing if you are. The proof will be in the doing."

"If you like," Dr. Brody said, "although I'm not quite sure how you wish to go about it."

Moving her chair so close her knee brushed against his, she said, "Give me your hand."

Brody did as he was told.

Elbows resting on the table, Adelaide cradled the doctor's hand in hers. Tracing the lines on his palm with her finger she asked, "Past, present or future—which would you like me to see?"

"Past," the doctor quickly answered, as if he'd made the choice ahead of time.

"All right," Adelaide said. "Past it is. Shall we begin?"

"I suppose so," Dr. Brody replied, then gave her a more assured "Yes."

Ignoring the chatter and clinking of cutlery on plates all around them, Adelaide closed her eyes. She took a deep breath and inhaled a scent that was medicinal and clean. It reminded her of waking up in the operating theatre at Bellevue with a dozen surgeons gathered around her. "Carbolic soap," she said, opening her eyes again. "A tool of Listerism. You used it then, as you use it now, because you believe in things that can't be seen." Examining the doctor's graceful yet strong fingers, she added, "And it reminds you of who you used to be."

Glancing at the handkerchief folded in the breast pocket of his coat, Adelaide saw that the monogram, though elegantly stitched, was faded. It wasn't something he'd gotten for himself. It was a gift from long ago, from someone he'd loved, so he hadn't the heart to replace it. "You live alone," she said, "but that wasn't always the case. You had a wife, but she's been gone for several years."

Brody looked towards Heaven, then lowered his gaze and closed his eyes.

"She believed in God," Adelaide said, pushing forward, "but you're not sure He exists. She promised she'd send you a sign, but you've never received it." Fingers resting on his wrist, Adelaide felt the doctor's heartbeat begin to race. Leaning close, she whispered, "You're starting to wonder if you ever will."

Dr. Brody could barely breathe—not because she'd laid bare his past, but because she'd exposed his heart. How could this lilac-scented bohemian know so much about him? She'd spoken of things he'd never shared with anyone. What a gift she had. What a beautiful mind she'd been given. When Judith had pointed her out to him, he hadn't been able to take his eyes off her scars, couldn't help but think of how he might've done things differently if he'd been the one to put the scalpel to her skin. Now that he was in her presence, those thoughts, along with her scars, had faded away. All he could think of was how rare she was, this woman who could see into a heart he'd thought was no longer even there.

"Thank you, Miss Thom," he said, wondering if she knew how right she'd been. Oh how he'd like to spend hour after hour in pursuit of how her brain worked!

"You're welcome," Adelaide replied, her palms moist, her face flushing. "It was my pleasure." She wondered if she shouldn't be thanking him instead. She'd almost forgotten how it felt to blush.

My Dearest Eleanor,
Please meet me at Lady Liberty's Torch at
eleven a.m. I must speak with you today. It's urgent.
Come alone to the usual spot.
This is a private matter.
Yours,
L.N.

Seeing Is Believing.

THE NOTE WAS slipped under the shop door by an anonymous hand.

Perdu, first to see it, pinched the letter in his beak and delivered it to Eleanor.

"Good bird," Eleanor said, rewarding the raven with a hunk of stale bread.

While the bird pecked at the treat, Eleanor read the brief missive and thought, *Something's gone wrong.* The clock on the shelf read quarter to eleven. Was that right or had the infernal thing wound down again? Leaning close, Eleanor listened for the steady click of its works. Everything seemed to be in order.

She tucked the note inside a small leather satchel at her waist. She'd owned the bag since she was young, had carried it with her everywhere—through the meadow behind her mother's cottage, into the woods at the edge of the meadow, along the banks of the river that would one day lead her away from the place she'd called home. Each time she opened the little bag she was reminded of her childhood, of days spent gathering roots and blossoms for her mother and muddy worms to present to Perdu as treats. These days she used the purse for holding things she needed in her daily doings— pencil and paper, a phial of salt, a ball of beeswax pierced with pins and needles, a trio of engraved measuring spoons (*pinch, dash, smidgen*), a few coins to give to the needy, and a packet of parchment envelopes for collecting botanical specimens in the park. Opening a small wooden cabinet under the counter, she brought out a few other items she thought she might need—among them, mandrake root for protection and a tangle of dried oarweed stalks (as she suspected the young woman might be late with her courses).

She wished she knew when Adelaide would be back from breakfast. She really didn't like the thought of leaving Beatrice alone on her first day on the job. Ten minutes to eleven. No time left to fret. Slipping beneath the counter again, she fetched three paper-wrapped parcels and placed them on the shelf. One was labelled "Mrs. Anna Stewart," another "Miss Lorna Gowan" and the third "Mrs. Judith Dashley." Thank heavens she'd already filled the orders. At least that much had gone according to plan.

Beatrice was across the room, washing the front window, with Perdu overseeing her efforts. The shop was free from customers, but Eleanor had no idea how long the lull might last. Saturday mornings were unpredictable, as women tended to come through the door in fits and starts. She suspected their ebb and flow was dependent on things like the phase of the moon, the latest play at Booth's Theatre, the season of the year, the sales at Macy's, the state of the weather.

With any luck the shop would stay quiet at least until after noon and surely she wouldn't be gone any longer than that. Walking over to Beatrice, Eleanor gave the girl's shoulder a soft tap.

Beatrice dropped the rag she was holding into a wash bucket at her feet. The air around her was scented with vinegar and lemon. "Let me know if I've missed any spots. I'll happily go after them again."

Eleanor found the girl's enthusiasm endearing. Had she ever been that eager? "You're doing a fine job," she said, giving Beatrice's arm a reassuring squeeze. "In fact, I was wondering if you might be up to the task of looking after the shop while I run a quick errand?"

Beatrice crinkled her brow. She didn't want to seem unwilling. She wanted to do her best, but she wasn't sure she wanted that much responsibility just yet. "I could run the errand for you," she volunteered. "I studied several maps of the city before I came. I'm sure I can find my way around, given a few landmarks."

"It's very kind of you to offer," Eleanor said, "but I'm afraid the task is mine alone."

"In that case," Beatrice said, "I'd be glad to look after the shop." She hoped she appeared more confident than she felt.

"Are you sure you're all right with this?" Eleanor asked. "If not, I can close up until I get back."

"Please don't do that on my account," Beatrice said. "I promise if I feel the slightest bit uneasy, I'll turn the sign in the window and lock the door."

"All right then," Eleanor replied. "Here are the things you'll need to remember."

Wiping her hands on her apron, Beatrice gave an eager nod.

"First," Eleanor said, pointing to the shelves behind the counter, "don't trouble yourself with every jar and tin. Orange pekoe, Darjeeling and jasmine are the most popular choices among the fashionable set, so if you offer them as 'our preferred teas,' chances are you won't need to bother with anything else. They're kept in those three large containers to the right of the stove."

"I see them," Beatrice said, pointing to a trio of squat, wide-mouthed crocks.

Realizing she hadn't bothered to label the jars, Eleanor asked, "And you know how to tell the teas apart?"

"Yes," Beatrice answered. "They're among my aunt Lydia's favourites."

"Excellent."

"But suppose someone isn't content to choose one of those three?" Beatrice asked.

"Explain to them that you're new and that those are the teas you brew best. If they seem put out, offer a sweet on the house."

"Right," Beatrice said. "On the house."

"And if a customer presents you with a question you can't answer, don't guess or make up some silly story. Just admit that you don't know and tell them they're welcome to wait until I come back. Whatever you do, don't lie."

"No," Beatrice said, shaking her head. "I mean yes. I won't guess. I won't lie."

"Good."

As Eleanor started for the door, Beatrice spotted the parcels on the counter. "Miss St. Clair," she called, "what are those?"

"Oh, heavens," Eleanor said, rushing back. "Well noticed, dear girl. They're orders waiting to be picked up—special requests."

"Do you get many of those?"

"Yes indeed. If a lady tells you there's something out of the ordinary she'd like me to make, then write it down and place it in the shop's ledger. The book is under the counter."

The clock's chimes sounded eleven times, chiding Eleanor. "I'm sorry, but I really must go. You're sure you'll be all right?"

"Don't worry about me. I'll manage until you return," Beatrice answered.

Perdu waddled behind his mistress and tugged at her skirt.

"I'll be back soon," Eleanor said, bending down to speak to her pet. "Be good," she whispered. "No magic while I'm gone."

Once Eleanor was out the door, Beatrice spread her arms wide in the middle of the shop floor and twirled.

Perdu whistled with approval.

Although she was nervous, Beatrice couldn't help but feel she'd been given the perfect opportunity to prove her worth. Yesterday things had been so topsy-turvy she'd wondered if she'd ever feel right again. Today, aside from the brief vision that had appeared in the mirror during breakfast, things seemed better, maybe even fortuitous. There were so many questions she had for Miss St. Clair (and Miss Thom, too, if she could penetrate her reserve), but they'd have to wait. Curtsying to the raven, Beatrice rehearsed her best greeting in anticipation of her first customer: "Welcome to St. Clair and Thom's Tea and Sympathy. How may I serve you today?"

Upstairs, a window that overlooked the street rattled in its sash.

Perdu hopped to the counter and tilted his head towards the ceiling. "Hush!" he warned. "She's coming."

No sooner had the bird spoken, than a woman came through the door dressed in a long black cloak.

"Welcome to Tea and Sympathy," Beatrice said, hands folded at her waist. "How may I serve you?"

"Is the seer here?" the woman asked, looking past Beatrice to the back of the shop. "Is she available for consultation?"

"I'm afraid Miss Thom is out," Beatrice replied. "But I imagine she'll return soon, if you'd like to wait."

"How long will that take?"

"I can't say for certain."

The cloak the woman was wearing nearly swallowed her whole. Beatrice could tell by the tone of her voice that she wasn't pleased. The only bright spot on the woman's person was a small brass bell that dangled around her neck, its jangle as impatient and tinny as its owner's words.

Pointing to the clock behind the counter the woman asked, "Is that the right time?"

"I believe so," Beatrice answered.

"Then no, I wouldn't like to wait."

Thinking fast, Beatrice asked, "Would you like to leave your name? Or a message for Miss Thom?"

With a sneer the woman replied, "Tell her God sees who she is and what she does." Looking Beatrice up and down she clicked her tongue. "Caught in Satan's web at such a tender age. Don't you know this place is designed to lead women astray? God bless you, my child. May you soon see the light." And with that, she exited the shop.

Leaning on the counter Beatrice looked at Perdu. "Was it something I said?"

Perdu hissed and ruffled his feathers, looking as if he'd sprouted a sooty lion's mane.

Beatrice shrugged off the woman's words, and wondered how she should pass the time. She'd spent much of the morning washing cups, saucers and windowpanes, and filling honey pots. What was left to be done? Everything seemed to be in order. Lighting the stove, she put a kettle on, thinking she might as well brew herself a cup of tea. As she waited for the water to boil, she turned to the crocks of tea near the stove and said, "Orange pekoe for me, please." Fetching a cup, saucer and teaspoon, she made a half pirouette, cut short when the toe of her left shoe got caught in a gap between the floorboards. The cup went airborne, but Beatrice caught it in one graceful swoop before it crashed, sacrificing the teaspoon for the china. When she bent to retrieve the spoon, she spied a large book sitting on the shelf beneath the counter, overflowing with scraps of paper and coloured ribbons that stuck like snake's tongues from between its pages. Was this the ledger Miss St. Clair had mentioned that was meant for special orders? Lifting the heavy volume to the counter, Beatrice decided it might be in her best interest to inspect it. After all, as Aunt Lydia would say, fortune favours the prepared mind.

Perdu watched from his perch, not the least bit surprised.

Beatrice opened the book's cover and found the following verse.

> *This book belongs to none but me,*
> *For there's my name inside to see.*
> *To steal this book, if you should try,*
> *It's by the throat you'll hang high.*
> *And ravens then will gather 'bout,*

To find your eyes and pull them out.
And when you're screaming 'oh, oh, oh!'
Remember, you deserved this woe.

Beatrice looked to Perdu for direction. "I'm not stealing it," she said. "I'm only looking."

The raven chortled and croaked, "Only looking."

Taking his response as permission, Beatrice turned the pages one by one. Botanical sketches gave way to herbal remedies, which in turn led to recipes for everything from "dream tea" to "angel water." In and amongst these entries were other, more intriguing accounts of fairy rings, demon banishing and dream interpretation. Curious symbols and diagrams were annotated with instructions such as "charm against thieves," "talisman against the stupidities of wine" and "incantations for luck, love, and the dispelling of spirits." Eyes fixed on a page titled "Wish Magic," Beatrice spotted an illustration that looked remarkably like the charm she'd made for herself in Stony Point. "A Witch's Ladder" was written beneath the diagram in red ink.

Between a section called "The Oration of the Salamanders" and another called "Against Maladies and Accidents" was an entry that made Beatrice's blood run cold.

A VERSE *for* MAKING ONESELF OBLIVIOUS *to* TORTURE.

To avoid suffering under the question of a malevolent being, or when put to the stake, rope, rock, rack, pricking, scolding, dunking or screws—swallow a note on which the following words have been written in your own blood.

Before she could read any further, the shop's door opened again to admit a pleasant-looking woman with a sweet-faced boy clinging to her skirts. The woman, who was carrying a large bouquet of flowers, was having great difficulty getting through the door.

Coming to the rescue, Beatrice held the door for her, and gave the boy a friendly wink. "I've got it," she said. "Please come inside. Watch your step."

As the woman fussed with her skirts, the boy leapt over the threshold. Running to the back of the store he hid under Adelaide's fortune-telling table, peeking at them from beneath the fringe of the tablecloth.

"Welcome to Tea and Sympathy," Beatrice announced. "How may I serve you?"

"Well you can start," the woman replied, "by telling me who you are."

Beatrice's cheeks flushed. "Miss Beatrice Dunn," she stammered, "the newly hired help."

Circling around Beatrice, the woman scrutinized her carefully, then nodded with approval. "Lovely to make your acquaintance, Miss Dunn. I'm Mrs. Judith Dashley, friend of the proprietors."

"Mrs. Dashley!" Beatrice exclaimed, recognizing the name from one of the parcels that was waiting on the counter. "So pleased to meet you."

Judith smiled with the satisfaction of someone who enjoyed being known. Clutching the bouquet, she asked, "Would Miss Thom happen to be about? I've brought her a present."

"I'm afraid not," Beatrice replied, shaking her head.

"Oh dear," Judith said. "I'm not quite sure what to make of that."

"I beg your pardon?" Beatrice asked.

With a sigh, Judith plucked a wilted petal from an otherwise unblemished white rose. "It's nothing," she said. "Or it could be something . . . and that could be a good thing, I guess. Yes, let's hope for that."

In addition to the rose, the pretty bouquet contained geranium, heather, white chrysanthemum and ivy. Beatrice guessed that if she had the floriography right (and she was sure that she had), the flowers were meant to be a peace offering. Holding her hands out to Mrs. Dashley, she asked, "Would you like me to put those in some water?"

Judith happily surrendered the bouquet. "Yes, please," she said. "How very thoughtful of you."

Beatrice took the flowers and set them inside a water pitcher. "Miss Thom should be back soon. I'd be happy to make you some tea if you'd like to wait for her return."

Nodding, Judith settled herself in the window seat at the front of the shop.

"What kind of tea would you prefer—Darjeeling, orange pekoe, jasmine?"

"Hmm . . ." Judith pondered, finger to her chin. "Darjeeling, I think . . . no, wait, orange pekoe. No, begging your pardon, it's Saturday isn't it—so let's make it jasmine. Saturday mornings and jasmine tea go together nicely, wouldn't you agree?"

"Jasmine it is," Beatrice said, relieved.

As she prepared the tea, Beatrice heard laughter waft from under Adelaide's table. She wondered if she should offer to make something for the little boy as well—warm milk, toast with honey, a slice of lemon tart? No, wait, on second thought, perhaps she shouldn't. Mothers had hard and fast rules about indulging their children, and she didn't wish to do anything that might offend Mrs. Dashley. For the time being, she'd leave well enough alone.

Perdu, however, couldn't resist the urge to meddle with the lad. Hopping to the floor, he waddled towards the table and stuck his head under the tablecloth. In a low, throaty whisper he said, "Boo."

The boy let out a gleeful squeal.

Beatrice stifled a laugh.

As she delivered the tea to Mrs. Dashley, she was amazed to find the woman staring at the street, seemingly deaf to her child's excitement. Such calm, she thought. Such nonchalance. "This tea smells divine," Judith said, sniffing at the ribbon of steam that was whirling from the pot's spout.

"Would you like me to pour?" Beatrice asked, at the ready with honey and milk.

Motioning to the seat across from her, Judith suggested, "How about you fetch another cup and join me? Drinking tea should never be a solitary endeavour."

"That's very kind of you, Mrs. Dashley," Beatrice said, "but I'm not sure Miss St. Clair would approve."

"Miss St. Clair isn't here," Judith argued, "and I insist."

"All right then," Beatrice replied. "If you insist."

On her way back to the counter, Beatrice spotted a shiny marble rolling towards her along a groove between two floor-boards. Catching it, she picked up the sweet blue orb and stared at the tiny constellation of bubbles trapped within it. This must belong to Mrs. Dashley's boy, she thought. Did he know he'd lost it? Walking to Adelaide's table, Beatrice lifted the edge of the tablecloth expecting to find him there. Much to her surprise, he was gone.

"Everything all right?" Judith called from across the room.

"Yes," Beatrice replied as she glanced around the shop to see where he might've got to. "I'll be right there." The last thing she wanted was to get him in trouble. Tucking the marble in her pocket, she fetched a cup along with the parcel Eleanor had set aside for Mrs. Dashley.

"Ah yes," Judith said, giving the parcel an affectionate pat. "Eleanor's Sweet Dreams Tea—have you had the pleasure of trying it?"

"No," Beatrice answered, wondering if it was the same tea that was mentioned in the book she'd found.

Holding the package to her nose, Judith inhaled deeply. "It works like a charm. I'd been having the most terrible time falling asleep, but this tea fixed all that. Just one cup an hour before bed and I drift off like a baby. Miss St. Clair has given it a fitting name—I've been having the most wonderful dreams since I started drinking it."

"Really?" Beatrice asked as she poured tea into Mrs. Dashley's cup.

"Beyond belief," Judith said, offering, passing, accepting, honey, sugar, milk. "Just last night I dreamt of a secret room, hidden from everyone in the world except me. It looked identical to the parlour in my house on Marble Row, only everything was white—the furniture, the draperies, the fixtures, the flowers. There was no clock, no mirror, no letter tray, no doorbell. Nothing was expected of me, and no one came to call except for one delightful visitor, my dear little Billy."

"Your son?" Beatrice asked, puzzled as to why Mrs. Dashley would consider her child a visitor in her own house.

"That's right," Judith replied. "Did Eleanor tell you about him?"

"No," Beatrice said, remembering that Eleanor had instructed her not to lie. "She didn't."

Judith took a sip of tea and smiled. "He was such a beautiful child, so full of joy and life. I can't believe it's been five years since he's been gone."

Gooseflesh blossomed on Beatrice's arms as the sound of a child's footsteps seemed to race in circles around the shop.

Perdu ruffled his feathers and nervously sidestepped on his perch.

Oblivious, Judith closed her eyes in wistful thought.

Beatrice tried to make sense of it. Hand in her pocket, she felt for the marble she'd found on the floor. It was solid, round and real, even if nothing else was.

In an instant, the boy appeared again, this time from behind his mother's chair. He stared at Beatrice with sunken eyes, his pale face shining with the sweat of sickness. Despite the form he'd now taken, his clothes were tidy, his countenance keen, and from the way he looked at his mother, Beatrice sensed that he loved her with all his heart and that he desperately wanted her to know it.

Unlike the frightful Gypsy woman, the boy's spirit didn't scare her. Perhaps it was because he was only a child, or because his mother was so incredibly kind, but any uneasiness she felt was soon replaced by an overwhelming sense of duty and care. Turning to Mrs. Dashley she quietly said, "He's here."

"Who?" Judith asked with a confused stare.

"Your son."

"Didn't you hear me? He's been gone for years."

Unable to take her eyes off the boy, Beatrice said, "I believe his spirit remains."

The colour drained from Mrs. Dashley's face. "My dear girl," she said. "I want to think well of you, I really do, so please don't toy with me. Did Miss Thom tell you to do this?"

"No," Beatrice said, shaking her head. "She did no such thing."

"Are you a medium?" Judith asked. "Some sort of spiritualist?"

"No," Beatrice said, regretting her impulse to help. "Please believe me when I say that I don't want to frighten you, or upset you in any way. I wish I could explain exactly what it is I'm seeing, but I'm not sure I can."

"Try," Judith said, desperately. "I'm listening."

The boy remained at his mother's side, as if he too were waiting for Beatrice to speak.

Taking a sip of tea to calm herself, Beatrice considered how to begin. Should she steer clear of mentioning the darker details of Billy's appearance? Yes, she thought, that would be best. His mother remembered the toll the boy's illness had taken on his body—no need to revisit those horrors. She cleared her throat and said, "There's a young boy here with a round face and dark curls. He came in with you when you entered the shop. He's all of six years old, maybe seven. He's missing a front tooth."

"Billy—" Judith cried, looking around in all directions. "Is it really you?"

Turning to the ghost, Beatrice asked, "Is that your name?"

The boy nodded.

"He's a fine lad," Beatrice said. "A real charmer."

Looming in front of Beatrice, Billy put his face to hers, nose to nose.

"A little too curious for his own good," Beatrice said, leaning back in her seat. "He's got a small, crescent-shaped scar on his left cheek. A souvenir from a nasty spill."

Billy gestured for Beatrice to gaze into his eyes. When she did, she caught a glimpse of a lovely parlour with large windows and flocked wallpaper. "He was playing too close to the edge of the mantel," she said. "He slipped and fell."

Judith gasped.

"Good thing the stove wasn't hot," Beatrice went on, rubbing her hands together as if to warm them by a fire. "He only suffered a nick, no stitches required. You'd told him a hundred times not to chase the dog through the house. He knows, Ma. He knows."

"Yes," Judith said, caught between laughter and tears, "that's right. I did."

Sticking his hand inside his coat pocket, Billy brought out a crumpled paper bag.

"What've you got there?" Beatrice asked.

"Peanuts," the boy answered with a grin. Then, holding the sack next to Beatrice's ear, he shook it and teased, "Get 'em while they're hot!"

Beatrice's mouth went dry. Parched with thirst she licked her lips, tasted salt on the tip of her tongue.

Perdu bobbed his head and let out a hungry squawk.

Billy took up the greasy, rumpled bag again, this time holding it out to his mother.

Imitating the boy's actions, Beatrice said, "He's clutching a sack of roasted peanuts like a prize and saying 'Get 'em while they're hot!'"

Judith's hands went to her face as she began to sob.

Tugging at Beatrice's sleeve, Billy begged, "Please tell my ma I'm sorry. I don't want her to be sad."

"It's all right," Beatrice said attempting to comfort mother and son, "all will be well."

Billy moved to his mother's side and placed his hand on her shoulder.

Through her tears, Judith instinctively reached to touch her hand to his.

Moved by the sweetness of their bond, Beatrice felt as if she, too, might cry. Clutching the marble tight in her fist she closed her eyes. In her mind she saw the parlour again, now with a Christmas tree in the window, decorated top to bottom with candles, beads and bows. Underneath the tree sat several toys all bearing tags that read "For Billy"—a hobby horse, a tin soldier, a pair of skates, a wooden puzzle, an India rubber ball. Bells and carols sounded in her ears, heralding a vision of mother and son. Holding hands, the pair twirled in uneven circles like a wobbly wooden top before skittering into a happy heap on the floor.

Judith attempted to recover from her tears. "Please forgive me," she said, "I didn't mean to make a fuss."

"I'm the one who should apologize. I never meant to cause you heartache."

"You didn't," Judith insisted. "You've only brought me happiness, I swear it."

She leaned towards Beatrice. "Every minute of every day since my dear boy's passing, I've tried to imagine what had become of him, and I just couldn't figure it out. Was he in Heaven? Was he lost? Nothing anyone said has brought me peace. I fretted over Billy after his death more than I did when he was alive. I've never felt such worry in my life! It's weighed on me something fierce . . . right up to the moment you mentioned those silly peanuts. They were his favourite treat. He used to beg for pennies to give the vendor whenever we visited the park, pulling at my sleeve until I gave in. Bless you, my dear girl! Bless you again and again and again. Bless you and my darling Billy and those wondrous peanuts!"

Beatrice sat trembling, not knowing what to say. The woman was staring at her with such reverence and awe. Looking at the boy, she noticed his form was growing less distinct, his presence waning. "He's leaving now," she said. "He's fading away."

Judith begged, "Can't you make him stay?"

"I'm afraid I don't know how."

"Quick then," Judith said, "ask him something for me before he leaves?"

"Of course," Beatrice replied. "What is it?"

Hand to her heart, Judith asked, "Is he safe?"

Looking to the boy, Beatrice waited for an answer.

With a solemn nod, Billy kissed his finger and crossed his heart.

"Yes," Beatrice said, "he's safe."

May my mind be free from worry, my eyes clear of tears.
May my heart be filled with calm instead of fear.
In times of darkest turmoil, may the light of hope shine bright,
Fuelled by the knowledge that all will soon be right.

Lady Hibiscus.

ELEANOR STOOD ON the balcony of Liberty's torch waiting for Lucy Newland to arrive. It was Lucy with whom she'd
had the affair, whom she'd chased the day before (but never
found), who'd left a cryptic note under the door requesting
they meet in the park. Yesterday, Lucy had needed to speak
with her "soon." This morning, whatever was on her mind had
become "urgent." Eleanor wished the young woman had
given at least some small clue as to what was troubling her.

Holding fast to the railing, Eleanor kept watch on the
pathway that led to the base of the popular attraction. Couples
were walking arm in arm while nurses pushed baby buggies
around the block. Two girls were making a game of bouncing
a ball, chanting their progress as they played. "Twenty-one,
twenty-two, twenty-three, twenty-four . . ." When a gangly
boy scampered between the pair and interrupted their fun,
the girls shouted curses at his back. "May you sprout a dog's
tail! May your papa go to jail! May you step on a crack and
break your mama's back!" Eleanor saw no sign of Lucy. Had
she already been here and left? Reading the note again she
checked to make certain she'd gotten the place and time

correct. *Meet me at Lady Liberty's Torch at eleven a.m.* Yes and yes. It was just like Lucy to make her wait.

They'd met in early May when Lucy's aunt Mrs. Ida Scrope had brought her to the shop. Lucy had been a month away from marrying Cecil Newland, a successful real-estate magnate determined to leave his mark on every square inch of Manhattan. "The poor girl is beside herself with nerves," Mrs. Scrope had explained. "Have you anything to soothe her jitters?"

Taking a bottle of nerve tonic from the shelf, Eleanor had placed it on the counter in front of the fidgety flaxen-haired bride-to-be. "This should do the trick. Take one teaspoon in the morning, another at noon, and one more before bed—no more, no less. There's a verse on the back of the bottle designed to give comfort in times of distress. Don't hesitate to recite it whenever you feel tested."

The following day, Lucy had returned to the shop, this time without her aunt. With her hands behind her back, she approached the counter.

Fearing the tonic hadn't agreed with her, Eleanor had asked, "Is there anything else I can assist you with?"

"Yes and yes," Lucy had replied, giving her a smile. "Would you mind closing your eyes?"

Taken aback, Eleanor had said, "Why would I do that?"

"Indulge me," Lucy had urged. "You'll be glad you did."

Feeling foolish, Eleanor had followed Lucy's orders. After some shuffling about, Lucy had announced, "All right, Miss St. Clair. You can look."

A marble mortar and pestle, tied with a bright red bow, sat on the counter. "Is this for me?" Eleanor had asked, cupping the mortar's beautiful bowl in her hands.

"A token of my appreciation."

"That's not necessary," Eleanor had said, ready to return the gift.

"Yes, it is," Lucy had insisted.

"Why?" Eleanor had asked.

"Because I woke up this morning feeling more myself than I have my whole life."

Eleanor had had enough companions over the years (the most notable, a dark-eyed nurse named Florence with a predilection for ether) that she understood when certain cues were being given. A lick of the lips here, a well-timed compliment there, could get the point across nicely, efficiently. Sensing the young beauty's gesture was meant to test the waters, Eleanor had placed the mortar and pestle front and centre on the shelf and said, "Yes, it does seem to agree with you."

Two days later, Lucy had paid Eleanor another visit, this time with an errand boy trailing close behind carrying a large rosemary plant in a pretty brass pot. After Lucy had paid the boy for his help, she'd turned to Eleanor and asked, "Care to take a stroll with me through the park after you close shop? It's a lovely evening and it would be a shame not to take advantage of it. Please say you'll come."

The invitation had made Eleanor feel as if she was being courted, and she'd quite liked it. Her other affairs had been more accidental in nature—brief, enjoyable encounters that had filled a need. She'd never been the sort to seek out opportunities for love or lust. She'd thought herself to be more like Princess Odoline, happy to reject romantic overtures in favour of keeping company with books. Her mother had been right. Women were complicated creatures. Still, if Lucy, with her confident gaze and winning smile, insisted upon pursuing her, she wasn't going to turn her away. Impending nuptials be damned, it was spring.

They'd stopped for ice cream (Lucy's treat), then strolled along the garden paths until it was near dark, eventually finding their way to the top of the torch. The structure itself was a wonder to behold, a magnificent marriage of glass and copper metalwork. Lucy, with the last rays of the day's sunlight shining on her rosy cheeks, had leaned into Eleanor and said, "You're not like anyone I've ever known. Will you dine with me tonight?" Then she'd dared to caress Eleanor's hand. "My parents have gone to Boston, and except for the cook and maid, I'm quite alone in the house."

"Yes," Eleanor had replied, "I'd like that."

Eleanor hadn't planned on keeping the affair from Adelaide, but when things with Lucy had felt tantalizing and fresh, she'd chosen to follow her lover's lead and not say a word. The last thing she'd wanted was to unleash the barrage of questions Adelaide would be sure to heap upon her. Adelaide had always been quite free in her talk of her own exploits, but Eleanor had found it easier to play the stoic than confess to things she wasn't sure Adelaide would understand.

In a moment of weakness on their last night together before Lucy's wedding, she'd turned to her lover and asked, "Why didn't you choose to lie with your future husband instead?"

"Why would I? It's my last chance to make him wait."

Eleanor had hoped Lucy might make him wait forever.

On the sixth of June, as Lucy was becoming Mrs. Newland in an orange-blossom-bedecked affair at Trinity Church, Eleanor had stood near the shop window for much of the day, half expecting her to come running through the door.

"What's the matter with you?" Adelaide had asked. "Who are you waiting for?"

The day slipped by without a word from Lucy. A week passed and the only news Eleanor received was by way of a wedding announcement torn from the society page and delivered by Ida Scrope. "It was an astounding success!" she had reported. "Not a petal or pearl out of place. Whatever magic you performed on behalf of our dear Lucy, it certainly worked."

After reading the glowing account of bouquets, topiaries, tulle and lace, Eleanor had crumpled the paper in her hands and sighed. *The dashing groom and his radiant bride will be touring Europe for the summer. They intend to welcome visitors to their Manhattan residence in September.* Tossing it into the fire, she'd thought, *Lucy's made her choice.*

In August the bride had reappeared, once more seeking Eleanor's help. "I need something to keep my womb clear," she'd said, nervously turning her wedding ring around her finger. "I've run out of the regulating powders I purchased while abroad." She'd offered Eleanor no apology, expressed no regrets, shown no sign of being a reluctant wife other than not wanting to be a mother.

Swallowing her hurt, Eleanor had handed her a tin of tansy tea. "Drink a cup of this once a day for a full week before your courses are due. So long as you've kept proper track of things, it should provide all the help you need."

"Is there no verse to recite this time to soften my trials and woes?"

Was the young woman teasing her? Eleanor had been tempted to write something cruel on the receipt (*you've made your bed, now you must lie in it* came to mind), but she chose to take the high road instead. "The tea should suffice."

After that, Lucy had returned to the shop at least once a week—sometimes alone, sometimes with her aunt—never showing a hint of regret or longing on her lovely face. Last week when she'd asked for something stronger than the tea, Eleanor had given her a tincture of Queen Anne's lace along with instructions on how to use it.

This morning, when Eleanor had read the note that Lucy had slipped under the door, she'd assumed it could only mean one thing—she was pregnant. Why hadn't the tincture worked? And why leave a note rather than come back to the shop? If it was so important they meet at eleven in the park, why wasn't she here? Did she ever think of anyone but herself?

Just as Eleanor was about to leave, she heard footsteps on the stairs that led to the balcony. Turning, she caught sight of Lucy, decked out in a lavender walking suit and feather-laden hat. Making an attempt to smooth the wrinkles from her plain linen dress, Eleanor only said, "You're late."

"In more ways than one," Lucy replied, moving to Eleanor's side.

"I was afraid that might be the case. Did you take the tincture as I instructed?"

"You never mentioned how horrible it tastes. I couldn't stand it so I stopped."

Eleanor shook her head. "No wonder you're in a bind. How many days are you past due?"

"It doesn't matter," Lucy said, dismissing Eleanor's concern.

"It most certainly does," Eleanor chided. "I need to know how late you are, so I can decide how best to help you."

Lucy sighed. "What if I don't want your help?"

"Then why are we here?" Eleanor asked.

Lucy didn't reply.

"Do you want a child?" Eleanor asked, wishing she knew whether or not Lucy even wished to be married.

"I don't know what I want anymore," Lucy said. "I'm tired of thinking. Please tell me what to do."

It was all Eleanor could do not to leave her there. "Why don't you ask your aunt for advice, or better yet, your husband. I'm sure Mr. Newland would have something to say about the matter."

"That's not fair."

"Life's not fair."

Tears in her eyes, Lucy leaned close and whispered, "He found the bottle and threw it out. I tried to explain it away as best I could, but I'm sure he didn't believe me."

"He knows what it's for?"

"He seems to, yes."

"Does he know where you got it?"

"I don't think so," Lucy replied, "but it's hard to say what he does and doesn't know, or just what he's thinking. He gets so terribly angry sometimes. He said it's only a matter of time until he uncovers all my secrets. I can't imagine what he might do if he found out about us."

Eleanor placed a hand on Lucy's arm. "For what it's worth," she said, "you're always welcome to stay with me."

"What a scandal that would be!" Lucy said with a forced laugh.

Eleanor frowned. "I'm concerned for your welfare."

"You might consider your own before making such an offer. The consequences could be devastating."

"I'm not afraid of the consequences," Eleanor said. Despite the girl's fickleness, she still cared for her. If Lucy was in danger, she had to take a stand.

"Perhaps you should be," Lucy replied. "We'd both be ruined and I've no doubt that your fate would be far worse than mine. Society would turn its back on me, that's a given, but I can always run off to Paris or London to ride out the storm. You, my dear, would be tossed in the Tombs once the police got wind of the services you provide to the women of the Ladies' Mile. We were so careful to never speak of love! Why must you insist on being so self-sacrificing now?"

"This isn't about love," Eleanor retorted. "It's about liberty."

"But I'm not the one who would be thrown in a cell." Lucy shook her head in disbelief. "I don't know why I came to you about this. I quite like the way I live—my house, my parties, my dresses, my friends."

"But is that life really yours?"

Lucy's face softened. "If this is about what we shared together, please know I've no regrets. If we were living in another time or place—if I'd been your dark-eyed nurse, or you were my distant cousin, we could walk hand in hand down sidewalks or through ballrooms and no one would say a word. But you being who you are and me being who I am, our friendship was fated to end."

"My offer stands," Eleanor said. Her mother had never turned away a woman in need. *That is who we are. This is what we do.*

"I can't afford to take such a risk," Lucy said. "I've too much to lose."

"They're only losses if you perceive them to be," Eleanor insisted. "Think of what you might gain."

"By that same logic, I'm only a prisoner if I think myself one. I'm not like you, dear Eleanor. I'm weak and spoiled and afraid. It's simply not in me to be brave."

Those were the truest words Eleanor had ever heard Lucy speak.

"Here," Eleanor said, fishing in her satchel for another bottle of the tincture she'd brought with her just in case. "Ten drops beneath your tongue each morning for five days straight. It's sure to bring on your blood so long as you're less than two weeks past due. If you're any further along than that, you'll need something stronger and I'd need to look after you."

Lucy took the bottle. "This time I'll be more careful with it."

"Careful or not, it won't do you any good unless you take what's in it." Eleanor sensed that Lucy had no intention of using the tincture. There was a dullness in her eyes that said she was resigned to be more child than woman, more possession than partner in her marriage. "Send word if you need anything else," she said, reaching out to touch Lucy's hand.

Nodding, Lucy gave a weak smile. "I'll have Aunt Ida bring me something from time to time to remember you by."

"Hibiscus tea?" Eleanor asked, knowing it was her favourite.

Delivering a kiss to Eleanor's cheek, Lucy said, "Yes. I always liked hibiscus best."

Eleanor stayed awhile at the torch after Lucy left. In the gardens below, she spotted an old woman sitting by the fountain feeding the birds. The woman had once told her that the web of footpaths within the park had been arranged in such a way that anyone who visited more than once would rarely walk the same path. She'd claimed this was because the place was enchanted, guarded by the spirits of those buried far beneath the tea roses and locust trees. "Take care that you never tell a lie here," she'd warned, "or the spirits will follow you home."

Tossing the last of her crumbs, the old woman rose to trail after a group of pamphleteers making their rounds through the park. Two ladies dressed in white led the ragtag parade, carrying the standard of the National Woman Suffrage Association. Every so often the Bird Lady would bend down to collect a stray notice or bit of debris. Eleanor had seen her follow other groups in the past—the Daughters of Light, who were raising funds to build a proper base for Lady Liberty; Congregationalists from the Church of the Good Shepherd, who wished to rid the world of sin; the gentleman members of the Fraternal Order of the Unknown Philosophers, who had a question for every answer. After she'd collected all she wanted, the Bird Lady would sit on a bench with needle and thread and sew her precious scraps into paper stars and give them away to any passerby who bothered to approach her. To most, the shabby tokens were nothing more than trash, but to those who looked upon the woman's offerings with kindness, they were delicate artifacts shaped by skilled hands. Eleanor had kept every star the Bird Lady had ever given her. She planned to string them in a garland and hang them in the shop window come Christmas. Every fold, every stitch the woman made was filled with care and thought; somehow the Bird Lady found meaning in what the rest of the world tossed away. Although she didn't often speak to Eleanor, on the occasions when she did, the lilt in her voice reminded Eleanor of her mother.

She wondered if the wise Madame St. Clair could've convinced Lucy to flee her situation. As a child Eleanor had watched in awe as her mother had said whatever she thought whenever she wanted to whomever she pleased, mostly to great success.

"When do I get to do that, Maman?" she'd asked. "When do I get to say whatever I wish?"

"When it pains you not to," her mother had replied.

"What if I'm too scared?"

"All the more reason to speak your mind."

Known for its beautiful fountain, lovely trees and pleasant walking paths, Madison Square Garden is equally inviting at night. Every evening after sunset, spectators gather there to witness a great sight atop the Erie ticket building just opposite the park. It's there that the enterprising Mr. Eno has installed an enormous stereopticon (or Magic Lantern) along with a presentation screen three storeys high. Scenes of the world (Niagara Falls, the Grand Canyon, the Amazon River) are intermingled with advertisements, bible verses and the news of the day, each image dissolving into the next at a steady pace in the skilled hands of the lanternist. Although most observers come with an understanding of how the contraption works, they are still inclined to marvel whenever the screen is lit. The days of witchcraft and sorcery may be happily past, but man is not above believing in magic when science is so convincingly turned to spectacle.

—*Sights and Wonders of the City:*
A Guide to New York, 1880

Phantasmagoria.

ADELAIDE LOVED NIGHTFALL in the park, the way the glimmer of lights—from windows, street lamps, lanterns on carriages—made it seem as if there were stars twinkling on the ground. When she was a child she'd stay out all day and not go home until well after dark. (It was that or catch her mother accommodating the landlord while drinking herself into a sordid mess.)

She hadn't returned to the shop that afternoon, hadn't gone back to the hotel either, all in an effort to avoid Judith Dashley. After window-shopping up and down the length of Ladies' Mile, she'd decided to end the day in the park. She felt quite at home watching the buskers and beggars find their places, as if they were about to perform a pantomime of her past.

Let the lady stew, she thought, as she settled on her favourite bench. I'll mend whatever needs fixing tomorrow.

She knew Judith had meant well by introducing her to Dr. Brody, so why had her kindness felt so intrusive? If anything she should thank the woman for her efforts, because for a fleeting moment that morning, with Dr. Brody's hand in hers, she'd felt the excitement of having someone new to figure out. But then she'd bungled that up as well—she'd been too forward too fast, too revealing with her words. In her experience, most men became unbearably squeamish when faced with hard truths. It'd been a long time since she'd read a man's palm, and even longer since she'd felt a man's hand on the small of her back. Was she interested in the good doctor? Yes. Did she wish to fall in love? Absolutely not. And there lay the root of her problem. She hated to disappoint Judith, but she highly doubted that whatever might happen between her and Dr. Brody (or any man) would ever last. While her encounter with him had served to reinforce the notion that she was in dire need of something new to pursue, she was quite convinced that any involvement with him would wind up being a limited engagement.

What then should I focus my energies upon? she wondered. Things were going well enough at the teashop, but they could always go better. She wasn't like Eleanor, who was perfectly content with paying the bills and getting by. She dreamed of a larger clientele, of greater success, of enough money to buy out the landlord, Mr. Withrow, who was always belittling their role as businesswomen and threatening to raise the rent.

When they'd first opened the shop, all Adelaide had wanted was to repay Eleanor for her kindness, and make a fresh start for herself. With the heady early days of starting their business now behind them, she'd begun to feel restless and bored. Any new ideas that sparked in her brain never seemed to catch fire. She'd thought that reading cards for the ladies of Fifth Avenue would hold her interest for a good long while, but their problems were far too much alike for her taste. She felt that something was about to change (it simply had to), but she wasn't sure if she should run to or from it.

Considering her options, Adelaide wondered if the new girl, Beatrice, might hold the key to attracting more business to the shop. With her alabaster skin, shiny hair and home-spun charm, she might pull even the most reluctant passerby into their orbit. In the sideshow, they'd called her kind "a draw." Adelaide had been one herself. Maybe she could teach the girl how to tell fortunes. If Beatrice's mind was as keen as her attitude, then it wouldn't be too difficult a task. Her looks could certainly make up for any intuitive inclination she lacked. Eleanor, of course, would be sure to say that she was taking advantage of the girl's eager nature, and there'd be some of that, yes. But it would all be for the greater good of their venture. In any event, she'd need to observe the girl, spend time with her, which also might help her shake her own malaise. In the meantime, she had Mrs. Stevens' proposition to consider. If only she could get Eleanor to see the benefit of using her craft to wrangle at least a few of the hotel's wayward ghosts.

Evening chimes sounded from the bells of a nearby church. *One, two, three, four, five, six, seven, eight, nine.*

As spectators gathered to watch the latest round of images featured in the magic lantern show, a young girl wearing a shabby gingham dress passed through the crowd and stopped in front of Adelaide. Wisps of dark hair dangling in her face, she splayed a handful of playing cards like a fan. With a shy smile she said, "Tell your fortune, ma'am?"

"How much?" Adelaide asked. There was something about her hungry eyes and sunken cheeks that made her feel as if she were being shown a vision of her younger self.

"Three pennies a card," the girl replied. "A nickel if you like what you hear."

"All right then," Adelaide said, reaching for a card. "Let's see what I get."

"Choose carefully," the girl instructed. "Take your time."

Running her finger across the top edges of the cards, Adelaide studied the girl's eyes. When her lashes fluttered ever so slightly, Adelaide plucked a card from her hand. "Nine of Hearts," she announced, presenting it to the girl for evaluation.

"Excellent choice, ma'am," the girl cooed. "The best one in the deck. That's no lie."

Adelaide gave the girl a smile. Not because she felt lucky in her choice, but because the little soothsayer had just proved her worth. The Nine of Hearts was universally acknowledged among Gypsy fortune tellers to be the luckiest card of all. "What does it mean?" Adelaide asked, feigning ignorance.

"It means you get to make a wish," the girl replied. "And by and by, it'll come true."

Just then, a group of women in velvet-trimmed cloaks came towards them on the footpath, singing hymns and distributing religious tracts.

> *Sowing in the morning, sowing seeds of kindness*
> *Sowing in the noontide and the dewy eve;*
> *Waiting for the harvest, and the time of reaping,*
> *We shall come rejoicing, bringing in the sheaves.*

One of the women stared at the girl like a cat in want of prey. She reminded Adelaide of the Christian ladies who went slumming down on Chrystie Street when she was a child. They came from parish halls and ladies' societies to peer into the windows and lives of the less fortunate, one hand holding a skirt out of the muck, the other a peppermint-scented handkerchief to the nose. "Poor dear," they'd say while dropping pennies into her hand, taking care not to touch her. Then they'd invite her to their Bible study meetings so they could tell her she was nothing but a sack of sin. As soon as all those wretched *r*'s started coming from between their lips—*refuge, reform, religion*—she'd grab one of their biscuits and race out the door.

"Tell me more about my card," Adelaide said, motioning for the girl to sit next to her on the bench. She wasn't about to let this child get swept up in the Christian ladies' fervour.

"It's like I said," the girl replied, lighting on the bench's edge. "A wish come true."

"Wishes are serious business," Adelaide said.

"I'd say so," the girl replied with a wink.

Reaching inside her pocket, Adelaide pulled out a shiny dime and handed it over. "This is for you."

"Thank you, ma'am." The girl stared at the coin as if she couldn't believe her own luck. "That's awfully generous of you."

"There's more where that came from next time I see you," Adelaide promised.

"I hope it's soon then," the girl said, already looking for her next mark.

Watching the girl slip back into the crowd, Adelaide made her wish. *May she always find a way to survive.*

> *Bringing in the sheaves, bringing in the sheaves.*
> *We shall come rejoicing, bringing in the sheaves.*

The women's voices faded as they moved through the park. In their wake another voice sounded, off-key and broken by time. The Bird Lady was spouting profanities as she picked up dropped copies of the women's pamphlet: "God's Wishes for Women."

"Burn in Hell!" she shouted. "God damn you all!" Spotting Adelaide, she stopped in her tracks.

"Hello," Adelaide said, greeting her as sweetly as she could. She knew how much Eleanor revered the woman.

The Bird Lady sidled near, so close that Adelaide could smell the rot in her teeth, and asked, "Sit with you?" She reached out to touch the scars on Adelaide's face. "Sit with you?"

"All right," Adelaide said, and when the woman sat, she took her grubby hand in hers and held it in her lap. "Sit with me awhile."

The Bird Lady laid her head on Adelaide's shoulder and heaved a pitiful sigh that shuddered and creaked through her tired body.

"He's coming," the Bird Lady whispered. "He's coming for her."

On the other side of the park, Reverend Townsend waited for Sister Piddock and the rest of the women from his congregation to finish their rounds. He'd promised that he'd escort them (and any other they'd found) back to the church for refreshments and prayers afterwards. Their clucking chatter annoyed him no end, but their devotion was a sure sign that he was winning the fight against sin.

> *Bringing in the sheaves, bringing in the sheaves.*
> *We shall come rejoicing, bringing in the sheaves.*

The Reverend turned his attention to a young girl who was making her way towards him (the same waif who'd read Adelaide's cards). As she passed into the glow of the street lamp nearest to where he stood, he could've sworn for a moment the dishevelled child looked more otherworldly than human. Was she a demon? An angel in disguise? Another witch? Blinking away the vision, he figured he was seeing things. After all, he hadn't slept last night. He'd stayed on his knees in fervent prayer just as the two men in black had instructed him to do. And at first light Lena McLeod's body was gone. A miracle! A sign that all he'd done was right. Perhaps the girl standing before him was another test of his faith. *Thy will be done*, he thought, smiling down at her.

"Tell your fortune, sir?" the little soothsayer asked, staring up at the Reverend.

"Oh child," Townsend replied, "that's the Devil's work." Putting his hand on her shoulder he asked, "Why do you indulge in his deceptions?"

With a cheeky grin the girl replied, "I need to eat."

"Come with us then," Townsend said, guiding her towards the sisters. "The ladies of my church will give you food and rest."

"And what will *you* give me?" the girl asked.

"All that you deserve," Reverend Townsend replied.

With a lively skip the girl fell in line behind the women. As she did, a single card fluttered from her pocket and stuck between two pavers. The Ace of Spades, foretelling misfortune, difficulty and a treacherous path.

If you wish to upset the law that all crows are black, it is enough if you prove that one crow is white.

—WILLIAM JAMES

Dr. Brody's Ghosts.

QUINN BRODY BEGAN the evening just as he'd hoped— snifter of brandy in his hand, new book on the table, fire crackling before him as he sat in a worn leather chair in his father's study. Even as a boy, he'd preferred the dusky, book-filled room above all others in the house. Back then, his mother had held sway over what did and didn't make its way inside the Brody residence, except for the study. It was there that Quinn had first witnessed the wonder of electricity inside a Leyden jar, watched Pepper's ghost get conjured via magic lantern, climbed the spiral staircase to the roof to view the moon through a refracting telescope. It was there that he had learned to love science.

After his mother died, Quinn's father spread the tools of his trade throughout the house. The conservatory became a laboratory, the downstairs cloakroom a makeshift *Wunder-kammer*. Before long there was little discernible difference between the dining-room table and a mad scientist's work-bench. Saturday mornings the lonely widower visited estate sales in the countryside to rescue vast caches of philosophical equipment from abandoned barns and tumbledown shacks.

Crucibles, notebooks and leather-bound tomes were strewn on every surface. The smell of coal, sulphur and molten metal belched from every chimney, wafting up from the alchemist's cauldrons that Mr. Brody kept bubbling over roaring fires throughout the year.

As the elder Brody's obsessions grew, the world around him changed. The house, an exceptional example of the Italianate style just west of Madison Square, was suddenly on the edge of the Tenderloin, bordered by saloons, theatres, dance halls, clip joints, gambling dens and bordellos. To protect his possessions from questionable elements, Mr. Brody had affixed ironwork grates and bars to all accessible windows and doors, causing the house and his place of business to appear like a pair of giant birdcages.

During the last year of his life, the only people the old man trusted to cross the threshold were his son, his long-time housekeeper, Mabel Stutt, and the gentlemen members of the Unknown Philosophers. Identical signs placed on the front of the house and shop read, NO ADMITTANCE SHALL BE GIVEN TO PREACHERS, TAX COLLECTORS OR T.A. EDISON.

After his father's death, Quinn conducted a meticulous inventory of the many items that cluttered the place, precipitated in part by the upcoming symposium of the Unknown Philosophers to be held at the Fifth Avenue Hotel. As a tribute to his father, they'd asked him to deliver the opening evening's lecture and he'd agreed, figuring it was also a good place to share the latest findings of his own research: the finer points of his theories on spirit detection and communication with the afterlife (so long as he could gather satisfactory proof). With the symposium less than a month away, he'd turned the study into a space devoted to his work, adding to his father's kit a working model of Holtz's electro-static influence machine, a Bennet gold-plate electroscope and a collection of various and sundry pendulums and plan-chettes. The greatest and perhaps most important item in the study, however, was something Quinn's father had directed him to unearth from the back of the shop before he'd died—a strange-looking contraption he'd simply called a "spiritoscope."

Made to be attached to the top of a table, it featured a wooden board fitted with casters that could roll freely under the hands of the operator and a "spiritual telegraph dial" (patterned after the cast-iron dials used on early telegraph machines). Letters of the alphabet were arranged around the circumference of the dial, which was a little larger than the face of a grandfather clock, with the numbers one through ten inside that ring. At the one, three, five, six, seven, nine and eleven o'clock positions the following words and phrases appeared: YES, NO, DON'T KNOW, THINK SO, SPELL OVER, MUST GO, MISTAKE.

"It's for testing spiritual mediumship," Mr. Brody had explained. "Any and all who claim they can speak with the dead are welcome to try it. The dial is positioned so the operator can't see it. Any messages received from the Great Beyond are therefore free from bias."

"Have you ever had any luck with it?" Quinn had asked, wondering why his father had never spoken of the machine before.

"Only in exposing frauds," his father had answered. "It's terribly accurate when it comes to detecting liars. Perhaps you'll have better luck. I've placed a message in a bottle and stashed it in the rafters. Once I'm gone, see if you can get the machine to work. If the message comes through word for word, then you'll know you've heard from the other side."

Not long after his father's passing, Quinn had sat himself down at the machine and waited to see if the board might move beneath his fingers, but nothing happened. He'd also taken a turn sitting opposite the dial with pen and paper, and invited his father's spirit to move the needle on his own. On that occasion, the pointer had twitched ever so slightly to the left, and then gone still. That twitch may have been all his father could manage, but it'd been more than enough encouragement for Quinn. Now all he needed to do was find a medium through whom his father's spirit might freely act. It couldn't be just anyone, of course, but someone preternaturally sensitive to ghostly transmissions. Perhaps Miss Thom, with her uncanny knack for discerning the past, would be willing to give it a try?

Flustered by their breakfast conversation, he'd had an awkward parting with the soothsayer and they'd made no further plans to meet. Even when Quinn had been married, he'd never been quite clear on what it was women wanted from men (or to be more precise, from *him*). In fact, he'd often thought that his wife's acceptance of his proposal had been an accident. Not that it mattered anymore. She'd been gone so long he barely remembered what their life had been like. Did he wish to be paired with anyone ever again? Maybe yes. Likely no. Who would take him in his current state—without youth, ambition or a right arm? Still, he had to admit he wanted to see Miss Thom again. Before he let himself be discouraged from the attempt, he sat down at his desk with pen and notepaper.

Dear Miss Thom,
~~*I appreciated*~~ (No, that wasn't quite right.)

Dear Miss Thom,
~~*I greatly enjoyed our conversation*~~ (Too boring?
Too trite?)

Dear Miss Thom,
I greatly enjoyed our enlightened exchange this
morning at the Fifth Avenue Hotel.
May I converse with you again, at your
convenience?
You name the time and place, and I shall obey.
Sincerely,
Dr. Quinn Brody

Laying his pen aside, Quinn sensed a presence in the
doorway, the weight of a familiar, pressing gaze.

"May I help you, Mrs. Stutt?" The housekeeper had a terrible habit of standing in the shadows, as if she meant to catch
him doing something he shouldn't.

"*Nein*," she said. "If you're not needing me for anything,
I'm off to bed."

The grey-haired woman had been a fixture in Quinn's life
since his youth, and it seemed his father's passing had affected
her nearly as much as it had him. Earlier in the day, he'd caught
her crying, hunched over a stray button she'd found in the
bottom of her sewing kit. She'd meant to reattach it to his
father's favourite frock coat before he died, but hadn't gotten
the chance.

"Perhaps you'd like some time away?" Quinn had offered, wanting to make things better for her. "With pay, of course. I'd be more than happy to make all the necessary arrangements."

"*Nein*," Mrs. Stutt had replied, drying her tears. "What I'd like is for you to tell me what you want for supper."

Unlike his father, who'd often invited Mrs. Stutt to sit with him to discuss knackwurst or the weather, Quinn preferred to dine alone, to think alone, without interruption. Mrs. Stutt could cook whatever she wanted, he didn't care. He'd happily live on bread, cheese and cold cuts, day in and day out, if she'd allow it. He knew he was a disappointment to her.

Still standing in the doorway, Mrs. Stutt waited to be dismissed.

"You're free to do as you wish," Quinn said. "I've got a new book that wants to be read. I'll be awake a while yet."

"Very well then," Mrs. Stutt said. "*Guten nacht*, Dr. Brody."

"Goodnight, Mrs. Stutt. Pleasant dreams."

As the housekeeper took her leave she muttered under her breath, "*Geister zeugen Träume*." Ghosts beget dreams.

The novel Quinn had chosen for his evening's entertainment turned out to be a bust. More romance than adventure, much of *Dr. Heidenhoff's Process* concerned itself with a pair of young lovers who were, by turns, brooding, flippant, arrogant and insufferable. By the time Dr. Heidenhoff arrived on the scene, it was very near the end, and the character's scientific reasoning, intriguing as it was, was highly flawed and unconvincing.

As he placed the book on the shelf, he felt a nasty pinch between his shoulder blades. The leather straps that fastened his false arm to his body never stopped chafing his back. He'd tried wrapping the straps in muslin, but no matter what he did, the buckles and fittings found new and cruel ways to dig into whatever soft flesh he had left. His father had planned to replace the arm with a more comfortable and useful limb, but had never gotten around to completing the project. Taking his watch from his pocket, he placed it on his father's desk, then set about the task of unbuttoning his waistcoat, collar and shirt.

Tick-tick-tick-tick, the watch nagged.

He could hardly wait to be free of the weighty, wooden albatross tethered to his body. He would've removed the bothersome thing hours ago, but he knew it troubled Mrs. Stutt to see his sleeve limp without it. *Tick-tick-tick-tick.*

Thump!

His government-issued limb made a sickening thud as it dropped to the floor, causing Quinn's heart to pound and race. In an instant he was overcome with a sense of dread, his thoughts descending into the chaos of the war. The desk turned into an operating table made from two barrels and a plank. The flames of the fire became a distant battlefield lit with flashes of orange and red. Rows of furrows lay before him, dotted with blue jackets soaked in blood. In a blink, a heap of sawed-off legs, arms, hands and feet appeared at his side. The smell of gunpowder and chloroform filled the air. The soldiers at the Stump Hospital circled around him—one with no legs, one with no eyes, one with a copper nose; a dozen more falling into fits and convulsions at his feet. Then he was staring at his own body, naked and writhing under the knife of a surgeon who was sawing, cutting and slicing him to pieces. Bit by bit, hunks of his flesh got tossed aside until there was nothing left.

Trembling and drenched in sweat, Quinn went to his father's desk and tripped a lock on a hidden drawer. Why should he continue to be haunted when relief was so close at hand?

Tick-tick-tick-tick.

Stump propped on a tufted pillow, Quinn reclined on a woven mat and meditated on the opium pipe that sat on a tray beside him. *Yen tshung* was what the Chinese called the sleek, silver-saddled length of bamboo. *Yen hop*, the lacquered opium box. *Sui pow*, the sponge to cool the bowl. *Yen dong*, the small lamp that cast a friendly yellow gloom upon his face, reminiscent of the light from a waning campfire. *Yen hock*, the needle he used to tease and pull at the balled-up pill of *chandoo* until it turned soft. The substance reminded him of molasses taffy, yet its pleasures weren't nearly so innocent. He made sure he was precise with the dosage, because he didn't want to get hooked. He'd promised himself that he wouldn't fall too far under the poppy's spell. Still, he thought it a better choice than swilling a bottle of laudanum or getting piss drunk.

As he inhaled the nutty and sweet-tasting smoke, he did his best to allow the opium to ease his mind. The weight of him melted into the floor, his worries sinking down, down, down, along with it. Dancing skeletons and floating burial shrouds soon turned into a trio of rouge-lipped can-can girls in frilly skirts. *Tick-tick-tick-tick.*

One of the dancers broke away from her sisters to sit on the edge of the stage.

"Charlotte," Quinn said, recognizing her at once. "My dearest wife."

Her auburn hair fell to the small of her back, free from ribbons or pins. Leaning forward, Quinn tried to kiss her, but she averted her face.

He'd spent a blur of days keeping vigil at her bedside while she lay dying. Time and again he'd wondered, why couldn't she have been blessed with a better end?

"Kiss me," he begged, "I miss you."

She shook her head and disappeared.

Tick-tick-tick-tick-tick-tick-tick.

"Dr. Brody . . ." a second woman called. Another can-can girl come to taunt him.

"Dr. Brody," she called again, this time from the corridors of the Salpêtrière, the asylum in Paris where he'd studied under Jean-Martin Charcot. *"Aidez-moi!"*

She was young, full of figure and far more affectionate towards him than she should've been.

"Nadine," he whispered. "You got out again."

Her mother had tied Nadine to the gates of the asylum with a note pinned to her dress: *La fille de Lucifer.* Professor Charcot was more than happy to take her into his care.

"Aidez-moi!" she'd cried as Charcot and his students poked and prodded, pricked and scratched her as she lay strapped fast to an examining table. Not Brody, never Brody.

"Elle est hystérique!"

"Elle est délirante!"

"Elle est une sorcière!"

On Tuesdays she'd been brought to the lecture hall to be hypnotized and observed by the public transfixed by Charcot's *musée pathologique vivant.* The heat in the room was unbearable, the size of the crowd absurd. Hypnotized, she'd spoken of a handsome prince who'd fed her sweets, given her jewels and then repeatedly raped her. (On the ward, she wrote him lengthy letters filled with curses, and signed them "*du diable*.")

"*Aidez-moi*, Dr. Brody!" she'd wailed. "Help me!"

Quinn had watched as the young woman's ruffled skirts fell from her body, leaving her naked. Embarrassed, he'd given her his jacket.

In it, Nadine had slipped through the asylum gates unnoticed.

Tick–tick–tick–tick.

The last can-can girl gracefully straddled Quinn's lap. Wrapping her legs around him, the pretty one-eyed dancer gave him a crooked smile and said, "Giddy-up."

Quinn slipped his ghostly hand beneath her skirts and stroked her bare thigh.

Lips grazing his ear, Adelaide whispered, "How long has it been since you've been loved?"

Before Quinn could answer she was gone.

The little oil lamp twinkled before him, urging him back to his pipe. Another bowl would bring about another sweet release, followed by a pleasant stupor.

Then again, he could resist. He could pull on his coat and hat and go for a walk. The fresh air might do him good.

Before he could make up his mind, his belly lurched. Thank heavens there was a bucket nearby, waiting for the slippery lump that'd gathered in his throat. Those new to the pipe, like him, often suffered from surges of the fiend's remorse.

Tick . . . tick.

Retching until his stomach was empty, he thrust his hand in his pocket to search for a handkerchief. Clutching the keepsake Charlotte had given him all those years ago, he wiped his nose and mouth on his sleeve instead. As he settled on his pillow, he thought of Adelaide Thom. Would she be the one to bring him proof of the afterlife? Would she be the one to ease his longing?

Taking the pipe in hand, Dr. Brody made his choice. The day would end with more forgetting.

The lunatics were told that there was to be a dance in the Amusement Hall, a building in which concerts and balls are given to the inmates of the asylum. A merry air was played on the piano, and in a few minutes the lunatics were dancing and capering about in high glee.

The Lunatics' Ball.

THE AMUSEMENT HALL at the lunatic asylum on Blackwell's Island was a clean, open room sparsely furnished with an upright piano and half a dozen chairs lined up against the far wall. The light was dim but festive, twinkling from strings of brightly coloured lanterns hanging from the rafters. Several gentlemen who'd come by ferry from Manhattan were milling about the space, waiting for the female inmates to arrive. A small band played in the far corner of the room led by a fiddler who held his ensemble together with great flare, dancing a spirited jig as the viol, bass, guitar and banjo accompanied him.

The women—around thirty altogether, varied in age, race and education—were brought to the hall by a pair of orderlies. Some of them were quite eager to dance, practically running to take their places on the floor. Others reluctantly shuffled into the room, heads bowed. Hand-picked to attend the ball because of their good behaviour during the week, the inmates had been scrubbed and dressed for the occasion, their faces still red from rough rags and harsh soap, their hair tucked into neat braids or buns, their calico gowns unadorned and out of date. They looked like farm girls out to a country dance.

Among them was Sophie Miles—tall and lean, with large hazel eyes and honey-coloured curls. She'd been at the asylum for a year and nine months, and in that time she'd gone from being considered a danger to others to a shining example of recovery. The doctors were impressed with her progress, the nurses were coming around, and her sister inmates (who either feared or adored her) believed her to be a witch. What was the truth? All of it, she guessed. She was willing to do whatever it took to gain her freedom.

She'd been sent to the madhouse for throwing vitriol in a woman's face. The judge had told her she should be grateful— it was better than being locked up in the Tombs. Neither the cops nor the judge had believed her when she'd told them that she was right to do what she'd done. That smug bitch of a soothsayer had snubbed her, laughed behind her back. Miss Zula Moth had no idea of the kind of witch she'd wronged. The judge had described Miss Moth's injuries in detail: the agonizing pain; the gruesome scars on her face; the loss of her eye. "Lucky for you the young woman didn't die," the judge had grumbled. "Yes sir," Sophie had replied. *Pity she didn't*, she'd thought.

Tonight was Sophie's third time attending the ball and she had grand plans for the evening, hanging her hopes in the old saying, *Three times a charm*. Last week she'd spotted a man who'd seemed an ideal candidate to help her get out of the asylum. She'd smiled at him from across the room and she was sure she'd caught his eye, but he'd left before she'd had the chance to speak with him. Tonight he would not get away.

When she spotted him coming in at last, she clutched a small poppet she'd stuck in her pocket, one which she'd fashioned in his likeness, and whispered, "Come to me."

The well-dressed gentleman looked right at her and she gave him a shy smile and a wave. She'd chosen him because beneath his confident-looking exterior was a man who harboured a fair amount of self-doubt. She could see it in the way he'd taught himself to swagger even though he required the use of a cane. He was afflicted by things that couldn't be mended, and not just his wooden leg. Even within the walls of a madhouse he was the odd man out. He didn't possess the agility required for dancing a polka or reel. Hooking arms with a partner to swing her around was completely out of the question. He was a wounded animal. Easy prey.

The man made his way across the room and stopped in front of Sophie. "Mr. Bartholomew Andersen," he said, holding out his hand.

"Sophie Miles," she replied, with a soft Southern lilt, taking his hand briefly in return.

"Wonderful music," Andersen remarked.

"Yes," Sophie replied. "I like it very much."

"And where do you hail from, Sophie?" he asked, as if they were at a cotillion rather than an asylum.

"New Orleans, originally. It's where I was born."

"I'm from Baltimore myself."

Sophie swayed a little in time to the music and longingly looked at the dance floor.

"I'd ask you to dance," Mr. Andersen said at last, raising the cuff of his trouser, "but I'm afraid I wouldn't be much of a partner."

Sophie glanced at the wooden leg and shrugged. "I wouldn't say that." Daintily picking up her skirt, she dosey-doed around him for the rest of the song, occasionally brushing up against him, shoulder-to-shoulder, elbow-to-elbow.

When the song was over, Sophie took Mr. Andersen's hand in hers. Pointing to different women in the room, she listed why they had been consigned to the asylum, in an effort to show him that she, too, was out of place. "Intemperance. Hysteria. Jealousy. Nymphomania. Immoral life. Self-abuse. Preventing conception. Religious obsession. Setting fires. Kicked in the head by a horse. Mental excitement. Opium habit. Domestic affliction. Grief. Desertion of husband. Bloody flux. Brain fever. Death of child. Quackery. Uterine derangement. Vicious vices. Over-action of the mind. Syphilis. Greed. Parents were cousins. Rumour that she murdered her husband. Seduction and disappointment."

"And you?" he asked, just as she'd hoped.

"Superstition," she said with downcast eyes.

"That certainly doesn't seem reason enough to be locked away in a madhouse. What sort are you talking of?"

"Belief in witchcraft," Sophie answered, "and its practices."

Just then, the bandleader raised his bow and called for quiet. In a booming voice, he announced, "Grab your partners, gents, 'tis the Sweetheart Waltz!"

Another gentleman who'd been eying Sophie from across the room approached. "May I have this dance?"

Blushing, Sophie looked at Andersen. "I believe it's spoken for."

Leaning his cane against the wall, Andersen placed an arm around Sophie's waist and took her hand in his. Together they swayed to the music, their eyes locked. As the last chorus swelled, the former soldier felt as if the leg he'd lost was suddenly whole and perfectly steady. Turning Sophie around with ease he exclaimed, "I do believe you've bewitched me!"

Smiling, Sophie said, "Perhaps I have."

The Dumb Supper is the most respectful way to
summon the dead. Although traditionally held on
All Hallows' Eve (the time of year when the veil is
thinnest), it can be performed at other times, in other
seasons, should the need arise. The rules of the ritual
must be strictly obeyed, lest unintended consequences
follow. Reverence and respect are required throughout.
—*From the grimoire of Eleanor St. Clair*

The Song of the Sibyl.

BEATRICE HAD NEARLY paced a hole in the teashop floor
while waiting for Eleanor to return. Everything with Mrs.
Dashley had ended well, all things considered, but the epi-
sode had left the girl terribly unsettled. Worst of all, while
Beatrice was still trying to make sense of what had happened
with the boy's ghost, Mrs. Dashley had made it clear that
she was eager to try to contact him again as soon as possible.
As she was leaving, she'd squeezed Beatrice's hand and
exclaimed, "What an angel! What a gift! You're the answer
to my prayers."

She didn't want to be the answer to Mrs. Dashley's prayers. What she wanted was for someone to answer the questions that were racing around in her brain. How had this
come to pass, and why? Was the book she'd found under the

counter what she guessed it to be? Did it have anything to do with what was happening to her? Should she pack her things and catch the next train to Stony Point? After her spill at the pier, did she even have enough money to do so?

As soon as Eleanor walked through the door, Beatrice rushed to her. "Might I have a word with you, Miss St. Clair. May we sit?" Perdu waddled behind Beatrice, feathers puffed, chest thrust out, displaying all the confidence the girl lacked.

Eleanor could see the worry in her eyes. "Did everything go all right while I was out?" Taking a seat at the table by the window she asked, "What is it? What's the matter?"

Beatrice sank into the opposite chair. "I'm not quite sure, but something strange happened while you were away."

Perdu flew to perch on the back of Beatrice's chair.

Eleanor could swear he meant to protect the girl.

With her encouragement, Beatrice described all that had gone on as best she could, from Billy's footsteps running across the shop floor, to his greasy bag of peanuts, to the marble she still clutched in her hand. Presenting it to Eleanor she said, "I need you to know this is no game. The things I've been seeing—the Gypsy woman from yesterday and Judith's son—they're real to me, in some ways more real than you or Miss Thom. Their thoughts come into my awareness unbidden, without my permission. They aren't like anything I've ever seen. As a child I used to stay awake at night, staring at images of ghosts, ghouls, devils and witches in a book of spectropia until my eyes were so tired they saw things that weren't there. I can assure you, these encounters were nothing like that. I've either gone mad or I'm seeing ghosts, or both."

"You're not mad," Eleanor said. "But I do believe that you can see spirits."

"How can you be sure?" Beatrice whispered, her hands trembling.

"About which?" Eleanor asked. "The madness or the ghosts?"

"Both."

Eleanor reached out to the girl and clasped her hand. "Do you trust me?"

Beatrice nodded. Eleanor got up and slipped behind the counter to fetch her grimoire. She carried the heavy book across the room and set it on the table in front of the girl.

"Are you a witch?" Beatrice blurted, unable to hold the question back any longer.

"Yes," Eleanor answered, placing her palms on top of the book.

Perdu hid behind Beatrice and gently tugged at her braid.

Eyes closed, Eleanor said, "I see you've opened the grimoire."

Beatrice tried to think of an acceptable excuse. Could she blame the bird? Certainly not. Why would she? It wasn't his fault. "Yes," she admitted, praying Eleanor didn't have plans to turn her into a toad or boil her in a cauldron. "But I didn't mean to."

Eleanor opened her eyes and smiled. "I'm glad you found it. It'll make things easier from here on in."

Remembering her run-in with Adelaide during breakfast Beatrice asked, "Is Miss Thom a witch too?"

"Yes," Eleanor answered, "I suppose she is." Staring into Beatrice's eyes she added, "As are you."

"Me, a witch?" Beatrice asked. "I'm afraid you're mistaken."

"No," Eleanor said. "You're just afraid."

Perdu leaned his head against Beatrice's and made a noise in her ear that sounded for all the world like a purring cat. None of this seemed real. "How can I be a witch?" Beatrice asked. "So far as I know, I haven't any in my family. I've never heard of one in Stony Point. There's one rumoured to live in Sleepy Hollow, but I've never even caught a glimpse of the woman. I crossed the covered bridge near her house once, on a dare, when I was little. I held my breath and walked backwards the whole way. Could that be what caused this?"

"No," Eleanor laughed. "I don't believe so."

Beatrice shook her head in disbelief. "Beg your pardon, but until today, for me witches were the stuff of fairy tales. How can I be one if I don't believe they're real?"

"It's complicated."

"I was afraid of that."

Perdu hopped into Beatrice's lap.

"No doubt your thoughts are jumbled," Eleanor said. "Don't bother trying to untangle them. That's not how this works. This isn't like sums or telegraphy or scientific equations. It isn't something you can easily figure out."

Picturing herself with a wart-ridden face and wearing a pointy hat, Beatrice stroked Perdu's feathers to calm herself. "Why is this happening to me?"

"I believe you opened yourself to magic when you tied your knots and made your wish."

"Does this happen to everyone who makes a witch's ladder?"

"No," Eleanor said. "The magic working within you is more powerful than most. Your desire to discover if magic truly exists in the world is what allowed it to find you."

"What if I don't want to be a witch?"

"I suppose you could reject it," Eleanor replied, "but it can't be undone without great effort, and I wouldn't want you to come to any harm."

Beatrice's mind was reeling. "How do you know all this? Have I been bewitched?—by you, or Miss Thom, or someone else?"

"I saw you in a dream before you arrived," Eleanor admitted.

"A good dream?"

"From what I can remember, yes."

"Tell it to me."

Eleanor sighed. "Most of it left me the minute I opened my eyes. All I recall is that you and the girl in my dream are one and the same."

"And she's a witch?"

"Yes."

"And that led you to believe that I'm one too?"

"The dream and many other things, including what you experienced today. But if you'd like, I can perform a test to confirm it."

Visions of dunkings and hangings and burnings at the stake filled Beatrice's mind. The passage she'd read in Eleanor's spell book suddenly seemed painfully prescient. "What kind of test?"

"We'll need to speak with my mother."

"She's also a witch?"

"Yes."

"Is it far for her to come?" Beatrice asked.

"She's never far," Eleanor answered. (At least that's what she'd promised Eleanor when she'd died.)

"How long will it take her to get here?"

Looking to the clock, Eleanor considered the hour, the moon, the day of the week, the direction of the wind, the time of year. "Until tonight," she said. "Unless she can't be disturbed." She opened the grimoire to a page near the middle and said, "Read this. We've much to do if we want to be ready by midnight."

RULES *of the* DUMB SUPPER

1. Preparations shall be carried out in an orderly fashion—ingredients for dishes gathered, linens set aside, serving utensils and dishes cleaned, candles anointed, the room blessed. Instructions shall be made clear to all participants.

2. The table shall be set backwards—forks on the right, knife and spoon on the left, and so on.

3. A place must be set and a candle lit for each spirit you wish to contact. Their chair shall be shrouded in black. Personal items or tokens may also be included so the spirit feels welcome and at home.

4. All dishes served are meant to honour the dead as well as feed the living, so choose the menu wisely with consideration for the spirit's preferences and appetites.

5. The meal itself is to be served backwards—tea and sweets first, wine (or spirits) last.

6. A scrying mirror may be set before the place of the spirit.

7. Each participant may choose to bring an offering or write a message for the deceased to bring with them to the dinner.

8. Participants shall enter the room facing backwards, eldest to youngest.

9. A bell shall be rung to begin the rite, and then again to end it.

10. Once the rite begins, the living must remain silent until the rite has ended.

11. The rite shall begin at Midnight.

The two women spent the rest of the day preparing for the ritual. For the sweets, they baked soul cakes filled with honey, spices, raisins and currants. For the tea, Eleanor sent Beatrice back and forth to the pantry to gather the ingredients for "seer's steep"—star anise, calamus root, wormwood, mugwort, rose petals, lavender, peppermint and chervil. The rest of the meal would consist of her mother's favourite autumn foods: mashed turnips, sautéed mushrooms, pickled beets, cheese curds, black grapes, stewed apples, pumpkin soup with fresh cream, and noggins of mead.

Eleanor had been pleasantly surprised at how well the girl had taken the news that they were about to call upon another spirit. She'd grown up holding yearly dumb suppers with her mother at l'Hermitage, but she'd never had to organize one herself.

After sunset, Eleanor directed Beatrice to walk down the block, past the park, to the monument where General William Jenkins Worth was buried. "Scrape off a few bits of the lichen clinging to the tomb. I need it to make the incense I'll use to bless the room. Be sure to leave an offering in exchange for what you take." Giving Beatrice a handful of pennies, she said, "This should be more than enough."

As she approached the tomb, Beatrice looked all around, hoping she wouldn't get caught. Lifting her skirts, she stepped over the decorative border and slipped behind the grave, crouching near the edge of the towering obelisk that marked the site. Decorated with symbols and inscriptions lauding the General's heroics, it wasn't nearly so large or magnificent as Cleopatra's Needle. Still, it occurred to Beatrice, as she scraped her knife along the granite, that this was the second such object she'd touched in as many days. Tucking the lichen into a small purse, she carefully placed the pennies along the top edge of the plaque that bore the General's name.

Eleanor sang a tune under her breath as she ground the lichen in her mortar, mixing the powdery orange flakes with bits of sage, yew, cedar, myrrh and a sprinkling of henbane seeds. She'd given Beatrice the task of making hag's tapers—mullein stalks dipped in melted beeswax. "The smoke from the tapers will help to guide Maman from beyond the veil," she explained.

Beatrice nodded, then asked, "What's that song you were singing?"

"'J'ai vu le loup,'" Eleanor answered. "'I Saw the Wolf.' My mother used to whistle it while clacking a pair of sheep's ribs to keep time. Before the burnings, witches sang it as they danced at their Sabbaths."

"I can see why," Beatrice said. "It's lovely."

Smiling, Eleanor thought of her mother. *We'll make a witch of her yet, Maman.*

When it came time to set the places around the table Beatrice asked, "Will Miss Thom be joining us for the supper?"

"I hope so," Eleanor replied wondering what was keeping Adelaide out so late, again. "It would be a shame for her to miss it."

"And what about the place for our ghost?"

"Our *guest*," Eleanor corrected. "Leave that to me."

Climbing the stairs, she went to her room to fetch several items from an old wooden trunk—a dagger, a chalice, a mirror, a bell and a cloak. The dagger, worn with age, had a handle made of antler. The chalice, though tarnished, was made from the finest silver. The mirror, meant for scrying, was of polished obsidian, stowed inside a leather case to protect it from damage and demons. The brass bell, no bigger than an egg, was inscribed with angelic script. Holding it upside down in her palm Eleanor silenced the clapper with a small rag, to ensure it wouldn't sound prematurely. Last but not least, she scrutinized the cloak that was waiting in the bottom of the trunk. Simple in design yet exquisitely made, the cloak, with its pointed hood and crescent-shaped clasp, was a beautiful shade of blue, akin to the wash of azure that paints the sky as twilight turns to night. Her mother had told her its origins. "The woman who was first to wear this cloak was also the one who made it. She tended the sheep to get the wool. She grew the woad to dye it. She spun the wool into yarn. She wove the yarn on her loom. She poured the silver to make the clasp. She sewed each stitch by the light of the moon. Every fibre of the garment contains her determination, her sweat, her blood."

Eleanor hugged the cloak, burying her face in its folds. It smelled of woodsmoke, sweet grass and beeswax. "I need you,

Maman," she whispered. "Please come." The key Eleanor was wearing around her neck grew hot against her skin, prompting her heart to open and her tears to fall.

The opening of the trunk brought Bright out of hiding. The minute the Dearly saw what Eleanor was up to, she knew what was in store. "Twitch," she hissed, after Eleanor had left the room. "Come here!"

"Why for?" Twitch asked, yawning and stretching his spindly arms above his head.

"We need to move a ghost."

"Again?" Twitch complained.

Tugging on Twitch's arm, Bright pulled him into the air and guided him towards Adelaide's room. She hovered over Adelaide's mother's ghost (who was curled up in a washbowl, snoring). "We need to oust her now. I don't want her to interfere with the supper."

"Where to this time?" Twitch asked.

Forcing the chimney's flue wide open, she said, "Up and out!"

The Gypsy woman snorted and turned in her porcelain bed.

"I don't have a good feeling about this."

"Don't you care about the girl?" Bright needled.

"Beatrice?" Twitch asked, eyes gleaming.

"Who else?"

Twitch couldn't deny that the beautiful young woman had stolen his heart. "Well, all right then, let's put her out. How do you want to do it?"

"By hook or by crook," Bright replied with a grin. Then she roused the dead Gypsy from her sleep so she could tell her something between the truth and a lie.

"You're sure she needs me?" the befuddled ghost asked, unsure as to why the fairy was in such a rush.

"Your daughter's not home yet. Who knows why."

"Who knows why she does anything," the Gypsy replied.

"She should be here asleep in her bed. Don't you wonder where she's got to?"

The ghost knew her daughter could take care of herself. But it'd been a long time since she'd seen the whole of the night sky, or given a fright to gaily-dressed ladies who'd had too much to drink. If the fairy was willing to let her out, then who was she to argue? "You'll let me back in?" she asked, just to be sure.

"Of course," Bright replied, nudging Twitch with her elbow.

"Of course," Twitch parroted. "Of course."

Had the Dearlies made the ghost a promise they didn't intend to keep? Not quite. Bright would gladly let the wayward spirit in, *if* she could find her way back. Flying up the chimney, the eager ghost swallowed great gulps of soot and smoke, savouring the dirty air.

Bright quickly threw a handful of graveyard dust on the fire, then watched it spark and hiss. "That should keep her from coming back any time soon."

"She's going to be angry," Twitch warned, shaking his head.

"She's always angry," Bright said. "It had to be done."

It was quarter to midnight when Adelaide finally appeared. She'd fallen asleep on the park bench with the Bird Lady at her side. When a policeman had poked her with his stick, she'd woken with a start and found the old woman was gone. She was hungry, thirsty and tired. She wanted her bed.

Finding the shop with the table set, blinds drawn, strewn with lit candles, she wondered if she might already be asleep and dreaming. "What's all this?" she asked while reaching to pinch a grape off a plate that was overflowing with fruit.

"Don't," Eleanor said, rushing to push Adelaide's hand away from the offering. "If you've ever considered yourself my friend, you'll listen carefully and do as I say."

Adelaide stopped where she stood. Not because she was offended, but because there was something in Eleanor's voice that said there was more at stake than their friendship. Taking hold of her partner's hand she said, "Tell me what to do."

Beatrice stood near as Eleanor explained the strange things that'd been happening in the shop and everything that was about to take place. She could tell from the expression on Adelaide's face that she, too, had never participated in such a rite.

"What if I forget something?" Adelaide asked.

"You won't," Eleanor said. "You're the girl who sees everything, remember? Watch, observe, listen. Use your gift. It's what you do best."

At one minute to midnight, everything was in place—food and drink on the table alongside the sacred tokens of Madame St. Clair's past. A small cauldron served as a centrepiece, sending curling billows of smoke wafting through the air. Beeswax candles anointed with oil of myrrh burned bright about the room. A single taper glowed before Madame St. Clair's chair.

Bright and Twitch sat on the stairs, waiting for the proceedings to begin.

"Join hands," Eleanor said to Adelaide and Beatrice. "It's time." Closing her eyes, she began the rite.

Earth, air, wind, fire,
In a circle we conspire,
To make ourselves dumb so we might see,
Across the veil to summon thee.
As we are, so you once were
As you are, so we shall be.
So may it be
So may it be
So may it be

The hands on the clock touched twelve, but the chimes did not strike.

Eleanor took the bell in hand and rang it three times.

One by one, each of the women moved through the room, their backs towards the table—first Eleanor, then Adelaide, then Beatrice. Once they were seated, Perdu made a graceful swoop and landed on the back of Madame St. Clair's chair.

They ate the first course in silence.

Eleanor savoured her share, allowing each bite to conjure memories of her mother.

Adelaide fought the urge to devour the sweet in one go.

Beatrice wondered if she'd be able to finish everything on her plate. Her nervousness had returned with a vengeance, and she could hardly swallow.

Thankfully, as the meal progressed, their nerves were soothed by feelings of sisterhood and friendship. When the soup was gone and the last course over, Eleanor reached for her cup of mead and held it aloft, making a voiceless toast to her mother. Adelaide followed suit, as did Beatrice (as did Bright and Twitch with thimbles full of May dew).

The flame of the candle that'd been placed at Madame St. Clair's seat began to dance and flicker. A rhythmic clacking sounded in the room, seeming to come from all directions.

Throwing his head back, Perdu imitated the sound in his throat. *Click-clack, click-clack, click-clack, click-clack.*

Beatrice stifled a laugh.

Adelaide tapped her teaspoon on the edge of her plate, keeping time with the raven.

Eleanor did nothing to stop her.

Between the clicks and clacks someone began to whistle "J'ai vu le loup."

The cloak draped on Madame St. Clair's chair began to move, undulating to the music. As the tune grew to a frenzied pitch, the wise-woman's spirit appeared, inhabiting the garment. Her skin was wrinkled, her bones gnarled, but her eyes shone bright as the full moon on a clear night. "Hush!" she said, then gave a roaring laugh.

Adelaide dropped her spoon, sending it tinkling to the floor.

Madame St. Clair turned to her. "As you are, I once was. As I am, so you shall be."

No sooner had she uttered those words than the ceiling above the table turned into a night sky dotted with stars. The walls of the shop disappeared, giving way to a dark forest. Wind rustled through trees, punctuated by the hoot of an owl and the distant howl of a wolf. The scents of moss, pine needles, leaf litter and smoke filled the air.

Eleanor kissed her finger and held it out to her mother.

Adelaide pinched the fleshy part of her forearm to make certain she was awake and not dreaming.

Beatrice bit her lip in fear, tasted blood on her tongue before it trickled down her throat.

Perdu took hold of the hood of Madame St. Clair's cloak with his beak and gave it an impatient tug.

The spirit laughed as she addressed the raven. "Old friend," she said, "you've tricked us all, haven't you? Now that I'm on the other side, I can see who you are. Do not forget the Mothers are watching you. So long as you behave yourself, your secret will be safe."

The raven cocked his head and nodded.

"Dear Eleanor," Madame St. Clair said, turning to her daughter. "You're wondering how I'm feeling, being called here this night? I will tell you I'm disturbed but not surprised. But it matters not. That is the way of all spirits. I wait for the past. I remember the future. Time means nothing." She caressed the objects before her—the dagger, the chalice, the mirror. Cradling the mirror in her hands, she gazed across its black surface searching for signs. "For you, my child," she said, "I see blessings from beyond, from all the Mothers who have ever lived and all the Mothers yet to come. You are as strong and wise as the Bright Ones who came before you, from Heidr to the Queen. Your strength comes from on high, but you needn't be a nun."

Adelaide looked at Eleanor and gave her a wink.

"And you," Madame St. Clair said, turning to Adelaide. "Why have you chosen to forget your name? The tree has not forgotten you, Moth. Do not ignore the magic it gave you." Holding her hand in front of her face, she blew on her fingertips until a perfect golden pear appeared in her palm.

"Eat of its fruit," she commanded. "It will help you remember."

Adelaide reached for the pear and took it. She sank her teeth into the fruit's ripe flesh, and felt its juice run down her chin. It was the sweetest, most delicious thing she'd ever tasted.

"Beatrice!" Madame St. Clair exclaimed, now clutching the girl's witch's ladder in her fist. "You tied these knots to make your wish and by so doing bound your fate. Do you deny it?"

Eyes wide, Beatrice shook her head. She thought she might be sick.

Wriggling in Madame St. Clair's hand, the charm slowly changed from a tangled length of string to a writhing, hissing snake. Holding fast to the serpent, Madame St. Clair opened her mouth again to speak, only this time it was unclear as to whether it was her voice or the snake's. "This realm of the living is a palace of forgetting. Birth gives us life, but leaves us blind to all other worlds. We witches, we wise-women seek to touch all that's been forgotten. Isn't that the stuff of your dreams, dear girl?

"Your wish was your choosing and now you have been chosen—to remember the worlds before the present, to see those who've passed beyond the veil, to hear the whispers of the Fay, to learn the sacred order of nature, to speak the language of dreams. The world has need of more witches. Sibyl, oracle, seer, prophetess, hag—it is their hearts that wish to beat within you, their souls you see in the face of the Moon. The Mothers are always watching. They've seen you cross paths with a sacred stone and confer with an ancient jinni. They've watched you sleep in the house of witches, and heard you speak with spirits. They are here with us now, come to bring you a message. *The first witch not born but made shall renew the work of the Mothers. She shall lead her sisters through the fire."*

Madame St. Clair slumped in her seat, her spirit fading fast.

In the forest an animal drew near, snarling and breaking branches underfoot.

Disappearing into the darkness, Madame St. Clair cried, "Le Loup!"

With that, every candle in the room went out.

Twitch bolted upright and looked at Bright, who took his hand and held it tight.

Ringing the bell three times, Eleanor whispered, "Don't be afraid."

Beatrice sighed.

Adelaide smiled.

The clock struck midnight at last.

September 25, 1880.

Waning, third quarter moon.

Neptune, Saturn and Jupiter, aligned.

CLEOPATRA'S NEEDLE STUCK

Engineering woes, lack of personnel and a spate of rainy weather have conspired to bring the Great Obelisk's journey through our fair city to a temporary halt. In the week since the ancient monument's landfall at the 96th Street Pier, its movement has stalled, largely due to what Chief Engineer Lieutenant-Commander Henry Honeychurch Gorringe calls "unforeseeable delays."

The ascent up Ninety-Sixth Street has proved more troublesome than originally anticipated, causing Gorringe and his fellow engineers to re-think their approach. The method initially devised for moving the obelisk through New York's streets lasted just long enough to get its precious cargo across the Hudson River Railroad line. Shortly thereafter, the tremendous weight of the stone caused it to fail. The former method has now been abandoned in favour of a modified "marine railroad," which should, according to Gorringe, easily accommodate the load. This revised plan will require more manpower for the duration of the obelisk's trek—to grade the ground ahead of the caravan, reposition the track beams, move timber and other materials and sink anchors to stabilize the device. Able-bodied men with experience in railroad construction are encouraged to apply for immediate employment. Work should resume as soon as there is a break in the weather.

Egyptomania Takes Hold.

The delays in the movement of the monument haven't quashed Manhattanites' excitement over the Needle. Visitors have been steadily making their way to see it, despite the stone being clad in a protective sheath of wood planking. Crafty treasure hunters have also been caught with chisels in hand, hoping to steal a bit of granite for themselves. "Who can blame them?" one bystander said. "Everyone who's seen the obelisk for themselves has walked away in a wild state of excitement. Ladies swooned, lovers made wishes, and an elderly gentleman prayed he'd be sent another wife—all in the short time I was near it."

A-B-R-A-C-A-D-A-B-R-A
A-B-R-A-C-A-D-A-B-R
A-B-R-A-C-A-D-A-B
A-B-R-A-C-A-D-A
A-B-R-A-C-A-D
A-B-R-A-C-A
A-B-R-A-C
A-B-R-A
A-B-R
A-B
A

The Witches of New York.

IT RAINED EVERY day for a week after the dumb supper, and the three witches did their fair share of thinking and worrying and scheming about the best way to proceed. When Saturday arrived with more rain rolling down the windows, Eleanor rose early from her bed, slipped on a dress and snuck downstairs before Adelaide and Beatrice were stirring.

For the past six mornings she'd performed six different spells to keep the shop protected and safe. What had happened the night of the supper had been astounding (even to her), but it had worried her as well. She could still hear her mother's panicked cry of *Le Loup!* She had no idea who or what "the wolf" might be, but she knew the sound of fear in her mother's voice. The words had clearly been meant as a warning, much like those of her family's motto, *Always needed, ever hunted*. Even if Eleanor couldn't say for certain why her mother had sounded the alarm, she figured that being more vigilant couldn't hurt. After all, she wasn't alone in this. She had Adelaide and Beatrice to consider and protect.

On Sunday she'd spread salt and tea leaves between the floorboards to keep all evil at bay. Monday she'd hung a mirror facing the shop door to reflect all negativity back to its source. Tuesday she'd placed an old shoe filled with bent nails beneath the threshold, to dispel whatever dark magic might be cast upon this place. Wednesday she'd dipped her finger in water in which a mandrake root had been bathed, and traced pentagrams on the windows, doors and mirrors to seal every portal from any dark forces that might wish to enter. Thursday she'd burned bay, juniper and sage in a large brass censer and wafted the smoke through every room, swinging the thing floor to ceiling, front to back and kitty-corner. Friday she'd swept the shop top to bottom with a crooked-handled hickory broom, collecting bits of lint and dust. Tossing the litter out the door she'd recited the following verse, *Under the watch of a waning moon, I sweep out the old to make room for the new.*

This morning she planned to pin a piece of parchment over the entryway, inscribed with an ancient charm spelled out in a magical cypher to invoke the aid of beneficent spirits against disease and misfortune. Her mother had made use of it time and again at their little cottage, swearing by its power to protect and heal. Whenever Eleanor was feverish or ill, her mother would write the charm on a scrap of paper then hang it with linen string around her neck to rid her body of all sickness and evil.

Perdu watched from his perch as Eleanor stood on a chair and fixed the charm in place with three brass tacks.

Sensing the bird's gaze, Eleanor finished her task, then set the chair aside and fetched a hunk of cheese for him.

Ruffling his feathers, the raven stretched out his neck and pinched the treat in his beak.

Eleanor couldn't stop wondering what her mother had meant when she'd told the bird, "You've tricked us all." What did her mother's ghost know about Perdu that she didn't? "Tell me who you are," she urged as she watched her pet gobble down the morsel.

The raven replied with a stubborn chortle, shaking his head. She'd asked him the same question every day since the dumb supper, and each time he'd refused to answer. She'd try again tomorrow.

It bothered Eleanor to think Perdu might be keeping something from her. The raven had been a constant companion, following her through meadow and forest, sleeping by her bedside every night of her life. Together they'd heard knockings, rattlings and voices from the ether; seen feathers, goblets and flaming cauldrons float and dance above the kitchen table.

On one occasion Perdu had had the misfortune of being (briefly) possessed, his feathered body inhabited by a strange spirit who spoke in a bullying, unearthly voice. "Skip through the graveyard! Ring the coffin bell! Dance beneath the full moon, then follow me to Hell!" Madame St. Clair had chased the entity out of Perdu by spitting in the bird's face and reciting a series of banishing spells from the *Petit Albert*. Later she'd explained the incident away, saying, "There's nothing to worry about, my dear. Perdu's the same sweet bird as always. One of Old Scratch's minions just thought he could steal his feathered cloak and not get caught. The pesky imp should've known better. When it comes to demons, witches always have the last laugh!" Contrary to her reassuring talk, Madame St. Clair had insisted the bird drink nothing but holy water for nine days straight. Perdu had then proceeded to hack up nine balls of lead shot, one for each day.

By and large, the other ghostly beings who'd visited their home had come in the form of harmless apparitions—gauzy and transparent, prone to take their leave shortly after they'd appeared. Seeing her mother's spirit take on such a magnificent form had caused Eleanor to wonder if what she'd witnessed was real. When the dumb supper was over and the gaslights lit, she'd turned to Adelaide and Beatrice and said, "Tell me everything you saw." In short order the three witches realized that they'd seen and heard much the same things, and pledged not to speak of what'd taken place to anyone outside themselves. Pricking their thumbs with the tip of Madame St. Clair's dagger, they'd sealed the promise in blood.

To Eleanor it'd been abundantly clear what should happen next. She and Adelaide were to assist Beatrice in gaining her full powers as a witch. Surprisingly, Adelaide had agreed. "How do we begin?" she'd asked, her eagerness causing Eleanor to wonder exactly which spell had been cast upon the magical pear she'd consumed (and how she might go about learning it). Beatrice, still reeling, was understandably reticent. "I'd like some time to think on it, if it's all the same to you."

"Right," Adelaide had replied.

"That's very wise," Eleanor had said. "Take as long as you need." The last thing she wanted was for the girl to feel pressured in any way. If everything her mother had said was true, then she wasn't about to do anything that might keep

Beatrice from fulfilling her promise. In the meantime, she'd set Adelaide the task of holding Judith Dashley off until things had settled.

After a quick visit to the Fifth Avenue Hotel, Adelaide had returned to the shop to report, "I've got good news and bad news."

"Out with it," Eleanor said.

"The good news is that Judith has promised she'll not breathe a word about Beatrice's gift to anyone without our permission."

"And the bad?"

"The cat's already out of the bag."

"Who did she tell?"

"Mr. Dashley."

"That's to be expected," Eleanor said. "Anyone else?"

"Quinn Brody."

"Who?" Eleanor asked, unable to place the name.

"He's a mind doctor, an alienist who also dabbles in chasing ghosts."

That last remark gave Eleanor pause. "You know him?"

Cheeks turning pink, Adelaide replied, "We've met."

"And?"

"Leave him to me."

Eleanor tried to keep her mind on daily business at the shop. Her regular customers came and went, buying tea and sweets and making their usual special requests. Beatrice donned her apron and moved about the store, happy to pretend she hadn't a care in the world. For the first few nights after the dumb supper, she'd stayed up late re-reading *Strange Tales of Gotham* and writing letters to Lydia, most of which she didn't intend to send. On Wednesday, at quarter to midnight, she'd finally gone to Eleanor and said, "I'm ready to learn. I'd like you to teach me all you know."

Since then, Beatrice had spent her evenings studying Eleanor's grimoire while absent-mindedly feeding Perdu hunks of bread. Eleanor had made herself available for any questions the young novice might have, watching with a fair bit of pride as Beatrice wrote page upon page of notes in a small notebook of her own. She'd never thought she'd have someone to teach her craft to, and she only hoped that she'd be able to do everything right. Her mother had been extremely patient and thorough in her teaching, never scolding her for being distracted, or for wandering off to paddle along the river with Perdu, or for sitting for hours in the crook of a weeping willow tree, daydreaming. If she hadn't learned all she needed to know in order to be a good tutor, she had no one to blame but herself.

For Beatrice's first lesson, Eleanor had given the girl a small gift, a witch's purse to carry in her pocket or to wear around her neck. She told her, "It's a place to store sacred herbs, stones and amulets to assist you in your work." Guiding the girl through choosing the proper herbs to place inside it, she'd explained how different roots, leaves and flowers have the power to enhance certain spells. "There are herbs for luck, herbs for love, herbs for divination, and so on."

"Which herbs do you think I should start with?" Beatrice had asked, giving the purse's strings a nervous tug.

"Those for protection," Eleanor had answered straight away. "Horehound, to guard against demons, sorcery and fascination. Caraway for protection against malevolent entities. Toadflax to keep the evil eye at bay. Thistle for strength, and to confuse your enemies."

Following Eleanor's instructions, Beatrice had placed each of the herbs inside the bag, then tucked the purse inside her pocket. She was glad for any help she could get.

In her effort to discern what, if anything, Dr. Brody had made of Judith's talk of her encounter with Beatrice, Adelaide had boldly tracked him to where he lived so she might address the subject head on. After an evening's worth of conversation with the doctor (which she'd quite enjoyed), she'd come to Eleanor with a surprising plan. "I propose Beatrice meet with Dr. Brody."

Eleanor asked, "Why on earth would she do that?"

"He's already aware of her talent for speaking with ghosts. What harm could it do?"

"I thought you said you'd take care of things with him."

"I have, I swear it. This will only lead to good things, I can feel it. Don't you trust my good sense?"

"I do," Eleanor replied, "but that doesn't mean you're not up to something."

Adelaide folded her arms. "I say we let Beatrice decide for herself."

Eleanor sighed. "I hope for her sake you know what you're doing."

Beatrice had decided to say yes to Adelaide's plan. Although the dumb supper had led her to be more inclined to believe in magic and less inclined to feel she was out of her mind, she was still left wondering how everything that'd happened to her had transpired. If a man of science wished to try and shed some light on her situation, then she was willing to give him a few hours of her time. Adelaide had spoken well of Dr. Brody, so she had high hopes for her visit with him. In short order a date and time was set— Saturday, September 25 at ten a.m.

When the day of her appointment arrived, Beatrice began the morning trying to decide which dress to wear.

"The red calico," Adelaide urged.

"Whichever you like," Eleanor said with a shrug. "It should be your choice."

Reaching for the dress she'd worn her first day in the city, Beatrice inspected the place where the skirt had ripped when she'd fallen near the obelisk. To her surprise, the tear was no longer noticeable. She'd never made such fine, even stitches in her life! It was as if nothing had happened. Had Eleanor repaired it? Pleased, she pulled the dress over her head and buttoned it up the front. She hoped that when the day was done she'd feel just as satisfied about her decision to meet Dr. Brody.

The previous morning a steamer trunk had arrived with the rest of the things she'd requested from her aunt. Upon receiving it, Beatrice had penned Lydia a note of thanks, making sure to include all the news she thought she'd be expecting—a description of the teashop ("quaint, cheerful, bustling"), a glowing review of her employers ("wise, amiable, independent") and a light-hearted complaint about the relentless rain ("if it goes on much longer, some enterprising gentleman will have to erect an ark in Central Park"). As she'd done with her previous missive, she'd omitted any and all details of the magic that'd befallen her. Sealing the envelope, Beatrice glued a three-cent stamp to the upper right-hand corner, one that bore the image of George Washington in stately profile.

Gazing at the envelope, she could swear that General Washington had turned his head ever so slightly to give her a disapproving scowl. ("Why haven't you told your aunt the truth?") He was right to question her, of course, but where would he have her begin?

Whenever something odd had happened in Stony Point (a rare thing indeed), the townsfolk were quick to try to put things into a shape they could understand. One spring, after one of Mr. Wheeler's nanny goats gave birth to a two-headed kid, the town square soon filled with people exclaiming, "My heavens!" "What a sight!" "Have you seen it?" "What could be the cause?" "Have you ever heard of such a thing in all your life?" By the end of the day, a half-deaf grandmother, a travelling salesman and Mr. Walter Rose, the town apothecary, had come forward with stories that made Mr. Wheeler's goat seem not so special after all (of a two-headed calf, a six-legged sow, and a dog that could whistle "Dixie" through its teeth). The poor kid died early Easter morning, and the talk between the pews at the First United Presbyterian Church turned more towards sympathy than sensation. "I guess it wasn't meant to live." "I suppose it's just as well."

What on earth would the people of Stony Point make of Beatrice now? The closest thing she could think of to match her own odd experiences were the occurrences she'd read about in Lydia's copy of *A Compendium of Miracles*. She'd especially enjoyed the accounts of young girls who'd had miraculous visions, and had often imagined herself in their place—something akin to being a mouse caught in a lion's maw and living to tell the tale. How sad she'd been to discover that more often than not, the girls hadn't found a happy ending. It's a risky thing for a girl to admit she's witnessed a miracle.

Joan of Arc, witch. Also known as the Maid of Orleans. Burnt at the stake for heresy and witchcraft, at Rouen, in 1431. Joan had her first vision at the age of thirteen while sitting in her father's garden. The message brought to her by Saint Catherine, Saint Margaret and the Archangel Michael was so beautiful that she cried when it came to an end. By nineteen she was dead.

Bernadette of Lourdes had fared a bit better. *On February 11, 1858, Bernadette Soubirous (fourteen years of age) had a vision while gathering sticks along the banks of a river. It was there, in a small grotto near the water's edge, that she first saw a lady dressed in white with a long veil covering her head and a perfect rose on each foot. This began a fortnight of visitations by a being who would later identify herself as the Immaculate Conception.* At first, Bernadette's mother thought it was a trick of the Devil. Many people in the girl's village demanded she be put away in an asylum. In the end, the Lady promised Bernadette she'd make her happy "not in this life, but the next." Bernadette was sent to a convent where she spent the rest of her days embroidering altar cloths and vestments. "The Virgin used me as a broom to remove the dust. When the work is done, the broom is put behind the door again," she was supposed to have said. She died at thirty-five.

Even Brooklyn could boast its own "enigma," a young woman who never left her room and lived mostly on air. *Mollie Fancher, "the Fasting Girl," fell victim to a terrible accident in 1865 when she was seventeen years of age. After being dragged behind a streetcar, she lost the ability to see, touch, taste and smell, but thereafter was able to go for long periods of time without food or drink.* According to several reports, Mollie had also gained the power to read without seeing and to predict future events. Was she still lying in her bed after all these years? Did anyone bother to visit her anymore?

The spirits Beatrice had seen hadn't been angels, and she had no idea as to whether or not her "gift" had come from God. Was it temporary or long-lasting? Was she right to pursue it or should she let it go? She supposed there were many instances where people chose to ignore the frightening, curious or miraculous events that'd occurred in their lives, thinking, *Who would believe me if I told them?* Beatrice wondered what her aunt might advise if she confessed her experiences. She guessed Lydia would say just what she'd always said whenever she'd gone to her with something perplexing. "Let's be practical about this, Beatrice. Do you know all there is to know about the matter? If not, then perhaps you should take the time to find out."

That's just what Beatrice intended to do. Tying a ribbon around the end of her braid she made a wish: *May this day hold more answers than questions.*

Adelaide pinned a spray of pheasant feathers to the hat she planned to wear to accompany Beatrice to Dr. Brody's house. Setting the velvet bonnet high atop her curls, she turned her head to appraise her work. Not too bold. Not too sweet. Just right. She was anxious to see how Beatrice would perform, pleased to be spending time with Quinn, again. When she'd gone to his house, he'd invited her to call him by his first name. Was that how she should address him today? With Beatrice along she figured she'd better stick with "Dr. Brody." Inspecting her face in the mirror, she patted the slightest bit of rouge onto her lips. Then she mouthed the words, "You're looking well today, Dr. Brody."

What a brilliant creature he was! With such lovely eyes! Just thinking of him made Adelaide cross her ankles and tighten her thighs. He was endearingly shy, yet she knew he was hungry for her: he had a habit of biting his lip whenever his eyes dropped to her mouth. (Perhaps a little more rouge was in order?) No, today was to be about Beatrice.

She couldn't help but think that the something she'd been feeling was about to happen had already begun and it had everything to do with the girl. When the dumb supper was over and their blood oath made, she'd snuck up to her room with what remained of the pear, and carefully plucked the seeds from its core. Then she'd placed the seeds one by one inside a small, slender phial and hung it by a chain around her neck. She'd worn the thing every day since, keeping the seeds close to her heart as if they were a religious relic. From time to time she'd shake the phial so she could hear the seeds rattle. To her, their tiny sounds were like the rumble of thunder, testifying that everything she'd seen, heard, smelled, touched and tasted that night was real. Was this what it was like to be spiritually transformed? If so, then she'd become a True Believer.

Although she didn't profess to understand every device Quinn had shown her in his study, she'd learned quite a lot about the nature of his research, including his hopes of finding a medium who could get his father's spiritoscope to work. In light of all she'd experienced during the dumb supper, it'd all seemed tremendously compelling and meant to be.

Too bad Eleanor wasn't going to come with them for today's visit, but she'd said an outright no. "You go. I'll stay. Beatrice doesn't need an audience watching her every move." Adelaide had felt the sting of Eleanor's disapproval, but she was convinced she was in the right. She'd been careful not to push or cajole Beatrice in any way. She was simply opening doors and allowing magic to blossom in an effort to help the girl discover her own path. Although her methods might not be ones that Eleanor preferred, Adelaide had to be true to herself, didn't she? She had to use her own gifts in her own way, get back to her old self, as it were. Wasn't that what Madame St. Clair had compelled her to do? Whenever she stopped to consider Beatrice, everything came clear. She could see what the girl needed, sense where she was headed.

Today could prove to be the way forward, for everyone. Great things were on the horizon!

Beatrice came downstairs with Adelaide trailing close behind.

"Your hat's a little crooked," Adelaide said when they reached the bottom. "Shall I make it right?"

"Yes, please," Beatrice replied, holding still while Adelaide deftly straightened it.

"There," Adelaide said, adjusting a hatpin to keep the bonnet in its proper place. Lightly tugging Beatrice's braid, she coaxed it into lying flat and inspected the ribbon that was tied to its end. "I've a wider ribbon in grosgrain that would look quite lovely with your dress. I'm happy to fetch it if you like."

"I'm happy enough with this one. I wouldn't want to make us late."

"Nonsense," Adelaide said. "Dr. Brody is sending a carriage for us, and the driver will wait. I know just where the ribbon is. I'll be back in two shakes."

Eleanor watched the pair with amazement. If someone had told her the week before that Adelaide would be so accommodating towards a shop girl (or to anyone for that matter), she wouldn't have believed them. *Miracles never cease.* Leaning towards Beatrice she lowered her voice and said, "If you're doing this just to impress her, please know you don't have to."

"No, I want to," Beatrice insisted. "I'd like to hear what Dr. Brody has to say."

"All right then," Eleanor replied, "but don't let her bully you into anything."

Taking her witch's pouch from her pocket, Beatrice dangled it in the air. "No worries," she said. "I'm prepared."

Perdu squawked from his perch near the window. A carriage had stopped in front of the door. Its driver sat hunched, hat tipped, collar turned against the rain.

"I believe that's us," Adelaide said, as she came back down the stairs brandishing the ribbon. Taking Beatrice's arm, she said, "We'll change it on the way."

"Take care," Eleanor said, giving Beatrice a little wave. Staring at Adelaide she added, "Be good."

"Be good," said Perdu, his eye on something no one else could see.

The aura of a medium which thus enables an immortal spirit to do within its scope things which it cannot do otherwise, appears to vary with the human being resorted to; so that only a few are so endowed with this aura as to be competent as media. Moreover, in those who are so constituted as to be competent instruments of spiritual actuation, this competency is various. There is a gradation of competency, by which the nature of the instrumentality varies from that which empowers violent loud knocking and the moving of ponderable bodies without actual contact, to the grade which confers power to make intellectual communication of the higher order without that of audible knocking. Further, the power to employ these grades of mediumship varies as the sphere of the spirit varies.

—Professor Robert Hare, *Experimental Investigation of the Spirit Manifestations*

Study.

DR. BRODY WATCHED the skies as he waited for Adelaide and Beatrice to arrive. He'd thought he might escort the women on a walk if the weather had been agreeable, but he was glad he'd chosen to send a carriage instead, since it seemed yet another deluge was threatening to pour forth from the slate-coloured sky.

On this particularly dreary Saturday, the sidewalk in front of Dr. Brody's house was mostly bare, the traffic on the street slow. Even the smoke coming from the chimney pots along the rooftops seemed to be dragging its heels, eking its way into the sky in stubborn, reluctant puffs. A few sleepy-faced gentlemen strolled past, clearly on their way home after spending the night down on Sisters' Row. The exclusive bordellos were situated on the other side of the street in seven adjacent townhouses, each one managed by a different sister from the same family. Descended from prominent New England stock, they required all of their gentlemen callers to wear formal evening attire and come bearing chocolates and flowers. The eldest sister, Miss Julia Hapgood, had knocked on Quinn's door from time to time to deliver engraved invitations for their private parties. EVENING DRESS. INVITATION ONLY. ALL PROCEEDS GOING TO THE ORPHANED CHILDREN'S FUND. Although he'd never set foot in any of their houses, he respected the sisters' attention to detail and discipline. Theirs were the loveliest-looking houses on the street by far.

In an effort to put his own house in order, Dr. Brody had asked Mrs. Stutt to sort out the rooms he thought the ladies might see during their visit (the front foyer, the study, the downstairs water closet). For his part, he'd gone to the florist in search of something to brighten the house and walked away with a gaudy bouquet of chrysanthemums, marigolds and carnations in shades of yellow, orange and pink. On his way home he'd crossed paths with a desperate-looking flower girl at the corner of Fifth Avenue and Broadway, and had purchased the last blossoms from her basket—six wilted roses in a striking scarlet—in hopes that the poor child could get off the streets for the day. Once home, he'd inserted the roses one by one into the florist's arrangement, battling their urge to droop by propping their heads on the sturdier stems. The scarlet of the blooms reminded him of the suit Miss Thom had worn when they'd first met. She, like the colour of the roses, was not for the faint of heart. Although they'd only crossed paths twice, she had already proved herself to be a woman of rare intelligence and wit. And, he had to admit, incredibly alluring—from her delicate hands to her soulful gaze, from her pouty lips to the unabashed way she spoke her mind.

"Dr. Brody," Mrs. Stutt said, entering the study. "Would you like me to prepare tea now, or wait until your guests arrive?"

"Let's wait," the doctor answered, half lost in his thoughts.

"And will you be wanting luncheon as well?"

He pondered the housekeeper's question, wishing he'd thought of it himself. If the meeting went as he hoped, then his guests might well be in need of refreshment. "Perhaps," he said.

"Where will it be served?" Against her wishes, he'd asked her to leave the dining room in its perpetual state of messiness. He hadn't the heart to remove his father's experiments from the table just yet.

"If it comes to that, we'll take lunch in the study," Dr. Brody replied.

"And will it?" Mrs. Stutt pressed.

"I suppose it might."

"I'll assume it will."

"Very well then," Dr. Brody said, checking his watch for the time.

Mrs. Stutt cocked her head in thought. "It's two for tea?" she asked, as if she'd forgotten.

"Two," Dr. Brody answered with a nod.

"Two, besides you, correct?"

"Yes. Three altogether."

"Two gents, two ladies, or one of each?" Mrs. Stutt fished.

"Two ladies," Dr. Brody answered, wondering what the word for "subtle" was in the German language. His housekeeper wasn't. "Miss Thom, who you've already met, and her companion, Miss Dunn."

Plucking a bruised petal off one of the roses before it could fall, Mrs. Stutt grumbled, "Miss Thom."

"Is there anything else?" Dr. Brody asked, feeling as if he'd already provided her with more than enough information.

"*Nein*," Mrs. Stutt said, stuffing the rose petal into her pocket. "Just ring when you'd like your tea."

When the carriage arrived, Dr. Brody went out to meet his guests at the curb. Umbrella in hand, he greeted them both then ushered Adelaide and Beatrice up the steps and into the house.

Once they were in the study, Beatrice found it difficult to know where to look first. Every book and object that lined the shelves was of immense interest. It was all she could do not to pick each one up for closer inspection. When she came across an old bottle with a scroll of paper inside, she paused to peer at it. Covered in dust and sealed with wax, the bottle looked as though it might've been used to conceal a pirate's treasure map. As she reached to touch it, the scroll began to spin. When she withdrew her hand, the scroll went still.

Glancing over her shoulder to make sure neither Adelaide nor the doctor had noticed, she decided she'd better leave well enough alone for now.

Dr. Brody was seated at his desk on the other side of the room, arranging pen and paper. Meeting Beatrice's eyes, he tried a little small talk. "Miss Thom says you're new to the city?"

Adelaide, who was gracefully reclining on a nearby couch, gave Beatrice a supportive smile.

"Yes and no," Beatrice answered. "I spent much of my youth in Stony Point, but made occasional trips to Manhattan with my aunt. This is the first time that I've chosen to stay."

"I thought we might begin with a few questions," Dr. Brody said, picking up his pen.

"Should I sit or stand?" Beatrice asked, her mouth suddenly dry.

"Whichever you find most comfortable," Adelaide offered.

"Yes, of course," Dr. Brody agreed. "Do as you please."

"Then I'd just as soon stand. If you don't mind." She preferred to stay where she was, near the bookshelves, comforted by the musty scent of old books and leather bindings.

"Why don't we start with something simple," Dr. Brody suggested. "If you wouldn't mind, please state your age."

"Seventeen," Beatrice replied, gazing at the gilding that graced the books' spines.

"Place of birth?"

"Albany, New York."

"Have you suffered any grave illnesses in your lifetime?"

"No."

"Any mental deficiencies diagnosed in yourself or your family?"

"No, and not that I know of."

"Any tragedies or traumas to yourself or those close to you? Accidents? Fire? Thievery? Near drownings or the like?"

Beatrice thought of her mother and father, pale and sickly, lying in their beds as she stood in the doorway with tears streaming down her face. Where had her parents' spirits gone after they'd passed? Why hadn't they appeared to her yet? Was there any chance she'd see them again? "My parents died when I was ten."

"What caused their passing?"

"Smallpox."

"Is that when you started encountering spirits?"

"No, not then."

"You had no visions of your parents, heard no voices after their deaths?"

Beatrice shook her head.

"When did you have your first experience with the spirit world?"

"A little over a week ago—the day I arrived in New York."

"The day you communicated with Mrs. Dashley's deceased son?"

"No, I saw a different ghost the day before Billy appeared, a woman dressed in Gypsy garb. She was sitting at a table in the back of the teashop."

A chill went up Adelaide's spine.

"She seemed quite real to me at first, but then I saw she wasn't made of flesh. She turned into a ghoulish spectre right before my eyes. I thought she meant to kill me."

Head down, Dr. Brody penned line after line. "Did you believe in ghosts before that day?"

"I suppose I did," Beatrice said, pulling a book from the shelf. *Experimental Investigation of the Spirit Manifestations.* "At least I hoped they were real."

"Had you ever tried to communicate with spirits, say, through pendulum or planchette?"

"No, I've never done anything like that."

"Ever attend a table-tipping or séance?"

"No."

"Ever heard knockings or rappings that might be construed as ghostly transmissions?"

"No," Beatrice said, "but I know Mr. Morse's code for communicating by telegraph."

"How resourceful!" Dr. Brody said with a chuckle. "May I ask how you came to learn it?"

Thumbing through the book's pages Beatrice replied, "I'm self-taught. I thought I might find employment as a telegrapher, but Miss St. Clair and Miss Thom took me on, so I didn't pursue it."

Adelaide gave the girl an encouraging nod.

"How many times have you made contact with a spirit?"

"Just twice," Beatrice answered, careful not to mention the dumb supper. Closing her eyes, she hoped he wouldn't press further. She'd never been good at lying.

"And how did the spirits make contact with you?"

"Mostly through my mind."

"In a familiar language, I take it?"

"Yes, although it was more thought than conversation. As if a sense of knowing suddenly sprang up between me and them."

After a few minutes of hasty scribbling, Dr. Brody laid down his pen. "Thank you, Miss Dunn, this has been most enlightening."

"Are we finished?" she asked, still clutching the book.

"Not quite," he answered. "I was hoping you might be willing to submit to a test using the spiritoscope?"

Beatrice looked at Adelaide.

"It's the device I mentioned to you," Adelaide said. "It translates messages as they pass from a spirit through your hands. You'll be acting much like a telegraph operator does when she sends messages over the wires."

Reassured, Beatrice turned to Dr. Brody. "Do you have a particular ghost you wish to contact?"

Thinking of his father, the doctor glanced towards the bottle on the shelf. He'd fetched it from the attic earlier that morning. He'd purposely not mentioned it to Adelaide so there'd be no chance she could tell Beatrice what it was (either on purpose or by mistake). "I'd rather not say," Dr. Brody replied. "I wouldn't want to taint the experiment with my expectations."

Adelaide went to the spiritoscope, pulled out the chair behind it and gently urged Beatrice to sit. "I imagine you'll find it a more reliable and pleasant form of communication with the spirit world than you've experienced thus far. If it doesn't feel right, then just say the word. Nothing ventured, nothing gained."

"All right," Beatrice said. "I'll try."

Once she was comfortably seated, Dr. Brody explained the procedure she was to follow while using the machine. "Place your fingertips ever so lightly on the transmitter board and wait for a spirit to guide your hands. You'll be blindfolded for the duration of the test so as to lessen any chance of distraction. I ask that you not speak while the test is in progress, unless you feel it's absolutely necessary. Miss Thom and I will be nearby, recording any activity on the dial, and observing your progress."

Adelaide placed a reassuring hand on Beatrice's shoulder.

"Thank you," Beatrice said with a smile.

"Are you ready, then?" Dr. Brody asked, holding a silk scarf in his hands.

Beatrice nodded.

After securing the scarf over Beatrice's eyes, Dr. Brody motioned for Adelaide to sit at his desk. "If you'd be so kind, I'd like you to record whatever the needle dictates so I can be free to observe both the machine and Miss Dunn."

"I'd be happy to," Adelaide said, settling behind the desk.

"Miss Dunn," Dr. Brody said, "please place your hands on the board."

Beatrice nodded. No sooner had her fingertips touched the wood than she felt a ghostly pair of hands gently come to rest on hers. Although she was blindfolded, she could see the hands in her mind's eye—spotted, wrinkled, twisted by time, unmistakably masculine. Any fear she had was soon replaced by an overwhelming sense of wonder. With a gentle push, the board began to glide and move across the table.

I A-M T-O-B-I-A-S B-R-O-D-Y.

I T-E-L-L N-O L-I-E-S.

I B-R-I-N-G Y-O-U A M-E-S-S-A-G-E F-R-O-M T-H-E O-T-H-E-R S-I-D-E.

As the needle nervously edged around the dial, it paused and hovered over each letter Mr. Brody's spirit wished to indicate.

Dr. Brody shook his head in disbelief.

Adelaide did her best to keep her amazement in check as she faithfully transcribed each letter of the message.

Beatrice swayed forward and back with the board's movement, as if she were a child on a swing, being pushed ever higher into the air.

W-H-A-T Y-O-U S-E-E-K

Y-O-U S-H-A-L-L F-I-N-D

I-F Y-O-U U-S-E Y-O-U-R W-I-T.

E-V-E-R-Y P-R-O-B-L-E-M

C-A-N B-E S-O-L-V-E-D

I-F Y-O-U D-W-E-L-L W-I-T-H-I-N I-T.

After several minutes of this ethereal push and pull, Beatrice felt the spirit's hands come to a stop. "Is that all you wish to say?" she whispered under her breath, waiting for the ghost to respond.

Y-E-S, the spirit replied before leaving the needle to rest on the phrase "MUST GO."

With that, Mr. Brody's bottle tumbled from the shelf and shattered on the floor.

Plucking the scroll from the broken glass, Dr. Brody pulled loose the ribbon with his teeth and broke the wax seal. "The messages are the same," he said, clutching the paper like a prize. "Word for word."

Adelaide rushed to his side to see for herself.

Beatrice was still seated at the spiritoscope. As she listened to their exclamations of wonder, she felt another presence draw near. A second pair of hands placed themselves on hers—feminine and familiar, thumbnails marked by little moons, a wedding band shining on a ring finger. The board tentatively danced and floated beneath their touch, a mother guiding her daughter in a message that was long overdue.

Sadly, no one saw it.

HOW a WITCH SAVED our DREAMS

Long ago, the First Witch came face to face with a Demon who meant to do the World great harm. This Demon, whose name we shall not mention (because to do so would cause him to feel flattered and smug), wished to rid the World of all dreams, good and bad. He knew, as all witches know, that dreams are the surest way for beings of flesh and blood to discover the Mysteries of Life. This knowledge made him terribly jealous, because Demons cannot dream.

The Demon was further upset, in his boorish way, over the way dreams provide hope to people in troubled times. (Something else that Demons cannot abide.)

To destroy this precious boon of mankind, the Demon knew he would need to rid the World of the source of all dreams—a race of otherworldly beings whose sole responsibility is to make and deliver dreams to humans as they sleep. Throughout the ages they have been called by various names—angels, memunim, oneiroi, sandmen, Dearlies—but their true name is known only to themselves, a precious secret keenly guarded and strictly kept, for if a human were to utter it, they would never be allowed to dream again. (Perhaps you might be tempted to cry, "How sad, how unjust, how unfair!" but I beg you to hold your tongue. It is the prerogative of the Fay to do as they see fit. If there were no consequences for mis-behaviour in our dealings with them, there could be no magic between us. We witches do not question their punishments, so long as they do not question our curses.)

The Demon, wishing to discover the Dearlies' secret name, hid in the branches of a Hemlock tree on the edge of their sacred grove at Twilight on the night of their Great Gathering. What he didn't know was that the First Witch had also come to the outskirts of the grove, her ears plugged with cotton flowers and dandelion fluff. She'd come there to leave an offering of thanks for the Dearlies, a few trinkets she'd gathered together in hopes of adding to their delight—a thimble filled with salt, nine buttons made from brass, a spool of silver thread, and a needle dipped in gold.

In years past, the Witch had never dared stay to watch the Dearlies frolic for she'd feared their merriment might prove too riotous for her senses, leaving her deaf, dumb and blind. This year, as the sun fell below the horizon, she drank a potion made of toadstools and harebells so she might disguise herself as a rabbit in the tall grass near their fairy ring.

The rite was lit by foxfire and lightning bugs, their dances accompanied by beautiful odes depicting their illustrious past. Once the Demon heard what he was after, he snuck into the shadows. As he went, he heard the chance snap of a twig, alerting him to the Witch's presence.

Overpowered by hunger (as such monsters often are), the Demon seized the rabbit by her legs and held her in the air, ready to devour her whole. Struggling to break free, the Witch cried out in fear, her spell broken by her distress. The fairies, alerted to the intruders, threw a net of spider's silk over the pair and dragged them through the glen. Discovering the offerings the Witch had left for them, they blew salt in the Demon's eyes and set the Witch free. Taking the Witch's thread in hand, they guided it through the needle, then pierced the skin of the Demon's lips to sew his mouth shut. As they worked, they tied each of the buttons to the thread to secure their knots. No sooner had they finished than the thread turned to molten lead, searing the Demon's flesh and removing their true name from his tongue. Rather than doing away with the beast, they sentenced him to live, mute and anguished, with only brimstone smoke and the scent of rotting flesh to nourish him.

To thank the Witch for her kind deed, the Dearlies invited her into their circle to share an elixir made of Bog Myrtle and Mugwort, and to teach her the Language of Dreams. In three years' time (which seemed like three minutes to her), she returned to her village to live out her days as an interpreter of Dreams.

In these times, because so many have forgotten the Dearlies and their gifts (men are far more inclined to attribute their dreams to indigestion than magic), these marvellous creatures cling less frequently to our bedposts, and are more likely to be found in places they inhabited in the distant past. (If you've ever wondered why some locations—sunny meadows, mossy grottos, lonely castle towers—generate the most spectacular visions, you now know the reason.) But be not dismayed, the Dearlies will come whenever and wherever they're needed, so long as they are kindly coaxed and treated with respect. Demons of all stripes may try to thwart them, but the Dearlies stand invincible because of the kindness of the First Witch.

And that, my darling girl, is why witches' dreams are the best of all, and should never be dismissed.

Close your eyes and get some rest. We gain new worlds when we sleep.

—*From the grimoire of Eleanor St. Clair*
(as told to her by her mother).

Divinations and Dreams.

BEATRICE DID NOT mention her mother's visitation. The spirit's presence had been brief—there for but a moment, then gone. What could be done about it now? Nothing. Thus far, her encounters with spirits had been varied and strange, and she wasn't sure whether that was due to the nature of ghosts or the newness of her gift.

But during the carriage ride back to the teashop, Adelaide sensed something was amiss. "You're keeping something to yourself," she said. "And you might as well tell me because I'll keep my eye on you until I discover it myself."

Beatrice stared at a cascade of raindrops flowing down the edge of the carriage window. "I'm not sure I should," she said. "It won't do anyone any good."

Adelaide watched as the girl nervously tugged at one of the buttons on her glove. It was a sure sign something was troubling her from the past. If she was haunted in her mind and heart, it followed that she might also be haunted in the truest sense. "Did another ghost visit you while we were at Dr. Brody's?" she asked, wondering if her mother's spirit had attempted to make more dark mischief.

Eyes wet, Beatrice nodded, clutching at the folds of her dress as a child holds fast to her mother's skirts.

"It was someone you knew? Someone you loved?"

Caught in Adelaide's gaze, Beatrice surrendered. No matter what she chose to say she'd already been found out. Eleanor had mentioned that Adelaide's ability to peer into others' souls was beyond compare, but Beatrice hadn't felt the total weight of it until now. "It was my mother," she confessed.

"You're sure?" Adelaide asked. "It couldn't have been anyone else?"

"Quite sure," Beatrice replied. "I didn't see the whole of her, but I saw and felt her hands on mine, much the same as I did with Dr. Brody's father. She guided my hands to move the board but I'm afraid I don't know what she meant to say."

Adelaide bit her lip. The fault lay with her. "I didn't see the needle move around the dial."

"You were caught up with Dr. Brody's excitement over his father's message. I completely understand."

Adelaide shook her head. "I should have stayed where I was while you were at the board and kept my eye on the needle."

"You couldn't have known," Beatrice said.

Adelaide stared out the carriage window. *I would've if I'd been paying attention*, she thought. The situation with Beatrice was too important to be so inattentive. She'd already started to think about what should come next—a meeting with Judith and Marietta, a note to Quinn to arrange another round of experiments, a talk with Eleanor to convince her all was well. How could she have been so careless with the girl?

"It's all right," Beatrice said, "truly it is."

"No, it's not." Adelaide was touched that Beatrice would try to give her comfort when it should've been the other way around. Taking the girl's hand, she added, "Unless of course, you didn't wish to hear from her in the first place?" There was always a chance Beatrice's feelings might be akin to her own when it came to mothers.

"Why wouldn't I?" Beatrice asked, perplexed. "Wouldn't you, if you were in my shoes?"

"Have you forgotten that you've met my mother? In my case, I'd have to say no."

"I hadn't considered that." The girl looked even more distressed.

Adelaide gave Beatrice's hand a squeeze. "Count yourself lucky that you had the kind of mother who didn't require doubt, and that you've lived a life where embracing joy wasn't a dangerous endeavour. Missed messages aside, what did you think of the experience overall?"

"It was all very interesting," Beatrice replied, "the books and the scientific instruments were fascinating, and I liked Dr. Brody too. He's gentlemanly and so smart."

"I agree," Adelaide said, her cheeks turning warm.

Beatrice gave Adelaide a slight nudge with her elbow. "I believe Dr. Brody thinks quite highly of you too."

Nudging back, Adelaide said, "So you've taken up reading minds, have you?"

Beatrice laughed. "I suppose I should add that I quite enjoyed using the spiritoscope. The mechanics of it caused me to feel as though I was leaving less to chance, which leads me to wonder if the ghosts might feel the same? Mr. Brody's communication was so steady and sure, but then, of course, I have to take into account that he built the contraption himself." Thinking of her mother, she wondered if today might've been her only chance to receive a message from her spirit. In her heart, she hoped not.

"Does that mean you'd like to try it again?"

"I think so," Beatrice replied. "Yes."

"Excellent," Adelaide said. "I'll let Dr. Brody know."

As the carriage wheels ground to a stop, Adelaide picked up her skirts, but before she could exit the cab, Beatrice caught her by the arm. "Would you mind terribly if I spoke to Miss St. Clair about it first? I'd like to hear her opinion on the matter. It's been so hard for me to know how best to proceed with my new abilities, and she's been awfully kind about helping me find my way. Sometimes I wish I could gaze into a crystal ball and see exactly what's coming, but Eleanor says that's not how they work."

Adelaide wished she had two eyes so she could roll them both. "Yes, of course you should speak with Eleanor, about everything we've discussed and more. As far as looking into the future goes, I believe I can help with that. I imagine you're getting rather tired of feeling so unsure."

Walking through the shop door, Adelaide took Beatrice by the hand and led her back to her table for a consultation.

Miss Beatrice Dunn. Inquisitive, bright, full of promise. Unbearably lovely in every way.

Her question: What does my future hold?

Her cards: Prudence. Fortune. Hope.

Adelaide's answer: Heavens! I don't believe I've ever seen a more fortuitous spread.

"Is that good?" Beatrice asked, carefully inspecting the cards that Adelaide had placed in front of her. Each one held the image of a formidable-looking woman, more goddess than human in dress and stature. Prudence was dressed in Roman garb, a mirror in one hand, a spear with a large snake wrapped around it in the other. Fortune stood naked except for a scant piece of cloth draped across her middle and a length of cloth wrapped over her eyes. Wheel at her back, she was holding two purses fat with lucre. Hope, dressed demurely in a long flowing gown, was standing in the crook of an anchor. Her face was calm despite the stormy seas that raged beneath her feet.

"You see who those fine ladies are, don't you?" Adelaide asked. "Each one stands for someone you know. She who stands at the crossroads of decision, giving insight, wisdom and forethought; she who spins the wheel on behalf of those who seek her, never allowing despair to get the best of her, for she knows good luck is bound to come around again in time; and she who serves as an anchor for our souls, a refuge for our hearts, the last thing left in Pandora's box."

Pointing to each card, Beatrice assigned each of the goddesses a human counterpart. "Prudence is Miss St. Clair, Fortune is you, and Hope, I suppose, is myself?"

Adelaide gave a wide smile. "How perceptive of you. Well done."

Beatrice shook her head. "But I'm not quite clear on what it all means."

"I'd say it means we're good company for each other," Adelaide replied. "We're better together than apart. This bodes well for everyone's future—yours, mine and Eleanor's."

Out of the corner of her eye, Beatrice saw Perdu waddling towards her with a stray card pinched in his beak. "Is that for me?" she asked, as the raven drew near.

"What's that he's got?" Adelaide asked.

"One of your cards," Beatrice replied, showing it to her. The image on the card was that of a young woman, face to face with a snarling lion, her hand inside the beast's mouth. The girl's expression was serene even though the lion was clearly untamed. Thinking that the frightful-looking token had appeared by magic rather than chance, Beatrice asked, "What do you suppose it means?"

Courage. You will face an unexpected challenge that requires fearlessness and great strength.

Since the day she'd received the cards, Adelaide had never had one get away from her like that. Perhaps it had escaped to serve as a reminder of Beatrice's current situation? *Yes,* Adelaide thought, *let's leave it at that.*

Plucking the card from Beatrice's hand she swiftly shuffled it into the deck. As she turned her head, her vision went cloudy and off-kilter. Before her sat two Beatrices—one, lovely and inquisitive, just as she'd always been; the other, a pale, trembling wreck of a girl in great distress. Head bowed, Adelaide willed the vision to fade. When she looked at Beatrice again, the frightful image was gone. With a nervous laugh, she said, "It means I should pay better attention to what I'm doing."

Evening came and Adelaide left for dinner at the hotel with
Judith Dashley and Marietta Stevens. She'd invited Beatrice
to join her, but Beatrice chose to stay behind to wash dishes
and discuss the day's events with Eleanor.

"Do you think I should try using the spiritoscope again?"
Beatrice asked, drying a teapot.

Eleanor replied, "So long as you're mindful in what you're
doing, I don't think it could hurt."

"But you can't say for certain?"

Eleanor furrowed her brow, placed the pot on the shelf.
"Communication with the spirit world can be something
like baking a soufflé. You can use all the best ingredients,
follow the instructions to the letter, and still wind up with a
confusing mess—oftentimes because of something silly, like
heavy footsteps or a slammed door. Although I can't say for
certain how things will go the next time around, I can promise you this—I'll be right by your side should you choose to
pursue it."

"I'd like that," Beatrice said. Swirling a tea towel inside
another pot she asked, "What does it take to be a witch?"

Washing the pot's lid, Eleanor said, "Curiosity, attention,
tenacity, courage and an unshakable belief in things unseen.
What did it take to be Beatrice Dunn before all this began?"

"Much the same, I suppose," Beatrice said with a shrug.
Thinking of the card that'd escaped from Adelaide's deck she
added, "Excepting, perhaps, courage."

Eleanor frowned. "I don't believe that, not for a minute.
Think of what brought you here in the first place. I dare you
to say courage had no part in it."

Beatrice, embarrassed, smiled at her.

"My mother was right to say the world has need of more witches," Eleanor explained. "She worked diligently to help the many women who came to her for assistance. She healed their bodies, minds and hearts as best she could. Still, she felt she had to hide. I suppose in a sense I've been hiding here, too, albeit in plain sight. I often worry what might happen if certain people were to discover what I do. Throughout the ages witches have been hunted and put to death. I'm sure you've read the tales, heard the stories?"

"Yes," Beatrice answered. "But the witches in those tales were bad. They deserved what was coming to them."

"Ah-ha!" Eleanor said, wagging her finger. "That's exactly what the storytellers want you to believe. I guess you haven't come across 'The Princess Who Wished to Be a Witch.' The grimoire will show it to you should you wish to read it. Imagine what the world would be like if all mothers told that tale to their daughters."

"Do you believe everything your mother said about me during the dumb supper?"

"Yes."

"But why me? Why now?" Beatrice asked. "What good does it do me, or anyone else, if I'm a witch?"

"You've barely gotten started and you're already working magic. Think back to your encounter with Judith Dashley. She's been changed by your words, her heart healed."

"Is that what I'm supposed to do then?" she asked. "Spend the rest of my life talking to spirits?"

"Among other things," Eleanor said. "But I believe there's far more ahead for you than that. My mother's words indicated several gifts—the Wisdom of the Mothers, the Language of Dreams . . ."

"Do you believe in the Dearlies?" Beatrice asked. She'd read of them in the grimoire and found the notion of them intriguing. "Or is that just another tale? Sometimes it's difficult to tell the tales from the truth."

"The grimoire doesn't lie," Eleanor replied. "Its wisdom takes many forms within its pages—recipes, spells, sagas . . . and yes, even fairy tales. Every word within it holds truth. As fanciful as it might sound, the Dearlies are real. Have you had any dreams since you arrived?"

"No," Beatrice said, "at least not any that I can remember. It's no wonder, though. I've had a dreadful time getting any rest, because of, well, everything, I guess. When I sat with Mrs. Dashley she mentioned a tea you'd given her to help her sleep. Do you think it might help me?"

Fetching a large canister from behind the counter Eleanor said, "Let's find out, shall we?"

The tea was made from mugwort, peppermint, chamomile, rose petals, valerian root, burdock, yarrow and bog myrtle, and as the canister said, *the perfect tonic to ready the body for sleep and the mind for dreaming.*

Beatrice watched as Eleanor measured the mixture into a teapot then added hot water so it could steep.

"There are a few things you can do to entice the Dearlies, too," Eleanor said. "You must let them know they're needed. Here is how you go about it."

Listening intently, Beatrice took down Eleanor's instructions in her notebook. *Place a drop of honey on top of each bedpost. Tie a sprig of lavender above your head. Fill a muslin pouch with anise seeds and tuck it inside your pillow. Sprinkle marigold petals on the floor beneath your bed.*

"Last but not least," Eleanor said, "the Dearlies adore anything that shines, like raindrops on holly leaves, or morning dew on spider webs. If you've anything that sparkles and glints—a ring, a hair comb, a ribbon with silver thread—wear it to bed."

"I've just the thing," Beatrice said, remembering her mother's glass brooch with the wren's feather inside it. "Should I be worried about nightmares, though?"

"Some witches believe you should always guard against them, but I only do so if they make pests of themselves, returning again and again, refusing to leave me alone. Nightmares are like the rest of our dreams, they come to us for a reason. The Dearlies make them with your exact dimensions in mind. A dream always fits."

Pouring herself some tea, Beatrice hoped Eleanor was right.

"If you wake in the night," Eleanor said, "come tell me your dreams. It's been a while since I've made sense of them for someone else, but I'm happy to try. As my mother used to say, 'An uninterpreted dream is like an unopened letter.' The more you pay attention to them, the more they repay your attention. At the very least, write down every detail you can remember, whether it's at midnight or first light."

"I will," Beatrice said, suddenly feeling quite tired. She hadn't even taken her first sip of the tea, but the scent spiralling from her cup was already working its magic. "Who listens to your dreams?" she asked, stifling a yawn.

"My mother did, when I was young," Eleanor replied, "and there's always been Perdu."

"Not Miss Thom?" Beatrice asked, thinking she would've been a more likely choice.

Eleanor laughed. "Attempting to wake Adelaide from sleep is like trying to wake the dead. Who knows, someday soon, I might tell my dreams to you."

Notebook tucked under her arm, cup and saucer in hand, Beatrice bid Eleanor goodnight. "Thank you for the tea," she said, "and the advice."

"Goodnight, dear Beatrice," Eleanor replied. "May your dreams be all you need them to be."

Bright sat on the edge of Beatrice's saucer staring at Twitch. "Is she asleep?" she asked, impatiently tapping her foot. Twitch had insisted on singing to the girl each night, mostly lullabies in the languages of the Fay. "We don't have time for a serenade," she complained. "There's work to be done, at last!"

"My, she smells heavenly!" Twitch swooned, hovering over the girl, sniffing her hair, her cheeks, her lips.

"That's just the mugwort on her breath," Bright said, arms folded. "Don't let yourself get incapacitated by her glamour. It grows more powerful every day." Walking along the rim of Beatrice's cup, she peered into its bowl to take stock of how much tea the girl had consumed. "It's still half full," she observed. "We'll need to work fast."

Twitch crouched near the brooch Beatrice had pinned to the neck of her nightdress. Clouding the pretty trinket with his breath, he polished the glass with his coat sleeve until it shone bright. He was more excited about Beatrice's dream than he'd been about anything in his entire life. He and

Bright had been planning it for days, constructing the details, bit by precious bit. He'd thought of it each night as he'd sung to her in her sleep, each day as he'd trailed around her room, sharpening her pencils with the edge of a rose thorn, re-mending the hem of her dress with fairy silk. Gently blowing her a kiss, he whispered in her ear, "Sweet dreams, dear Beatrice."

She was flying through the air, high above the city, over rooftops and trees in a cloudless, moonlit sky. She was surrounded by hundreds of witches, careening about on broomsticks, robes trailing in the wind, hair loose, eyes wild. She was not afraid. To her, they were the most beautiful creatures she'd ever seen—powerful, intelligent—free from all care. She followed wherever they led. This was where she belonged.

Their destination was half familiar, half strange—Madison Square Park transformed into a witches' lair. The footpaths glowed with enchantment, the tree branches were strewn with bells, bones and poppets. The flames of Lady Liberty's torch were no longer made of glass, but fire. It raged and hissed and shot overhead as the witches danced around it dressed in veils that trailed to the ground. They were singing in a language she'd never heard but somehow understood. They spoke of the Land of Dreams, the Realm of the Dead, the Wonders of the Otherworld. They called to Hecate, to Circe, to the Morai "to open our minds, to strengthen our spells, to bless our works."

When their rite was finished, they turned and looked upon Beatrice, blessings and secrets flowing from their mouths like a thousand babbling brooks. As she marvelled at the sight, one witch stepped forward. Pulling the veil from her face, she revealed herself to be Adelaide Thom.

"Look!" Adelaide commanded, pointing to the scarred hollow above her cheek.

Beatrice did, and was startled to find that Billy Dashley's precious toy, his shining blue marble, had replaced Adelaide's missing eye. As she stared at the glowing orb twinkling in the firelight, she was transported to an endless corridor lined with chandeliers and mirrors. Ghostly figures flitted all around her, their reflections appearing more as wisps of smoke than flesh. Most of them were unknown to her, but there were a few she recognized—Dr. Brody's father holding the dial of the spiritoscope; Adelaide's mother wearing her tattered silk scarf; Billy Dashley clutching his bag of peanuts, giving her a toothy smile; and her own beloved mother extending a lonely, empty hand. As Beatrice reached for her, the ghost changed into the spirit of Madame St. Clair. "Be still," the witch ordered, reaching through the looking glass and placing a crooked finger on Beatrice's mouth.

Beatrice blinked and Madame St. Clair disappeared, her own reflection taking the witch's place. Her eyes were lined with charcoal and she wore a crown of gold on her head as if she were a queen, or a priestess, or perhaps even a goddess. "This is who you are," Madame St. Clair's voice announced.

No sooner were the words spoken than the corridor went black as pitch. Lost and afraid, Beatrice clung to the wall, hoping to find her way out. The glassy surface beneath her fingers turned to stone, cold and damp and covered with glyphs like those that were carved into the obelisk. In the darkness, she heard a creature draw near, growling and snarling and gnashing its teeth.

"This way!" Eleanor's voice called from the right.

"Follow me!" Adelaide's voice called from the left.

Not knowing which way to turn, Beatrice tore a string from the hem of her dress and began tying knots along the length of it. "By knot of one, my spell's begun. By knot of two, it will come true. By knot of three, so may it be. By knot of four, this power I store. By knot of five, my spell is alive."

With the fifth knot, a door appeared in front of her, fitted with a forbidding iron lock.

"By knot of six, this spell I fix. By knot of seven, the future I'll leaven. By knot of eight, my will be fate. By knot of nine, what's done is mine!"

With that, a key appeared around her neck, hot to the touch, as if it'd been freshly pulled from the forge and quenched in oil.

Putting the key in the lock, Beatrice made to turn it, but was shaken from her dream by the sound of breaking glass.

Perdu squawked and spat and sounded an alarm. "Fiend!" he cried. "Fiend, fiend, fiend!"

Twitch tugged at Bright's arm. "Your cheeks . . ." he whispered, watching them turn blue.

"I know," Bright replied, hands to her face as she helplessly watched Beatrice rise from her bed.

Hearing Eleanor and Adelaide tramping down the stairs, Beatrice threw on a wrap and followed them. The three women huddled together near the door, bathed in the dim glow of lantern light. A rock had come through a window-pane and settled amongst a scattering of glass shards. They might've thought it simple vandalism had there not been a message attached.

Eleanor picked up the rock and examined the crude note.

"What does it say?" Adelaide asked.

Peering over Eleanor's shoulder Beatrice read the words aloud, "I know what you are."

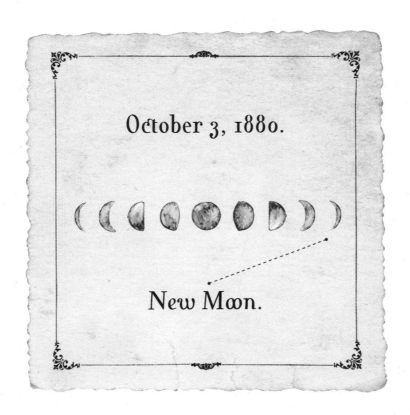

October 3, 1880.

New Moon.

Late, late, yestreen
I saw the Old Moon in the New Moon's arms.
I fear, I fear, my Master dear,
That we shall come to great harm.
               —The Ballad of Sir Patrick Spens

The Sibyl, with frenzied mouth uttering things not to be laughed at, unadorned and unperfumed, yet reaches to a thousand years with her voice by the aid of the god.

—Heraclitus

Into the Fire.

The witches were seated around a table in the teashop, enjoying a quiet dinner of brown bread and onion soup. They could've been dining at Delmonico's (Judith Dashley had offered to treat them), but Beatrice had declined the woman's invitation in favour of having supper in, just the three of them. She'd wanted to be surrounded by peace and quiet and familiar faces before they made their way to the Fifth Avenue Hotel where she'd agreed to perform a demonstration with Dr. Brody's spiritoscope for Mr. and Mrs. Dashley, and Marietta Stevens.

Sopping up the last of her soup with a piece of crust, Adelaide glanced at the clock to check the time—quarter past seven. They were expected at the hotel for eight. "I'm going on ahead," she announced. "I'd like to make sure everything's in order."

"We'll be along shortly," Eleanor said, speaking on Beatrice's behalf. "I thought Beatrice might like to have a cup of tea to sort her thoughts."

Beatrice gave Eleanor a grateful nod.

It was just the kind of response Adelaide had expected from Eleanor. In fact, she was surprised her partner hadn't found some excuse for them to call the whole thing off. Since that rock had come crashing through the window, Eleanor had been jittery, on edge. Mr. Withrow, the landlord, had spotted the broken pane before she could get the glazer in to fix it.

"You'll have the repair done and paid for before the next rent is due," he'd grumbled, "or else you'll be out on your ears. I don't know why I even agreed to rent to a pair of petticoats."

Adelaide had tried to calm Eleanor by saying, "As soon as it's fixed, Withrow will forget it ever happened." Shaking her head, Eleanor had replied, "I doubt it."

And she was not wild about the idea of the demonstration at the hotel. "Participating in a few supervised experiments at Dr. Brody's home is one thing, but getting pulled into his search for ghosts is quite another. Can't he conduct that sort of research without Beatrice? And why must the hotel's owner and the Dashleys be present? It's looking for trouble, especially when Beatrice still has so much to learn about her gifts."

"How horribly maternal of you," Adelaide had retorted. "It's Beatrice's choice. Who are we to ask her to wait when the stars are so magnificently aligned? The signs, as you would say, couldn't be clearer. Everything—from Beatrice's arrival, to Dr. Brody's research, to the sudden influx of ghosts— points in this direction. Oh Great Witch of the Bronx River, how many portents do you require?"

Arms crossed, Eleanor had said, "I haven't even met this Dr. Brody of yours. How can you be certain he's not playing Beatrice and you for fools?"

"Have you forgotten I, too, have gifts? Or aren't they worth trusting anymore? If anyone should be worried about getting hoodwinked, it's Dr. Brody. This city is rife with false prophets and seers who'd happily pull the wool over his eyes. And he's not *my* anything. He's a decent man with an open mind."

"You're saying that because you fancy him," Eleanor had accused.

"I make it a practice not to fancy anyone: it's a horrid way to live."

"I have eyes," Eleanor had countered. "Your cheeks turn crimson at each mention of his name. But what does Dr. Brody know of magic? Just because he has an interest in all things supernatural, that doesn't mean he respects Beatrice's gifts."

"Before you condemn the man, you should take the trouble to get to know him," Adelaide said stiffly.

"Very well then," Eleanor had relented. "I'll defer my judgement until I see the good doctor's work for myself. That is, if I'm allowed to attend this grand affair?"

Dr. Brody was standing with Mr. Dashley in a private salon on the second floor of the Fifth Avenue Hotel. The room, richly appointed with Persian rugs, rosewood panelling, crystal chandeliers, overstuffed chairs and a half-dozen porcelain vases filled with palm fronds and tuberoses, was generally reserved for lectures and meetings held by the hotel's elite clientele. Mrs. Stevens had been kind enough to lend it to them for the evening, so long as she was allowed to witness the proceedings. Quinn would've happily continued his experiments at home, but Adelaide had suggested they try their luck at the hotel instead, since the place was supposed to be crawling with ghosts. So there he was, at half past seven on a Saturday night, preparing to help a young woman talk with spirits. Who would've imagined it?

"Is the table where you'd like it?" Mr. Dashley asked. "I can call the porter if you'd like it moved."

"It's fine where it is," Quinn answered. He'd spent the last hour adjusting the various components of the spiritoscope in relation to its position on the table. Moving the table would mean he'd have to go through the entire process again. As he checked the angle of the machine's dial one last time, the powerful scent of tuberoses filled his nose and caused him to sneeze. Fiddling in his pocket for his handkerchief, he stared down the offending flowers. "What the porter can do," he said, pointing to the many vases around the room, "is get rid of those." Mr. Dashley called the porter and one by one the vases disappeared, whisked off to some other part of the hotel to spread their overwhelming scent.

"Better, eh?" Quinn said, looking pleased.

"Much," Mr. Dashley replied, then hoped he hadn't just quashed some act of generosity by his wife. Judith hadn't mentioned she was going to send flowers, but he wouldn't put it past her. Short, stout and balding, Dashley was a veritable giant when it came to intellect, but never certain of himself when it came to his wife. He found it difficult to express feelings, although he, too, had been hit hard by their son's death, so entrenched in sorrow that he'd feared it couldn't be lifted up without a system of fortified levers and wedges. Many men in his position might've drunk themselves into oblivion or thrown themselves into their work, but Alden Dashley had never had much of a taste for drink, and he didn't have to work in any true sense of the word. Judith's family's fortune was the engine that pulled the train of their financial success. He was just the conductor, keeping things on track— legal matters, real estate, business investments and such. In the wake of their son's death, Judith had found distraction and solace in her quest to make contact with the spirit realm. While he'd supported her efforts, he'd found he'd needed to take a different tack. To that end, he'd joined several benevolent societies and lodges including the Freemasons and the Odd Fellows. But it wasn't until he'd gone into Mr. Brody's shop in search of a new magnifying glass that he'd finally found the sort of camaraderie he'd been looking for. Joining the Fraternal Order of the Unknown Philosophers had been a welcome balm for his weary heart. And now he had grown very fond of the late Mr. Brody's only son.

"Thank you for agreeing to attend this evening's proceedings," Quinn said, resisting the urge to tinker with the spiritoscope any further.

"I'm always happy to come to the aid of a fellow Philosopher," Mr. Dashley replied. "Besides, Judith has been going on about Miss Dunn ever since they met. I'd be in hot water if I passed up the opportunity to make her acquaintance. I'm quite curious to see what all the fuss is about. With you involved, I dare say I'm even hopeful something miraculous might transpire." His tone at the end was wistful, his gaze far off.

Dr. Brody recalled just then, with some embarrassment, mind that the ghost child Beatrice had seen in the teashop was Mr. Dashley's son.

When Adelaide arrived, she surveyed the room to see if there was anything left to be done. She couldn't shake the feeling

that something was missing. "Flowers," she muttered at last.
She'd left the task to Judith, who was keen to be helpful with
anything involving the young Miss Dunn, telling her that
something understated, yet elegant, would be best. "Leave it
with me," Judith had said. "I'll find just the right blooms to
create the perfect ambience."

Approaching the porter, Adelaide asked, "Has there been
any mention of flowers for the room?"

"Yes, miss," the young man answered. "They arrived this
afternoon."

"Then where have they got to? I don't suppose they walked
off by themselves."

"No, miss," the porter replied. "The gentleman sent them
away."

Adelaide checked the time. It was too late to go chasing
after the flowers (and where was Beatrice? It was a quarter to
eight already). Just as she tried to think of a plausible excuse
for the missing bouquets, Marietta and Judith entered the
room. Mrs. Stevens was dressed in her usual black on black on
black, several strands of jet beads around her neck. Adelaide
admired the way the woman could make her perpetual
mourning look fashionable, when so many widows became
invisible, swallowed up by endless yards of crepe. Judith had
chosen to wear a mustard-coloured dress with a perky bustle
and matching hat. The felt topper was trimmed with velvet
ribbons and a stuffed goldfinch with glass eyes that stared
inquisitively from the brim as if it were a sailor on a ship's
prow. Six well-pressed housemaids trailed behind her, each
one carrying a large vase filled with the banished tuberose
bouquets. "Two on the mantel, two on the floor and two on
that table over there," Judith directed, as her husband regarded

her with wry affection. Shaking her head she turned to Marietta. "Thank heavens I spotted them in the lobby or they might never have made it upstairs."

As a pair of maids headed to the table that held the spiritoscope, Quinn intervened. Hands up, he politely suggested, "Perhaps those could go on the hallway table outside the door, instead?"

The maids looked at Judith.

"Do as the good doctor wishes," Judith said, giving Quinn a friendly nod. Then turning to Adelaide she breathlessly asked, "Where is our Beatrice?"

"She'll be here soon," Adelaide assured her. "She and Eleanor decided some tea was in order, to calm the nerves and clear the mind."

"Of course," Judith said. "Miss Dunn is remarkably wise for her age."

Adelaide wasn't sure if Judith's unwavering admiration for the girl was good or bad. Beatrice was an unbelievably forthright creature, but she knew nothing of managing expectations or brokering respect. If she wanted to make headway in this town, especially with the likes of Marietta Stevens, she'd have to temper her goodness with confidence and savvy. In Adelaide's opinion, it was the only way to survive.

Strolling around the salon, the women appraised their surroundings, with Judith glancing frequently at the door for sign of Beatrice.

Marietta soon turned her attention to the spiritoscope. "Is this the contraption the girl is to use? It looks like an outdated telegraph machine."

"What an astute observation," Adelaide said, motioning for Quinn to join them.

"Indeed," he chimed in. "That's exactly what inspired it. I'd be happy to explain how it works."

"Don't trouble yourself," Marietta replied. "I expect all to be revealed in the doing."

"If all goes according to plan," Quinn replied.

Adelaide kept quiet, thinking it might be best to let Marietta's remarks go unchallenged. She'd warned Quinn that Mrs. Stevens wasn't driven by emotion, but rather a constant state of waiting to be impressed.

But Judith couldn't leave well enough alone. "I, for one, think it's rather ingenious."

Mr. Dashley slipped his arm around his wife and gave her a quick affectionate squeeze.

Seeing this small act of kindness pass between the pair inspired Adelaide to stick up for Quinn. Tucking her arm through his she declared, "As do I."

Eleanor and Beatrice entered the hotel lobby at ten to eight. Taking in the extravagant decor, from the marble floors to the fluted columns to the gilded mirrors that lined the corridors, Beatrice now understood why her old classmate Joseph Wheeler had said the place made him nervous. All the same, she was eager to try her hand at the spiritoscope again. She hoped this time her mother's spirit might stay a while longer. Based on what she could remember of her dream (thus far, very little), she felt it might be possible, even probable. From time to time brief flashes of what she'd seen were triggered by mundane things—the sound of Eleanor or Adelaide's voice speaking a certain word, or the scent of woodsmoke in the air when the wind was from the west. Among the foggy images in her brain, she'd seen her mother's face, tender, yet fleeting. Clinging to that memory she'd made up her mind to do whatever it took to see her mother again. If it meant she had to endure a thousand experiments and meet a thousand ghosts, then so be it.

"This way," Eleanor said, motioning to the front desk.

As Beatrice followed, she was overcome by the feeling that she was being watched. The scents of furniture oil and lye soap stuck in the back of her throat. The sound of a young woman's laughter rang in her ears. When she turned to try to find the source, she spotted a pair of scrubber girls nearby, pointing at her and whispering. She watched with amazement as they passed in front of her, their bodies effortlessly gliding through a wall of solid marble.

A gentleman in an ill-fitting suit was at the desk in front of them. Waiting for the night manager to assist him, he swayed side to side, softly, almost imperceptibly, talking to himself.

Thinking he, too, might be a ghost, Beatrice reached out and touched the sleeve of his coat. Finding it real, she drew her hand back and looked to see if Eleanor had noticed her indiscretion. Happily, she hadn't.

At last, the manager looked up from a ledger on the desk and addressed the gentleman. "I'm sorry, Mr. Guiteau. Senator Conkling is unable to meet you tonight."

"It's important I speak with him," the man insisted. "Election Day is just a month away."

"Perhaps you can come back tomorrow? I'm afraid there's nothing more I can do for you today."

Disgruntled, Mr. Guiteau left the desk, swearing under his breath.

Beatrice watched him as he skulked away. One by one, shadowy figures came up from the floor beneath his feet and wrapped themselves around him. He seemed completely unaware of their presence, and they seemed frightfully determined to stay put. Unsettled, she quickly looked away.

"Who's next?" the night manager asked, eyes on Eleanor, silently judging her attire. Verdict, *unimpressed*.

"Miss Dunn and Miss St. Clair for Mrs. Stevens, please," Eleanor replied.

Licking the end of his thumb, he turned the page of the ledger and scanned it for their names. "Ah yes, there you are," he said with a surprised smile. "Just one moment and I'll get a bellhop to accompany you to the salon." Ducking back to a small office behind the desk he pulled the cord on a distant bell.

Suddenly feeling dizzy and sick, Beatrice reached for Eleanor's hand to steady herself.

"Are you all right?" Eleanor asked.

"I think so," Beatrice answered, hoping her queasiness would soon pass.

"You don't have to do this," Eleanor said. "We can send our regrets. No one will think any less of you, especially if you're unwell."

"I'm fine now. Really," Beatrice said, standing straight and smoothing her skirts.

Eleanor could see that Beatrice was struggling, but didn't quite know how to help her through it. Her thoughts turned to Lucy Newland standing on the balcony at Liberty's torch and the helpless feeling that'd come over her when Lucy had insisted she could take care of things on her own. That feeling had become far too familiar as of late.

A bellhop in a red wool jacket and cap appeared beside the desk. "Follow me," he said.

Beatrice spotted the table holding the spiritoscope as soon as she entered the room. It was just as it'd been in Dr. Brody's study, only now there were several chairs facing it, as if she were expected to put on a show. Adelaide had told her ahead of time who would be in attendance, but she hadn't met either Mr. Dashley or the formidable Marietta Stevens before, and her nerves flared again. Then Judith Dashley rushed across the room to greet her, taking her by the arm. "You look lovely this evening," she said, "and quite sophisticated too. It's so nice to see you again."

"Thank you, Mrs. Dashley," Beatrice said, not feeling sophisticated at all. She was wearing a dress in a beautiful shade of blue, borrowed from Adelaide. It had required a fair bit of corset tightening to fit her into it and it made her feel like an imposter rather than fashionable. Eleanor had tried to veto the gown, but Beatrice had decided it was best to give in to Adelaide's kindness. She didn't want her to think she was ungrateful.

"Come meet my husband," Judith said, leading Beatrice across the room. "Alden, dear," she called to Mr. Dashley, "here is our darling Miss Dunn."

Beatrice nodded and smiled and tried to look serene.

"Mr. Dashley is here tonight as a representative of the Unknown Philosophers," Judith explained. "But he also has a great interest in hearing from our darling boy."

"Of course," Beatrice said, wishing she could promise them Billy would appear. She, too, hoped for his return. She'd liked his sweet face. "He favours you," she said to Alden, without considering how strange her words might sound.

"Pardon?" Mr. Dashley said.

"He has your eyes," Beatrice said. "I saw his face quite clearly during his visitation."

Mr. Dashley stammered, "What a nice sentiment."

"And so true!" Judith exclaimed. "I can't tell you how many times I made the same observation when Billy was alive."

Next came Mrs. Stevens. Adelaide had described her as "a discerning woman who could dictate the course of our future" but had neglected to mention her formidable stature and intimidating stare. Thankfully the introduction was a brief affair, a simple exchange of names then a cut to the chase.

"Shall we dispense with small talk, Miss Dunn, and get things underway?"

Adelaide ushered Beatrice to the table where Dr. Brody was waiting to help her settle into her chair. "You've nothing to worry about," she said. "Everyone here wishes you well."

Eleanor, who'd been staying out of the way, now came to Beatrice's side and whispered in her ear, "Don't hesitate to bring things to a halt should anything give you pause. If you need my help, I'll be here."

"Thank you," Beatrice said with a nervous smile.

Handing Adelaide the silk blind to tie over Beatrice's eyes, Dr. Brody gave the girl a few final instructions. "We'll proceed the same as we did before. After I blindfold you, we'll take our seats. Adelaide will record any movement of the needle and I'll keep my eyes on the board. You may disengage from the spiritoscope at any time. All clear?"

"Yes, Dr. Brody."

Adelaide gently draped the silk scarf over Beatrice's eyes, pulled it taut and tied it in place.

"Are you ready, Miss Dunn?" Dr. Brody asked, taking his seat.

"Yes," Beatrice answered, taking a deep breath.

"You may place your hands on the board whenever you'd like to begin," Brody said.

Fingertips to the wood, Beatrice waited for a spirit to approach. From what she'd witnessed in the lobby, there were indeed a few ghosts lurking about the hotel. But several seconds passed and nothing moved, nothing came near. A minute on, she and the board remained still.

She heard a stray cough from Mr. Dashley, an impatient sigh from Mrs. Stevens, the restless tap of Adelaide's foot. She could also feel all eyes upon her, from Eleanor's warm, supportive gaze to Judith's pleading stare.

Should she say something? she wondered. Extend an invitation? "Hello?" she faintly whispered. "Are you here?"

Just as she was about to give up, she felt a tug at her skirt beneath the table.

"Hello, Billy," she said. "I'm glad you've come." Even blindfolded, she could see the boy in her mind's eye.

Judith reached for Alden's hand and excitedly whispered, "That's him. Our boy is here."

Alden responded with a measured nod.

Marietta rolled her eyes in disbelief and shifted in her seat.

Quinn looked concerned. Clearly there was a spirit present. Why wasn't it using the spiritoscope to communicate?

Adelaide glanced at Eleanor.

Eleanor mouthed the word, "Wait."

"Why don't you come out and see my new toy?" Beatrice suggested. "We can play a little game."

Billy frowned and shook his head.

"It's easy," Beatrice urged. "All you have to do is place your hands on mine, then make the needle spin to spell the things you wish to say."

"I can't," Billy insisted.

"Why not?" Beatrice asked.

"I can't make words," Billy replied.

Beatrice thought for a moment. "You mean you can't spell?"

Everyone laughed, except Mrs. Stevens.

Dr. Brody hurriedly wrote, *In future, must consider likelihood of spirit's ability to spell.*

Caring more for Billy's feelings than for making the machine work, Beatrice tried to coax the boy out of hiding. "Why don't you come out from there and give me a proper hello."

Once again, Billy shook his head.

"What's the matter?" Beatrice asked. "Can't you see who's here?"

Pulling his cap over his eyes he said, "Don't tell them where I am."

"Don't tell who where you are?" Beatrice asked, thinking the boy would surely want to see his parents.

"The Marys," Billy whispered, then disappeared.

With that, the same laughter Beatrice had heard in the lobby sounded again, this time ringing loudly in her ears. The overpowering smell of lye soap filled the air. The two scrubber girls were there, with several more by their side. Circling around Beatrice they flew up to the ceiling to hide in the chandeliers. The crystal fobs that hung off the lights tinkled and chimed in sympathy with their flight.

"What's happening?" Judith whispered to Adelaide, eyes wide.

"Shh," Adelaide replied, finger to her lips.

The board under Beatrice's hands grew hot to the touch, so hot she thought her fingertips might burn. Snatching her hands off the board, she felt a violent push against her shoulders. She smelled smoke, felt the searing heat of a fire at her back. Darkness surrounded her. There was no escape.

"Beatrice?" Eleanor softly called. "Are you all right?"

As she opened her mouth to speak, a scrubber girl clasped her hand around her throat, forcing words to come forth that weren't hers. "I am not she," a raspy voice sounded, that of a young woman with an Irish lilt. "I am one of many. Mrs. Stevens knows who I am. She saw me in life. She gazed upon me in death. She knows the secret my body kept. She alone can make it right. She must set in stone what should've been in life."

While everyone else sat stunned at these developments, Eleanor quickly moved to Beatrice's side. She feared for the girl's well-being should the spirit persist. None was so still as Marietta Stevens.

Head bowed, shoulders slumped, Beatrice began to sing.

> *The Marys have gone rotten,*
> *Dead and forgotten.*
> *Lying in their beds*
> *With their eyes wide open.*
>
> *The chill hand of death,*
> *Stole them in the night,*
> *As they danced in a fire*
> *That burned too bright.*

The chair Beatrice was sitting on began to teeter and shake.

"Beatrice," Eleanor called, trying to steady the girl, "can you hear me?"

Dr. Brody leapt to his feet and came to her aid.

"We can't leave!" Beatrice cried, the voice inhabiting her body now changed to a chorus of desperate wails. "We can't get out!"

Taking a silver charm from her pocket, Eleanor pressed it into Beatrice's hand. "Joan of Arc, Maid of Orleans, Witch of Domrémy, come to our aid, defend this girl."

"Help us!" Beatrice whimpered, her skin turning red, hair singeing at the ends. "We can't breathe!"

The smell of smoke filled the room. The chandeliers began to chime and sway.

Not knowing what else to do, Alden took his wife's hand.

The pear seeds in the phial around Adelaide's neck began to rattle.

Marietta put her hand to her mouth and shook her head.

"Send your angels to protect her," Eleanor implored, "guide her soul to the fore."

Falling into Eleanor's arms, Beatrice gasped for air.

"Beatrice," Eleanor cried, pulling the blindfold loose. "Are you with us?"

Adelaide abandoned her post and rushed to Beatrice's side. Together they held the girl's hands, waiting for her to reply.

"Beatrice," Adelaide whispered, "are you here?"

Eyelids fluttering, Beatrice answered, "I never left."

With that, the needle on the spiritoscope began to move.

Mrs. Stevens watched with astonishment as it spelled out the words M-A-R-Y D-O-N-N-E-L-L-Y A-N-D C-H-I-L-D.

There is a sort of Witchcrafts in those things, whereto the Temptations of the Devil would inveigle us. To worship the Devil is Witchcraft, and under that notion was our Lord urged unto sin. We are told in 1 Samuel 15:23, "Rebellion is as the sin of Witchcraft." When the Devil would have us to sin, he would have us to do the things which the forlorn Witches use to do. Perhaps there are few persons, ever allured by the Devil unto an Explicit Covenant with himself. If any among ourselves be so, my counsel is, that you hunt the Devil from you, with such words as the Psalmist had, "Be gone, Depart from me, ye evil doers, for I will keep the commandments of my God."

—Rev. Cotton Mather, *On Witchcraft*

The Preacher's Confession.

REVEREND FRANCIS TOWNSEND was crouched in front of the fireplace in his study, stirring hot coals with an iron poker. He'd hoped the mundane chore might help stir his thoughts as well, but the mesmerizing glow of the fire had the opposite effect. Taking his pipe from his pocket, he tapped a clump of ash from its bowl onto the hearth, then proceeded to fill it with a pinch of fresh tobacco. Perhaps a few hearty draws on the pipe's stem would clear his mind. Sticking a straw in the fire until it caught light, he brought its glowing end to the bowl and puffed hard.

Checking his watch he saw that it was half past eight. He was supposed to have his weekly sermon written by nine so he could hand the pages over to Sister Piddock. She, in turn, would then choose the appropriate hymns and readings for the Sunday service. That was the arrangement they'd made when he'd first taken the post at the Church of the Good Shepherd just over a year ago, and he'd grudgingly stuck to it. It was that, or choose the hymns himself and take the chance that Sister Piddock, who was also the church organist, might hit a string of sour notes leading up to his homily. Better safe than sorry. The music set the tone for his words, and his words set the stage for the salvation of his flock. Although he was sure the congregation could afford a more accomplished musician, he couldn't afford to lose Sister Piddock's support. Her appearance might be plain, to put it kindly, but her convictions were unshakable. She was obedient to her husband, strong in her faith, and quick to eschew anything that was meant to tempt the weaker sex away from home and family. She especially abhorred the current fashion for ladies to congregate in cafés and teahouses, indulging in idleness and gossip. Childless, she spent her days in the service of the Lord and the Reverend— looking after his vestments, polishing the offering plates, and keeping him informed of those members of the congregation who were in need of his special guidance.

It'd been at Sister Piddock's urging that Townsend had been offered his current position. After hearing him preach at her father's meetinghouse in Utica, she'd asked her husband and several upstanding members of the congregation to consider bringing him to New York. He'd delivered one sermon, "Fidelity to the Word, the Only Shield against the Devil's Malignity," and they'd offered him the job. "We've been praying for a true leader," Sister Piddock had cried, "and clearly God has answered our pleas by delivering you to us." (The previous pastor had been released from his duties after it was discovered he'd taken up the habit of visiting various gambling dens on Saturday nights.)

Reverend Townsend had felt it was the hand of divine Providence, as if he had been called to play a part in some grand holy plan. His grandfather, the Reverend Deodat Townsend, had always insisted that Francis was destined for great things, even when, for a short time in his youth, he'd been drawn to fisticuffs and rum. It was his grandfather who'd advised his father to send him to the seminary in Andover, and it was there Francis had learned not only of theology but of his family's storied past.

He came from a long line of God-fearing men going back to the famed preachers of Massachusetts Bay, who'd lived there when the colony was rife with witchcraft. It'd been his ancestors, in the years after the trials, who'd continued to be watchful for the Devil's workings within God's people. They, along with a few faithful followers, had formed a group called the Brethren, religious folk who wished to practice the strong faith of those who first settled the land. Carrying on the traditions of his forefathers, Reverend Deodat Townsend had become a travelling preacher, moving across the Frontier to spread the Gospel. He quickly gained a reputation for having a beautiful singing voice, knowing the Bible by heart, and having the ability to "put evil to flight." There'd been plenty to distract the people—preachers who peddled false miracles, salesmen of all stripes (hawking brushes, pots, scissors, knives and patent medicines), tawdry circus folk in gaudy tents (bearded ladies, legless men, snake charmers and fortune tellers)—but Deodat had something to offer that no one else had. Upon hearing stories of the magic and witchery that existed in the wilderness of the West, Deodat Townsend guaranteed, hand to God, that he could take care of whatever witchery might be troubling a place with no questions asked.

Francis had inherited his grandfather's personal effects after he had passed—a Bible worn and faded from much use, a small collection of relics from his days on the frontier, and a parcel of writings passed down from the Brethren (sermons, mostly, pertaining to the wages of sin). When Francis's mother had cleared out the room where his grandfather had died, she took all the bedding from the mattress and stripped the pillows of their linens. The pillow on which the old preacher had rested his head felt oddly cold to the touch. Slicing the ticking open, she'd discovered a wreath of feathers buried within the stuffing, large enough to fit on a man's head. She'd cradled the thing to her breast and called it a glorious sign—a feather crown made by the angels to show her that Deodat had made his way to Heaven. His father, thinking it evil, had thrown the crown into the fire. "It's a sign of dark magic," he'd said. "Proof that the witches who've plagued this family cursed him to die."

The one thing that Francis had gained from his grandfather that no one could cast aside was his fervent desire to banish evil. Yes, he knew that it was only by God's will that evil existed, but he also knew that the reason it was there was so that men of God could expose and destroy it. Only by such shining examples could the most rebellious naysayers be brought into the fold. Sometimes his intolerance for sin was so great, he became overwhelmed with a longing for stocks and thumbscrews, pressings and hangings. Choking on his impulses, he'd cried to Heaven with clenched fists, "Dear Lord, what would you have me do when the world allows so little punishment for sin?"

He was glad of the faith of his new congregation and the way they clung to his every word, but no amount of Temperance meetings or weekly Bible study could stop the storm of iniquity that was brewing outside the chapel doors. What would his grandfather think of the times in which he lived? Of this city, so rampant with sin? Surely he would say that it was filled with opportunities for righteous men to carry out the work of the Lord. Francis prayed every night for the chance to stand up to be led to the dwelling places of evil so he might cast it out.

Mr. Beadle's housemaid Lena McLeod had been one answer to that prayer. So had the little Gyspy girl he'd met in the park. The waif had been more a challenge to him than the maid, sent to him as a test. He'd been fooled into thinking that because she was a child there was still goodness inside her, but it hadn't taken him long to discover that was not the case. When he'd asked her to recite the first Bible verse that came to her mind, she'd spat at him and spoken a string of foul words instead. She'd acted sweet then insolent, repentant then wicked. When none of that had succeeded in breaking the Reverend's resolve, she'd pressed herself against him and tried to seduce him. She turned out to be a devil in a child's dress. Perhaps she'd been sent to torment him by Mr. Beadle's maid or some other deceased witch. His father had always warned that a witch's curse couldn't be undone just by killing the witch who spoke it. "Their words stay alive long after the fact. Sometimes gaining more power after death," he'd instructed his son. The Gypsy girl had come at him, eyes filled with fire, cursing and taking the Lord's name in vain. He'd struck her with the back of his hand and she'd fallen in a heap on the floor. Her scalp had blossomed red with blood as her eyes rolled back in her head.

Remembering the words of the two men in black suits who'd come to his door after Mr. Beadle's maid had died, he'd retreated to his bedchamber and prayed until dawn, hoping that they might return and do as they had done before. At first light he'd gone down to the cellar to discover that the little girl was gone, no trace of her to be found. Falling on his knees he'd said a prayer of thanksgiving, praising God for releasing him from the foul little devil. The Lord does indeed work in mysterious ways.

Checking his watch again, Reverend Townsend saw that it was nearly nine. Although he was tempted to leave the parsonage in search of greater challenges, he knew he should get on with composing his sermon. Walking to the bookcase, he pulled out his grandfather's Bible and read the inscription: *Let this book be the Light that guides you through the Storm.* In recent weeks, when he'd been at a loss for inspiration, he'd taken to the practice of Bible dipping to assist him in his work. Last Saturday, after letting the Bible fall open on its own, his finger had landed on 1 Timothy 2:12: *But I suffer not a woman to teach, nor to usurp authority over the man, but to be in silence.* The words had then flown from his pen to the page as if guided by providence of angels. He'd titled the sermon, "Against Intuition."

Women often say they have a "knowing," a "feeling," that something is right or wrong. They'll claim they've seen the answer to a great dilemma in a dream. Who are they to claim the gift of prophecy? What force compels them to speak such lies? More often than not their words are merely a ploy to get others to do their bidding. When caught, they say it was nothing but a silly, foolish game. They insist no one got hurt. But this sort of deceit is no laughing matter. It is a terrible crafty tool of women, especially when used upon trusting men—a tool of Satan himself. I say to all gentlemen, do not be fooled by women's talk of intuition. I say to all women, do not be used by Devils as a mouthpiece for Satan's foul words. The only special knowledge he'll afford to you is misery. The only thing you'll gain is regret.

Taking the Bible in hand, Francis set it on its spine. Closing his eyes, he prayed for the Lord to lend divine assistance. "Not my will, Lord, but Thine." As the book fell open and he placed his finger on the page, he discovered something he was sure he'd never seen before. Sticking up between the Bible's pages was a small unbound leaflet, written in a stranger's hand.

"An Attempt to Cure Witchcraft"

For, though it be Folly to impute every dubious Accident or unwanted Effect of Providence to Witchcraft, yet there are some things which cannot be ascribed otherwise. That the following Account will afford to him that shall read with Observation, a further clear confirmation, that, there is both a God and a Devil and Witchcraft.

Early in the year 1693, Reverend M. travelled from Boston to Salem. He had it in his mind that he might deliver a sermon to the good people there and also gather an accurate accounting of what had taken place during The Great Storm of Witchcraft. Upon his arrival he'd found that in the months since the witchcraft tryals, things had gone considerably quiet, especially when it came to Apparitions and Accusations. By and large, people spoke as if the thing had never happened, or at least as if they had no real knowledge of it. When pressed, no one could even point to the exact location of the hangings on Gallows Hill. "You must ask so-and-so," one man would say. "I know nothing," another would profess. "Perhaps Mr. D— can be of help, he has the longest memory of anyone in the Neighbourhood." These cries of ignorance went on and on from farm to farm and house to house, but Reverend M. would not be dissuaded. He was determined to stir the pot as it were, knowing that the Devil could not so easily be put to rest.

During his visit, two odd things occurred to further convince him that witchcraft in this Country was alive and well.

One: The leafs his sermon had been written upon were lost and the only explanation he could find was that they'd been stolen away by spectres. (This was later confirmed by yet another strange occurrence.) "These notes were before the Sabbath stolen from me, with such Circumstances that I am somewhat satisfied, the Spectres or Agents in the Invisible World were the Robbers."

Two: He held discourse with a Mrs. Carver (assumed to be an honest, God-fearing woman), who had been strangely visited with some shining Spirits, which were good Angels, in her opinion of them. "She intimated several things unto me, whereof some were to be kept secret. She also told me that a New Storm of Witchcraft would fall upon the Country, to chastise the Iniquity that was used in the willful Smothering and Covering of the Last; and that many fierce Opposites to the Discovery of that Witchcraft would be thereby convinced."

Not long after the good Reverend returned to Boston, he was called to minister to a young servant girl named Mercy Wylde who had fallen into fits one Sunday after church. Seeing that the girl (just seventeen years of age) was clearly afflicted in the manner of the Damsels of Salem, the Reverend determined that he should retire with her to a nearby house to assess her condition.

In the course of his examinations he began to suspect that the girl had been bewitched. Some time before, at the height of The Great Storm, Mercy Wylde, on her way home from market, had come across one Sarah Gowan who was chained to the wall of the prison. Sister Gowan, since hanged at Salem for witchcraft, called to the girl and begged for tobacco. Fearful of the woman, Mercy had refused and thrown sawdust in her face. The woman, revealing her true nature, cursed the girl to suffer for her unkindness.

In Reverend M.'s words: "I had many Entertainments from the Invisible World in the Circumstances of a Young Woman horribly possessed with Devils. The Damsel was cast into my cares by the singular Providence of God; and accordingly I kept Three Successive Dayes of Prayer with Fasting on her behalf, and then I saw her

Delivered. (For which I kept a Time of solemn Thanksgiving.) But after a while, her Tormentors returned, and her Miseries renewed; and I did alone in my Study fast and pray for her Deliverance. And unto my Amazement, when I had kept my third Day for her, she was finally and forever delivered from the hand of evil Angels; and I had afterwards the satisfaction of seeing not only her so brought home unto the Lord that she was admitted unto our Church, but also many others, even some scores of young people, awakened by the Picture of Hell exhibited in her sufferings, to flee from the Wrath to come."

The following is an account of the trials and tribulations of Mercy Wylde.

Reverend Townsend was taken away from the page by the insistent ringing of a bell. Sister Piddock had arrived to collect the Sunday sermon.

October 8, 1880.

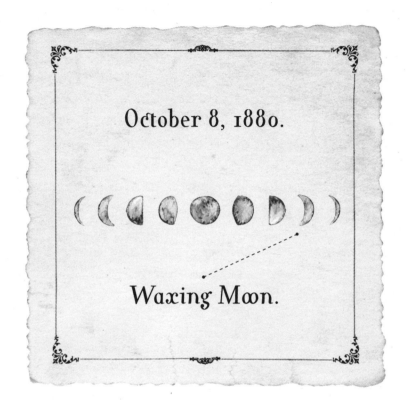

Waxing Moon.

FREEMASONS TO ASSEMBLE

Tomorrow, October 9th, at approximately three o'clock, a grand parade will take place along Fifth Avenue from Madison Square to Central Park. Some nine thousand Freemasons from within the city and without will assemble to march through the streets to Greywacke Knoll. This momentous gathering is to mark the dedication ceremony for the pedestal on which the Great Obelisk will one day sit.

Although the obelisk has only recently made landfall, the marble pedestal on which it once stood was transported through the city to Central Park in early August. While its journey was far simpler than the Needle's, it was still quite a feat to move it, requiring thirty-two horses in sixteen pairs to pull it to its destination. Since that time, the pedestal has been waiting for preparations at Greywacke Knoll to be completed, so it might be set in place and properly dedicated prior to the obelisk's arrival.

October 8, 1880

Dear Aunt Lydia,

What would you say if I told you I've been visited by ghosts? Regularly and often! I would've mentioned it sooner, but I wanted to be certain that I wasn't suffering from a passing illness that'd put me temporarily out of my head. Lest you think me mad, and I wouldn't blame you if you did, I can assure you that what I've been experiencing is quite real and true. The spirits talk to me and I with them just as naturally as I used to do with you while sitting at the dining room table.

As you might imagine, this has stirred up a fair bit of excitement at the teashop. Happily, Miss Thom and Miss St. Clair are inclined to be understanding of such things, due to their ongoing interest in the unseen world.

I hesitate to describe how it all works because to do so would surely take several more pages, and even then I'm not sure I could do it justice. Suffice to say it's all happened rather suddenly. Perhaps one day soon you'll come for a visit so I can demonstrate my new abilities for you in person.

Your loving niece,
Beatrice

An Unsent Letter.

BEATRICE FOLDED THE NOTE, tucked it inside an envelope, then threw it into the fire. She'd write a less revealing, more reassuring missive to replace it, later, one that still extended an invitation for Lydia to visit. One that included the parade but not the ghosts.

Settling herself on the floor of her room in front of a small parlour stove, she propped the stove's door open to gaze at the fire's dancing flames. She'd recently learned the practice of scrying from Eleanor, and found it to be a fitting way to end the day. It helped her push unimportant thoughts aside and focus her mind.

"Hold a question in your thoughts and let your sight go slack," Eleanor had instructed. "Watch carefully. Be patient. Eventually a vision will appear within the flames. Give whatever comes to your attention measured thought and consideration. Scrying allows us to see with sight beyond our own."

"How will I know when I've seen what I'm meant to see?" Beatrice had asked. "Surely there must be some sign of assurance that comes along with the visions? Gooseflesh, flushed cheeks, a whisper of affirmation?"

Shaking her head, Eleanor had replied, "That's something you'll have to discover for yourself."

Although Eleanor had described several ways to scry—staring into a bowl of water, gazing upon a darkened mirror, keeping watch on the night sky—Beatrice found she preferred the fire. She'd always appreciated the warmth and comfort a fire could provide, always felt a certain reverence for its potential for destruction. The idea that flames could also hold insights meant only for her was tremendously appealing.

Since the night of her demonstration at the hotel she'd felt the urgent need to learn all she could about the art of witchcraft, as quickly as she could. Everyone who'd been in the salon that evening, including Adelaide and Eleanor, had been concerned that what'd transpired with the scrubber girls' spirits had taken a terrible toll on her. Instead, it had firmed her resolve to embrace her destiny wherever it might lead.

As she watched the fire consume what was left of the letter, she thought of how she'd felt while under the influence of the maids' spirits. Even when the ghosts of the scrubber girls had been speaking through her, she'd never felt frightened or consumed by their presence. Her soul hadn't been possessed, as everyone had feared, but rather she had felt as if she was acting on the girls' behalf. Given the depth of their sorrow and anger, allowing them to speak through her had seemed the best way for her to properly convey their message. Not that she'd thought through any of that in the moment, but she'd always been fully aware of what was taking place and she'd been willing (even glad) to be the ghosts' vehicle.

Predictably, Adelaide and Eleanor had landed on opposite sides of the fence when it came to advising her on what to do next. Eleanor wished to err on the side of caution. "I'm fearful of what might happen if you move too soon, too fast. Don't be afraid to take your time with things. There's no need to rush." Adelaide had been absolutely giddy over the prospect of her undertaking regular communications with spirit. "Perhaps you could hold consultations here at the shop. Enlist one or more of your ghostly companions to look into situations on 'the other side' on behalf of the living."

"That's not how it works," Eleanor had protested.

Though encouraged by Adelaide's enthusiasm, Beatrice had sided with Eleanor on that point. She couldn't just call forth spirits with a snap of her fingers or get them to do her bidding as if they were ponies in a circus. Spirits, of all sorts, shapes and stripes, were everywhere, all the time (unless otherwise banished from a place), and prone to make themselves known to her however and whenever they liked. Eleanor had done an excellent job of keeping them out of the teashop, but whenever Beatrice set foot outside the door, she was confronted with a deluge of the dearly departed. It was confusing and alarming each time it happened, and she'd soon gone to Eleanor for more advice. "Is there anything that can be done to make them less . . . eager?"

"Don't feel you have to talk to each and every one that vies for your attention, or you'll surely go mad," Eleanor had said. "They're fully aware that your gifts are taking hold. They see them in you as clearly as I see the freckles on your nose. You must foster the power to open and close yourself to their supplications as you see fit."

"How do I do that?"

"Through strong will and practice. It's not dissimilar to throwing off unwanted advances from a gentleman. Be confident as you make your way through the world. Hold your head high. Don't be afraid to cast an uninterested eye on those you wish to repel, be they living or dead. Wave them off, speak your peace, shout if you must. Be direct. There's no need to be polite. Even then, some may pester and persist. In such cases, you'll need to resort to more extreme measures."

"Like what?" Beatrice had asked, intrigued, but also frightened.

"There are incantations, charms and spells in the grimoire. Look them up. Learn them well. There are even a few potions for pests of flesh and blood, but remember, no matter what magic you choose to practice, the most effective way to deter any being from your presence, ghostly or otherwise, is to let them know who you are."

"What do they care?" Beatrice had asked, puzzled by the notion. "Who am I to them?"

At that point, Adelaide had sauntered over from her table in the back of the shop. "You are Beatrice Dunn," she'd said. "You're a witch. You're not to be trifled with." At least she and Eleanor had seen eye to eye on that.

She was glad for their advice, especially since tomorrow she'd be retuning to the hotel to assist Dr. Brody with his evening lecture for the Unknown Philosophers' Symposium, "Communication with the Afterlife: a Scientific Approach." The plan was for Dr. Brody to inform the audience of his research and for her to demonstrate the spiritoscope (hopefully with the scrubber girls' cooperation). The latter seemed quite possible now that the maids had become more docile and predictable in their communications.

The change in them had come about after Mrs. Stevens had hired a stone carver to go to the cemetery and make things right on Mary Donnelly's tombstone. "Thank heavens," Mrs. Stevens had exclaimed upon hearing news of the ghosts' new-found spirit of cooperation. "And thank heavens for men who think more of my money than of archaic rules about who should be buried where."

To show their appreciation, the Marys had ushered Mr. Paran Stevens' ghost into the salon to deliver a message to his wife.

T-H-E-R-E I-S N-O O-N-E S-O D-E-A-R A-S M-Y D-A-R-L-I-N-G M-A-R-I-E-T-T-A.

The spiritoscope had stayed put there since Beatrice's first encounter with the maids. Adelaide had escorted her each day to the hotel to meet with Dr. Brody, the trio working diligently to document Beatrice's connection with spirit. Several tests had been conducted, with the spiritoscope and without, and the results of their efforts had been quite encouraging.

Impressed with their efforts (and her husband's recent communication), Mrs. Stevens had insisted on providing them with whatever they needed to further the work. She sent delicious meals from the kitchens: roast chicken with pearl onions in cream sauce, leg of lamb with honeyed carrots and mint jelly. A porter was placed on call to cater to their every request; and, after Marietta had conducted a lengthy consultation with Adelaide, a gorgeous gown was brought to the room for Beatrice to try on. The latter had come shortly after Adelaide had suggested to Beatrice that she might wish to perform under an alias, at least for this particular engagement. "Something to pique the audience's interest. Something exotic and alluring." Although Beatrice hadn't cared much about being seen as exotic or alluring, she'd thought the idea practical, as it would preserve her true identity and eliminate the chance that word of her performance would get back to Stony Point. In the end they'd settled on the Egyptian Sibyl, in honour of her brief encounter with the Great Obelisk.

The gown was a beautiful creation made of layer upon layer of black crepe de chine, decorated top to bottom with gold embroidery depicting various Egyptian figures and glyphs. It came with a matching headdress bearing sphinx-like sidepieces striped in black and gold. The costume had once been worn by Mrs. Stevens' daughter, Minnie, who'd attended the Delmonico fancy dress ball of 1875 as Cleopatra. "Are you sure she won't mind?" Beatrice had asked, worried something awful might happen to the dress while she was wearing it. "Heavens no," Marietta had answered. "Now that she's become Lady Paget and moved to Belgrave Square, her ball gowns all come from Paris, encrusted with gems and jewels."

Detecting a hint of sadness in Mrs. Stevens' voice, Beatrice had gratefully accepted the woman's kind offer, but insisted the dress stay at the hotel for safekeeping until the night of the symposium.

Under Adelaide's direction, the evening was shaping up to be more spectacle than demonstration. She'd been especially excited when she'd discovered that the symposium was to fall on the same date as the Masons' parade, figuring it might well boost the size of their audience. "If all goes well," she'd enthused, "who knows what might come next?"

That was the question on Beatrice's mind as she watched the fire spark and crack. Like the stray bursts of flame that occasionally sprang forth from the dying embers, odd surges of magic had been occurring now and again in her daily life. Along with her encounters with spirits, other strange things had happened, some of her own making, some completely unexpected. She'd managed to execute a number of simple spells from Eleanor's grimoire—making a candle's flame increase or diminish with her mind, calling creatures to her side as she sat on a bench in the park (birds, bees, the odd squirrel, a stray dog), willing Perdu to say specific words without her speaking them aloud—but she'd also woken up in the middle of the night speaking a second language as if it were her mother tongue. It was unlike anything she'd ever heard, and although the meanings hadn't stuck in her mind, she couldn't shake the feeling that one day, with a bit of patience, they would.

She'd written a few of the words on scraps of paper, spelling them as they had sounded. Then she'd pinned them to the wall alongside several newspaper clippings she'd collected since she'd arrived in the city. Like her room in Stony Point, the walls of her garret had quickly become papered with strange and curious ephemera.

Haunted by Dead Wife: Husband Dies of Shock after the Ghost's Visits. A House to Let.

Faith in Ghosts: Mrs. Stymus Sues Mr. Howell for the Rent of her Haunted House.

Is it a Resort for Ghosts? Some Things That Have Excited the Residents of a Staten Island Village.

Woman Accuses Neighbour of Witchcraft.

The Brooklyn Ghost—The Proprietor of the Ghostelrey Determines That it is Old Nick.

Mrs. Lahey's Dreams of a Stranger's Death. Her Premonitions Are Proved True.

A Considerate Ghost Throws Stones About a House for a Year but Injures No One.

Children Witness Their Delancey Street Teacher Face her Doppelgänger at School.

Sorting through the stories day after day, she'd begun to wonder if she should do more than just collect them, but investigate their meaning. Perhaps one day she'd make a *Census of Astonishments*, much like Mr. Pratchett's *Compendium of Miracles.*

Gazing into the fire, she held that thought in her mind, not as a question but as a desire. Such things would have to wait, though. She'd have to get through tomorrow first. She could hardly believe the symposium was only one sleep away. Eyes heavy, she watched the fire's flames undulate amongst the hot embers in waves of blue, orange and gold. Perhaps she was too tired for her scrying to prove fruitful tonight.

Just as she was about to shut the door on the stove, the coals shifted and hissed. From between them, a glowing face looked out, more beast than man. It wore a twisted smirk, its lips ragged at the edges.

"Who are you?" Beatrice asked in a frightened whisper.

Staring at her, the beast refused to answer.

"Be gone!" she ordered, thrusting an iron poker into the stove to stir the coals.

With a burst of sparks the fire surged, and the face disappeared.

God is therefore pleased to suffer Devils sometimes to do such things in the World as shall test the mettle of His followers. Evil is therefore placed in the paths of the faithful so that we might overcome it. It is to His glory that these Devils be cast out by the hands of the righteous.

—from *An Attempt to Cure Witchcraft: The Story of Mercy Wylde*

The Devils Also Believe and Tremble.

THREE PROSTITUTES IN frilly skirts stood under a street lamp near Madison Square Park. Teasing each other and every man who walked by, the trio traded puffs on a cigarillo and passed a half-empty bottle of schnapps hand to hand to hand. Their reedy laughter bounced off the brick buildings behind them while the tacky remains of stale beer stuck to the sidewalk beneath their boots.

A few feet away, a gang of guttersnipes occupied themselves with tossing dice against the curb.

"Double sixes!" one boy exclaimed, bull's eye lantern dangling from his grimy hand.

"Again?" another boy groused.

"Them dice is for sure loaded," a third complained.

The youngest whore, Jenny Greene, rubbed the rabbit's foot that was hanging around her neck, then stuck her hand in her pocket and counted the coins sunk deep within it. Ten quarters, six dimes and an assortment of nickels and pennies. It'd been a good night so far, but ooh-boy that bottle of schnapps was almost empty and she sure could use more booze.

"Hey there, sweetie-pie," she called to one of the boys, "if you fetch me a growler, I'll let you keep the change." Even if he made off with what she gave him, or drank down half the bottle before handing it over, she still wouldn't have lost as much as she stood to lose by missing out on the next john if she went for the booze herself. She was next in the pecking order. It was her turn to score. She considered herself quite smart when it came to the arithmetic of want.

"Shut your trap, you dirty slut," the boy hollered as his gang mates showered him with elbow jabs and guffaws.

"Stubby-fingered little pecker," Jenny grumbled, flicking a stone to the street with the toe of her boot. Once upon a time, any beast with a cock between its legs—man, boy, dog, horse—would prance at her slightest look. With a haughty shrug and a fuck-you chin, she withdrew her offer. These boys were uppity. The boys downtown might be rougher around the edges, but at least they understood the value of tit for tat.

Jenny usually spent her evenings trolling for johns by the docks on the East River, but she'd heard from a reliable source that the saloons surrounding the square would be crawling with out-of-town gentlemen who were there to march in a big parade in honour of a new monument or statue or some such nonsense. So many things got "erected" these days—bronze giants with wreaths on their heads, tall steeples on stone churches, towering buildings with flags flying at attention on sturdy poles. How could she be expected to keep track of it all? She didn't give a hang why the men were coming, only that their pockets would be jangling with silver and their heads muddled with drink. Tying her lucky rabbit's foot around her neck, she'd convened a meeting with the two other girls who boarded in the house where she lived to see if they might be interested in trying their luck at the park.

"Who's up for cruising Madison Square?" she'd asked. "I heard tell the place will be crawling with johns."

"I'm in," Elsie Trew had replied while cleaning her teeth with an orange stick.

"Me too," Mae Blum had chimed in, pinning her hat atop her head.

When Jenny had first met them, she'd thought the two were sisters. In low light, they could easily be mistaken for twins. "We get that a lot," they'd confessed. "And we don't mind it a bit. It has its advantages in certain situations." They weren't exactly fast friends of Jenny's, but more friendly competitors who were willing to loan her a couple of dollars when she was short on rent. In fact, she was currently in debt to Elsie, and she hoped that by inviting her along for the evening some of what she owed might be forgiven. She'd grown tired of the way the girl stared at her during suppers at the boarding house, as if every morsel she put in her mouth had been stolen off someone else's plate. She'd also figured if there were as many men around the park as she'd been told there'd be, she wouldn't be out anything by having them come along. (She certainly couldn't service them all, now could she?) Besides, there was safety in numbers. It'd be a mighty long trek back to the boarding house if she had to walk alone.

Swigging the last of the schnapps from the bottle, Jenny spotted a gentleman walking towards them. Sizing him up, she announced to her companions, "He's mine."

"I say we let the gent choose for himself," Mae announced.

"I thought we agreed to take turns."

Elsie shook her head. "And I thought you were good for your rent money, but seeing as how it's getting late and you still haven't made right on your debt, I'd say he's fair game."

Jenny didn't want to bicker. She guessed if the man heard them arguing, he'd just as soon move along. He was only a few blocks from the Tenderloin where he could get anything he wanted. She had to seem easy, right and ready, if she wanted him to bite.

Squinting in the man's direction Mae sneered, "He looks like a preacher."

"How can you tell?" Jenny asked.

"The wide-brimmed hat, the long frock coat, the cross hanging around his neck, the arrogant, uptight gait."

Elsie gave an indifferent shrug. "You can have him, then."

Mae smiled and teased: "I'd like to see her try."

Spurred by the dare, Jenny pulled up the hem of her skirts to reveal a good portion of her leg as the man drew near. "A quarter for a suck, two for a fuck," she teased. Why should she be coy? Preachers had cocks too.

The man stopped in front of her.

Sidling closer, Jenny flashed a flirtatious smile, working hard to turn his disdain to desire. She'd fried much bigger fish when she was still a child. Back then, she'd had a place in a house that specialized in providing "fresh maids" for its clients, and her favourite caller had been a young priest named Father Whitby. He'd especially liked it when she'd fluttered her lashes and said, "Forgive me Father, for I have sinned." She'd especially liked it when he'd called her his angel and referred to her quim as his "holy vessel." Those were the days!

Too bad the woman who ran the place had decided it was time for her to move on. She missed the wine that'd flowed freely there and the feather bed where she'd slept each night. Perhaps if this gent was truly a man of God he'd pity her enough to take her home with him. Perhaps he had a feather bed just waiting for her to slink between its covers. Rubbing her shoulder against his she whispered, "It won't take long. You'll be glad for it, I promise."

With a nod he grabbed Jenny by the arm and led her down the street. The large silver cross fastened at his collar glinted in the lamplight.

"You like it rough?" Jenny asked. She wasn't averse to a spanking now and then, but he'd have to pay extra if he wanted it like that. "I'll let you leave a mark for a dollar, so long as it's below the neck." For two, he could have someone else watch, so long as they didn't touch her. For three they could both have a turn. For five, she'd take it in the ass, but she made a point of never offering that up front. The man had to ask. She'd once been told by a very wise whore (who also happened to be her mother), *everything has a price.*

Looking over his shoulder, the man pushed Jenny into a dark alley. Tossing a silver dollar to the grimy cobblestones he said, "Pick it up."

She did as she was told, then shoved the coin between her breasts. Back turned, she stroked her rabbit's foot three times for luck.

Arms folded, the man stared at her, waiting.

Spotting a low stack of wooden crates, Jenny bent over them, bracing herself with one hand while pulling her skirts up with the other. In her experience, men who didn't talk much didn't have a sense of humour, didn't want the trouble of kissing, didn't wish to see her face when they fucked. That was fine by her—she'd already gotten paid.

As she waited for the sudden thrust of his cock, she could hear his ragged, excited breathing behind her. Suddenly, she felt his hand take hold of the hair at the back of her neck. Before she could sense anything was wrong or let out a scream, a blade slashed across her throat. Falling to the ground, she reached for the hem of his coat. With the shudder of her last breath she heard him say, "Depart from me, ye cursed, into everlasting fire, prepared for the Devil and his angels."

Watching the life fade from the whore's face Reverend Townsend thought he might weep for joy.

He'd gone to the park to get some fresh air and to search for whatever foul presences might be lurking about. He'd prayed to the Lord that he might be allowed to see things more clearly, be shown the working of devils, bold and unabashed, and it seemed his prayers had been heard and answered. Sinners, devils, witches walked the crowded streets everywhere he went.

He'd been tempted (ever so briefly) by the whore's pale skin and rouged lips, but after he'd kissed his cross and recited a psalm, he'd seen her for what she was, eyes flashing with brimstone, lips wet and thirsting for blood, cloven hooves peeking out from under her skirts. What else could he have done but put the malignant wretch to rest?

God was testing him. Waiting for him to prove his worth. One day soon he, too, might be tasked to save a soul in the form of his own Mercy Wylde.

October 9, 1880.

Waxing Moon.

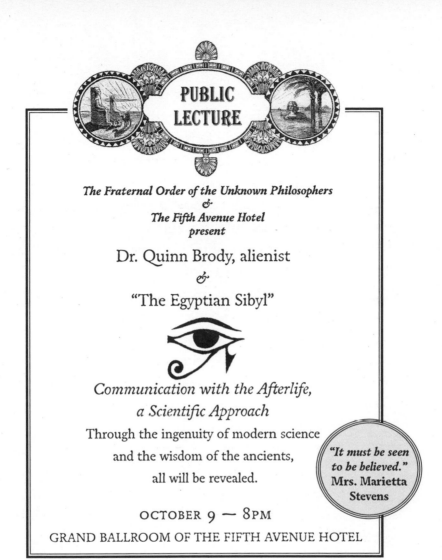

The Fraternal Order of the Unknown Philosophers
&
The Fifth Avenue Hotel
present

Dr. Quinn Brody, alienist

&

"The Egyptian Sibyl"

Communication with the Afterlife,
a Scientific Approach

Through the ingenuity of modern science
and the wisdom of the ancients,
all will be revealed.

"It must be seen
to be believed."
Mrs. Marietta
Stevens

OCTOBER 9 — 8PM

GRAND BALLROOM OF THE FIFTH AVENUE HOTEL

The Final Fitting.

BEATRICE WAS STANDING, dressed in Minnie Stevens'
ball gown, on a low wooden stool in the middle of Judith
Dashley's suite. She held her body still and straight while
a nimble-fingered seamstress circled her, pins stuck in a

cushion strapped to her wrist, a half-dozen more pinched between her lips. Although Beatrice appreciated the woman's efforts, she wished she'd finish the job so she could be free to go downstairs to the hotel lobby and take in the lectures and displays on offer at the symposium.

Earlier that morning, Alden Dashley had delivered a stack of programmes to the teashop and it hadn't taken Beatrice long to find several things that piqued her interest. Pencil in hand, she'd starred the items that most appealed to her—a lecture titled "Women as Inventors"; a presentation by a group called the Followers of the Obelisk; and a travelling bookseller touting an outstanding selection of antiquarian tomes dealing with the occult. Eleanor had chosen to stay behind and mind the shop. Adelaide was taking care of any and all last-minute preparations for their evening presentation. Beatrice had agreed to meet her at the base of Lady Liberty's torch at three o'clock so they could distribute notices for the lecture to interested bystanders who were waiting for the Masons' grand parade. Until then, she was free to do as she pleased, so long as Judith approved of the dress's fit.

As the seamstress put the final touches on the dress's embroidered sleeves, Beatrice kept her eye on the curtains on the other side of the room. The damask panels were moving to and fro, much as they would if a cat were weaving in and out between them. The only trouble was, the Dashleys didn't own a cat.

Judith, noticing Beatrice's distracted state, asked, "Is that my Billy? Is he here?"

Trying her best to keep still, Beatrice whispered yes.

The seamstress let out an impatient cough.

"I knew I sensed him," Judith said. "Ever since that day with you in the teashop I've become increasingly attuned to his presence. I can feel him come and go—sometimes he gives a little tug on my skirt, or rolls a pen out of Alden's reach. I don't know why I never noticed it before. Do you think it might be due to my keeping company with you? Is it possible I've been touched by magic? Sympathetically, of course."

Beatrice just smiled and held her breath as the seamstress slid several pins through a length of lace at the nape of her neck.

Judith's mouth turned down. "You don't suppose *they're* here, too, do you?"

"Who?" Beatrice asked as soon as the seamstress moved on to the dress's hem.

"The scrubber girls." Judith gave a shudder.

The seamstress winced as she pricked her thumb with a pin. Saying a silent prayer she sucked the blood from its fleshy tip. *God protect me from the things I cannot see.* She'd heard tales from the night porter of the unhappy spirits that haunted the hotel corridors.

Shaking her head, Beatrice replied, "They're not here, at least not in your suite. Nor do I think they ever will be. They're much happier now that they're at ease with their fate."

"Thank you for entertaining such questions," Judith said, flushing. "I don't mean to impose on you."

"It's the least I can do," Beatrice said. "You and Alden have been incredibly kind."

Holding out her hand, the seamstress motioned for Beatrice to step down from the stool. "All finished," she announced as she waited for Judith's approval.

Eyes gleaming, Judith clapped her hands. "It's simply ravishing!"

Sewing basket in hand, the seamstress took a bow, then took her leave.

Judith rushed to fetch a small box that was sitting on a nearby table. "While I have you here," she said, "I'd like to present you with a little gift."

"Oh, Mrs. Dashley," Beatrice protested, "you shouldn't do such things."

"It's just a trifle," Judith said. "A small thank-you from me and Alden and the rest of the Philosophers."

Beatrice took the box from her and gently opened its lid. Nestled in a bed of green silk was a little doll with a card that read: "Miss Fortuna." The plaything had dark curls under a pointed velvet hat and was dressed in a long red gown with moons, owls, bats and snakes embroidered on the skirt, like the Gypsy fortune tellers in children's books and European romances. She held a crystal ball in one hand and a tambourine in the other. Her legs were stiff and affixed to the base of a wooden top. Under her skirt, Miss Fortuna held a secret, or more precisely hundreds of them—page upon page of coloured paper shaped, stitched, folded and inscribed to form a never-ending book of tiny prophecies.

"You spin her around to find your fortune," Judith had said, demonstrating how the toy worked. "Wherever the pages fall open is where your luck lies. The fortunes are written inside."

Giving the doll a playful turn, Beatrice tried it for herself.

Pages fluttering, the toy spun around several times then wobbled to a stop.

Hand to her heart, Beatrice read her fortune.

Courage always. Without it there is no hope.

Dr. Brody sat in the hotel reading room, cup of coffee in hand, programme for the symposium laid out before him on the table. He was glad to have a few moments to himself. He enjoyed eavesdropping on the hum of ideas, boasts and complaints that got bandied about the place. Brody found comfort in the predictable din (so long as he wasn't required to participate in it).

"Hello there, St. Nick," a familiar voice sounded, accompanied by the clap of a hand on his shoulder.

"Andersen," Brody replied, turning to greet his old acquaintance. The burly army hero didn't look half so well as he had the last time they'd met. His skin was pale, his eyes dark, his suit rumpled and smelling stale. "How have you been?" Brody asked, wondering if the poor fellow might be suffering from a lingering illness, or was simply down on his luck.

Andersen pulled up a chair. Wiping sweat from his brow, he tugged at his tie to loosen it. "Never better," he said with a tired smile. Leaning close he added, "I'm glad I've run into you. I'm in need of your professional opinion."

Brody shook his head. "If it's medical advice you're after, you might be better served by a full-time practitioner. My work these days centres more on the mind and less on physical ailments."

"And that's exactly why you're the right man for the job," Andersen insisted. "I need a doc who's well-versed in the business of examining brains."

"Yours?" Brody asked, thinking the stress of the war might've finally proved too much after all these years.

"No," Andersen replied. "There's a girl I've come to fancy out on Blackwell's Island."

"At the asylum?" Brody asked.

"She's one in a million," Andersen boasted. "A diamond in the rough. As lovely and witty as any woman I've ever known. And far saner compared to most. For the life of me I can't figure why she's not been let out."

"There must be some reason she's there," Brody said, hoping to bring Andersen to his senses. Still he knew all too well that it was possible (and regrettably easy) for a perfectly sane woman to get put away against her will.

With a laugh Andersen said, "Would you believe she got locked up for witchcraft? Some scuttlebutt about practicing it . . . or was it believing in it? Either way it's a bunch of nonsense."

"I see," Brody said, torn between wanting to learn more and wishing he hadn't asked.

"Come out with me tonight and meet her for yourself," Andersen suggested. "No doubt you'll come to the same conclusion as I have, that it was all a big mistake."

"I'm afraid I can't," Brody replied. "I have another engagement."

"Right," Andersen said, looking dejected. "Maybe another time, then? Perhaps you could talk some sense into the staff there. Put in a good word as to the strength of my character. The opinion of a doctor such as yourself, a respectable society gent, could go a long way towards springing my girl from that hellhole."

Brody knew the asylum, like many public madhouses, was overcrowded and poorly maintained. He also knew that if someone of note had been the one to send the girl there, the chances of her getting out were slim. Without studying the woman's case at length, he wasn't sure he could make an informed plea. But clearly Andersen was desperate. "I'll consider it," he said at last.

"Thank you," Andersen said. "Do you think you could make it sometime soon? Else I might just have to break her out by other means."

Brody could see he wasn't joking. The spell the girl had cast on him was strong and fast. "We'll talk soon," he said, excusing himself from the table. "Be well, Andersen."

"Take care, St. Nick."

Brody found a quiet corner and read over his notes for the evening lecture. It was still hours before he and Beatrice would take the stage, but he wanted to be sure his thoughts were in order. He'd left the minor details of the evening's presentation to Adelaide. Her eagerness to engage in spectacle went far beyond his practical nature, but he could see that it was all in an effort to show how much she respected his work. She had faith in his methods (and, dare he think it, in him), which was something he'd never felt before from a woman. As much as he'd loved his wife, she'd never shown any interest in his profession. He'd been a medical student, on his way to becoming a surgeon, and she'd forbidden him to mention anything related to medicine in her presence. He'd respected her squeamishness, but that didn't mean he hadn't felt let down by her lack of interest. Adelaide, despite her bold, impulsive nature, was a welcome companion and a true equal. If the night turned out to be a success, he planned to express exactly those sentiments to her, put his cards on the table, as it were.

He also planned to suggest they resume their research in his study rather than carry on at the hotel. He hoped to coax his father's ghost into a longer conversation so he might ask him a few pressing questions.

What are your surroundings like on the other side?

What of time? Is it measured? If so, how do you keep track of it?

What of the senses that your body used in life? Do you see, hear, smell, touch?

What is your relationship to the physical world? Why do some spirits move objects, while others do not?

How do you travel from one place to another? Is distance of no consequence?

What, if anything, is beyond where you are now?

He thought if he could gain the answers he sought, he might publish them in a short book. It would, no doubt, be a risky endeavour, but wasn't that the sort of risk that every scientist had to be willing to take? To profess truth despite the looming spectre of ridicule.

And there was another subject he'd like to explore in the privacy of his study. Hearing Andersen speak of his girl and her plight, he'd remembered the card Adelaide had given him the day they'd met. "Miss Adelaide Thom. Mind Reader. Seeress. Witch." She'd mentioned the word a few times since, seemingly in jest, and once, he'd heard Beatrice speak it with shy seriousness. *Witchcraft.* Could their abilities be attributed to some greater mystical force or were they just bandying the word about for effect? Incredible as it seemed, it would explain much of what he'd witnessed while in their presence. There'd been talk of witchcraft at the Salpêtrière—some inmates claiming they were born into it, others threatening to use it to curse the place—but Charcot had dismissed it, saying their claims of sorcery were merely archaic explanations for hysteria. He had been incredibly dismissive, and the procedures he'd used to prove his theories, to document and cure hysteria, had been damaging and dangerous—no better than the trials put to women during the witch hunts of old. The women were treated as if they were criminals and kept like animals in cages. Spirits broken, they'd spent their days crying for mercy and freedom.

If Adelaide, Beatrice and Eleanor (who he suspected was of the same magical persuasion) wished to confess their practices to him, he would surely listen. If they were good enough to allow him into their world, he'd do whatever he could to protect them.

Much like Dr. Brody, Eleanor had decided not to interfere with Adelaide's plans. She'd chosen instead to stand patiently on guard until she was needed. Beatrice was bright and observant and determined, and that would go a long way towards keeping her from falling too far under Adelaide's spell.

"She seems so strong, so unafraid," Beatrice had said once to Eleanor in private. "Has she always been that confident?"

Eleanor had tried to set the record straight. "Adelaide isn't strong because she's confident. She's strong because she's always afraid."

The sooner Beatrice realized that Adelaide had weaknesses, the better. She didn't want the girl to be too eager to follow her every whim. Dr. Brody seemed to have already fallen into that trap, but she figured a man who'd lost an arm in battle could probably take care of himself.

She didn't blame Beatrice for being enthralled with Adelaide or even for wanting to be like her. She'd suffered from that same cycle of admiration-envy-infatuation when she'd cared for Adelaide after the attack. It's what had led her to agree to go into business with her and to suspect that Adelaide had powers that were yet to be made manifest. But it wasn't Adelaide's charm that'd led Eleanor to become her friend. It was discovering the parts of Adelaide that Beatrice had yet to see—her vulnerability, her tender heart, her fear of love. She hoped that Adelaide might reveal those things to Beatrice sooner rather than later, for all their sakes. Who knew what wondrous things might occur when that took place? Adelaide had said it herself, and she'd claimed she'd seen it in Beatrice's cards: "We're better for knowing each other, we're stronger together."

The words her mother had spoken at the dumb supper still lingered in Eleanor's mind, and she'd been struggling to see any signs that might guide her in instructing Beatrice. Everyday rituals that'd been foolproof when she'd lived on the river now felt cumbersome and meaningless. The rhythms of the city intruded on her senses as if they had messages of their own to give, but more often than not, she felt caught between two places, belonging to neither.

Since the rock crashed through the window, she hadn't seen any more signs of trouble. But that didn't mean the person who'd thrown it wasn't lurking about, waiting to strike. She'd been checking her tea leaves, observing the bees, waiting for a dream to be delivered . . . If a sign had been given to point the way, she'd missed it. Beatrice's powers were increasing each day. Was she losing hers in the inverse proportion? Surely her mother would've mentioned that, if it was to be her fate.

Perdu waddled to Eleanor's teacup and tapped his beak on its rim.

Eleanor looked at the cup and discovered a tiny stalk stuck to the edge of the bowl. *A single stalk means a message is on its way. Press it to your palm, and clap your hands together. If the stalk stays put, the message will be fair. If it switches hands, it will be fickle. If it falls to the floor, it will be foul.*

Pinching the stalk between her fingers, Eleanor placed it on the palm of her right hand. She clapped her hands once then looked to see where the stalk had landed. It clung to her left palm for a moment before floating to the floor.

The bells on the shop door jangled and a young man came into the store. "Telegram for Miss St. Clair," he announced, handing an envelope to Eleanor.

"Thank you," she said, motioning for Perdu to give the lad a tip.

Perdu dipped his beak into the change jar and fished out a dime.

The boy laughed as he shoved the coin in his pocket. "Thanks much," he said, tipping his cap.

TO: MISS ELEANOR ST. CLAIR

FROM: MRS. CECIL NEWLAND

I REQUEST YOUR COMPANY AT MY HOME TONIGHT.

7 O'CLOCK.

URGENT.

I have seen wonderful Snares laid for Curious People, by the Mouths of Damsels possessed with a Spirit of Divination.

—Rev. Cotton Mather

Parade.

The weather that afternoon was terrifically inviting. A cloudless blue sky and a high yellow sun made every bit of brass, copper, silver and gold (from buttons to buckles, from medals to sword hilts) shine that much brighter. Scores of Masons rushed here and there decked in their regalia—stewards, deacons, wardens, knights, sword bearers, worshipful masters—greeting one another with secret handshakes and sacred phrases, their sashes pressed flat, their feathered chapeaux set straight, their fringed aprons flapping.

Two gentlemen, decidedly ignoring the proceedings, played checkers under a poplar tree in Madison Square Park. They knew the place would soon fill with noisy parade goers, that Fifth Avenue would turn into a bustling boulevard of pomp and brass bands and horseshit, but they didn't feel the need to concern themselves with any of it. They'd come there every Saturday for the past thirty years, since before the Fifth Avenue Hotel was even thought of, and they weren't about to let a rowdy gathering of nine thousand Freemasons in their ridiculous garb ruin their long-standing tradition.

"Nice weather we're having," one of the gents said, scratching his head beneath his cap. His checkers were black.

"Indeed," his friend replied. His checkers were white. Moving one of his pieces to the end of the board, he crowned it king. "Warm for October, wouldn't you say?"

Mr. Black turned his head sideways, as if changing his perspective would change the game. "I suppose," he replied, hesitating over his turn.

"What's there to suppose about?" Mr. White asked. "It's positively balmy. I was tempted to fling my coat over my shoulder and walk in my shirt sleeves all the way here." Pointing to one of his pieces he said, "There's your move—you have to take it."

"Humpf," Mr. Black snorted, seeing he'd fallen into a trap. "This weather's nothing out of the ordinary, you know. There's been a warm spell in Manhattan every October since 1792."

After Mr. Black made the move he'd been waiting for, Mr. White took three of his friend's checkers and crowned one of his own, king. "You don't say."

"It likely started long before that, though the records of the *Old Farmer's Almanac* only go back so far." Making the only move he could, Mr. Black saw he was going to lose the game. At least he'd been right about the weather.

"Funny how folks forget," Mr. White observed, taking the last of Mr. Black's pieces off the board.

Tossing a nickel into the old tin cup they used for a kitty, Mr. Black nodded and said, "Good game." There was plenty of daylight ahead, plenty of time to plot and scheme. They wouldn't play their final round until sunset, winner take all.

Mr. White set his pieces on the board one by one. No need to ask if Mr. Black wanted another go. "Then why do you suppose we're so quick to say, 'How warm! How strange!' when it's not unusual at all?"

Mr. Black also readied his men for battle. "People like the feeling they get when they think they've stumbled upon something miraculous. It's a proven fact."

Adelaide arrived at the park with a stack of notices tucked under her arm. She'd decided to get there early so she could claim a spot near Lady Liberty's torch and size up the crowd. It was only two o'clock, yet the square was already crowded with politicians, preachers and protesters, as well as a variety of vendors selling everything from roasted peanuts and steamed oysters to a multitude of obelisk-related souvenirs. One enterprising confectioner had even set up shop near the fountain, selling chocolate-covered dates in obelisk-shaped boxes complete with gold-leaf glyphs.

As Adelaide perused the wares in a nearby cart—bracelet charms made from Egyptian coins, figures of Anubis, Osiris and Horus cast in coloured wax—she thought how glad she was that she'd seized upon the idea of Beatrice becoming the Egyptian Sibyl. The city was abuzz with Egyptomania. Why shouldn't they make the most of it? The crowd filling the sidewalks to watch the parade was growing by the minute. She couldn't remember seeing such a crowd in her life, except for the day President Lincoln's funeral procession had passed through the streets. Back then she was nothing but a curly-headed imp at her mother's hip, but the sombre affair had made an indelible impression. She hoped today would turn out to be equally unforgettable, yet in a far more festive way.

"How much for this?" Adelaide asked the woman who owned the cart, pointing to a silver propelling pencil shaped like the obelisk. It was mechanical, practical, novel. She thought she might give it to Quinn as a gift, if the price was right.

"Four dollars," the woman answered with a squint.

"That's too much." Adelaide shook her head.

"It's a steal," the woman argued. "I'm practically giving it to you. It's an exact replica. Look close and you'll see it's accurate down to the last glyph."

Adelaide had no way of knowing if the markings were authentic or mere chicken scratches. "Two dollars," she countered.

"Three dollars and I'll throw in a programme from the big to-do they're having at the Fifth Avenue Hotel. I hear they've got a girl on tonight who calls herself the ''Gyptian Sorceress' or some such. Should be something to see."

"You don't say," Adelaide said, handing over the asking price. Her enthusiasm alone was worth the extra dollar. "I'll take them both."

Gift in hand, Adelaide turned to leave.

"Wait, wait, wait, miss," the woman called. "Would you like to see something really special? I'll bring it out, only for you."

"All right," Adelaide said, "let's have a look."

The woman bent behind her cart then reappeared with a lacklustre piece of stone the size of a lump of coal. "It's from Cleopatra's Needle," she whispered. "The genuine article. The only one I got."

Guessing that the sad little piece of rubble probably came from a stonecutter's trash heap, Adelaide waved it away. She knew a gaff when she saw one. No doubt the woman had at least a dozen more such "relics" hidden behind her cart. "Good luck to you," she said. "All the best."

"Hurry back if you change your mind," the woman called after her. "I'll try to hold on to it, but I can't say how long it will last."

Making her way to the base of the torch, Adelaide passed between two groups of women who were clearly at odds with each other.

Several members of the National Woman Suffrage Association had gathered near the fountain with their colourful VOTES FOR WOMEN banners prominently on display. Distributing the latest issue of the *Ballot Box* they chanted, "Men, their rights and nothing more. Women, their rights and nothing less!" Across from them, the Ladies' Bible League from the Church of the Good Shepherd countered the suffragists' efforts by handing out literature of their own titled, "Votes for Women: Against God's Order."

One of the women from the Bible League waved a tract at Adelaide. "Repent, dear sister, and change your sinful ways!"

Adelaide recognized her by her sour expression. Over the past few weeks the woman had taken up the habit of standing outside the teashop and peering through the window. Only once had she bothered to come through the door, and, sadly, Adelaide hadn't been there to greet her. She'd scared poor Beatrice half to death when she'd accused her of serving Satan and leading women astray.

"Repent, I say!" the woman cried in Adelaide's face. "Repent and be saved!"

Grabbing the tract and tossing it to the ground, Adelaide lifted her veil, faced the woman and snarled until she backed away. This was indeed turning out to be a memorable day.

"Pretzels! Get yer fresh pretzels!" a boy's voice rang out above the crowd. "One for a nickel! Three for a dime!" Isaac Markowitz, son of the man who ran the bakery next door to the teashop, was coming down the path with a basket of salty treats strapped to his front, a sign for his father's store hanging down his back. "Pretzels! Fresh pretzels!" he shouted again, as he came towards Adelaide.

"I'll take one," she called to the boy.

"Here you go, Miss Thom," Isaac said, sliding her pretzel into a small paper sack.

Tucking a quarter in Isaac's front pocket Adelaide said, "Keep the change."

"Thank *you*, Miss Thom," Isaac said, smiling broadly.

Settling on a bench at the foot of the torch, Adelaide bit off a hunk of the pretzel as she waited for Beatrice. There were plenty of society folk out and about, gentlemen reading *Frank Leslie's Illustrated*, ladies promenading with parasols on their shoulders. The people that held Adelaide's interest, however, were those whom the rest of the crowd mostly chose to ignore—the young pickpocket lifting a watch from a distracted sap, the flower girl admiring a rich girl's smart dress, the Bird Lady singing songs to herself one after another. Just as Adelaide was about to take the last bite of her pretzel, a stray dog came towards her through the maze of skirts and suits. Black and tan with blazes of white on its muzzle and chest, it reminded her of the pair of Swissys that'd pulled the rag lady's cart through the neighbourhood where she'd lived when she'd served as a lady's maid. The woman had owned next to nothing but she'd always made sure her dogs were well fed. Each hound had a collar decked with bells that jingled as they walked. This poor dog didn't have a collar, its ribs showed every which way, and it had the hunch and tremble of a creature that had been beaten. Taking pity on the hound, Adelaide tossed the remaining hunk of pretzel to the ground at her feet. She understood what it was like to have loyalty rewarded with a kick in the ass.

Tail between its legs, the dog snatched the bread and wolfed it down.

Pointing towards Isaac, Adelaide told the dog, "Follow that boy."

The dog obeyed and slunk away.

Adelaide hoped that's not what she'd become, a pitiful used-up stray trailing after Beatrice and Quinn in hopes of licking up their scraps. She truly had an interest in what they were trying to accomplish and was more than happy to play a part, but what would happen once they figured out they didn't need her? She'd hardly spent any time alone with Quinn; whenever they'd had a few spare moments to themselves they'd spent them talking about Beatrice. *What might Beatrice become? What should we do to encourage her, educate her, protect her?* Admittedly, much of Quinn's obsession with Beatrice was of her own making, she'd pushed so hard to shine the light squarely on the girl. Until now it'd seemed the best course of action, one that would inevitably lead to recognition, perhaps even fame and fortune. That was the path she'd always taken—choosing limelight over lamplight, lust over love.

Why couldn't she read Quinn better? Was she losing her touch? Maybe the trouble was she'd come to care too much for him. (If that was the case, she really had to put a stop to it.) She could see the interest in his face, so why didn't he see fit to act on it? Was it her disfigurement? Was he planning to cut her loose "out of respect" once he'd had his fill of Beatrice's abilities? Men frequently used that word as an excuse to shy away from topics they didn't want to discuss. Plenty of women had come into the shop weeping over a gentleman's respect. "He broke it off with me, out of respect." "He respected me too much to let it go on any longer." "He said he couldn't respect himself if he held me back from something greater." Bollocks. If Quinn didn't act on his attraction to her soon, she'd be the one to end it. Not out of respect, but because she had no room in her life for games of the heart.

Perhaps he'd decided he'd rather have Beatrice. She wouldn't blame him. The girl had lots she couldn't offer—beauty, cheerfulness, naïveté, and an unparalleled rapport with ghosts. (Though she hadn't seen any signs that Quinn was drawn to Beatrice so far.) Oh how she hated herself for feeling jealous! Was jealousy also destined to go hand in hand with love? If so, she didn't want any part of either. She'd seen where love could lead by watching her mother stand on the porch of a boarding house cursing at a young whore to give her back her husband. If her mother had ever held any witchery in her blood, the pathetic wretch had lost the better part of it the moment her heart had been broken by a man. She'd given whatever power she'd had away—to love, to drink, to laudanum and, eventually, to the river.

Pulled forth by her daughter's thoughts, the spirit of Adelaide's mother rose from the bubbling waters of the park fountain. After shaking a penny loose from her ear, she took her skirts between her hands and attempted to wring them dry. *Chrissakes*, she was sore and damp and groggy from being stuck in the fountain's rusty bladder. *What time is it? What day is it?* Noticing the bustling crowds she wondered whether another president had died. Or was she stuck in a ghostly dream, sent back in time to Lincoln's funeral procession?

It was that damn fairy's fault, she was sure of it. Everything had been a jumbled mess since she'd been tricked into leaving the teashop. She wasn't sure what the foul pixie had done, but she knew it wasn't good. Dizzy and confused, she hadn't been able to make her way back to where she'd been. It was as if the teashop had up and disappeared. Every time she flew down the block, the sign, the door, the whole storefront went missing. She couldn't remember the number of the building. The confusion she felt was akin to waking up after a night of drinking and fucking to find spunk stuck between her legs and her head filled with nothing.

Spitting out three snails, a handful of watery worms and a plug nickel, her memories began to stir, but not in any particular order. Last week, last month, last year, some time ago, she'd gone to the park in search of her daughter. In a strange turn she'd seen not one Adelaide, but two. One was the young woman her daughter had become—the nattily dressed one-eyed seer who called herself Adelaide Thom. The other was the child she had abandoned—the slim, shining, smart-mouthed waif her lost husband had named Moth. She'd chosen to follow the little one through the confines of the park. Over the course of the next while (minutes, hours, days, weeks), she'd trailed after the child, who had a terrible habit of hiding in places even ghosts couldn't see. Was she real? Was she a memory? Was she a spirit, like her? She'd seen the girl fall prey to a terrible man, a man who meant to harm her, and even though she'd tried everything in her power to warn her, the girl wouldn't listen. She'd shouted in the Bird Lady's ear, but the die had already been cast. Some dark force below the pavers had been determined to hold her there, not allowing her to follow the child to her fate. Where was she now? Where was her daughter?

As she searched the park for the little girl, she spotted Adelaide. She's here! Safe and sound! All grown up again. Hovering to Adelaide's right, she swooned over her daughter's beauty. *Look here! That's my girl! So elegant and lovely!* Circling to Adelaide's left, she cringed. *How hideous! How sickening! What's happened to her? Look at my child, the poor, pathetic wretch!*

Rising high above the crowd, she spotted the man who'd led the sweet little girl away. "Watch out!" she cried. "He's here! He means to catch a witch!"

Beatrice rushed across the avenue from the hotel to the park. It was almost three o'clock: she was nearly late. She'd been held up by the session put on by the Followers of the Needle, enthralled by one of the members' accounts of having her rheumatism cured after visiting the obelisk aboard the *Dessoug*. The woman spoke so fervently about her miraculous healing, it'd been all Beatrice could do to hold herself back and not share her experience with the room. But remembering Adelaide's strict instructions not to speak of her connection to the Needle until the symposium, she'd kept her thoughts to herself.

Moving towards the spot where she and Adelaide had agreed to meet, she began to feel uncomfortable amongst the crush of strangers, overwhelmed by the persistent shouts of vendors, the startling racket of gunshots and the swell of brass bands as the parade marched ever closer. She was sad the obelisk itself wasn't going to be part of the celebrations, but the latest report in the papers had said that Mr. Gorringe was now predicting that it might take until the New Year for it to reach Central Park. She supposed the man she'd met the day the Needle came ashore wouldn't be attending today's festivities, either. He'd seemed to take his guardianship of the stone quite seriously and she couldn't imagine him leaving his post.

Beatrice could sense a contingent of spirits drawing near. The sound of drums in the distance, the sea of uniformed men, the clomp of horses' hooves had brought a ghostly parade of soldiers (five Union, two Confederate) to her side. The scent of gunpowder filled her nose while the strains of a melancholy tune rang in her ear. *Me, oh my, I love her so. Broke my heart I had to go. Only time will heal my woe. Johnny has gone for a soldier.* "Move along," she whispered, waving the ghosts away. "I can't speak with you now." Thankfully, they relented, and no one among the living had noticed her odd behaviour.

Ahead of her, she spotted a young woman who looked for all the world like Joan of Arc. Dressed in armour from the waist up, with her chestnut hair and scarlet skirts flowing, she appeared more vision than human, shrouded by the invisible waves of heat that were rising from the stone path. Could this out-of-place Joan be a spectre too? Tracking the young woman with her eyes, Beatrice hastened after her. She needed to find out for herself whether or not the girl was real.

When she finally caught up to her, she discovered it was all a good-natured ruse. Joan, sword strapped to her side, was standing with the suffragists, cigarette holder in one hand, the standard of the NWSA in the other. "Blazing hot today," she exclaimed as she chatted with her sisters.

"Better than being on the stake," one of the women teased.

"I get enough of that," Joan retorted, "eight shows a week."

Beatrice guessed she must be the actress who was starring in *Joan's Lament* on Broadway near Union Square. She'd seen broadsheets for the play plastered on brick walls around the square. Although she was flesh and blood, she was still a wonder to behold. She hoped Adelaide had gotten a chance to see the girl. No doubt she'd approve of the suffragist's flair for the dramatic.

Thinking she might send some of the NWSA literature to Lydia, she started to approach the women to ask for a copy of their paper.

Before she could reach them, a man drew near. "Miss?" he said, his voice hoarse, his dark imperial beard nearly hiding his mouth. "Might I trouble you for a moment?" From the tailored cut of his suit to the gaudy signet ring that glinted on his finger, it was clear he was a man of considerable wealth. Even the handle of his walking stick was a cut above, a silver ram's head with two gleaming emeralds for eyes.

Not wishing to be rude, Beatrice stopped to hear what he had to say.

"I am Mr. Gideon Palsham," the man said, giving Beatrice a polite bow.

"Miss Dunn," Beatrice replied with a wary nod.

"Lovely to make your acquaintance, Miss Dunn."

"Likewise," Beatrice replied, wishing she knew where Adelaide was and how long this might take. The torch was just up ahead, but they'd stepped off the path, close to a group of women who were standing in a circle reciting psalms.

"Correct me if I'm wrong," Mr. Palsham said, "but didn't I see you at the hotel a short while ago, at the meeting of the Followers of the Needle?"

"Yes, I was there," Beatrice answered.

"I knew it!" Mr. Palsham exclaimed, placing his hand on Beatrice's arm. "I was seated in the same row, only a few seats over."

Not liking the thought that he'd taken notice of her, Beatrice flashed a nervous smile. "I'm afraid I really must go."

Gripping her arm so she couldn't leave, he smiled and spoke with pleasant ease. "I hope you'll forgive me for being forward, but I couldn't help but notice your reaction when that lovely woman told her remarkable tale of her miraculous recovery after being in the presence of the Needle. The expression on your face was simply sublime. Angelic. Transcendent."

Beatrice held her breath, not knowing what to do or say.

"Something tells me that you have a tale of your own to tell. I can only assume that perhaps you've had a similar experience? Have you also been in the presence of the Needle?"

"Yes," Beatrice admitted, immediately regretting her answer. "I mean, no," she said, shaking her head, as she tried again to pull away from Mr. Palsham. His gaze was uncomfortably intense, his grip powerful, unyielding. For a moment she swore his eyes glowed bright, as if there was fire within them. Her belly lurched. She thought she might be sick.

"Which is it, Miss Dunn?" Mr. Palsham pressed. "Yes or no?"

The bells from a nearby church tolled the hour, *one, two, three*. Dogs barked from all corners of the square as the parade came closer.

"I have to go," Beatrice insisted, looking around for help.

"You seem confused," Mr. Palsham said, grabbing her around the waist. Lips pressed against her ear he hissed, "I saw you the day the obelisk crossed the tracks. I saw you touch it."

Suddenly, someone loomed tall at her back. "Unhand her," Reverend Townsend commanded, his voice ringing in the air.

Mr. Palsham let loose of Beatrice. Briefly looking at the preacher, he gave a polite nod as if he was handing off a dance partner in the middle of a waltz. Without a word, he slipped into the crowd.

"Are you all right?" Reverend Townsend asked, now standing at Beatrice's side.

"I think so," she answered, still queasy and shaken. Just as she was about to thank him for intervening, Adelaide appeared.

"There you are," she said to Beatrice while giving Reverend Townsend a suspicious stare. "I was starting to think you weren't coming." Handing the preacher a notice for the lecture she said, "If you want to see more of her, you'll have to come to the hotel tonight."

Beatrice linked arms with Adelaide as they walked towards the torch. She'd never been so happy to see anyone in all her life.

The Bird Lady trailed after them, picking notices from the ground whenever they dropped from Adelaide's hand. Cloudy eyes shining, she rattled a string of stinking oyster shells tied to her wrist. "He's here!" she sang. "He's here! He means to catch a witch!"

The speedy gleams the darkness swallo'd;
Loud, deep, and long the thunder bellow'd;
That night a child might understand
The devil had business on his hand.

—ROBERT BURNS

The Coming Storm.

RATHER THAN WAIT for Sister Piddock to come knocking on his door, Reverend Townsend planned to go to hers. He hadn't begun composing his sermon, yet he felt sure that the message he'd deliver the next morning would be nothing short of inspired.

This evening, there was more important work at hand.

He'd saved that poor girl (the angelic maid with the lovely eyes) from certain danger in the arms of a foul gentleman, only to have her fall into the hands of a witch! That one-eyed wretch, that horrible woman, was by far the greater threat. He was sure he'd smelled sulphur when she was near.

He'd spotted her earlier in the day when she'd turned her grotesque visage towards Sister Piddock and scared the dear lady half to death. It'd been all he could do not to seize the hag and slit her throat then and there. He was sure, of course, that's what she'd wanted—to beguile him into taking a course of action that would leave him looking like he, rather than she, was in league with the Devil.

The evil sorceress clearly had the maid bewitched. What

else could explain the docile way in which the damsel had responded to her touch, her words, her commands? No one but a foul temptress could get so perfect a creature to do her bidding. Nothing but witchcraft could place so firm and convincing a hold on the unblemished.

Ah, but his God was a clever God! Just when the Reverend had thought the girl lost to him forever, the witch herself had provided him with the means to find her again. Now all he needed to do was to get to her before she fell further under her tormentor's spell. The Lord's Providence had put her in his path and he wasn't about to abandon her in her time of need. Hers was a soul in distress waiting to be freed from the Devil's grasp. Only then could she become the full measure of her God-given self and serve as a shining example to others. He could feel the Lord's reason moving through him, making his blood run hot with divine guidance. He could see himself standing at the pulpit with the girl at his side— reformed, refined, reborn. What better way to increase the faithfulness of his fold than by having her stand before the congregation and testify of her woes? What better way to neuter a witch? If he got rid of the witch first, there was a good chance whatever curses she'd cast would live on, but to have one whom she'd afflicted rise up against her would surely break the spell. Once the damsel was saved—once he had his Mercy Wylde—and the witch's evil confirmed, he'd set his sights on the witch herself.

"Oh Lord," he cried, falling to his knees, "I will not shrink away from this calling! I will follow your path to the end of your choosing. I am prepared for whatever you would have me do—to save the girl in her innocence, or save the world from her if she be innocent no more. I believe that devils and witches still roam the earth just as I believe in your goodness. No matter what becomes of me, I will rest easy in the knowledge that I have followed your will.

"Bless me that I might be successful in my efforts, give me the strength, courage and resolve I need to execute your wishes. To Thee I will give thanksgiving, I will sing hymns of praise. Not my will, but Thine shall be done."

After kissing his grandfather's Bible three times along the spine, he tucked a small chemist's bottle in his pocket wrapped in a cotton handkerchief, slid his knife into its sheath, and tied a cross of hazel wood around his neck. His goal was clear, his faith keen, his blade sharp.

Standing at Sister Piddock's door, he handed her a slip of paper.

> *Psalm 73:27*
> *For, lo, they that are far from thee shall perish:*
> *Thou hast destroyed all them that go a whoring from thee.*

"Is this all there is?" she asked, confused as to how she was supposed to choose the Sunday hymns from such an unsavoury verse.

"The scripture is all we need," Reverend Townsend answered, heart pounding, anxious to get on his way. "I trust the Lord to guide me. I suggest you do the same."

Yes, of course, Sister Piddock thought. *The Reverend's given me a test of faith.* "Our God is a knowing God," she said with a solemn nod. "I will pray and find a way."

"He will provide," Reverend Townsend said, tipping his hat.

"Amen."

"Amen."

Eleanor sensed a storm was on the way the minute she left the teashop—the hairs on the back of her neck pricked to attention as the melancholy scent of turning leaves hung heavy in the evening air. There was no sign of lightning yet, but she had no doubt it would arrive soon.

She'd always adored autumn storms—from the quiet that came before the rain when the birds and bugs went silent, to the raucous cracks and grumbles that echoed between the clouds, rife with the possibility of goblins and ghosts. Dancing on the porch of their cottage her mother had often sung an ominous little tune as the first raindrops hit the slate roof, a reminder of the dangers of getting caught in a tempest.

Beware the oak, it draws the stroke. Avoid the ash, it prompts the flash. Creep under the thorn, it saves you from harm.

Madame St. Clair believed that any trees that got burned or struck by lightning should be treated with great respect and that whatever wood remained, be it barely scorched or charred black, contained magical powers. Amongst her most prized possessions was a spoon made from the branch of an ash tree that'd been severed from its trunk by a blinding, terrible strike. She'd used the spoon every day to make soups and sauces, potions and brews. Whenever she got called to visit a house where trouble was stirring, she'd carried the spoon along with her and used it to knock on the door to dispel any anger or hard feelings. Halfway to the Newland residence Eleanor wondered if perhaps she should've stuck the worn relic inside her satchel along with the other items she'd packed for her visit with Lucy.

She hadn't heard from Lucy since their conversation in the park and the last time her aunt had visited the shop, she'd claimed she hadn't spoken to her niece in quite some time. "I suppose our Lucy is fine," Mrs. Scrope had said, shaking her head in dismay, "but I wouldn't know. Just last Monday I stopped by the house unannounced and the maid turned me away. 'Mrs. Newland doesn't wish to be disturbed,' she'd said, arms folded, barring the door. I suppose Lucy has every right to refuse visitors, especially during her confinement, but I'm her family for heaven's sake!"

Tucking a small packet of hibiscus tea in Mrs. Scrope's bag, Eleanor had given the woman a sympathetic nod. "I'm sure it was a maid's mistake. Please wish Lucy well for me next time you see her?"

With a troubled sigh Mrs. Scrope had replied, "I'll tell her you asked after her."

Reaching the Newlands' door now, Eleanor wondered if she should bother. While it was possible that Lucy needed to see her, it was equally as possible that she might've called her there as part of some twisted game. Eleanor was prepared for the latter, but she was also prepared to help the young woman if she truly needed her. She'd brought a host of remedies along—ginger root for morning sickness, raspberry leaf to strengthen her womb, oarweed and a long slender hook if she wanted to turn things the other way and let the child go. She hoped it wouldn't come to that, and she hoped she wouldn't have to stay long. She'd promised Beatrice she'd come to the lecture and she didn't want to be late. After ringing the doorbell, she kissed the brass key tied around her neck, and made a silent wish that her mother be on her shoulder should anything go wrong.

"This way, ma'am," the maid said, showing Eleanor into the Newlands' drawing room.

To Eleanor's surprise, the only person there was Lucy's husband. Dressed in a silk smoking jacket, Cecil Newland was sitting by the fire, a decanter of whiskey and a half-empty glass at his side—the perfect picture of a man of wealth taking his leisure. "Care for a drink?" he asked, pouring more whiskey in his glass. The strong scent of alcohol blossomed in the room.

"No, thank you," Eleanor replied. Looking to the clock on the mantel she wondered where Lucy might be. It was already quarter past seven. Where was she?

"Care to sit?" Mr. Newland asked, gesturing to the chair next to his.

"I'll stand until Lucy arrives."

Mr. Newland threw back his drink. "She's not here," he said, wiping his mouth with his sleeve. Eleanor suspected he'd started drinking long before she'd arrived.

"I'll leave you to it then," she said.

Eyebrow arched, Mr. Newland asked, "You didn't know she'd gone?"

"No," Eleanor replied. "In fact I'm more than a little confused. She sent me a telegram this morning asking I meet her here at seven."

"I sent the telegram," Mr. Newland said. "So I suppose this means she's up and left us both. Such a pity. She seemed so fond of you." Fumbling, he reached for a small book on the table next to his chair. Turning to a page marked with a white ribbon he began to read aloud.

"'June first. Saint C. has a devilishly delicate touch with her tongue! So playful. So masterful. So completely disarming. I tremble whenever I recall our last tryst. I'm counting the hours until I can be with her again. I need to have her naked body next to mine, feel her lips on my flesh. There is no better joy or complete pleasure. Nothing in this world compares to it . . .'" Peering up at Eleanor, he asked, "Shall I go on?"

Her face flushed hot. When she didn't respond, Newland slammed the book shut and tossed it on the table. The decanter took the brunt of his anger, wobbling to and fro, and nearly toppling.

Eleanor tried her best to stay calm. "I assure you, Mr. Newland, I have never been and never will be a threat to your marriage."

Mr. Newland sneered at her. "I believe it's too late for such assurances."

Perhaps it was, Eleanor thought, but her conscience was clear. The fate of his marriage was between him and his wife.

Pouring more whiskey in his glass Mr. Newland asked, "Do you know why men drink?"

Eleanor shrugged. "I haven't the faintest."

"We drink to celebrate. We drink to gain courage. We drink to the beauty, good nature and fidelity of our wives." Tossing the glass at the fire he shouted, "I can't do that tonight!"

Eleanor flinched as the glass shattered and the fire flared. Backing away from him, she said, "Why have you called me here?"

Reaching into the pocket of his smoking jacket, Mr. Newland pulled out a small pistol. "I wanted to see you face to face. That's what gentlemen do in these sorts of situations.

We face our enemies, our rivals. A gentleman never slinks around like a coward behind another man's back."

Stay still, she thought. *No sudden movements.* "Is that what you think I am, a coward and a rival?"

"I think you're abhorrent. I think you're a freakish ghoul who wishes she were a man."

Eleanor calculated how many steps it would take to get to the door. "Trust me when I tell you that's the last thing I wish. I've no interest in being anything other than what I am."

Mr. Newland stroked the barrel of his pistol, toyed with the hammer. "It's a shame duelling has gone out of fashion here in the East. These days, dishonest men die such ignominious deaths. They get shot in the back in stairwells or alleyways, sometimes in the best parts of town. They never see it coming. Where is the romance, the honour in that? Tell me, Miss St. Clair, what do women do when they wish to punish their enemies? Sharpen their scissors? Pick a poison? Cast a spell?"

She felt threatened, but his head was muddled, his hands shaky. His aim would be poor. "Do you intend to shoot me, Mr. Newland?" she asked.

Tucking his pistol back in his pocket, he pointed his fingers at her instead. Squinting one eye, he took aim and pulled an imaginary trigger. "Satisfying as it would be," he said, "it'd leave too big a mess. The cleanup alone would take hours. Not to mention that the scandal that'd follow would be incredibly appalling. Tedious. Boring. I favour more elegant means of revenge."

Now he was toying with her, behaving as if he were holding the winning hand. She realized whatever he had planned wasn't going to play out here. "If you're not going to shoot me, then I really must be on my way," she said. "I'm expected elsewhere."

Newland glanced at the clock and smiled. "By all means," he said waving Eleanor out of the room. "Leave my house, you cunt. Enjoy your evening."

Beatrice was sequestered in a small room adjoining the hotel's Grand Ballroom. The space was usually reserved for the storage of music stands and other paraphernalia used by the house orchestra, but Adelaide, with Mrs. Stevens' blessing, had commandeered it for use as a dressing room. After the room's original contents had been moved elsewhere, other items were shuttled in one by one to accommodate Beatrice's needs—a full-length mirror, a clothing rack, a folding modesty screen, a table for accoutrements, two slipper chairs and a large, overstuffed fainting couch. Beatrice would've been happy to dress in Judith's suite and make her way to the ballroom from there, but Adelaide had insisted she take the room, saying, "The mystery dissolves the minute you're seen off the stage."

Staring at a porcelain vase that was overflowing with yellow roses, Beatrice picked up the card that'd accompanied them. WITH BEST WISHES AND HIGH REGARD. JUDITH AND ALDEN DASHLEY. The flowers were beautiful and perfect and smelled divine and it'd been awfully kind of Judith and her husband to send them, but their presence made Beatrice feel as if she were an ingénue on opening night rather than a participant in a scientific presentation. She only hoped she could live up to everyone's expectations.

She, Adelaide and Dr. Brody had finished their preparations a good hour before the event was supposed to start. The
stage was set, the spiritoscope was in good order, but she
hadn't been able to stop herself from asking, "What will we
do if no spirits come forth?"

"Don't say such a thing!" Adelaide had exclaimed, making
a sudden gesture as if she were spitting something foul from
her mouth. Her Gypsy roots were showing.

Dr. Brody had responded in a more practical fashion. "You
can tell them of the supernatural experiences you've had in
the past couple of weeks. I've no doubt the audience would
find it highly informative."

"Pish!" Adelaide had said. "Isn't there something we can
do to assure at least one ghost will show up? Surely there's
some way you can entice them to appear?"

Beatrice had forced a smile and said, "I'll try."

The answer she'd really wanted to give was the one she
imagined Eleanor would have offered. *It doesn't work that
way.* Why had she even brought up the possibility of there
not being any ghosts? The scrubber girls were here, there and
everywhere—in the water closets, in the dining hall, in the
corridors—one of them was bound to make an appearance.
She guessed she was nervous, and unsettled by the frightening run-in she'd had with Mr. Palsham in the park. The full
weight of what had happened was only now sinking in. What
if he'd not let go of her? Had he meant to do her harm? Was
his the face she'd seen last night in the fire? She decided it
was best not to mention it to Adelaide, at least not until the
lecture was over.

Adelaide had taken her hand and led her to the little room
so she could get dressed at her leisure and settle her nerves.

But once she had cinched, buttoned and pinned Beatrice into Minnie Stevens' ball gown, she'd been quick to take her leave. Had Beatrice somehow offended her? Was Adelaide tired of her company? Sometimes she wished she could trade places with Adelaide as she was sure she was better equipped to handle this sort of thing. She was growing tired of constantly wondering if she was out of her depth.

The room had no clock and Beatrice didn't own a watch, so every few minutes she'd poke her head out the door that led to the wings behind the ballroom's stage to ask Adelaide for the time. The last time she'd done it, Adelaide had impatiently stalked to the door and announced, "It's seven thirty." Her tone was decidedly frosty. "The audience will be arriving soon. I don't want there to be any chance of anyone seeing you until the lecture begins. Not even the slightest glimpse between these curtains. Don't be such a child. Get back in there and close the door. I'll come get you when it's time."

She tried to do as Adelaide said, but when she couldn't get the elaborate headdress to sit correctly on her head, she decided it was best to fetch Adelaide to help. Slowly opening the door to the wings, she looked to see if Adelaide was close by. It was then she caught a glimpse of Adelaide and Dr. Brody entwined in an intimate embrace. She'd known they were fond of each other, but to see them kissing with their bodies pressed together was a blush-inducing shock nonetheless. Thinking better of interrupting the pair, she wondered where Eleanor might be. She'd promised she'd be there before the event started, to recite a spell of good fortune on her behalf. Why hadn't she arrived yet? Pulling her wrap over her dress Beatrice snuck out of the room and down the long corridor that led to the lobby. She figured so long as she was covered up, no one would guess that she was the Egyptian Sibyl.

Hiding behind a marble column in the entrance, she searched for Eleanor. The place was filling fast, ladies fanning themselves in the hot, close air; men clutching their pro-grammes with their hands behind their backs. A porter rang a shiny gong suspended from a stand. "Five minutes until seating begins!" he called. "Five minutes!" By the clock in the lobby it was seven forty.

Beatrice spotted several familiar faces in the crowd, including Judith and Alden Dashley, who were holding court with several members of the Fraternal Order of the Unknown Philosophers. Mr. Guiteau was back again (along with his attendant shadows), passionately informing the receptionist of his urgent need to speak with Senator Conkling. Billy Dashley and a pair of scrubber girls darted here and there among the living, playing hide-and-go-seek. As she watched them have their fun, Beatrice thought she caught sight of Mr. Palsham, the man who'd frightened her so terribly in the park. Standing on tiptoe, she tried to get a better look at the gentleman, but before she could confirm it was him, he was gone. Across the room, the preacher who'd come to her aid was looking straight towards her. She pulled the hood of her wrap over her head. There was no sign of Eleanor.

Hands clammy, Beatrice headed out the ladies' entrance to the street, hoping to meet Eleanor at the door. A cool breeze was stirring, rustling the fading leaves that clung to the tops of the trees. A few stray drops of rain fell as lightning flashed in the distance behind a wall of clouds. Beatrice began to count, *one Mississippi, two Mississippi, three Mississippi, four*

Mississippi . . . A grumble of thunder brought her count to a halt. The centre of the storm was about a mile off.

Where was Eleanor? How could she have missed her? Was she still at the shop?

Walking down the street, Beatrice thought, *I won't go far. Just a few steps down the block, and I'll turn right back.* Staring up at the magic lantern show just off the park, she saw the notice for their lecture in letters three storeys high: IT MUST BE SEEN TO BE BELIEVED.

What have I gotten myself into? She could run to the shop, leave the dress on the bed and find her way to the train station. If the trains travelling north along the Hudson didn't run this late on Saturdays, she could always go to Joseph Wheeler's cousin's saloon in the Bowery. It wasn't ideal, but surely they'd give her a place to lay her head until morning. Then it'd be back to Aunt Lydia and Stony Point and her reliable yet unremarkable life.

Crossing the street, she came upon a stretch of sidewalk where a new building was being erected. Rickety-looking scaffolds stretched high above her head. A dark figure was perched on one of the boards leaning against the brick. A mason who'd fallen asleep on the job? A man without a home? To her recollection, the building hadn't even been started when she'd walked to the hotel that morning, but that was the way of the city, she supposed. In the short time she'd been in New York, the city had been constantly changing, one man's idea of what was tremendous elbowing out another's for something taller, newer, better, like bullies who stepped on sand castles on the beach.

The wind picked up and the rain along with it. Drivers perched on their carriages turned up their collars and tipped their hats over their eyes. Lightning spread in wiry fingers between the clouds—brighter, sharper. *One Mississippi, two Mississippi, three Mississippi.* Thunder echoed between the buildings—louder, closer. Does the lightning choose the tree, or does the tree call to the lightning? Eleanor had told Beatrice that it was her deep desire to discover if magic existed in the world that had allowed magic to find her. Beatrice couldn't help but wonder if she was strong enough to withstand its attentions. One by one, several street lamps in front of her sputtered out, leaving her in a long stretch of darkness. It began to pour. She was almost to the shop. If she turned around, she could make it back to the hotel just in time.

What should she do?

Footsteps sounded behind her, gaining fast.

Before she could quicken her own pace, she was grabbed by the waist. Putting a gloved hand over her mouth, the man in black didn't give her the chance to decide.

Lost and Found.

ELEANOR ARRIVED AT the hotel dripping wet. She'd trudged through the rain, completely shaken by her conversation with Mr. Newland, wondering where Lucy had run to and if there was anything she could do about her husband's veiled threats. For now, she'd simply have to be on the lookout for whatever he might have planned. It was one thing to protect the shop from wayward ghosts, it was quite another to safeguard herself from physical harm. Cecil Newland was used to getting whatever he wanted, whenever he wanted it, without a care for the consequences. If he wished to hurt her, she was sure he'd find a way to do it and come out unscathed.

Shrugging off her wrap, she hurried to the Grand Ballroom knowing she was late. The clock in the lobby had just struck eight, its bells fading out of earshot as Eleanor snuck to the side of the stage. The room was stifling, the audience impatient for the lecture to begin. At least she could take some comfort in the fact that events like these never started on time.

"Where's Beatrice?" she asked when she'd found Adelaide standing with Dr. Brody, heads bent together in deep discussion.

Adelaide looked up, worried, irritated, frantic. "I was hoping she was with you. I thought she might've gone back to the shop for something she'd forgotten."

"I wasn't at the shop." Now wasn't the time to explain where she'd been. "When did you notice Beatrice was missing?"

"No one's seen her for the past half-hour," Adelaide said. "She was in her dressing room, ready to go at half past seven. The next time I checked on her she was gone."

It wasn't like Beatrice to up and disappear—and it wasn't like Adelaide to be so anxious. "Can you think of any reason as to why she might've slipped out? It's awfully hot in here. Perhaps she took a stroll down one of the back hallways and lost track of time."

Adelaide bit her lip.

"The hotel staff has searched high and low but so far they've had no luck," Brody said. Putting his hand on Adelaide's forearm he added, "That's not to say they won't, though. I'm sure she'll turn up."

Mrs. Stevens strode to the doctor's side clutching a black lace fan. "Eight o'clock has come and gone, Dr. Brody. We can't delay much longer."

"Five minutes more?" Adelaide suggested, trying to hide her panic. "We'll still be on the proper side of fashionably late."

"Five minutes it is," Marietta said, her eyes doubtful. "In the meantime I'll make an announcement to pacify the masses. People are already talking of leaving."

As Mrs. Stevens took to the stage, Dr. Brody pulled Adelaide and Eleanor aside. "If Beatrice doesn't show before our five minutes are up, then I'll do the presentation without her."

"How will that work?" Adelaide said shaking her head. "What will you say?"

Looking out at the fidgeting crowd Dr. Brody replied, "I'll say she's taken ill. People will be understanding about that, won't they? Or at least the thinking members of the audience will."

Eleanor gave Dr. Brody a supportive nod. "I think it's a wise solution."

"People won't understand," Adelaide protested. "They're here for a show, to see a sensation. You'll get booed, you'll get heckled, they'll head for the door and leave you talking to empty chairs. This was to be your big night. What of your research, your career?"

"My research will be the same tomorrow as it is today," Brody said. "What's important is that Beatrice is found, safe and sound."

"He's right," Eleanor said. "I'll go to the shop to see if she's there."

Taking hold of Adelaide's hand, Dr. Brody said, "You should go with her. I'll be fine on my own."

Adelaide frowned at him, hesitant.

"When you find her," Dr. Brody added, "please let her know that she's under no obligation to come back. If she shows, I'll count it as a happy surprise. If she doesn't, I've no hard feelings."

Adelaide leaned up and kissed his cheek. "Good luck out there."

As the two women made their way to the lobby, Eleanor whispered to Adelaide, "I'm not placing the blame on you, but I can see that you feel guilty. At some point I fully expect you to tell me what you think you did to make her run off." Holding her breath she waited for Adelaide to rail against her words, to storm off without her, but that moment never came. They walked arm in arm from hotel to home in silence.

The lights were out in the shop and the windows upstairs

were dark. Putting her key in the door, Eleanor found the lock had already been tripped. "Beatrice?" she called moving to turn up the gaslights.

"I'll look upstairs," Adelaide said, twisting the wick key on an oil lamp and striking a match to light it. After turning the flame down so it burned low and steady, she settled the lamp's glass chimney in place and took the light in hand.

Eleanor followed her as she climbed the stairs.

"Beatrice?"

"Are you here?"

Silence. Adelaide briefly cast the light into their own rooms before heading to the garret.

"Hello?"

"Beatrice?"

"Are you all right?"

"Are you unwell?"

Adelaide took the lamp into Beatrice's room but the girl wasn't there. "Where do you suppose she's gotten to?"

"I don't know," Eleanor answered, lighting a second lamp so they could search the room for clues. She'd been up here several times since Beatrice had arrived, but she'd never stayed long enough to take stock of how the girl had made the space her own. It was an endearing sight. Books were piled by the bed. Notes, spells and news clippings covered the walls. The witch's ladder she'd brought with her from Stony Point was safely coiled inside a bottle that rested on the window ledge. Spotting a notebook that was lying open on the bed, Eleanor picked it up to inspect it. It was turned to the last page, which was blank except for the words *Census of Astonishments* written in large, flowery script. The rest of the book was filled with observations and musings, but nothing out of the ordinary for a young witch. Placing the book where she'd found it, Eleanor felt a pang of remorse for having snooped, but what else was she to do?

Adelaide sat on the floor rummaging through the trunk the girl's aunt had sent to Beatrice. "All her dresses are here, except for one," she announced. "The red calico is missing, but she was wearing it today until she changed into the gown for the lecture. It's still in the dressing room."

"She'd never run off in that gown," Eleanor said, fear creeping up her spine.

Clutching a length of striped grosgrain ribbon in her hand, Adelaide replied, "You're right. She wouldn't." She'd gifted the ribbon to Beatrice after she'd let her borrow it for their first visit together to Dr. Brody's house. Beatrice had tried her best to return it, saying, "I can't, it's yours, I'm afraid I'll ruin it." Smoothing the ribbon between her fingers, Adelaide bowed her head, overcome with guilt.

Eleanor took one last look at the clippings on the wall. "It doesn't look like anything's missing."

"Nothing except her," Adelaide said, sitting on the edge of Beatrice's bed, a single tear rolling down her cheek.

"Oh Adelaide," Eleanor said moving to comfort her. She knew how rare a thing it was for her to cry.

Trembling, Adelaide confessed, "I was short with her when I had no good reason to be. She was nervous about the presentation, and I called her a child and left her alone instead of staying with her and making her feel at ease. You've been right all along. All I've ever done is push her, trying to turn her into something I wanted her to be."

"Hush now. You mustn't talk like that. I'm sure she didn't see it that way, any of it. Beatrice adores you. I don't know how many times she's told me she wished she could be more like you."

Wiping her cheek, Adelaide said, "But that's the thing, isn't it? She's not like me, nor should she wish to be. What was she thinking, going out alone in the city at night? She doesn't belong out there."

"She's stronger than you think."

Adelaide thought of the tragic tales she'd grown up with—young women being seduced, raped, battered, stabbed, murdered, and then tossed in back alleys or steamer trunks and left to rot. She'd known many girls, herself included, who'd been used up and discarded as ruined goods. They were girls who wished (maybe once, fleetingly, or maybe hour upon hour) that they were dead. When they'd cried for help, no one listened. When it was over (and over and over and over) they were told, "There are worse fates than this. You deserve what you got." Looking at Eleanor she said, "You don't know what it's like."

"I know your story and I believe every word. And you forget that I came to know the city on my own before I met you."

Adelaide stood and straightened her skirts. Chin up she said, "I'm going out."

"Please don't," Eleanor begged. "It's late. It's raining. You'll catch your death . . ."

"I'm no good here," Adelaide said. "If I stay, I'll go mad. I know where to look, who to talk to. Don't fight me on this."

Taking Adelaide's hand in hers, Eleanor spat in her friend's palm and then traced a star on her skin. Closing her eyes she whispered, "Light before, light behind, light above, light below. May you stay safe wherever you shall roam."

"I'll be back soon," Adelaide said. "Wait up for me?"

"Always," Eleanor replied.

Eleanor saw Adelaide to the door. For the first time since she'd returned to the shop she wondered where Perdu was. He hadn't greeted them when they'd arrived and he wasn't sleeping on his perch. "Perdu?" she called. "Where are you?"

A faint chortle sounded from beneath the counter.

"Come out here," she coaxed. "Come on out. It's all right."

The raven flapped to the top of the counter and began pacing back and forth along the length of it, craning his neck and crying, "Fiend! Fiend! Fiend!"

"Perdu, what's wrong? What's happened?"

The bird quivered and shook as Eleanor gently looked him over from beak to tail. No feathers were missing and there were no signs of injury. Still, it was clear that something had happened to frighten the poor pet.

"Fiend!" he cried again, breaking loose from Eleanor's touch.

She remembered the open door. Had she forgotten to lock it before she'd left for Lucy's or had someone broken in? Had this fiend taken Beatrice? Moving through the shop she looked for missing items, broken glass, drops of blood. But nothing seemed amiss. The teacups were hanging from their hooks on the wall, their saucers evenly spaced on the plate rail behind them. The honey pots, sugar bowls and creamers sat innocently waiting to be filled. There was no evidence of a burglary, no signs of struggle.

"Fiend!" the bird bellowed as if he were sounding an alarm. Ruffling his feathers, Perdu lit on the top shelf behind the counter and began pecking his beak against a glass jar. *Ting, ting, ting,* he tapped. *Ting, ting, ting,* three times more.

Seeing what the bird was pecking at, Eleanor let out a gasp. "*Merde*," she said putting her hand to her mouth.

The jar that Perdu was focused upon wasn't one of Eleanor's. Cobalt blue with a cork stopper, it was fitted with a label that bore a skull and crossbones. Bringing the container down to the counter, Eleanor removed the cork and inspected it with care. "Arsenic," she said, eyes wide with fear. Staring at the many tins and jars that lined the shelves, she had the chilling thought that perhaps everything in the tearoom, every jar of honey, every tin of tea, every container of sugar had been opened and tampered with. Slumping on a stool, she put her head in her hands. This was just the sort of treachery Cecil Newland would exact.

Flapping back to the shelf, Perdu chose a jar of hibiscus tea and began to peck at it, *ting, ting, ting . . . ting, ting, ting.* Chortling, low in his throat, the bird said, "Who's a good boy?"

Knot in her belly, Eleanor replied, "You are."

Shaking his head, Perdu tapped the jar again, *ting, ting, ting . . . ting, ting, ting,* then he repeated his throaty, ghoulish question, "Who's a good boy?"

"You are?" Eleanor asked, wondering if there might be method in the raven's madness.

Ting, ting, ting . . . ting, ting, ting.

Taking the second jar from the shelf, Eleanor opened it and discovered a ring of white powder stuck to the rim. Clearly the bird knew all that'd happened. With any luck she'd soon know too.

Thinking there might be a way to assist the raven with his task, Eleanor grabbed her broom from the closet and pointed the end of the handle at the next jar on the shelf. *Ting, ting, ting,* she lightly tapped the glass and waited for Perdu's response.

The bird stared at her with a gleaming, curious eye.

Ting, ting, ting, she tapped again, looking to the jar. "Safe?" she asked, hoping he'd cotton on.

"Safe!" he croaked, vigorously nodding yes.

Eleanor moved on to the next jar.

After Perdu had declared five jars in a row to be safe, Eleanor gently ran the broom along the rest of her stock as if she were a child running a stick along a picket fence. "All safe?" she asked, praying he'd confirm her hunch.

"Safe!" he crowed, nodding and flapping his wings. "Who's a good bird?"

"You are," she declared.

Sitting in the front window, Eleanor kept watch for Adelaide and Beatrice and anyone who might bring her news. Pulling apart a loaf of Mr. Markowitz's black rye, she tossed a hunk to Perdu then took a piece for herself. The chewy loaf tasted of molasses and malt, and helped to settle her churning belly. She had no doubt that Cecil Newland had ordered someone to do the dirty business with the arsenic, but had he ordered them to take Beatrice too? She didn't think he would dare such a crime—it carried too much risk— but she needed to rule out the possibility. Running to the counter she fetched an egg from a wire basket. "Who wants a treat?" she asked Perdu.

The raven cocked his head. "Perdu," he answered, sidling onto Eleanor's shoulder. "Perdu, do."

Cradling the egg in her hands, Eleanor said, "Tell me who was in the shop tonight?"

"Perdu?" the bird replied, before emitting a series of bubbling coos. Anticipating the slither of yolk down his throat made him hopeful, eager.

"Yes," Eleanor said, with a supportive nod, "and was Beatrice here too?"

The raven shook his head.

"She wasn't?"

"No," he said, clucking his tongue.

"Then who else was in the shop?" Eleanor said, continuing to tempt Perdu with the egg. "I know you weren't alone."

Staring out the shop window, Perdu pecked at the glass. He puffed up his feathers until he was twice his normal size. "Fiend," he said in a low, menacing whisper.

With that, Eleanor cracked the egg on the edge of a saucer and gave up her interrogation. If the bird had recognized the intruder, he would've said so.

As Perdu scooped runny egg into his beak, Eleanor hid the arsenic and the hibiscus tea in the broom closet. Adelaide came through the shop door just as she'd closed the cupboard. Looking at Perdu, Eleanor put her finger to her lips. The bird flew to his perch and tucked his head under a wing.

"Any luck?" Eleanor asked as a dejected Adelaide settled into the window seat.

"None," Adelaide said.

"Tea?"

"Yes, please."

Turning to the shelves, Eleanor chose a jar marked "sweet ease," and went about brewing a pot to calm their nerves. As the water came to a boil, Eleanor whispered a few words over the leaves, first in French then in English. "*Ne laissez aucun mal à s'abattre sur nous.* Let no evil befall us." She trusted Perdu, of course, but a few good words couldn't hurt. She wondered how long she'd feel the need to bless every tea leaf, sugar cube and drop of honey in the place.

Settling across from Adelaide, she made sure she took her first sip of tea before Adelaide took hers. The bright notes of the herbs within—lavender, lemon balm, spearmint and passionflower—were the only tastes she sensed on her tongue. Closing her eyes, she thanked Heaven for Perdu.

Before long the shop's bell rang, startling both women to their feet.

Adelaide rushed to the door.

Dr. Brody was there, cheeks flushed, beer on his breath. Beatrice wasn't with him.

"How did it go?" Adelaide asked, inviting him into the shop. She wasn't quite ready to break the bad news.

Eleanor stood close by, waiting for the penny to drop.

"It was splendid," Dr. Brody said, teetering into the room. "Well actually, it was horrid at first. Most of the crowd left, except of course for the Philosophers and all but one of the North Orange Diviners, and several members of the Followers of the Needle. Mrs. Stevens was just glad there wasn't a riot. After I gave a brief lecture of my findings, and Judith Dashley gave a stunning account of Beatrice's abilities, we adjourned for the evening. I would've been here sooner but the Philosophers insisted we make a toast or ten to my dear father." Squinting, Dr. Brody looked around the room. "How's our girl? Is she faring any better?"

Adelaide guided him to a chair. "I think you'd better sit," she said, staring helplessly at Eleanor.

Eleanor scurried behind the counter. "I'll put on the kettle for more tea."

Upstairs, Twitch was face down, sobbing into Beatrice's pillow.

"Don't worry," Bright said trying to comfort him. "She's a strong, resilient girl."

"How could this have happened?" he whimpered. "We gave her the right dream. I touched all her garments with magic . . ."

Bright placed her hand on the small of his back. "We did all we could do. It isn't up to us."

When the Devil with his confederate and concomitant Spectres came unto this poor girl, it was their custom to cast her into such horrible Darkness that she imagined herself in a desolate cellar, where Day or Night could not be distinguished. Her eyes were open, moving to and fro after the Hellish Harpies that fluttered about her and she was little able to see anything else.

—from *An Attempt to Cure Witchcraft: The Story of Mercy Wylde*

Taken.

BEATRICE WAS HUDDLED on a straw mattress in the corner of a cold, dark cellar, head down, knees hugged to her chest. Shivering, she tried to remember how she'd gotten here but her aching head couldn't muster the answer. Every part of her was sore, from her leaden limbs to her face, and the harder she worked to make sense of things, the more she felt her memory slipping, falling off the edge of reason. Touching the nape of her neck to explore why it hurt, she realized all that remained of her hair was a mess of choppy ends. It had been cut close to the base of her skull. She couldn't remember the mincing of shears or how Minnie Stevens' ball gown had been taken from her, leaving her in nothing but her thin cotton shift. Whenever she swallowed, blood seeped from a gash inside her bottom lip and there was a mass of tender, swollen skin around her mouth. There was an odd smell in her nose, a strange taste in her mouth, medicinal yet sweet.

As her eyes adjusted to the darkness she noticed scant traces of light from between the floorboards above her head and the narrow gap under the door. The walls were stone, the floor dirt. There was no washbasin, no mirror, no way for her to tend to her wounds. Aside from the mattress there was a wooden bucket in the corner, a few pebbles in the dirt, and a large wooden support beam standing at attention in the middle of the room. The air was damp and musty except for an occasional waft of pipe smoke that met her nose, perhaps from the rooms upstairs. Hauling herself up she went to the door, where she discovered there was no knob or latch to loose. She leaned against its wide wooden planks, but it wouldn't budge. She was starting to wonder if she hadn't been thrown into the Tombs. But what for? Hearing the sound of a fly buzzing, she turned her attention to the bucket on the other side of the cellar. The pail was half full of vomit. Holding her breath against the stench, she wondered if the bucket's contents were hers, as if the ownership of such muck mattered. Trembling, she couldn't help the tears that now streamed down her face.

"Help!" she cried.

Instantly she heard footsteps above her—heavy pacing at a steady, even gait. Occasionally a loose board would creak and complain under the weight—it had to be a man. Remembering Mr. Palsham's determined grip on her arm, she wondered if it might be him. She was sure she'd spotted him in the lobby of the hotel. If he'd seen her the day she'd touched the obelisk, had he been following her ever since? As she strained to listen for other sounds that might tell her where she was, she heard the man speak. Although she couldn't quite make out what he was saying, his words had a cadence, like prayer or madness or song. Unlike Mr. Palsham's raspy voice, though, this man's had a pleasant tone and rhythm. Dare she call out again? Perhaps whoever it was would take pity on her and come to her aid.

"Help me!" she wailed. "Please, let me out!" She shouted until her throat was raw. When her voice failed she pounded on the door.

The light above her went out. The footsteps faded, but she was not alone.

October 10, 1880.

Waxing Moon.

Forerunner, or foretelling. Among the signs and portents that make themselves manifest in the daily world is the forerunner or foretelling. These mystical signals occur in anticipation of, or at the time of, someone's death. There have been many such signs recorded over the ages in various places around the world. The most prevalent include: three knocks on the door when no one's there; a dog howling in its sleep; a bird flying into a house through an open door; a favourite picture falling off the wall; the dream of a loved one bidding goodbye; the sound of church bells ringing in the middle of the night.

—*From the grimoire of Eleanor St. Clair*

Church Bells and Seekers.

ADELAIDE, ELEANOR AND Dr. Brody kept vigil at the teashop through the night. On Dr. Brody's recommendation, the three put together a plan of action for the following day: Dr. Brody would speak with the hotel detective and make the rounds among the staff; Adelaide would meet with Mrs. Stevens and the Dashleys to tell them of Beatrice's disappearance and to enlist their help; Eleanor would visit Police headquarters to file a report at the Office of Missing Persons. As their minds grew muddled from constant worry and their bodies weary from lack of sleep, Brody suggested they take turns keeping watch so each might get some much-needed rest.

Eleanor was the last to take her turn. During her watch, she thumbed through her grimoire looking for spells that might aid them in their search. Pausing on the page that addressed forerunners she thanked Heaven that any such signs had been absent thus far. Stopping on an entry titled, "Eye of Illumination," she remembered her mother practicing the spell whenever she'd feared someone might've used magic against her.

In the wake of evil, take a sharp needle and prick the shape of an eye into the palm of your left hand. While guiding that hand over any item, person or space you fear may have been touched by wickedness, close your eyes and repeat the following words: "May my blood sense what my eyes can't see." If dark magic has been cast upon you, the eye will glow and burn. Further steps must then be taken to protect yourself from harm.

Eleanor took a needle from her sewing kit and carefully pricked her palm. Slowly making her way around the shop she held her hand over every inch of the place as she recited the chant over and over again. Although she was certain she and Perdu had uncovered the extent of what must have been Cecil Newland's mischief, she worried something else might be afoot. Upon completing the spell, she stood in the centre of the shop and heaved a great sigh, relieved to find that there were no traces of dark magic to be found there. She was more confused than ever as to what had happened to Beatrice.

At sunrise she took a pencil in hand and made a list of other steps she might take to help find the girl. She had a feeling it was going to take more than keen minds and good will.

1. Ask Maman.
2. Ask the bees.
3. Ask Perdu (again).
4. Ask the Dearlies.
5. Read the Leaves.
6. Look to the mirror.
7. Consult the "Book and Key"

Dr. Brody rose shortly after dawn, shrugging into his jacket and rubbing his stubbled chin.

"Tea?" Eleanor asked, setting a kettle on the stove.

"Please," Dr. Brody replied, though what he really wanted was a cup of the coffee he'd lived on in the army: hot black sludgy fuel that could wake the dead.

"How'd you sleep?" Eleanor asked, dumping three generous spoonfuls of the strongest tea she had into the pot.

"Fitfully, and you?"

"The same."

"No sign of her?"

"None."

Then a flustered Adelaide came downstairs. "What's that racket?"

"Hmm?" Eleanor said, fetching another cup.

Holding up a finger for silence, Adelaide paused to listen. "There," she said. "There it goes again. Don't you hear it?"

"Hear what?" Dr. Brody asked with a shrug.

"I think it's a dog," Adelaide answered. "It's been yowling for the past hour."

Eleanor bit her lip. "Howling?"

Adelaide shook her head. "No, not howling. It's more like whining." Getting nothing but blank stares she headed for the door. "I'm going to see if I can't find it."

Eleanor kept on with the tea.

Quinn looked out the window after Adelaide.

The stray dog Adelaide had fed scraps to in the park was standing on the stoop of Markowitz's Bakery whining and scratching at the door.

The shop was closed for the day, but peering through the window, Adelaide spotted the portly baker. She knocked on the door.

"Miss Thom!" Mr. Markowitz exclaimed as he opened the door with a friendly smile. "How are you this fine morning?"

The dog cowered behind Adelaide's skirts.

"Tired," Adelaide grumbled. "I'm usually not up this early."

The baker waggled his eyebrows. "Late night?"

"Yes," Adelaide confessed, "but not nearly as much fun as I'd like it to have been."

"So sorry to hear that," Mr. Markowitz said looking genuinely concerned. He liked people to be happy, especially the women next door. "Would a basket of turnovers help cheer you up?"

Adelaide wasn't one to refuse the baker's kindness. "That would be lovely," she said, stepping inside the shop and closing the door behind her. "If it's not any trouble."

"No trouble at all. I just took a batch out of the oven."

The dog resumed its frantic bid to get inside the bakery.

"You didn't happen to see Beatrice last evening, did you?" Adelaide asked.

"Can't say that I did," Mr. Markowitz replied. "But you know me . . . early to bed, early to rise."

Adelaide nodded. "How about this morning then? You're usually up before dawn?"

Flipping the turnovers one by one out from their baking tins he replied, "Yes I am, but I haven't seen her. I can't keep track of you young ladies. So many pretty faces running willy-nilly all over the city with rouge on their lips and minds of their own. Where I come from, all three of you dear girls would've been married and holding babes in your arms by now." Turning, he caught the look on Adelaide's face, and the smile dropped off his. "Is Miss Dunn in some sort of trouble?"

The previous night she had searched for Beatrice in the park and along the streets near the hotel, stopping to give her card to every rough, nighthawk, carriage driver and whore she encountered. "Something like that," she said. She didn't want to worry the man too much. "If you see her, could you feed her some turnovers and send her home?" His golden treats were enough to soften even the most stubborn heart.

"I will," he said, handing the basket of baked goods to Adelaide. "My treat. No charge."

"Thank you," Adelaide said. "You're very kind."

As she opened the door to leave, Mr. Markowitz's son Isaac shot from the back room and outside before her. "Cleo!" he exclaimed, wrapping his arms around the dog's neck.

Mr. Markowitz raised a rolling pin in the air and bellowed, "That mangy hound's not to set a single muddy paw inside my shop!"

"But Papa," Isaac protested, "she's got no home."

Mr. Markowitz stared the boy down. "No."

"Please," Isaac begged.

Grumbling, the baker stomped back to his work.

"How about Cleo comes to stay with me?" Adelaide proposed, taking pity on dog and boy.

Cleo cocked her ears, wagged her tail.

"And I can come visit her at your place?" Isaac asked. His eyes were as hopeful as the dog's.

Adelaide nodded. "Any time you like."

"Isaac!" Mr. Markowitz shouted from the back of the shop.

"Coming, Papa!" Isaac shouted back.

Giving the boy a little wave, Adelaide hung the basket from her arm. "Come on Cleo, let's go."

Dog at her side, Adelaide entered the teashop and waited for Eleanor's reaction. She was half certain she'd get the same response as Isaac had gotten from his father.

Setting a saucer of raw stew meat on the floor for Perdu, Eleanor looked up at her friend and then at the dog.

Head low, tail wagging, nose catching the scent of the meat, Cleo slowly approached the raven.

Feathers ruffled, Perdu hissed and defended his breakfast.

Giving a sharp bark, Cleo ran between Dr. Brody's legs.

"Who's this?" Dr. Brody asked, scratching the dog behind its ears.

The dog's tail wildly thumped on the floor.

"Cleo," Adelaide answered, watching the pair with some astonishment. If Eleanor didn't fold, perhaps he'd take the pup.

"Nice name," Dr. Brody said, still scratching.

Taking another saucer from the shelf Eleanor grudgingly asked, "Is she staying?"

Adelaide smiled. "I suppose she is."

Eleanor put several pieces of meat on the saucer and placed

it on the floor. "Come on then," she said to the dog, "eat up before Perdu decides it's his."

Adelaide, Eleanor and Brody stood in silence watching the dog eat, each hoping that their kindness towards the stray might somehow hasten Beatrice's return.

She underwent a sort of plague, which I don't remember that I ever observed in more than one or two bewitched persons besides her. Her tortures were turned into frolics, and she became as extravagant as a wildcat. Her imagination strangely disordered, she was always excessively witty in talk; never downright profane, but yet sufficiently insolent and abusive. Knowing it was not her true self she was displaying, I had no hesitation in putting a stop to it.

—from *An Attempt to Cure Witchcraft: The Story of Mercy Wylde*

Witch's Mark.

THE GHOST OF Lena McLeod hovered in the cell where Beatrice slept. Although her body had been promptly fetched after she'd hung herself, the men who'd collected it couldn't keep her spirit from returning to the parsonage.

Staring at Beatrice she laughed, she swooned, she wept. Would this girl pay attention to her? The other one hadn't listened to a thing she'd said.

"Wake up," she called to Beatrice. "Wake up!"

Beatrice stirred, exhausted and hungry, her throat aching with thirst. Squinting across the room she noticed a bright light eking its way through a crack in the wall. Within the glow was a spirit, or was it an angel? As it drew near, she realized it was no heavenly being.

Head listing, the ghost stared at her, an angry red ring showing around her neck, face mottled in the colours of a nasty bruise—yellow, purple, blue.

"Who are you?" Beatrice asked, unsure but not afraid.

"Who are you?" Lena repeated, touching the tip of her finger to Beatrice's forehead.

Adelaide's voice sounded in Beatrice's head. *You are Beatrice Dunn. You are a witch. You're no one to be trifled with.* "I'm Beatrice," she answered, "Beatrice Dunn."

"Are you a witch, Beatrice?"

She paused to think. Would a witch have gotten herself into such a mess? Was that why she was there? Were Adelaide and Eleanor looking for her? Were they in any danger? Maybe she was better off just being a girl from Stony Point.

"Well are you a witch, or aren't you?" the ghost demanded. "I don't imagine you'd be here unless he thought you were."

"Who?" Beatrice asked.

"The Reverend."

Beatrice wondered what a reverend could possibly want with her.

"He's terrible," Lena said, frowning.

The taste of blood blossomed in Beatrice's mouth. Her head throbbed.

Tugging on the hair at the back of Beatrice's neck, Lena said, "You don't know the half of it."

"Where am I?" Beatrice asked.

"The parsonage," Lena replied.

"How long have you been here?"

"Nearly a month, I think. Three days alive, the rest dead."

"Did he kill you?" Beatrice asked wondering how many days she might have.

Laughing, Lena answered, "He thought he might, but I didn't let him. I beat him to it! He couldn't kill me and they couldn't catch my ghost."

"They?"

"The Collectors. A pair of ghouls dressed in black suits and gentlemen's skins. They snatch up witches' bodies once they're dead."

Beatrice swallowed hard. "They work for him, this Reverend?"

"No, they work for someone much worse. I don't dare say his name, but I'll spell it for ye."

A pebble rolled across the floor to Beatrice's feet.

As Lena spelled the name, "P-A-L-S-H-A-M," the pebble etched a series of letters into the dirt. *M-A-L-P-H-A-S*.

A chill travelled up Beatrice's spine. "Is that who put me here?"

Footsteps sounded on the stairs leading to the cellar.

"Hush!" Lena cried as she disappeared into the crack. "He's coming!"

Beatrice used her foot to erase the markings from the dirt.

The door opened with a jolt and a tall, dour-faced man entered the room, tin pail in one hand, lantern in the other, a thick wooden rod slung at his hip. The heels of his patent leather boots thudded on the dirt floor. His dress was more like that of a military man than a man of God, his trousers tucked into his boots, his coat decorated with braided stitching, his lapel adorned with a shining medal that bore a silver cross. An engraving in the centre of the medallion read, *To give light to those that live in darkness.* Hair slick with oil, dark moustache neatly trimmed, he had an intense, greedy look in his eyes that led Beatrice to think he expected her to be impressed by him.

Stepping back, she put distance between them and tried to quell her fears.

"My child," he said. "Don't be afraid. I'm Reverend Townsend, the pastor of the Church of the Good Shepherd."

Looking him in the eye she asked, "Why am I here?"

"I saved you," he said, setting the lantern and pail on the floor. The pail contained a crusty hunk of bread and a small canteen. "Don't you remember?"

She recognized him now. "You scared off that man, yesterday, in the park."

Smiling he said, "And I saved you again last night, outside the hotel."

Could the ghost have been wrong? Beatrice wondered. Maybe he didn't wish to do her harm after all. Then again, if he'd meant to save her, why had he brought her here?

Inspecting the wooden bucket in the corner, Reverend Townsend frowned with disgust.

"I'd like to go home now," Beatrice said moving towards the door.

"Not yet," he said, blocking her way.

"Am I not free to leave?"

Gripping the wooden rod at his side, his eyes narrowed. "Not now."

The rod was a formidable weapon, fitted with a leather grip and sporting an iron tip. Beatrice knew he'd use it to stop her if she tried to flee. "If you let me go, I'll not tell a soul," she begged. "I swear it."

"Don't try to trick me. That's the Devil talking through you, and I'll not hear it."

"Please," Beatrice begged, "let me go home."

Grabbing her by the shoulders, Reverend Townsend shook her hard. "That foul woman has bewitched you! She's got you under the influence of devils and demons."

A series of memories flashed in Beatrice's mind. The cruel hateful look the Reverend had given Adelaide in the park. Her muffled screams as a moist rag covered her mouth. The sound of his voice in her ear before everything went dark.

"Let me go!" she demanded, struggling to break free.

Holding her fast he hissed, "Fight all you want. Say whatever the Devil tells you, but do not think that you can hide it." Turning her loose for a moment, he snatched the hunk of bread from the pail, then seized her again. "Eat this," he said holding the bread in her face, "if you wish to prove me wrong."

Although her belly was churning with hunger, the bread smelled foul, like urine. Lips tight, she turned her head, repulsed.

Lena McLeod's ghost flew out of hiding and whispered in her ear. "Gobble it down, my dear! Keep it in your belly for as long as you can."

Beatrice closed her eyes and opened her mouth to accept the Reverend's challenge. Taking the bread on her tongue she did her best to swallow it, but besides having a terrible odour it was sickeningly thick with salt. "I can't," she whimpered in apology to the ghost, before gagging the thing up and spitting it out.

Reverend Townsend began to pray. "Thank you Lord for exposing the evil that dwells within the afflicted. May she be cleansed by your might so she might walk the path to righteousness."

Breaking from his grasp, Beatrice dropped to her knees and grabbed at the canteen.

Pulling it out of her hands before she could drink from it, he held it over her head.

"Please," Beatrice hoarsely pleaded, "I need water."

Reverend Townsend uncorked the vessel and put it to her lips. Grasping her by her hair, he let her briefly drink. "That's enough," he said. "We mustn't indulge your appetites, not while that witch still has a hold on you."

Beatrice slumped to the floor. It was clear the Reverend was a madman. She wished he would leave her alone so she could think. She needed to survive long enough to go free.

Reverend Townsend used the cold iron tip of his rod to lift the hem of Beatrice's shift. She wasn't sure if he was toying with her or searching for something.

"Where are my clothes?" she asked, scared that he intended to violate her, worried that he already had. "Where's the dress I was wearing last night?"

"That witch's garb?" he sneered. "It's been done away with. Turned to ash." Smacking the side of the rod against the palm of his hand Reverend Townsend said, "Disrobe."

"No," Beatrice said, shrinking away from him, clutching at the thin white fabric of her gown.

"Disrobe!" he ordered again, this time grabbing her by the arm.

She tried to scream but her voice was gone. Wild with fright, she kicked his shins, scratched at his face, bit his hand so hard it bled.

Reverend Townsend cracked his stick against the side of Beatrice's head.

She fell to the floor in a heap.

Head aching, Beatrice opened her eyes to find she'd been stripped naked. Her hands and feet were bound with rope, and she was gagged. The scent of smouldering coal filled the air, coming from a scuttle near the door. Reverend Townsend was circling around her, lantern in hand, chanting a strange rhyme.

> *By lamplight and fire's spark,*
> *Help me find the witch's mark . . .*
> *By God's will and grace divine,*
> *Help me spot the Devil's sign . . .*

He went once, twice, three times around before he found the thing he was searching for. "There!" he exclaimed, shining his lamp on the pale freckled skin of Beatrice's left thigh. "I've found it."

She knew exactly what he'd spotted. The dark red stain on the tender curve of her leg had been there since her birth.

Crouching next to her, he placed his hand on her leg, then circled the mark with his finger. "She's touched you," he said, his voice soft with indignant wonder. "She's poisoned your body as well as your mind. She's marked you as her own." Taking his rod to the other side of the room, he knelt and muttered a secret prayer. When he returned to Beatrice's side, the iron end of the stick was smoking and hot, the emblem of a double V on its tip glowing red.

She flinched at the sight of it, fearing what was to come.

"Be still," he said holding her fast with a steady hand. "It will soon be gone."

Turning her head she closed her eyes as he came at her with the heated brand. A fettered wail caught in her throat as her flesh sizzled and burned.

The Office of Missing Persons.

ELEANOR WAS SITTING on a bench at Police Headquarters waiting to speak with the men who ran the Office of Missing Persons.

She'd been there for three hours, staring at the two doddering gentlemen, Mr. Osmund and Mr. Kimball, as they went about their work. Although she was seated only a short distance away, the waist-high partition that separated her from their twinned desks might as well have been a brick wall, fifty feet long and five storeys high. With long grey beards tucked inside their waistcoats and white hair flowing past their shoulders, they were impassively hunched over a vast collection of ledgers in which they recorded the particulars of the city's vanished souls. Every so often they looked up from their desks to stare longingly into the distance as if they were a pair of apes caged within the menagerie at Central Park.

"Excuse me," Eleanor said, as she'd done every quarter hour since she'd arrived. "Could you spare a moment?"

Both men looked at her and then at each other.

"Mr. Kimball?" Eleanor said to the gentleman on the right.

"Osmund," the man corrected her. Pointing to his companion he added, "He's Kimball."

Eleanor swore the last time she interrupted the pair it was the other way around. Thank heavens they can tell each other apart, she thought, because surely no one else can.

"Mr. Osmund," she tried again, weary with waiting. "I've a missing person to report."

"Ah, yes!" he said with sudden enthusiasm. "We are aware that you're still here. Mr. Kimball will address your concerns."

Mr. Kimball scowled at his companion, then went back to his work.

Adjusting her skirt, Eleanor settled in for the next quarter hour. She hoped Adelaide and Dr. Brody were having better luck than she was.

Taking up a newspaper that'd been abandoned on the bench, Eleanor saw that it'd been folded open to the missing persons section.

Our lynx-eyed detective police need some widely spread organ to aid in their searches. Our illustrated paper is the only organ in America which combines immense circulation with amplest artistic resources. Perfectly reliable portraits pronounced by friends to be correct. Faithful facsimiles, striking likenesses, official information. Provided by G. Davis, exclusively for *Frank Leslie's Illustrated Newspaper*.

The listings of vanished persons were sandwiched between several notices for lost jewellery and missing dogs. Transcribed from police reports or placed by concerned individuals, they were meant to entice readers to take up the search. A few of them were accompanied by finely drawn illustrations.

Eleanor caught her breath as she counted how many women were on the list. Sixteen out of twenty this week alone, all under thirty years of age.

MISSING: GRETTA BUSKIRK: Twenty-two years old. Short. Thickset. Full features, pug nose, coarse voice. Has a small slit on right ear. Black hair, dark complexion and eyes, and speaks with a slight German accent. Last seen October 3rd at Broadway and Bowery. REWARD OFFERED, alive or deceased.

MISSING: BONNIE FLANNIGAN: Nineteen years of age. Light complexion, light brown hair. Green eyes. Petite. Last seen at Union Square on October 1st wearing blue calico dress. Last known words were to her sister, Polly. "Don't wait up for me tonight." Loved by family. Unaccountably absent. Dear Bonnie, please do not forsake us.

MISSING: LENA McLEOD: Twenty-five years old. Tall. Thin. Long brown hair. Blue eyes. Last known residence, Vinegar Hill, Staten Island. Was employed as a housekeeper at the Beadle residence. Brother from Scotland wishes to find her. He can be reached at the Seafarer's Mission in Fulton Landing.

Heart filled with dread, Eleanor couldn't bring herself to read any further. "Excuse me," she said, "Mr. Kimball, Mr. Osmund?"

As she waited for their response, another woman walked through the door. Lean and confident, she wore a dark tweed suit, a Phrygian cap, and carried a worn leather satchel at her side. Settling on the bench next to Eleanor she asked, "Been here long?"

"A few hours now," she replied. "I'd advise you make yourself comfortable. You may be in for a wait."

Wiping her hand on her skirt, the young woman held it out to Eleanor. Her fingers were smudged with charcoal and stained with ink. "Georgina Davis," she said. "*Leslie's Illustrated*. Pleased to meet you."

Eleanor accepted Georgina's hand. "Eleanor St. Clair, and likewise."

Getting up from the bench, Georgina whispered, "Let's see if we can't move things along." Taking a small wax-paper sack from her satchel she held it in the air and gave it a hearty shake.

The clerks turned in unison, their eyes lit with childish curiosity.

"Georgie," Mr. Osmund said. "Good to see you!"

"Are those lemon drops?" Mr. Kimball asked. "For me?"

Georgina took aim and tossed the crumpled bag so it landed in the centre of the line where the men's desks were butted together. Smiling she teased, "Be good, boys . . . share and share alike."

Before long the two men were smiling and puckering while licking sugar from their fingers.

"I suppose you've come to gather names for the vanished persons column?" Mr. Osmund finally asked.

"That I have," Georgina replied. "But I believe the fine lady over there was here first."

Motioning for Eleanor to approach, the two men took up their pens, ready to assist her.

"I'll be damned," Eleanor muttered, shaking her head. "What witchery is this?"

Georgina gave her a wink.

Taking turns the men asked Eleanor a series of questions—first Mr. Osmund, then Mr. Kimball (and so on and so forth).

"Name?"

"Eleanor St. Clair."

"Not *your* name," Georgina whispered. "The name of the missing."

"Oh, sorry," Eleanor said. "Beatrice Dunn."

"Age?"

"Seventeen."

"Seventeen, you say?"

"Have you checked the theatres?"

"Or the Tenderloin?"

"Or the East River?"

Eleanor scowled and crossed her arms.

"Nationality?"

"American."

"Height?"

"Five foot and a bit."

"Say, five foot one?" Mr. Kimball asked.

"One and a half?" urged Mr. Osmund.

"Two?" offered Kimball.

Eleanor stood and pointed to a height just below her own.

"Five foot three," Georgina declared with a confident nod.

"Weight?"

Eleanor held out her hands to indicate the size of Beatrice's waist, then compared it to her own.

"One hundred and ten pounds," Georgina said. "Approximately. Hair colour?"

"Red."

"Clothes last worn?"

"A party gown of black silk crepe de chine, embroidered with Egyptian glyphs in gold."

"Sounds fancy," Mr. Kimball said, eyebrow raised.

Sighing, Eleanor brought out a carte-de-visite of Minnie Stevens wearing the gown, and placed it on the man's desk. "That's not her, but it's the same dress."

Mr. Kimball took the photograph and stared at it for a moment before handing it to Mr. Osmund. The two men looked at each other and rolled their eyes.

"Date and time gone missing?" Georgina asked, prompting the men to stay on task.

"Saturday, October ninth, between seven thirty and eight o'clock."

"In the evening?"

"Yes."

"Place last seen?"

"The Fifth Avenue Hotel."

"Oh, I see," Mr. Kimball said, as if that had explained it all.

"Hmmm," Mr. Osmund added, taking a similar tone.

"Is something wrong?" Eleanor asked.

The men exchanged knowing looks but refused to answer.

"To what would you attribute Miss Dunn's disappearance?" Mr. Kimball asked.

"I've no idea," Eleanor said. "That's why I'm here."

"If you had to guess?"

"She had no enemies, no troubles that couldn't be solved, at least not that I know of." Eleanor didn't want to complicate matters by mentioning the girl's involvement with ghosts. The pair of codgers would have a high old time with that.

"When it comes to girls of a certain age," Mr. Osmund explained, "we generally find they tend to follow certain paths . . ."

"Lunacy," Mr. Kimball offered.

"Or suicide," Mr. Osmund said.

"Abduction."

"Or seduction."

"Or succumbing to the drink."

"Or a wily madam."

"Or religious fervour."

"Or some other nefarious scheme."

"Did she have cause to run away from her family?"

"Or a bad situation?"

"Do any of these things ring a bell?"

Eleanor glared at them both and shook her head.

"The police need to know what they're looking for, my dear," Mr. Kimball pressed.

"A slobbery fool."

"A degenerate girl."

"A dead body."

"Any guess as to whether or not she was in her right mind?"

"When?" Eleanor asked.

"At the time of her disappearance?"

"Or any time for that matter."

Eleanor took a deep breath, trying to hang on to her temper.

Georgina placed a supportive hand on her arm.

"It's important to get the details right," Mr. Osmund chided.

"For our records," Mr. Kimball said.

"And these cards," Mr. Osmund added, taking a stack of small notecards from atop a tall crooked pile, one of several that sat precariously on a shelf near his desk. "They're used to alert police and press." Handing the stack to Georgina he said, "Here's this week's missing, Georgie. I put the best ones on top."

Briefly thumbing through them, Georgina handed them back. "These are last week's."

Scratching his head, Mr. Osmund looked them over himself. "So they are," he said, exchanging them for a different, larger stack. "My mistake."

With a shrug Mr. Kimball offered an excuse. "A ship went down in the harbour last Friday. We had twenty missing husbands in one night alone."

Mr. Osmund lifted the left leg of his trouser to reveal a wooden peg. Pounding the end of his false limb on the floor he teased, "Missing . . . my foot!"

Eleanor stood. She'd had enough. Handing Mr. Kimball one of the teashop's cards, she said, "Please contact me at this address should any news come to light. Thank you for your time."

"Don't forget your picture," Mr. Osmund said, waving Minnie Stevens' photograph in the air.

Teary-eyed, Eleanor snatched it from his hand and rushed out of the office.

Georgina followed. "Wait," she called. "I think I can help."

"How?" Eleanor asked, stopping short, her voice sharp with hurt.

Guiding Eleanor to an empty bench in the hallway, Georgina sat beside her and pulled a sketchbook from her bag. "I'd like to include Beatrice in this week's column. I'll include a drawing of her if you'd like."

Eleanor was grateful for the offer, but confused as to how it might work. "I don't have a photograph of Beatrice. How can you draw her if you've never seen her face?"

Georgina opened her sketchbook to a blank page. "I don't necessarily need a photo, in fact I prefer not to rely on them exclusively. Most are just fantasies anyhow, created by a photographer working in a room filled with painted clouds and stuffed peacocks. I'm guessing that you have a picture of Beatrice in your mind that's truer than any carte-de-visite. If you share the details of it with me, I can put it on the page, and that just might be enough."

Down the hall, a couple of roughs were harassing a prostitute. "I was minding my own business!" she yelled. "Why can't you mind yours?" A group of sad-looking beggars filed past and out the door. They were returning to the streets after spending the night on the police station floor.

"All right," Eleanor said, "what do you need to know?"

Head down, pencil in hand, Georgina began the process of piecing together Beatrice's likeness. "What would you say is the shape of her face? Round, oval, square, heart-shaped?"

"Somewhat round," Eleanor said, looking over Georgina's shoulder. "But not full like a child's. Apple cheeked, yet ladylike."

"What about the length of her hair? Or its style?"

"It's quite long," Eleanor answered. "Down to her waist. But I think she planned to wear it up last night. She was supposed to wear that headdress that's pictured with the gown, but it got left behind."

"And this was the gown she was wearing?" Georgina asked, pointing to the card.

"Yes," Eleanor answered, holding it steady as Georgina continued her work.

"And what about her eyes," Georgina asked. "Are they round, narrow . . . close together, wide apart?"

"They're quite large and round and blue."

Bit by bit, the image began to take shape.

"Are her brows heavy or thin, flat or arched?"

"Heavy, but arched."

"Her nose?"

"Narrow. Slightly upturned."

"Is her chin rounded, pointed, dimpled?"

"Round, but firm."

Georgina paused and tapped the end of her pencil against her lips. "You mentioned she has red hair . . . is she freckled as well?"

Eleanor smiled. "Her skin is speckled everywhere, like a bird's egg."

"Was she wearing the necklace that's pictured in the photo? Any rings on her fingers, earrings perhaps?"

"No," Eleanor replied. "She didn't want to borrow Miss Stevens' jewels for fear she'd lose them."

"Did she have anything else of value that might have been taken from her person?"

"Not that I know of."

Making a few notes beneath the sketch, Georgina asked, "What was her business at the hotel?"

Eleanor bit her lip. "You won't believe me if I tell you."

"Try me," Georgina said.

"She was there to demonstrate her ability to speak with ghosts."

Underlining the word "ghosts" three times, Georgina asked, "Truly?"

"Cross my heart," Eleanor replied.

"That's good, actually," Georgina said with a thoughtful nod.

"It is?"

"People love stories about ghosts."

Eleanor gave a tired smile.

"We're almost done," Georgina assured her. "Just a couple more questions. Does she have a sweetheart?"

"No."

"Do you know of any unusual circumstances surrounding her disappearance? Was she acting out of character? Did she leave anything behind?"

"No and no," Eleanor answered. "I have nothing that could serve as a clue."

"What would you say is the most common expression she wears on her face? Quizzical, coy, shy?"

Closing her eyes, Eleanor thought of Beatrice standing at her side in the shop, always asking questions, always keen to learn. "Curious," she said, "but determined."

"That's excellent," Georgina said as she put a few final touches on the sketch. "One last question. Can you offer a reward?"

Wringing her hands Eleanor paused to think. She supposed she could count on Judith to contribute. "Yes, I think so," Eleanor answered. "Would five hundred dollars be enough?" It was the first number that came to mind.

Georgina whistled through her teeth. "That should do it." Turning her sketchbook towards Eleanor she said, "What do you think?"

"That's her," Eleanor said, shocked by the likeness. "That's Beatrice." A wave of worry suddenly came over her. All the questions she'd been keeping in check nagged at her heart. Where was the dear girl? Had she taken ill? Fallen into the wrong hands? Was she whole? Was she safe? "When will the notice appear in the paper?" she asked.

"Not until Saturday, I'm afraid," Georgina replied.

"I see," Eleanor said, disappointed.

Noticing Eleanor's dismay, Georgina said, "But I can go to the press and print up some handbills in advance so you can post them at the hotel and any place else you like."

"How soon can you have them finished?" Eleanor asked, fishing in her pocket for something to offer as an enticement. "I'm willing to pay."

Georgina waved the offer away. "No need for that," she said. "You'll have them by tomorrow."

You must know, Achilles, that Prayers are the
Daughters of Jupiter. They are crippled by frequent
Kneeling, have their faces full of Cares and Wrinkles,
and their Eyes are always cast towards Heaven.
— Joseph Addison, *Essays, Moral and Humorous:*
Also Essays on Imagination and Taste

Prayers Are the Daughters of Jupiter.

AFTER A LONG day of searching for Beatrice, Dr. Brody
went home and retired to his study. He'd informed Mr. Pryor,
the hotel detective, of the girl's disappearance, then talked to
every maid, porter and attendant he could find. After walking the streets for hours visiting every place he'd thought she
might go, he'd decided it best to call it a day. He wasn't sure
what else he could offer Eleanor and Adelaide short of what
steps to take should Beatrice's body be found. That was advice
he hoped he wouldn't have to give.

Sitting at his father's desk he contemplated taking out his
opium pipe. Having dabbled without becoming addicted,
he'd managed to stay away from it for some time now, but in
his current state of mind, the allure of the poppy was strong.
Mrs. Stutt had gone to bed and he had no other plans for the
night. The pipe and the glow of its attendant oil lamp seemed
better company than sitting alone with his guilt—for he
didn't count himself blameless in this terrible mess. On the
contrary, he felt he'd been the worst offender. Eleanor had

always been the voice of reason; Adelaide, even in her over-wrought enthusiasm, had been honest about her intentions; and he'd . . . well, he'd held back from taking too firm a stance on any of it, never willing to admit his hopes for where things might be headed, fearing it might make him seem arrogant, presumptuous, unfairly ambitious. Perhaps if he'd spoken up, laid out a plan for the future, Beatrice wouldn't have felt the need to run.

As he tripped the lock of the desk's hidden compartment, a knock sounded at the front door. Quinn found Alden Dashley standing on his stoop.

"Dashley," he said. "Do come in. Have you news to share?"

Alden stepped inside and removed his hat and overcoat. "No news, I'm afraid, but I thought I might remind you of a possible diversion. Heaven knows I could use one while we're waiting for Miss Dunn's safe return. Judith took to bed early, exhausted from pacing the floor, so I thought I'd take a walk and wound up here. The skies are clear and both Jupiter and Saturn are in the southeast sky. I was wondering if I might nip up to your father's observatory to have a look."

"Of course," Dr. Brody said, thankful for Alden's company. He couldn't think of a better interruption unless it was Beatrice herself. "I think that's an excellent plan."

They climbed the spiral staircase to the tower Tobias Brody had built atop his house, and stood side by side in the modest cupola.

Alden waited patiently as Quinn cleaned the lenses on the telescope in preparation for viewing the planets. "According to the *Clipper Annual* tonight's the best night to see Jupiter's bands," Alden remarked.

"Is that so?" Quinn asked, adjusting the scope's height, angle and focus.

"It's in Pisces," Alden directed, "with Saturn below to the left."

Squinting through the eyepiece, Quinn soon announced, "I've got it." Taking a step back he motioned to Alden. "Here, have a look."

Alden peered through the telescope. "Isn't that something!" he exclaimed. "The mighty Jupiter and its four moons as well."

"I Explore God's Creation," Quinn recited under his breath—a saying his father had taught him to help him remember the order of the Galilean moons.

"The sight that Galileo saw that changed the World," Alden mused. "Would you like to have a go?" he asked, stepping back from the instrument.

Quinn took his place. Staring into the heavens, he thought of the Romans who'd named the heavenly object, and how they'd seen it as something brilliant and mighty, worthy of bearing the name of their greatest god. How wondrous and strange it seemed to him, that men, himself among them, could now view the planet with such clarity and discernment, and yet still understand so little about it. Through his father's telescope, this overgrown spyglass, the mighty Jupiter appeared inconsistent—wobbling, flawed, wounded. A fitting sight for this night, he supposed. Men strove so hard to become god-like, forgetting that the world, God's world, would never allow them to be anything but less than perfect. Did that mean that they should stop their striving? No, but perhaps it meant that he should've paused to remember his place, to consider not just Jupiter, but its moons too. Fixed and faithful, Io was closest, then Europa and Ganymede fell into line, and this night, at this moment, poor Calisto was far on the opposite side, lonely and distant and seeming terribly out of reach.

The teashop was quiet except for Twitch, who was regaling Cleo with talk of Beatrice's goodness and beauty, and Eleanor, who was reciting an incantation to bring about her safe return.

> *Upon the wind,*
> *Within the air,*
> *I send my thoughts to Beatrice Dunn.*
>
> *I prick my thumb,*
> *I draw my blood,*
> *I send my heart to Beatrice Dunn.*
>
> *As above*
> *So below*
> *Let all kindly spirits know*
> *By foot and flight they now must go*
> *To find our Beatrice Dunn.*

Perdu stood guard, perched over the door, ready to alert his mistress to any change, any news, any danger.

Adelaide had chosen to walk past the hotel and through the park one last time before giving up for the night. Spotting the

Bird Lady sitting alone near the fountain, she'd settled next to her to keep her company.

The ragged-looking old woman was silent as Adelaide confessed her guilt, her worries and her fears. Extending her hand, she took Adelaide's in hers and gently stroked it, but never said a word.

Taking her last calling card from her pocket, Adelaide tucked it under the ribbon that ran around the Bird Lady's hat. It seemed the safest place to put it. "If you see her, or if you hear anything about her, come find me at this address."

On the streets surrounding the park, word got passed from guttersnipes to whores, from roughs to carriage drivers.

"Did you hear about that girl gone lost?"

"The girl from the teashop?"

"The one-eyed soothsayer?"

"No, the pretty young one. The ginger."

In the corridors of the Fifth Avenue Hotel, word got passed from scrubber girls to bootblacks, from chambermaids to porters.

"Do you suppose she's run off with a dandy?"

"Do you suppose she's met her death?"

"Do you suppose they'll offer a reward for the one who finds her?"

"Anything's possible, I guess."

In the basement below *Frank Leslie's Illustrated News*, Georgina Davis was tucked away in the back corner of a cavernous cellar, treadle pumping, flywheel spinning as she lost herself to the give and take of the platen on an old Franklin press. She'd spent the evening sitting at a bench, working to carve Beatrice Dunn's image out of a square piece of boxwood, curled shavings piling around her, clinging to her skirt. She'd set the finished engraving, along with several rows of type, in the press's bed, making a wish as she went, that her work might conjure up the girl whom Miss St. Clair had lost. The creaky *tick* and *ping* of the machine seemed to sing to her as it churned. "You may delay, but time will not."

Beatrice was still bound and gagged and lying on the floor of the parsonage cellar. Reverend Townsend had come and gone several times throughout the day to chastise her, to pray over her, to make certain her bonds were secure. There was never any mention of food or drink or kindness. There was much talk of God and sin and judgement. No indication he ever planned to let her go.

The ghost of Lena McLeod had come and gone as well. The lonely spirit had hovered near, to tell Beatrice tales of her own plight and to give her advice. "Deny all, but believe in your heart."

With what little strength she had, she tried to wriggle free from the ropes, but her attempts only managed to make her wrists raw and bloody. The cold damp of the cellar seeped into her bones, causing her to shiver and shake. Upon Reverend

Townsend's last visit for the night, she looked to him with pleading eyes and thought the word, *mercy*.

Lantern in hand, he'd turned from her and left her in darkness.

He who knows the Daughters of Jupiter, when they draw near to him, receives great Benefit from them; but as for him who rejects them, they entreat their Father to give his Orders to the Goddess to punish him for his Hardness of Heart.

October 11, 1880.

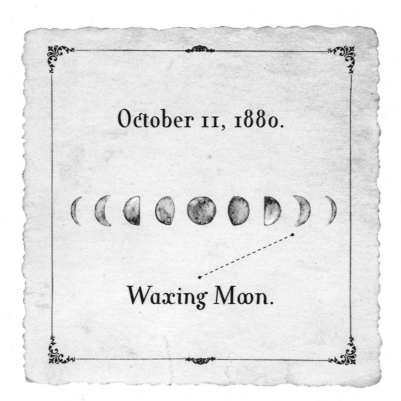

Waxing Moon.

NOTICE TO VACATE.

The Landlord of this property hereby gives notice of intent to raze the structure hereupon.

The tenants of said dwelling, namely the owners of the business ST. CLAIR AND THOM are advised to vacate the premises by NOVEMBER 1ST, 1880.

As of that date, any possessions, goods or effects remaining on said premises shall be confiscated and disposed of according to the landlord's discretion.

Let this notice serve as an official, binding document.

It shall not be removed from view.

Issued this day, OCTOBER 11, 1880

Cecil Newland

SIGNED: Mr. Cecil Newland, landlord.

E. M. Withrow

WITNESSED: Mr. E. M. Withrow.

Come, the Croaking Raven Doth Bellow for Revenge.

ON MONDAY MORNING, three sharp raps sounded at the teashop door. Eleanor held her breath as she went to answer it.

Mr. Withrow was there, hammer in hand.

"What's this?" Eleanor asked, of the notice now tacked to the door.

"It's your walking papers," Mr. Withrow answered with a smirk.

"If this is about the window . . . it's all fixed."

"Not my circus, not my monkeys," Mr. Withrow said, pointing to Cecil Newland's signature. "Mr. Newland's the proud new owner of this dump and he can do with it however he sees fit." With that he tipped his hat and walked away.

A sweet-faced waif stood in the shadow of the stoop, chewing on a stale piece of Mr. Markowitz's pumpernickel.

"Of course," Eleanor muttered, resisting the urge to tear down the notice. "Of course . . ."

The little girl looked up at Eleanor with sad eyes.

Eleanor dug a few coins out of her pocket and gave them to the girl. "Save some crumbs for me," she half-heartedly teased. "Soon I won't have a home either."

"Good luck to you, ma'am," the girl said before wandering away.

Inside the shop Eleanor paced the floor—bewildered and angry. "What will we do?" she said. "Where will we go? Why do men like Cecil Newland always manage to get what they want instead of what they deserve?"

Only Perdu and Cleo were there to hear her. The raven let out a cranky squawk of commiseration. The dog lay down at Eleanor's feet and rolled over.

Eleanor sat on the floor next to the pup and gave its belly a rub.

Adelaide had gone with Dr. Brody to Bellevue hospital and the City Morgue. They intended to check the medical wards, then visit the found persons gallery to see if Beatrice was among the unidentified dead. Eleanor had barely been able to stand the conversation that'd led up to their departure.

"I'm not saying she'll be there," Adelaide had said. "I just think it'd be wise to check."

"It doesn't seem right," Eleanor had argued. "Aren't there other things we should be doing than trolling through the morgue? Better ways to spend our time?"

"If you think of something, let me know. Until then, this is all I've got."

Dr. Brody had weighed in then, in an attempt to calm the waters. "Ruling certain things out can't hurt. In fact, it might serve to bring a little peace of mind."

But Eleanor couldn't shake the feeling that the morgue wouldn't hold any answers. Short of telling them not to go, what else could she say? She certainly didn't wish to argue with them. Since Beatrice had gone missing, the two had become a pair—she could hear it in the give and take of their conversations, see it in the way their bodies touched here and there. It was new, fragile, and despite all their worries, sweet. She didn't resent it for a minute, but with Beatrice gone it was difficult to see happiness as anything but out of place. Still, she couldn't deny that Brody seemed to be holding everything together, most especially Adelaide. There'd been moments when she'd felt that her friend was terribly close to running away, she was so guilty over Beatrice's disappearance. She just hoped Adelaide understood she didn't place any blame on her.

She needed Adelaide to be present, here with her, rather than running off every evening to the hotel or park. Where was the Adelaide who'd appeared after the dumb supper? The one who'd kept saying, "We're better together than apart." Eleanor was running out of magic she could perform alone.

But she wasn't ready to think the worst, not yet. That's why Adelaide's talk of the morgue had bothered her so. The very thought of Beatrice's body lying on a marble slab was like giving up. Eleanor had to believe that Beatrice was alive.

That morning she'd woken up feeling brittle and raw, yet hopeful. She'd turned the shop sign to OPEN, thinking someone might come through the door with good news, or that Beatrice herself would come skipping across the threshold as if nothing had happened. How long could this go on? How long before they learned the truth? Instead of answers they'd received an eviction notice.

Leaning over Cleo she put her head to the dog's heart, listening to the comforting throb and tick of it. She'd said yes to taking in the stray, thinking its appearance might be a sign—perhaps Cleo might be a benevolent spirit in changed form, come to guide the way. As she mused, the shop door opened, bells jangling.

"Hello," Georgina Davis called, "special delivery for Miss St. Clair."

"Over here," Eleanor replied, standing up, shaking her skirts.

"Everything all right?" Georgina asked. "I couldn't help but see the notice."

Eleanor let out a weary laugh. "When it rains, it pours."

"Sorry to hear that," Georgina said, setting a parcel on the counter. "Here are the broadsheets I promised. I thought you should have them as soon as possible. Any news?"

Shaking her head Eleanor said, "Thank you, and no." Georgina looked something like an overgrown pixie with her wiry limbs, inky fingers, and red felt cap askew. Another messenger sent by magical forces, perhaps. Unwrapping the parcel, she stared at Beatrice's image, blinking back tears. "You must've stayed up all night to get these done."

Georgina shrugged. "The sooner these notices get passed around town, the sooner someone might come forward with information. In my experience, the first hours and days are crucial to finding someone who's lost."

Eleanor nodded. "How long have you been working in the newspaper trade?"

"One year for the missing persons' column, three altogether for Mr. Leslie's papers. Mostly the ladies' beat—roller-skating clubs, women's societies, charitable organizations and such. If you need help distributing the notices, I'm happy to volunteer."

"I can't ask you to do that."

"Please," Georgina said, touching Eleanor's hand. "I'd like to."

"All right then," Eleanor said, turning the sign on the door to CLOSED. "Let's go."

Sister Piddock, making her morning rounds, stopped outside the teashop. She grinned ear to ear as she read the notice nailed to the door. "Our God is a wonderful God!" she exclaimed, clasping her hands together. "My prayers have been answered."

Reverend Townsend was coming up the sidewalk, contemplating Beatrice's fate in the brisk morning air.

"Good morning, Reverend," Sister Piddock said, giving him a wave. Noticing his hand was dressed with a bandage, she asked, "Have you injured yourself in some way?"

"A bite," Townsend replied, too distracted to lie.

"From a dog?" Sister Piddock asked, brow furrowed.

Reverend Townsend ignored the question. Let her think what she liked.

Cleo stood behind the door, crouched. Eleanor had left the dog and raven with strict orders: "No demons allowed in, no magic allowed out." Sniffing at the threshold the dog gave a low growl.

Taking a step away from the door, Sister Piddock said, "I wanted you to know that I thought your sermon yesterday was especially powerful. That story you told of the poor girl who'd been bewitched was very compelling. Will you visit her again? Do you believe she can be saved?"

"I will do all I can," the Reverend answered. "She suffers greatly. Much fasting and prayer is required."

"I shall remember her in my prayers, along with my prayers of thanksgiving," Sister Piddock said. Pointing to the notice, she smiled. "God has seen fit to remove mine enemy."

Reverend Townsend stepped forward and looked through the teashop window.

Cleo began to bark.

"The women who run this place are engaged in the Devil's work," Sister Piddock boasted. "One of them was even so bold as to set herself upon me the other day in the park. But now they will be put out."

"Was it Saturday?" the Reverend asked, remembering the one-eyed witch.

"Indeed it was," Sister Piddock answered. "But the Lord intervened and caused her to turn tail."

As Cleo continued to bark, Perdu hopped onto his perch in the window and peered out to the sidewalk. No sooner had he spotted the preacher than a terrible darkness came over his eyes. Within that darkness was a faint glimmer, and within that glimmer a faint noise—the sound of Beatrice crying. "Mercy," he croaked, causing the dog to fall silent. "Mercy . . ."

"Our God is a wonderful God," Reverend Townsend said, pleased with what he'd just learned. "He will provide."

"Amen," Sister Piddock said.

This Is the Place Where Death Delights to Help the Living.

A CROWD WAS gathered along a tiled hallway that skirted the west side of the City Morgue. Mothers, fathers, brothers, sisters, lovers, workmen, preachers, missionaries, roughs, prostitutes, paperboys and tourists—all were there to participate in the daily viewing of the unclaimed dead. Feet shuffling, elbows touching, voices hushed, the anxious onlookers waited at the gallery windows for the day's corpses to be revealed.

What drama would unfold today? What sadness, what ugliness, what evidence of brutality might they see? Some were there to search for loved ones, others only to satisfy their curiosity.

A curtain of glass and iron separated them from the dead. A patent lamp hung from the ceiling, its flame constantly burning, its flue set to draw out foul smells and bad air. Even with the hygienic contraption dangling above them, the men in the corridor cleared their throats loudly and often, while the women held handkerchiefs to their noses or sucked on candies flavoured with clove and mint. Consumed with thoughts of putrefaction, they were unaware that the soiled state and exhalations of their neighbours posed more of a threat to their well-being than the dead.

A pair of prostitutes, Elsie Trew in red velvet, Mae Blum in gaudy flounced skirts, held the railing at the far end of the viewing windows. They looked so much alike they could be sisters (but they weren't).

"I hope we don't see Jenny," Elsie said.

"I'm pretty sure we will," Mae replied as the spray of feathers in her hat drooped in the morgue's damp air. Their housemate, Jenny Greene, had disappeared from Madison Square and they hadn't seen her since.

"You think she's dead, or just hope she is?" Elsie asked.

"Oh, I know she is," Mae replied. "For a fact."

"That so?"

"I seen her tiptoeing across the telegraph lines and chimney pots last night. God strike me dead if I'm lying."

"I wish you hadn't said that."

"Why? 'Cause she's your friend?"

"No, because she still owes me two dollars for rent."

As the first body arrived behind the glass, the crowd leaned in for a better look. With deliberate care the coroner and his assistant lifted the cadaver from a wheeled stretcher and placed it on one of the marble tables that graced the gallery. This specimen was male, a gentleman of middle age, returned to the window for a second day of viewing. (Like the rest of the nameless bodies that came this way, he'd be displayed for three days before being carted off to a pauper's pit on Hart's Island. The only record of his having been in the gallery would be a portrait taken by the morgue's photographer and a breadbox-sized selection of his personal effects sent to gather dust in an out-of-the-way closet.) Naked, except for the length of gauze neatly covering his manhood, it was plain to see that whatever life he'd lived hadn't been easy.

His most notable disadvantage was his lack of legs. Both ended in stumps at the knees. A less pronounced but ragged scar that cut across his right shoulder possessed a similar sheen, all injuries sustained long ago. Among the tattered pieces of clothing the coroner had chosen to display with the corpse was a worn soldier's cap issued by the Union Army.

The coroner's description for the *Roll of Found Persons* read:

FOUND, October 10 at Pitt and Delancey Streets, male, approximately 40 years of age. Both legs missing from a previous injury. This unfortunate soul is thought to have been a veteran of the War Between the States, as the underside of the brim of his kepi is marked: *T.D.F. 13th N.Y.* Cause of death, consumption.

It wasn't unusual for the coroner to indulge in modest speculations about the deceased. Corpses that stirred his sympathy were often given captions in death. "Pretty blonde girl." "Portly matron with weary face." "Swarthy scar-faced gent." The sight of a clean liver on his examination table would lead the coroner to note, "The deceased was a temperate soul." A young lady found to be *virgo intacta* was described as "innocent and full of promise."

A gruff-looking man who was watching the proceedings clutched a torn-out page from *Leslie's Illustrated*. The entry for Gretta Buskirk was underlined and the words "reward offered" were circled with grease pencil. Hat cocked and eyes squinted, the man looked as if he were waiting for a racehorse to come into view around the clubhouse turn.

Sadly for him, the second body of the day belonged to a woman around fifty years of age, her dull brown hair streaked with grey, her belly bloated and veined, her sickly yellow skin mottled with angry purple bruises. Long scratches appeared along her thighs, some of them open and starting to rot. After today, her seventy-two hours would be up. The coroner had awarded her a single line in the *Roll of Found Persons*.

FOUND: October 9. Chrystie Street. Woman, grey hair, missing teeth, died from the drink.

The final cadaver to be brought to the gallery was another disappointment to the reward seeker: she, too, was not Gretta Buskirk.

FOUND: October 11, near Madison Square Park. Female, approximately twenty years of age. Hair, auburn. Eyes, blue. Cause of death: knife wound to throat.

Though kept as cool as the morgue could manage, the corpse was already showing signs of decay. It was clear she had been discovered days after she'd died, with the blue tinge to her skin and bites on her toes and fingers where rats had nibbled. Lips turned dark, gash in her throat stitched, wet hair swept back from her face: she looked more ghoul than girl. At the sight of her, a whisper went through the crowd: *murder*. The coroner folded the shroud down from the top, then up from the bottom, arranging it in such a way that the girl's remains were covered from her breasts to her thighs, but enough of her could be seen for someone who had been close to her to make an identification. He then arranged the girl's hair and turned her head slightly so something of her profile showed. He placed her hands on top of the shroud, one over the other, as if she were a sleeping princess waiting to be kissed awake.

Moving behind the marble slab, he hung the girl's garments one by one from an iron rod that ran the length of the back wall. Her undergarments were factory made and common, so he placed them together on one hook. Her dress was also shop-bought, nondescript, so it went up next. Her corset was by far the costliest item in the lot. Made from pink satin, heavily embroidered, and with silver clasps, he hung it against the dress's dark wool, making a backdrop for the young woman's prized possession. Lastly, he took up her mantle and boots, and a well-worn rabbit's foot strung on a piece of ribbon, and hung them side by side by side on three separate hooks.

On the other side of the glass two gentlemen dressed in black stared at the rabbit's foot, then bent their heads in consultation.

"Mr. Palsham isn't interested in her body," the one said. "Just the object."

"You're sure she's no witch, then?"

"There's nothing to her. The only thing that's been touched by magic is the charm."

"How do you propose we go about getting it?"

"When no one claims her, we will."

"And if someone does?"

"We'll offer to pay for the rabbit's foot."

"What if they refuse?"

"We'll persuade them otherwise."

Just then, Adelaide and Dr. Brody entered the gallery, Quinn finding the clearest path to the viewing windows. "Here," he said, taking Adelaide's arm, "this way." He wanted to get them in and out of the place as quickly as possible, for her sake. They fell in behind the two men in black, who blocked their view; they'd have to wait their turn. Resting her hand in the crook of Quinn's good arm, Adelaide lifted her veil, went up on tiptoes and craned in an attempt to see past the men.

Shaking, she came down off her toes, and clutched at Quinn's coat. "There's a girl . . . I can't see all of her but I think her hair is red."

Dr. Brody snuck a look between the men. "More auburn than red," he replied, but not the least bit convinced it wasn't Beatrice.

Adelaide assumed the worst. How would she break the news to Eleanor? "Please," she said, edging close to one of the gentlemen in front of her. "Make room for me."

The man turned and stared, then gave a slight tug on his companion's sleeve, who also turned to look down on her. Neither moved.

Adelaide assumed they were just another pair of insensitive souls gawking at the tangle of scars on her face. "Surely what's behind the glass is more interesting than this," she said, hoping to shame them into taking their leave.

"Let the lady have a look," Dr. Brody said. "You've had your chance."

Muttering one to the other, the men shoved past them.

Shaking off their rudeness, Adelaide stepped forward with Quinn and they took the men's spot at the window. It wasn't Beatrice. Blinking back tears, Adelaide found she couldn't see straight. She wiped her eye with a handkerchief, and it was as if the sight in her lost eye had been restored. When she looked again through the glass, she saw a dark figure standing over the young woman's corpse with a bloody knife in hand. She watched in horror as the corpse changed into a trembling, terrified Beatrice. Adelaide gripped the brass rail that ran along the length of the glass and closed her eye, a wave of dizziness causing her to feel as if she might faint.

"Adelaide," Quinn said, his arm circling her shoulders. "Are you all right?"

"It's not her," Adelaide said shaking her head. "It's not her."

"We've seen enough," Quinn said. "Let's get you home."

The ghost of Jenny Greene floated to the window and watched Adelaide leave. Then slipping behind the marble slab she stared at her cold dead body. Although she'd died days ago, she'd only been brought to the morgue early that morning. The coroner had cleaned her, stitched her up like a treasured rag doll. Then she'd been rolled into another building so a photographer could take her picture. The kindly gent had talked to her as he'd gone about his work, his friendly voice chattering away from behind his boxy camera. He'd said he was sorry no one had found her sooner. She'd shouted at him over and over, "I know who done it. I'll take you to him," but the photographer hadn't heard her. Once he'd finished his task, he'd disappeared to the darkroom to sniff away the wretched stench of her remains with an ether-soaked rag.

Looking at the other people lined up to see the dead, Jenny recognized the two girls she boarded with.

"I'm here!" she cried, as they came towards her body.

"I think that's her," Elsie said, putting her hand to her mouth. "I think it's Jenny."

"I'm not so sure," Mae said. "It's hard to tell, the body is so rotten."

Elsie pointed to the clothes hanging on the rod. "That's her corset there, the one she'd never let me borrow."

"Lots of girls have corsets like that."

"But do them same girls carry around a rabbit's foot on a ribbon?"

"Well so what if it is Jenny?" said Mae. "We can't claim her. We've got no money to bury the body."

"We could at least tell them her name."

"And run the risk that the coppers might think we done her in? No, thank you, ma'am. Let's get out of here."

Elsie took one last look at the body before they turned to go.

Nose pressed to the window, Jenny waved goodbye.

Once the pair was out on the sidewalk, Elsie asked, "You think it might be that preacher who did it? Who slit Jenny's throat?"

"Even if it was," Mae replied, "there's a tale no one would believe, especially not from a pair of whores."

"Ain't you scared?"

"Of what?"

"That it might happen to you?"

"I just won't go to Madison Square no more, and neither should you."

"Guess that rabbit's foot weren't so lucky after all."

In as much as the devilish workings of the witch persisted upon the girl (for they could be seen in the damsel's eyes) I continued to visit the haunted chamber in which she was kept. Through experiments and prayer I endeavoured to put a stop to the Invisible Furies rising within her and to turn her heart by whatever means God saw fit.

It is a dark dispensation of Divine Providence that such an innocent should be under the influence of the Fiends of Darkness. Although I could not see or hear the evil that entertained her (and I hope I never shall) it was made known to me by various means, most prominently by the words uttered from her mouth when a course of Godly questions were put to her. Oh how she begged to learn how she might thwart the temptations of that diabolical witch! For some time I carried on with the questioning, followed by much prayer and fasting. No exercise of religion gave so much vexation unto the evils that beset her as the singing of Psalms.

As the third night of her seclusion approached, the afflicted girl was finally and forever delivered. Prayers poured forth from her mouth, unbidden.

—from *An Attempt to Cure Witchcraft:*
The Story of Mercy Wylde

A Brand Pluck'd Out of the Burning.

AFTER RECITING A lengthy prayer of thanksgiving, Reverend Townsend rose from his knees and turned to his desk. Among the books and papers that littered its surface was a shallow brass bowl containing the coiled length of Beatrice's hair. The edge of the bowl was inscribed with the words, GOD LOVETH THE CHEERFUL GIVER. Taking the long red lock in hand, he admired its sheen, its softness, its fiery colour. He'd hated taking it from her, but he'd known that it had to be done. Vanity was generally the first weakness witches seized upon in the young women they wished to control. *They first used a thousand Flatteries and Allurements to induce her unto a compliance with the Desire of the Devil. They showed her very splendid garments, and thence proceeded onto greater glories, which they promised her if she would sign away her soul.* Did he need any more proof? How crushed the girl had looked when he'd told her he'd destroyed her dress, that terrible, whorish gown given to her by that witch. Tonight he would burn her hair as well, to cast out any dark workings that might dwell within its strands.

Although his path had been quite difficult, he felt progress had been made. Late last night he'd entered the damsel's cell to find her docile, the evil within her stayed. The witch's mark hadn't returned, and the brand that'd replaced it was flushed and bright with blood. To test the power of God's touch upon her, he'd loosened her bonds. She'd remained quiet and still, only groaning softly. Amen! Glory to God! And glory to Him for revealing the witch's dwelling to him through Sister Piddock. The good news that the foul women were being cast out onto the street was more proof that his prayers were working. *But there is cause to fear that she who afflicted Mercy is as dangerous and damnable a witch as ever was in the world. If only the words of this young woman were enough to prove it so.*

Beatrice woke from a fitful sleep, somehow returned to the straw mattress and dressed again in her shift. She would've thought she was back to where she'd started, but the painful, angry burn on her thigh and the aching lump at the side of her head told her different. She rose, gingerly, and made her way to the bucket in the corner of the cell. It had been emptied. Squatting over it, she urinated, then stoically wiped herself with the hem of her shift.

In front of her she spied a stray lump of ashen coal that'd escaped the scuttle the preacher had used to heat his brand. Picking it up she found a discreet spot on the wall, behind the mattress, and scraped two dark marks onto the stone, one for each night she'd been here. She tucked the coal inside a hole in the mattress to save it for future days, how few or many there might be. It felt remarkably good to make those two small marks: proof that she was here. Oh how she missed paper and pen and the flow of ink as her thoughts turned to words on a page. She'd never thought of writing as an act of defiance, but those two marks proved it to be so. Her need to leave something of herself was overwhelming. If she was to die here, she wouldn't let him forget she'd lived.

What kind of ghost would she be? Would she be carried off to some happy plane where her mother and father resided? Or would she be stuck in this dank cellar, sad and confused, like Lena McLeod?

Sitting back down on the mattress, she brought her mother's face to mind, loving, gentle, kind. Then she spent a good long while composing a letter to Lydia. She pictured her hand moving across the page, saw the words falling in line, one after another. *What wonders the city holds! How happy I am to be here! There are so many marvellous sights to see, so many opportunities ahead! If I don't see you before, I'll visit you for Christmas. I wouldn't miss your plum pudding for the world!*

Plum pudding. Eggnog. Roast turkey. Giblet gravy. Cherry cordial. Her hunger was its own animal, growling in her belly, pawing at her brain. To tame it she thought of Eleanor's dream tea, hoping the mere memory of the scents of lavender, mugwort and lemon balm would ease her mind. She thought of Eleanor's wise and patient teaching and Adelaide's style, and her sharp wit. She thought of Dr. Brody's dedication to finding the truth, Perdu's shining, curious eyes, Judith Dashley's kindness. Were they looking for her? She hoped they weren't in danger.

She thought of the ghosts who'd crossed her path, and all the strange, wonderful things she'd learned since she'd come to New York. Why had she walked away from the hotel? All she wanted now was to be back at the teashop, curled up on her bed. Closing her eyes she pictured the walls of her room lined with pages of newsprint and the notes she'd made from

Eleanor's grimoire. She saw the bottle on the windowsill that held her witch's ladder.

It was the one spell she knew by heart. She felt as if it lived inside her. She could do it now, make it here. She tore the hem of her shift and worked to unravel some threads. She had no feathers to tie to it and the hair on her head wasn't long enough to braid along the ladder's length, but she hoped that what Eleanor had said was true—*the more you strive to make magic, the more likely it is to find you.* If so, then it was worth trying to cast the spell.

Just then Lena's ghost appeared at her side, brought forth by the sound of ripping cloth. "Are you planning to do away with yourself?"

Beatrice replied, "Why would you think that?"

Sticking out her tongue, the lonely spirit tugged at an imaginary rope around her neck. "That's what I did." Looking around she said, "Though I'm not quite sure how you might go about it. There used to be a window over there with bars across it, but after I did the deed, a man came with a trowel and bricked it over."

"That's *not* what I mean to do."

"But what *are* you doing?" Lena begged. "Maybe I can help."

Finally freeing a long piece of thread from her shift Beatrice said, "I'm making a witch's ladder."

"To curse him!" Lena clapped her hands. "I've heard of such charms, but I never saw one. They say you can cause great illness that way, even death. I wish I'd known how to make one, I would've cursed him myself."

Beatrice wound the thread around her finger, thinking, then said, "I'm afraid I don't know anything about curses. I've only made one witch's ladder before, and it was to make a wish."

Grinning, Lena whispered, "A curse is just a wish turned on its head."

"All I want is to be free from this place," Beatrice said.

"What do you care how it happens?"

Tying a knot in the end of the thread Beatrice began to recite the spell. "By knot of one, my spell's begun . . ."

Lena reverently repeated the words.

The sound of Reverend Townsend's boots echoed on the stairs.

"He's coming!" Lena whispered. "You're done for if he finds the charm!"

Beatrice tucked the thread in the mattress alongside the piece of coal.

Reverend Townsend entered the cell, wooden rod at his hip, prayer book in one hand, a low stool in the other. Pipe clenched between his teeth, he shut the door and sat himself down on the stool. Opening the book, he brought out a notice that'd been folded and stuck between its pages.

Smoothing the paper flat, Reverend Townsend cleared his throat. "You are Beatrice Dunn?"

You are a witch. No one to be trifled with.

From where she sat, Beatrice could make out the word MISSING across the top of the page and what seemed to be a likeness of her face. "Yes," she said, incredibly relieved that people were searching for her. Maybe it would scare the preacher into letting her go.

He stared at her with great concern. "She means to find you."

"Who?" Beatrice asked. Did he know of Eleanor and Adelaide?

"The woman who bewitched you."

Lena tapped on Beatrice's shoulder and hissed in her ear, "Deny everything, or else he'll kill you."

Beatrice shook her head. "I'm not bewitched."

"That's what she wishes you to think."

"Who?"

"The witch."

"How am I to know her if she doesn't have a name?" Lena laughed.

Reverend Townsend scowled. "Do you believe in witches?"

"Deny it!" Lena urged.

Beatrice tried to keep a clear head, but Lena was so close she wasn't sure which thoughts were hers or the ghost's. "I don't know what a witch is."

"How can you be sure you've not been bewitched if you don't know what a witch is?" the Reverend pressed.

Beatrice brushed the spirit away. "If I were to come across any such person as you imagine, I should think I would know it."

"How?"

"By God's grace."

"Who is your god?"

"The god that made me."

The preacher smiled at her. "Do you believe in the Devil?"

"I do," Beatrice answered, staring him straight in the eyes.

"Have you ever seen him?"

"Only in the evil deeds of men."

"Have you ever seen strange creatures lurking about?"

"What sort of creatures?"

"Those not of this earth."

"Goblins or fairies?"

"If you like," Reverend Townsend replied.

"No. Never."

"Do you ever hear voices when no one's there?"

Lena flew in front of Beatrice's face and shook her head. "You must deny it!"

With innocent eyes, Beatrice said, "Only those who bid me to do what's right."

Reverend Townsend shifted forward on his stool. "As in angels?"

"If you like."

Closing his eyes the preacher paused for a moment of contemplation. Then looking at Beatrice, he said, "If you expect mercy from God, you must look for it in confession."

"I've nothing to confess."

"I beg you, dear girl, give glory to God and confess the name of your oppressor to me or all will be lost."

Beatrice couldn't bear the thought of Adelaide or Eleanor suffering, especially not because of her. She would not give this man their names. "If you wish to think me a witch, so be it. If you wish to kill me, then do so."

"I've said nothing of death," Reverend Townsend stammered. Gripping the handle of his rod, his eyes narrowed. "Who spoke to you of such things?"

"Nobody," Beatrice insisted.

"Is someone whispering in your ear? Tell me what they say—I demand it."

Lena frantically whispered in Beatrice's ear. "If you know the Lord's Prayer, recite it now."

Beatrice bowed her head and began to pray.

Our Father, which art in Heaven,
Hallowed be Thy name.

Thy kingdom come, Thy will be done,
On Earth as it is in Heaven.
Give us this day our daily bread,
And forgive us our trespasses, as we forgive them
    that trespass against us.
And lead us not into temptation, but deliver us
    from evil.
For thine is the kingdom, the power and the glory,
    for ever and ever.
Amen.

Heart softened, the preacher knelt in front of Beatrice. "Amen!" he exclaimed. "Praise God."

As he sang a psalm of thanks, Lena McLeod's ghost plucked a long red hair from the sleeve of his jacket. "Take this," she said and handed it to Beatrice. "Use it wisely."

My dear Beatrice,

I was glad to receive your most recent letter and to find that you are happy in your work and life in the city. Life here in Stony Point is uneventful, as ever. Just the way I like it.

With that in mind, I've decided to decline your invitation to visit for now. Autumn is here, winter not far behind and I would much prefer to make the trip in spring, thus giving you more time to get to know the place so you might give me a tour of your New York. Please understand that delaying my visit doesn't mean you're not welcome home anytime. Would you consider coming to Stony Point for Christmas? Miss St. Clair and Miss Thom are welcome to join you, of course.

I read about the grand parade put on by the Masons in honour of the obelisk's journey to Central Park. It seems as if you and your teashop were right in the middle of the celebrations! I hope it wasn't too noisy and taxing for a country-raised girl. Not that you haven't taken up and mastered every challenge that's ever been handed you. I know I rarely say it, since sentimentality isn't my forte, but I'm proud of your stick-to-itiveness and your pioneering spirit. I like to think perhaps I've even had a bit to do with it.

Be curious, smart, and safe, as I know you always are.

With affection,
Lydia

St. Clair and Thom.

ELEANOR MEASURED ROSE petals, hawthorn berries, St. John's wort, lemon balm and lavender into a waiting pot—a blend of buds and roots meant to soothe a broken heart. Catching a glimpse of Adelaide's face across the room, she added a second dose into the pot, thinking she'd better make enough for two.

Adelaide had returned from the morgue tired and shaken. Taking Eleanor aside, Dr. Brody had said, "I've an errand to run, but I'll be back this evening. I imagine it might be good for you two to spend some time together." The more Eleanor got to know him, the more she realized just how lovely he was. "Thank you," she'd said. "We'll see you tonight."

The two women sat at the table by the front window sipping their tea in silence. They'd agreed not to talk of the eviction notice, at least not for the time being. Since Beatrice had disappeared, every minute felt like an hour, every hour, a day. The end of the month seemed a lifetime away.

Eleanor retrieved Lydia's letter from the pocket of her apron and passed it to Adelaide. "This came in the post today."

Adelaide scanned it, then set it on the table. "I don't know what to say."

"Should we write to the woman? She'll be expecting a letter from Beatrice in return."

Adelaide shook her head. "She wrote the letter before Beatrice went missing. Maybe the girl is back in Stony Point, safe and sound. If we send a frantic note about not knowing where she is, whatever tale Beatrice has spun for her aunt will be torn to shreds."

"I have to believe if Beatrice was back home, she would've sent word by now. Even a telegram."

Adelaide poured more tea into her cup. "How long do we search for her?"

Eleanor crossed her arms. "How can you ask that?"

"I'm as worried as you are," Adelaide insisted. "But I also wish to be practical, for both our sakes. How long before we decide it's more likely she's dead than alive? What do we do when we've run out of places to look? Haunt the same spots, day after day, eventually becoming ghosts of ourselves?"

"She's only been missing for two days."

"It feels like a hundred."

Adelaide took inventory of Eleanor's facial expression, her body language, her posture: worried, fidgety, tightly wound. She decided to change the subject. "Did any customers come in today?"

Pointing to a stack of the notices Georgina had printed, Eleanor replied, "I kept the shop open for awhile, but then I went out to hand those around."

There was no escaping it. Not even for a minute.

Just then the bell on the door rang and Judith Dashley came bursting in, clutching the afternoon paper. "Tell me it's not her," she said, trembling as she spread a page of wrinkled newsprint on the table in front of them.

Special to The Evening Star. Police were alerted to a murder scene in the early hours of Monday morning when the body of a young woman was discovered in an alleyway near Madison Square Park. Her identity is unknown. The Head Coroner of the City Morgue estimates the deceased is approximately twenty years of age. Her hair is light auburn. Her eyes, blue. Cause of death: knife wound to the throat. Anyone with information concerning the victim or the crime is asked to contact Police Headquarters immediately. The body and the woman's personal effects will remain on display at the morgue until Wednesday.

Eleanor reached for Judith's hand. "It's not her, I promise."

"But how can you be sure?"

Adelaide made room for Judith to sit next to her. "I went to the morgue today. It's not her."

Judith gasped, eyes teary. "How horrible!"

Eleanor went to fetch more tea.

Judith attempted to calm herself. "I came by earlier to see how I might help, but I missed you both. Alden says I shouldn't be a pest, but I can't help it. And when I saw the notice on the door, I saw red. I went straight away to Mr. Newland's office to argue on your behalf."

Nearly dropping the fresh pot of tea, Eleanor exclaimed, "Oh Judith, you shouldn't have."

Judith sighed. "I had to try. Sadly, he wouldn't hear me out. He said 'business is business' and showed me to the door.

What a scoundrel Mr. Newland is! How dare he toss you out on the street!"

Adelaide poured for Judith. "Thank you for trying. Clearly Mr. Newland didn't know who he was dealing with."

After adding a dollop of honey, Judith picked up her spoon and gave it a vigorous stir. "You're not to worry. I'll take you in myself. You can move into the rooms next to mine. I don't care what Marietta Stevens thinks."

"Why would it bother her?" Adelaide asked.

Judith bit her lip. "She's worried about Beatrice, of course, as we all are . . . in fact, she's got the hotel detective on the case and her entire staff on their toes. She's even mentioned hiring a Pinkerton . . ."

"But . . ." Adelaide prompted.

Keeping her eyes on her teacup, Judith said, "Just don't expect her to openly show her support."

Eleanor shrugged.

Adelaide shook her head. "If she's upset about her daughter's precious gown, then she can go to hell."

"No, it's not that." Picking up one of the missing person's notices, she pointed at the text. "It's this."

LAST SEEN AT THE FIFTH AVENUE HOTEL.

"Beatrice is missing, and that's what she's most concerned with?" Adelaide sounded more resigned than angry. "Nothing like a scandal to show who your true friends are."

Judith gave Adelaide's hand a pat. Taking a sip of her tea, she turned to Eleanor, hoping that they could all think of something else for at least one moment. "I must tell you of the dream I had last night. Maybe you can make something of it."

"Of course," Eleanor said.

"It's the main reason I tried to find you this morning," Judith said. "Beatrice was in it, her face as plain as day."

Adelaide leaned forward.

"We were sitting at a table . . . you two, Beatrice and me. It wasn't here at the shop, though—it was in a place I've never been. The room was rustic—pot boiling over a fire, a broom leaning against the mantel, a long sturdy table set in the centre of the floor—the kind of place you imagine when you read a tale about a country cottage where fairies dwell. There were flower garlands woven through the rafters. We were laughing, and drinking tea."

"It sounds lovely," Eleanor said, thinking it sounded an awful lot like her childhood home. Wondering if it was a sign somehow sent by her mother, she asked, "What kind of flowers?"

"Forget-me-nots," Judith replied. "I remember because it's not something you'd ever see here in the city."

Adelaide asked, "What kind of tea?"

Sniffling the air as if it held the memory of her dream, Judith said, "Rosehip. Yes, I'm almost certain it was rosehip."

"Was that the whole dream?"

"Yes," Judith replied. "What do you think it means?"

Tears in her eyes, Eleanor said, "It means we shouldn't stop searching."

Judith nodded. "That's what I thought. What more can I do? I want to help. I've a NWSA meeting tomorrow. We can distribute some of those notices, if you can spare them."

Handing part of the stack to Judith, Adelaide said, "Yes, that would be good."

Eleanor moved behind the counter where she scooped several spoonfuls of tea into a jar. Tightening the lid, she gave the jar to Judith. "Tonight after dark, make a cup of this tea, then tuck yourself into bed and try to dream. If you see Beatrice again, come tell me. Who knows where it might lead."

Judith kissed both witches on their cheeks and scurried out the door.

As they watched her move off down the sidewalk, Adelaide thought of the vision she'd had at the morgue that morning. The picture of Beatrice she'd been shown wasn't nearly so lovely as the one Judith had seen. She'd thought of telling Eleanor but couldn't bring herself to do it. Turning to her friend she asked, "Do you think there might be something to Judith's dream?"

"I hope so," Eleanor said, thinking, *Hope is all we've got.*

The Witch of Blackwell's Island.

RAIN OR SHINE, snow or swelter, spring, summer, fall and winter, the women of Blackwell's Lunatic Asylum were led outside for a daily walk, or as the inmates called it, being put "on the rope." One by one the women were fitted with wide leather belts, then tethered by shackle, lock and chain to a thick, greasy line—two by two along the length of it, twenty-two women in all. A pair of nurses kept watch over them, one regularly shouting, "Hands to yourself!" the other crossly commanding, "Keep off the grass!" Nervously, the patients snaked their way along the gravel path. Some dragged their feet, others took to kicking stones. One tiny, meek woman, grateful to feel the warmth of the sun, turned her face to the sky as she shuffled along.

These were the first faces Dr. Brody encountered as he approached the asylum after his ferry ride across the East River from Manhattan. Surveying them, he thought, *Who knew that Hell was so close by?* He was glad he hadn't told Adelaide of his plans. She'd witnessed enough horror for one day.

He figured his chances of finding Beatrice here were slim, but he'd figured he should try. One of his acquaintances from medical school, Dr. Leonard Pitkin, had recently accepted a position at the place, so he'd sent a telegram announcing his intention to visit. He hoped Pitkin might allow him to search the recent asylum records for Beatrice's name. And while he was at it, he'd ask after Bart Andersen's girl, Sophie.

The main building was much larger than he'd imagined. The stone edifice was grand and gleaming, consisting of two long wings that stretched out in the shape of an L, providing two sides of the large courtyard. An octagonal tower rose from the centre, the ornate dome of its rotunda three storeys high, as if to house a band of distraught princesses being kept against their will. The rest of the yard was bounded by a thick wooden fence so tall one could only make out the tops of the masts and sails of the ships in the nearby harbour. Stepping through the main entrance, he was met with one of the great architectural wonders of New York, a grand interior staircase that spiralled to the roof of the rotunda like the twisted tail of a mythical serpent. Sunlight streamed from the dome above. To those visitors who went no further, there was nothing but reassurance to be found in both the grand space and the motto that graced the wide stone arch above the main door: WHILE I LIVE I HOPE. If the place was anything like the Salpêtrière, Brody thought, the corridors beyond were filled with Gothic nightmares and dark horrors. Making his way to the reception kiosk, he rang a bell to get the attention of the nurse on duty. "Excuse me," he said to the matronly woman who sat behind the desk, "I'm here to see Dr. Pitkin."

The round-faced nurse pushed back from her desk, causing the casters on her chair to squawk in protest. "Do you have an appointment?" she asked, her voice flat.

"No," Brody replied, "but I believe he's expecting me."

"Your name?"

"Dr. Quinn Brody."

The nurse sighed and rolled her eyes, then rose from her chair. "I'll see if he's available."

Dr. Pitkin seemed glad to see him. "Brody," he said with a kind smile, extending his hand before pulling it back with some embarrassment. "What brings you out to the island?" He was cheerful and well-pressed and Quinn wondered how long both would last.

"I'm here to inquire about a young woman who's gone missing," he said. "She's been gone since Saturday with no word to family or friends. I don't imagine she's here, but one never knows. She could've suffered a bump on the head or a terrible shock that might've rendered her senseless or dumb. Some well-meaning police officer could've brought her here, not knowing what else to do. I'm sure you've heard of such cases?"

Dr. Pitkin nodded. "Sadly, it's not uncommon for troubled girls to get brought out here, by police or even neighbours who make their own diagnoses of hysteria, brain fever or mania. Sometimes I think the coppers would rather leave them with me than deal with them on the streets."

"I can assure you this girl is of sound mind," Dr. Brody interjected, "but if something knocked her for a loop . . .'"

Dr. Pitkin smiled and raised a finger. "Say nothing more. Would you like to check the list of recent arrivals to see if she's on it?"

"If it's not any trouble," Dr. Brody said with a nod.

Dr. Pitkin looked to the nurse behind the reception desk.

"Happy to," she cheerfully replied, her attitude completely changed in Dr. Pitkin's presence. Clearly, she fancied him. Opening a large ledger, she asked, "What's her name?"

"Beatrice Dunn. She's been missing since Saturday night."

Licking her thumb, the nurse turned the pages of the register until she found the proper date. Running her finger down the page, she checked each entry, line by line. After several minutes, she finally looked up at Brody and said, "I don't see her name listed."

"Thank you for checking," Dr. Brody said.

Dr. Pitkin leaned across the desk and touched the nurse's hand. "Thank you, Nurse Brewster."

As the two men made to walk away, she called after them. "Wait. I see here that we had two unidentified girls come in on Saturday night. One couldn't speak, the other said she was Marie Antoinette."

Checking his watch, Dr. Pitkin turned to Dr. Brody and said, "They should be in the courtyard right about now with the rest of the inmates. Shall we go see if one of them might be her?"

In his walk from the ferry, Dr. Brody hadn't thought that any of the women tethered to the rope had resembled Beatrice, but it was worth taking a second look. "Yes," he said. "Please."

The doctors caught up with the women as the nurses were escorting them back into the building. Moving down the line, Dr. Brody looked each one of them in the eyes. They greeted him with scowls, laughter, smiles, winks and blank stares. One woman growled, then licked her lips.

An aged woman in the middle of the bunch flapped her arms and repeatedly moaned, "Oh dear . . . oh no . . . I'm going to soil myself!"

"Keep your pie and shit holes shut," the woman next to her groused.

Reaching the end of the line, Dr. Brody said to Pitkin, "She's not here."

"Sorry I couldn't be more help," the doctor said. "I'll look out for her."

Dr. Brody was about to take his leave, when he remembered Bart Andersen's desperate plea. "If I can trouble you for one more moment, Doctor, there's a patient I'd like to inquire about on behalf of a friend. He visits her quite regularly and seems to feel there might be grounds for her release."

"What's her name?" Dr. Pitkin asked.

"Sophie Miles," Brody answered.

"I know the case well."

"Would I be able to look at her file?"

"I'll get it for you."

Dr. Pitkin settled him in his office, and before long returned with a large brown envelope. Handing it over, he sat in the chair behind his desk and said, "Terrible crime she committed. But since she was completely out of her head, the court saw fit to send her here instead of the Tombs. I've seen some improvement in her since I've arrived and there are days when she seems quite recovered, but I'm not sure she'll ever be fit to leave."

Dr. Brody took the records from the envelope and scanned the page that detailed her admission to the asylum.

SOPHIE MILES. Aged 28. Found guilty of throwing vitriol in a woman's face resulting in grievous physical harm. The victim suffered the loss of her right eye and extensive facial scarring. The patient mentioned specific delusions and an outright belief in witchcraft. Her answers were presented in a manner that showed mental instability, violent excitability and a strong disrespect for authority. There is a deep concern for the safety of all those who might come into contact with her. All measures should be taken to subdue the patient at the first sign of agitation.

"She's not so unstable these days," Dr. Pitkin remarked. "She spends most of her time on the third floor, in the small parlour just off the fresh air pavilion. She has a fondness for sewing rag dolls. Would you like to meet her?"

Dr. Brody was shocked and unnerved by what he'd read. "I'm grateful, but not today. I should be getting back to the city."

Sophie Miles was, indeed, seated in a rocking chair in the corner of the parlour, sewing basket at her side. She was giving her attention to a small rag doll in her lap, the one she'd made in the likeness of Bartholomew Andersen, right down to his plaid suit, jaunty hat and peg leg. Holding the doll by its tiny hands she kissed its face, made it dance. "Why is it taking so long?" she asked. "Why haven't you gotten me out of here yet?"

Not an hour before, she could've sworn she'd received a sign of her impending release when she'd performed the little daily ritual she used to detect her future. Cupping her thimble to her ear she'd listened for the prophetic voice that lived inside it. Most days it spoke of simple things she could do to get ahead—"steal that fork," "trip that inmate," "pretend to like Dr. Pitkin"—but today she'd distinctly heard a man's voice within, speaking her name as his footsteps drew near.

The other women in the room were engaged in embroidery, cross-stitch, watercolours. One of them left her work to come close to Sophie and whisper, "Witch." Then another woman did the same, and another, and another. Slyly avoiding the eyes and ears of the room's attendant, they came at her, chanting under their breath, "Witch, witch, she's a witch . . ." not so regularly that they'd get caught, but often enough to drive her mad.

Sophie did her best to ignore their taunts. Putting her thimble to her ear again, she listened closely, but sadly the footsteps had vanished. The usual voice that spoke to her sighed and said, "He's gone away and it's all because of that evil bitch." Seeing the soothsayer's face in her mind's eye, Sophie muttered under her breath, "I'll not let her win." She tied a small noose out of red embroidery floss loosely around the poppet's neck. "Someday soon, love," she whispered to the doll. "Or else."

In the hours after the evil influence had fled, the girl came to her senses and to God. I prayed heartily through these precarious moments and observed her with great care.

Weak and trembling she suffered from the vapours, distressed by a final troubling thought from her oppressor: "You shan't be the last."

Still, I did rejoice that she had been saved! She no longer wished to engage in forbidden curiosities. Milk touched by her hands was no longer sour on my lips.

—from *An Attempt to Cure Witchcraft: The Story of Mercy Wylde*

The Third Night.

REVEREND TOWNSEND STOOD over his desk, puffing his pipe and inspecting a lacquered tray he'd filled with bread, oysters, apples, grapes and a pitcher of milk. After spending a good hour or two praying with Beatrice, he'd felt that all evil had fled the haunted chamber at last. Like Mercy Wylde had done, she'd shown all the signs of a damsel newly freed from her oppressor, from her weakened voice to her trembling limbs. When she'd begged for nourishment, he'd decided the girl's fast could end. What better way to show confidence in his faith and in the Lord?

He'd gone shopping for her meal himself. Walking home with his groceries, he'd passed by the teashop Sister Piddock had pointed out to him that morning. The store's sign was still turned to closed and several notices for the missing girl hung in the front window. How he'd rejoiced when he'd seen them! Let the whole city search for her. Let everyone know her name. Let them think she was taken, trapped, even dead. Then, when she came to stand before his congregation to tell her story of being enslaved by that foul witch, how much greater the tale would seem. When she spoke of her deliverance from the evil witch who seduced her heart, how much sweeter God's glory would be . . . how many more sinners would come to believe!

Setting his pipe on a saucer he'd tucked alongside a succulent cluster of grapes, he prepared to give thanks. As he knelt, his rod nagged against his leg, and he removed it from its loop and set it aside. Another act of faith. Hands clasped, he sang a psalm, then uttered a prayer.

> *But I will sing of thy power; yea, I will sing aloud of thy mercy in the morning: for thou hast been my defence and refuge in the day of my trouble.*
>
> *Unto thee, O my strength, will I sing: for God is my defence and the God of my mercy. Psalm 59: 16-17*

While the Reverend was singing, Beatrice was sleeping.

It'd taken all her strength to keep her wits about her through his questions, his accusations, his manic declarations of victory. By the time he'd left her, she was as certain of his madness as he was of her new faith. Hoping that things might turn her way, she'd taken up the thread she'd hidden in her bed and woven a single hair around it to complete the witch's ladder and its spell. "Freedom" was what she'd wished for, the final word she'd spoken before she'd tied the last knot. One could hope, one could pray, one could wish.

The Reverend had promised to bring her food when he came back tonight and perhaps fresh clothes and a warm bed tomorrow, if all continued to go "according to plan." She didn't know what his plan was, and she'd been too weak, too exhausted, too afraid to ask. She'd thought if she could eat something to get her strength up and then just make it through the night, then maybe she could come up with an escape plan of her own. She'd tried her best to stay awake, but once she lay down, her eyes had soon closed.

"Wake up," Lena called to Beatrice. "He's coming soon!"

Wiping the sleep from her eyes, Beatrice looked about the gloomy cellar and was met with a sight that made her think she was still dreaming. A great circle had been dug into the dirt in the middle of the floor, with a five-pointed star scratched inside it. A string of strange words was etched across the stone wall in black: *Titan gan eire ort.*

Lena whispered in Beatrice's ear, "'May you fall without rising.' It's a curse!"

"Why did you do this?" Beatrice hissed, fearing how Reverend Townsend would react.

"You cast your spell," Lena said. "I cast mine."

Hearing heavy footsteps on the stairs, she scrambled on hands and knees to wipe the circle and the star from the dirt.

The Reverend came through the door singing, carrying a tray of food. As soon as he caught sight of the wall, the floor and Beatrice, he threw the tray—plates clattering, oysters tumbling into the muck. The pitcher broke where it landed, spidery fingers of milk streaming forth, filling the points of the star. "You foul creature!" he shouted at Beatrice. "How dare you deceive me!"

Beatrice crept forward to grab the edge of his coat. "I swear I didn't do this. I woke to find it here. I was trying to get rid of it."

The preacher knocked her sprawling. "All I see is the Devil's work and a girl with the heart of a harlot."

Beatrice backed out of his reach, afraid he'd strike her again. "This isn't what it seems, and you don't know my heart."

He came at her, forcing her against the wall.

"Please," she begged. "I've done nothing wrong."

Seething, he kicked her shins. Then, as she crumpled to the floor, the small of her back, her gut.

"Mercy . . ." she whimpered, hugging herself. "Have mercy on me."

He began pacing as if he was the one who was trapped, muttering to himself and his Maker. "I thought she was the one. I thought she'd seen the light. Guide me, oh Lord, in what you would have me do . . ."

Beatrice shut her eyes, trying to keep from sobbing.

Kicking the tray across the room, Townsend stalked out of the cellar and bolted the door behind him.

Lena flew to Beatrice's side. "He means to kill you! He's gone to get the knife."

"Leave me alone," Beatrice said, crawling to the broken pitcher to upend what little milk was left into her mouth. She hurt everywhere, and yet she was so hungry. Spotting a single, intact oyster, she brought it to her lips and sucked out the meat.

"That shell's sharp, you know," Lena said. "Sharp enough to cut a man's throat."

Running her finger along its edge, Beatrice tried to picture herself attacking the Reverend. "I could never manage it," she admitted to herself as much as Lena, and it was then that she gave way to tears.

"Slit your own, then," Lena urged, "before he can do it. We'd be together, you and me . . . two ghosts against him."

The preacher's voice wafted down from the room above, angrily mumbling, likely praying, making it even harder for Beatrice to think. Among the spoiled food and shards of china sat Reverend Townsend's clay pipe, its bowl full of tobacco still gently glowing. Picking it up, Beatrice looked for a place to hide it. No matter what happened, at least she would've taken something from him.

The Fires of Saint Clarus. Each year, come summer, the people of La Haye-de-Routot, a small village in Normandy, celebrate the famed Saint Clarus by building a great bonfire in his honour. This spectacle takes place among a scattering of ancient yew trees very near where Saint Clarus was beheaded, and where Rollo, the Viking king, chose to abandon his pagan religion for Christianity. The villagers, who consider the rite sacred, gather en masse after dark, some setting chairs here and there around the fire for the comfort of the deceased who wish to attend. The most faithful of the followers have been known to approach the fire to collect glowing embers from its flames. Cradling the embers inside spent oyster shells they carry them home, believing that having a small part of the fire in their possession will bless their lives for the year to come.

—T. D. Pratchett, *A Compendium of Miracles*

Careful What You Wish For.

AS A CHILD, poring over Mr. Pratchett's collection of miracles, Beatrice had often imagined herself next to the crackling bonfire trying to pick out the ghosts from the villagers. As she picked up the oyster shells scattered on the cellar floor, it occurred to her that she might be able to make a fire of her own.

Setting the largest shell on the floor, she pulled a scant handful of straw from her mattress and made a little nest of it in the bottom of the shell. Then she collected whatever bits of coal she could find (most of the lump she'd hidden had gone to Lena's curse), and dropped them in. Lastly, she took Reverend Townsend's pipe and tapped what remained of the smouldering tobacco from its bowl into the shell. With soft, steady breaths, she fed the embers until the straw sparked and burned, and the coal cinders began to glow. Then she gently placed a second shell over the first to protect her treasure, leaving just enough space between them so the fire wouldn't go out.

"What've you got there?" Lena asked, circling around her. "What are you doing?"

Head bowed, eyes closed, all Beatrice would say was, "I'm going home."

Eleanor sat across from Adelaide at the centre table in the teashop. Five objects lay before them—Eleanor's grimoire, a porcelain teacup, a white feather quill, a small sheet of parchment and the bone-handled dagger that had once belonged to Madame St. Clair. "Are you sure you want to do this?" Eleanor asked, looking at Adelaide for signs of disbelief, or fear. "If you've any misgivings, then it's better I perform the spell alone. My hope is to use the charm to conjure a guide to take us to Beatrice. I can't say what form the guide might take or if it will lead us into peril."

"No misgivings," Adelaide said, staring at the dagger. "I want to help."

"Good," Eleanor said. "Two witches at the table makes the spell twice as able. Would you like to read it through one last time?"

Adelaide nodded. She desperately wanted the spell to work. She wanted to get it right.

The ESAUE Square.

Magicians, witches and mystics have long understood the power of placing numbers, letters or symbols in sacred combinations within a magic square. This square, described below, holds the potential to grant a heart's desire. This charm should only be used with utmost care and caution, for once its magic has been set in motion it cannot be reversed. Never draw the square in its completed form unless you wish to cast the spell.

At the time of the waxing moon, wound the thumb of your left hand with the blade of a consecrated knife. Draw enough blood to write the spell on a piece of parchment with a quill made from the feather of a white goose. Without speaking, spell out E-S-A-U-E in four directions to make the square. Then place the paper between the palms of your hands as if you are praying, and declare what you desire. To enhance the power of this spell, perform it with another who shares the same wish. Once the spell has come to fruition, destroy the charm by burning it.

"I'm ready," Adelaide said, giving the grimoire a shy, friendly pat.

Perdu perched on the back of an empty chair to act as witness. Bright hid beneath his wing. And Cleo, so far as they all knew only a dog, was sleeping at Adelaide's feet with Twitch tucked in the fold of her ear.

Eleanor reached for Adelaide's hand. This spell felt like something of a last resort. She'd seen her mother use it to great effect, only once having it yield less than ideal results. In that instance, a woman had come to l'Hermitage wanting Madame St. Clair to find her lost husband. The man had indeed been found, but to his wife's dismay, in another woman's bed. "Let that be a lesson to you," her mother had said wagging her finger at her daughter. "Those who use magic to find what they seek, may not always like what they find." Picking up her mother's dagger, Eleanor began the ritual by drawing its blade across the fleshy tip of her thumb. The first drop of her blood welled up in the wound, then shone like a ruby as it dropped to the bottom of the cup. Handing the knife to Adelaide, she bid her to do the same.

Adelaide made her cut quick and deep, then pressed with her forefinger to hasten the flow of her blood. It only took a few moments to collect what they needed for the spell.

Putting her finger to her lips, Eleanor reminded Adelaide that the next step was to be taken in silence. Dipping the quill in the cup, she stirred their blood three times clockwise before putting the tip to the parchment. They took turns writing the sacred word, penning the letters one by one— across, down, reversed, up.

As Adelaide set the quill aside after the last iteration, Eleanor picked up the parchment and blew the blood dry.

Laying it on the palm of her right hand, she waited for Adelaide's palm to meet hers, and then they threaded their fingers together, the charm sandwiched between their hands. Closing their eyes in unison, they chanted the verse:

> *In this square our wish resides*
> *Please send a soul to be our guide.*
> *The next one through the door to come,*
> *Will lead the way to Beatrice Dunn.*

Twitch flew to Perdu's side and burrowed between the raven's feathers. Tapping Bright on the shoulder he asked, "What happens now?"

Bright sighed, then whispered, "We wait."

A little girl stood near the fountain in Madison Square Park— the girl who'd told Adelaide's fortune, the girl Reverend Townsend had taken, the girl who'd survived him, the girl Adelaide's mother had mistaken for her daughter, the girl Eleanor had gifted the last coins from her pocket. She was debating whether or not she should wade into the shallow pool to steal a shiny dime that sparkled in the water. That was what the money was for, wasn't it? The small wooden sign that hung on the fountain's iron railing said so. MAKE A WISH, FEED THE POOR.

When the Bird Lady settled on a nearby bench, the girl chose to leave the dime for the ladies who collected the coins for the charity kitchen. For her it'd been a fairly good day, since her belly was fairly full. Fiddling in her pocket, she discovered the last of the pennies the woman from the teashop had given her that morning. Heaven knew she should probably save it, but for once she thought she'd like to make a wish.

A warm bed? A new family? All the bread she could eat? No, no and no. What she wanted more than anything was to not feel afraid. Ever since the Reverend had tricked her, taken her, beaten her and left her for dead, she'd felt his presence around every corner, heard his breathing whenever she closed her eyes. He'd called her a witch. She hoped he was right. She had a faint memory of someone telling her (had it been her mother? her grandmother? a stranger?) that she had witchery in her blood. Pinching the penny between her fingers, she kissed it, then tossed it into the water. "I wish he was dead."

No sooner had the penny splashed, than the ghost of Adelaide's mother rose up from inside the fountain, called by the girl's voice. It'd been weeks since anyone, including Adelaide, had thought of her, so her place among the living was quickly being lost. Was this strange watery grave to be her home forever? That damn fairy had proved more powerful than she'd imagined. Desperate to be noticed, she came towards the little girl, kicking up a whirlwind of wet leaves as she moved.

Thinking the shadowy figure might be the preacher, the little girl panicked and ran. As she flew past the bench where the Bird Lady sat, the old woman called out to her, "Careful what you wish for!"

The Reverend was still pacing the floor above Beatrice. The sound made her more anxious than ever. She had tied the witch's ladder around her ankle, and was cradling the pair of oyster shells that held her little fire, waiting for the preacher to come down the stairs and step into her plan.

"Here he comes," Lena hissed. "It's time!"

As soon as she heard his foot touch the creaky top stair, Beatrice opened her tiny fire to the air, then tucked it into the hollowed-out corner of her mattress. Feeding it with straw and breath, she willed the fire to catch. With any luck the flames would leap up and distract the preacher before he could kill her, and she could escape. His footsteps stopped midway on the stairs, then turned and retreated, just as the fire took hold in a flash, flames reaching for the rafters.

There was nothing Beatrice could do to stop it.

The frightened little girl ran out of the park and up the street to hide in the window well of Markowitz's bakery. Seeing lights in the teashop, she scrambled up the stoop and pounded on the door. The teashop woman had been good to her that morning, and might take pity on her now. "Please," she cried. "Please let me in!"

With a start, Eleanor let Adelaide's hand go and rushed to the door. No sooner had she flung it open than the girl ran into the shop to hide under the table.

"Mercy!" Perdu squawked when he saw her. "Mercy!"

The Dearlies flew from beneath his wings and took shelter inside a teapot.

Ducking her head beneath the table, Adelaide stared at the girl. "Don't I know you?"

Eleanor crouched down, then sat on the floor. "What's wrong, my dear?" she asked. "What's happened?"

The girl's eyes were panicked. "He's after me again!"

Cleo circled around the child and lay in front of her, keeping close watch on the door.

"Who?" Adelaide asked.

"Mercy!" Perdu cried.

Frantic, the girl stammered, "The awful man who always walks with the church-going ladies through the park. They say he's their preacher but I say he's the Devil. He locked me in his cellar with a ghost! I know he meant to kill me. He said I was a witch."

Eleanor looked at Adelaide as if to say, *This is it.* "But you got away from him?"

"He thought I was dead, but I swear he's after me again."

Adelaide put her hand on the girl's shoulder. "Can you take us to the place he kept you?"

The girl buried her face in Cleo's fur. Her only response was the trembling of her body.

"The dog can come with us," Eleanor offered. "She won't let anything happen to you."

Lifting her eyes to meet Eleanor's, the girl bit her lip, uncertain.

"And neither will I," Adelaide said, and as the girl turned to her, she pointed to the sheath on her boot where she kept her knife.

Beatrice pounded on the door as smoke filled the cellar. "Fire!" she shouted. "Please help! Let me out!" The smoke caused her eyes to sting, her throat to burn. Her skin was turning red from the heat, her blood felt as if it was about to boil. Surely, she thought, the Reverend could see the smoke seeping between the planks of his floor. Had he fled the house and left her here to die?

Suddenly she heard his boots thudding down the stairs. Arm over her nose and mouth, she stepped back from the door, desperate to escape.

No sooner did he come through the door than he lunged at her and seized her by the throat. Grim with anger in the fire's flickering light, he flashed a knife before her eyes. "You will not die by your own hand. That privilege will be mine."

With a swift knee to his groin, Beatrice managed to hurt him enough he let go. She stumbled back, and fell, and before she could get to her feet, he came at her again, this time grabbing her wrist, his fingers digging into the sore, tender flesh rubbed raw by the ropes he'd used to bind her.

Pain shot through her. Tears streamed down her face.

"I've got you now, you witch," the Reverend said attempting to haul her up.

Despite the pain, Beatrice resisted—her lungs tight with the effort, stealing her breath. As she struggled for air, Lena's voice sounded in her ear: "Remember my curse."

Flames flashed behind the Reverend and the rafters began to creak. Focused on handing Beatrice her punishment, he ignored the fire raging at his back.

"Once he falls," Lena cried, "he'll not rise again."

Beatrice fought him, shouting, "You'll not get this witch!" The scabs from her wounds broke open as he pulled, and she started to bleed.

Then, as he raised his knife, clearly meaning to end her, her wrist, wet with blood, slipped out of his grip. He toppled backwards, howling and flailing as his hair and clothes caught fire.

Lena's laughter filled the room as a single rafter gave way and sealed the Reverend's fate.

Beatrice fled for the stairs. As she flew through the door, it slammed shut behind her, and the bolt clanged to. The stairwell was filled with smoke. She could barely see or breathe.

"Beatrice," her mother called from the top of the stairs. "Come to me."

Looking up, she saw the silhouette of a woman on the landing, her hand outstretched. Unsure whether she was making her way to safety or Heaven, Beatrice climbed the stairs. Either way, she was going to be free.

Dr. Brody sat at his father's desk and stared at the dying coals of an evening fire he'd built in his study, debating whether or not to go to the teashop. He'd said he would stop by at the end of the day, but there didn't seem to be much sense in disturbing Eleanor and Adelaide at this hour. He had nothing new to offer, no information, no solutions that might lead to finding Beatrice.

He hadn't really expected to find Beatrice at the asylum, but he'd hoped he might. He certainly hadn't expected to stumble across the perpetrator of the acid attack on Adelaide. He supposed he could've guessed at some of the particulars that had led to the loss of her eye, but to read it on the page was a sobering thing. She'd never volunteered what had happened to her and he hadn't asked. He'd figured she'd tell that story, if and when she was ready.

But he wished he'd told her how beautiful she was the night they'd kissed at the hotel, that he'd professed his love for her then and there. Knowing Adelaide, perhaps she already knew how he felt. But how could he pursue happiness while Beatrice was still lost? All he could do was show his support, take the proper actions and hope that Adelaide could see that everything he did was from the heart.

He ran his finger around the dial of the spiritoscope, which he'd fetched from the hotel, thinking it was better to have it home than sitting in some broom closet. Oh how he longed for a ghost to direct his path! Where were Mr. Dickens' spirits of past, present and future? Was it just wishful thinking to hope they might appear? No. What Beatrice Dunn had shown him had been real. It couldn't be denied. "Father," he said, looking to the heavens, "send me a sign."

With a gentle clacking, the spiritoscope's dial began to turn. One by one it pointed out the letters, v-i-v-i-t.

She lives.

The little girl led the two witches to the parsonage with Cleo at their heels. As they drew closer, church bells began a slow, mournful toll. Eleanor stopped short, a chill up her spine. "Someone will die tonight," she whispered.

A team of horses pulling a fire wagon galloped past, spittle and sweat flying every which way in the cold night air. A half-dozen men clung to the ladders strapped to the truck's sides. A young boy, perched on top, clanged a leather hammer against a tinny gong, sounding the alarm. Adelaide smelled the smoke before she saw the fire. "Over there," she said, pointing to the parsonage as they rounded the corner. The building was falling in on itself, engulfed in a mass of flames.

"That's it!" the girl shouted, her eyes lit with glee. "That's the place." Then she danced away down the street, thankful that her wish had come true.

Eleanor slipped her hand in Adelaide's and made a silent wish that Beatrice had survived.

Cleo circled around them and began to bark.

"Look," Adelaide said, tugging on Eleanor. "I think it's her."

Beatrice, backlit by the fire, walked towards them, dirty and in a tattered shift, tears streaming down her cheeks.

Running to her, Eleanor and Adelaide embraced her as one, and held her tight.

By the time Brody got to the teashop, Beatrice had been fed and washed and was tucked safe in her bed with Eleanor and Adelaide taking turns watching over her. Perdu was perched on the headboard, and Cleo was curled at her feet. Twitch and Bright were snuggled up together on the windowsill contemplating her next dream.

When a knock came at the door, Eleanor went to answer it, wondering who might be calling so late. She and Adelaide had decided to keep the news of Beatrice's return to themselves until morning. What the girl needed tonight was rest.

"I'm sorry to impose," Dr. Brody said as Eleanor opened the door. Shyly stepping inside the shop he said, "I've news. A message from my father."

It was clear to Eleanor that it had taken the doctor a fair bit of resolve to say such a thing. "I see," she said, and smiled at him.

Stammering, he said, "I know it may sound foolish, but I'm sure of what I saw. Long story short, my father let me know that Beatrice is alive."

"She is," Eleanor said, taking his hand in hers. "Come see for yourself." It was all she could do not to laugh at the shock and wonder on Brody's face as she led him up the stairs.

At the door of Beatrice's room, he let out a small gasp, shocked by the sight of her ragged hair, her sunken eyes, the wounds and bruises that encircled her wrists.

Propped on her pillows, Beatrice called to him, her voice hoarse. "I'm sorry, Dr. Brody," she said. "I let you down."

"Dear girl," he said, his voice shaking a little, "you could never do that." Looking at Eleanor and then at Adelaide he said, "None of you could."

What wonderful beings they were, these women he'd come to care for, these women who'd helped him chase his dreams, these women he needed so much more than they needed him—these marvellous, glorious, Witches of New York.

October 12, 1880.

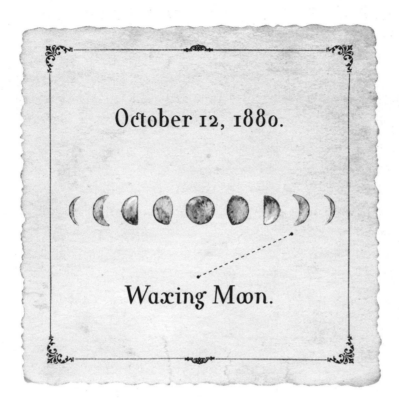

Waxing Moon.

RESPECTED PREACHER DIES IN TRAGIC FIRE

L ast evening at approximately ten o'clock, fire broke out in the parsonage of the Church of the Good Shepherd on Twenty-Third Street. A passerby sounded an alarm after smelling smoke and seeing flames shooting out the first-storey windows of the dwelling. Personnel from the Fire Department responded promptly, but by the time they arrived on the scene the wooden structure was fully engulfed.

The speed and aggressiveness of the fire has been attributed to the house's age and style of construction, which date back to the early 1800s. The building and its contents could not be saved.

As of this morning it has been confirmed that Reverend Francis Townsend, beloved leader of the church's congregation, perished in the fire. His badly burned remains were identified by one of his parishioners, a Mrs. Penelope Piddock. "He was a true soldier of God," she tearfully testified. "May the angels protect him, and Heaven accept him."

Funeral services for the late Reverend Townsend will be held this Friday at two o'clock in the Sanctuary of the Church of the Good Shepherd.

Miraculously, the church, a stone meeting house that dates from the same period as the parsonage, was spared the fire's wrath.

A collection for the poor will be taken in the Reverend's memory this Sunday during regular services.

479

Mr. Palsham.

THE COLLECTORS ENTERED Mr. Palsham's office unannounced. Hands folded at their waists, the pair stood impassively in front of his desk waiting to be addressed.

As was his habit, Mr. Palsham took his time. After sifting through the many papers, plans, schematics and blueprints that littered his blotter, he picked up a silver trowel from a velvet-lined presentation box that sat to one side of his desk. It was a gift from the Masons for his part in bringing the obelisk to New York. Holding the trowel's tip to his finger, he mindlessly spun it around by its wooden handle. Its blade glinted each time it passed through the sunlight streaming through the window, casting a flickering beam on his face. Beneath his bushy beard sat a constellation of scars. If he were ever to allow a barber to shave him clean, his mouth would bear the comical look of a carnival knock-down doll with a smile that had come unstitched. Leaning back in his chair he finally asked, "What brings you here?"

"Reverend Townsend is dead, sir," the first Collector said.

The second Collector gave a nod of confirmation.

"I am aware of it," Mr. Palsham replied. "He was weak. There are others who'll take his place."

The first Collector stared straight ahead. "And the girl is gone as well."

Mr. Palsham winced. The thought of Beatrice Dunn made him uneasy. She was different, special, almost frightening in her naïveté when it came to her power. Her glamour was brighter than any witch he'd ever seen (and he'd seen plenty). He'd made a mistake in thinking that bumbling preacher could do her in. "Perhaps it's for the best."

"You no longer wish to pursue her?" the second Collector asked.

"Only from a distance," Mr. Palsham explained. "It's not her time yet."

"And what of the others?" the first Collector inquired.

Mr. Palsham tapped the trowel on his forehead, thinking. "Leave them be, for now. They're worth more together than apart."

"Very well, sir."

"As you wish."

Setting the tool aside, Mr. Palsham asked, "Did you recover anything from the fire?"

"Only this," the first Collector said, placing Reverend Townsend's pipe on the desk.

"And this," the second replied, placing a blackened oyster shell next to it.

Picking up the shell, Mr. Palsham held it to his nose and sniffed, then ran his finger along its sharp edge. He could feel the magic lingering from where the girl had touched it with her will. In his long existence he'd brought about the demise of many witches merely by encouraging man's hate, man's greed, man's hubris, man's intolerance. These new witches would require careful consideration and planning. A small part of him was glad for the challenge. The hunts in Europe had gone so smoothly. Salem had been far too easy a task.

These women were another matter altogether. There was time yet, though, to observe them, maybe even turn them to his ways. Time was the greatest advantage a demon had.

Waving the Collectors away he said, "You're dismissed."

October 31, 1880.

New Moon,

All Hallows' Eve.

Home.

IN THE DAYS after Beatrice's return, everyone did their part to heal her wounds.

Among her first visitors was Georgina Davis, who'd dropped by the shop to see if anything had come from the notices she'd made. Much to her delight she'd found the girl was no longer lost. "I'll have her name struck from the missing persons list at once."

"Thank you for everything," Eleanor had said with a soft smile. "You've been a tremendous help."

"It's a rare thing to have a happy ending," Georgina had replied. "It's been a pleasure. I do hope we'll remain friends."

Eleanor's cheeks had turned bright pink, much to the surprise of everyone in the room.

Judith Dashley brought bouquets of fresh flowers nearly every day—chrysanthemums, roses, daisies, lilies. "To brighten your room and lift your spirits." Holding Beatrice's hand she'd admitted, "I missed not having you to confide in. You're one of the few people in this world who doesn't look on me with pity. All these years after Billy's death and I still feel the loss wash over me. People mean well, I suppose, but pity is such a dangerous pastime, prone to stir gentle madness in the head and poison the heart. Steer clear of it if you can, my dear. I promise, for my part, I'll never place such a burden on you."

"Thank you, Judith," Beatrice had said. "I couldn't ask for a better gift."

Dr. Brody had come bearing a small trunk filled with books from his father's library—titles covering such subjects as spiritism, psychical research and occult sciences. He'd hoped the girl might find them informative as well as entertaining. "I'll be anxious to hear your thoughts on them when you're up to it," he'd said. "How thoughtful of you," Beatrice had replied, already poring over one of the books.

Taking Brody aside, Adelaide had whispered in his ear, "And I'd like to hear your thoughts on animal magnetism, if you're feeling up to it." She'd made up her mind to not only entertain the notion of love, but to pursue it. This time it was Brody's turn to blush.

For their part, the Dearlies had delivered a handful of lovely dreams to Beatrice to aid in her recovery—visions of hidden rooms filled with gilded books, fairy circles lit with foxfire, secret spells that magically appeared in Eleanor's grimoire. When Bright announced that they needed to give the girl a nightmare, Twitch had protested, saying he refused to participate.

"It has to be done," Bright had insisted. "She needs to remember, not forget."

Curling one of the short strands of what was left of Beatrice's hair around his finger, he'd asked, "Isn't that terrible mark he left on her skin enough of a reminder?"

"It's not him we need her to remember," Bright had explained.

Giving in, Twitch had summoned Cleo to the end of Beatrice's bed so the dog would be there to comfort her when the dream took hold. "All right," he'd said. "Just this once."

Not keen to put the girl through it, either, Bright said, "Hopefully once will be enough."

Beatrice had tossed and turned the whole way through as her dream-self had tried to escape the clutches of Mr. Palsham. Unlike the time he'd caught her by the arm in the park, no one came to her rescue. His hands turned to clawed talons, his face into a ghoulish, horned fright. Fanged teeth glistening, hoarse voice growling he'd said, "Beware the demon's bite." She'd let out a terrible scream, bringing both Adelaide and Eleanor running.

"It's only a dream," Adelaide had said, stroking her arm. "All will be well. You'll be fine."

Taking Madame St. Clair's brass key from around her neck, Eleanor had placed it in Beatrice's hand. "A demon will never outsmart a witch," she'd said. "Remember the princess." Beatrice had worn the key next to her heart every day since.

Eleanor had seen to the girl's care around the clock, bringing her rosehip tea for strength and healing, and dressing her burns and bruises with a salve made from honey, chamomile, lavender and cobwebs. Beatrice had dutifully written down the recipes for each remedy. Eleanor had taken it as a sign Beatrice meant to carry on with them at the shop. "You're welcome to stay with us as long as you like," she'd told the girl. "Although, come November, I can't say for certain where that might be."

Judith had offered countless times to put them up at the hotel, but both Eleanor and Adelaide had turned down her invitations. As October had dwindled away, no solution had been found for their lodging or their business. Cecil Newland's eviction notice had seemingly secured his revenge.

Adelaide had given Beatrice hour after hour of companionship. Knowing what it was like to be bedridden, she'd sat nearby, reading her cards and her palm, and telling tall tales of the days she'd spent in a circus sideshow. Once Beatrice was up and around, they took a stroll every afternoon in the park. It was there that they, along with Dr. Brody, had hatched a plan for what to do next.

"What about *my* house?" Dr. Brody had said with a hopeful smile. "I can't believe I didn't think of it before. There's plenty of room and you can stay as long as you wish."

To Beatrice's surprise, Adelaide hadn't dismissed the idea, only teased, "What will Mrs. Stutt say? Won't she be scandalized?"

"A little scandal might be good for her," Dr. Brody responded. "I'll move into the carriage house out back to keep her from putting up too much of a fuss."

"We can't put you out of your own house," Beatrice had said, though inside she'd been giddy at the thought of having access to Mr. Brody's library at all hours. If it were up to her, she'd live, eat and sleep there for the rest of her life.

"Nonsense. The coach house is perfect for an old bachelor like me. Consider it done."

Slipping her arm through his, Adelaide had said, "But you'll come visit us from time to time, for suppers and entertainments and such?"

Leaning his head to hers he'd whispered, "You could not keep me away."

When they'd put the plan to Eleanor, both Adelaide and Beatrice had done their best to sweeten their proposal with various enticements. "The kitchen is enormous," Adelaide had pointed out. "So well equipped."

"And there's plenty of room out back for beehives and a garden," Beatrice had said.

But it hadn't taken much to convince Eleanor. Time was growing short, and she'd grown quite fond of Dr. Brody. His was a kindness that never felt forced or insincere.

They'd wasted no time, moving Perdu and their personal effects first, and then the contents of the teashop. Adelaide had wanted to find a new space for their business at once, but Eleanor had said she preferred they take their time. If she was going to enter into such a venture again, the place would have to be absolutely right. "I'll know it when I see it," she'd said. She had a picture in her mind of what it should be—more like her mother's cottage than not—and she wasn't sure such a place even existed in New York. Packing her jars, tins, cups and pots in boxes, she'd moved them into a back room at Dr. Brody's.

Mrs. Stutt had adapted to the situation quite well, quickly acquiring a deep affection for Beatrice and a great respect for Eleanor's skills in the kitchen. Adelaide, she learned to tolerate.

When the last day of the month arrived, all that was left in the shop were the bells that hung over the door and Eleanor's hickory broom. After Beatrice fetched the bells from their perch, Adelaide tied them to Cleo's collar.

Eleanor, as witches' tradition dictated, swept the floors back to front, one last time.

As she made her way down the stoop, chasing the dust from each step, she saw Isaac Markowitz staring gloomily in her direction. "Isaac," she called, "come give Cleo a proper send-off."

The boy scurried to the dog's side and wrapped his arms around her. "Don't forget me," he said in her ear.

"You can visit her any time, you know," Adelaide said. "It's only a few blocks."

"That's a world away!"

"Well you'd better get used to making the trip," Eleanor advised. "I've a standing order with your father, every Wednesday, for a loaf of his marble rye."

Beatrice smiled at the boy and he laughed.

Looking up the street, Eleanor asked, "Where do you suppose Judith is today? I thought for sure she'd come say goodbye. I'd gotten used to her moping about, wondering what she'll do without us."

Adelaide shook her head. "Who knows."

Beatrice gave a little shrug.

The pair looked at each other, then away, knowing something that Eleanor didn't.

Seeing the sun was low in the sky, Adelaide checked her watch. "Shall we hire a hansom?" she suggested.

"No," Eleanor said, shaking her head, "it's All Hallows' Eve. Let's walk."

They chose to stroll past the park—Eleanor with her broom on her shoulder, Beatrice and Adelaide on either side of her. Cleo followed behind, bells jangling against her red patent collar.

A group of Fantasticals paraded past them on the street, dressed in patchwork clothes and gaudy masks, carrying turnip lanterns and banging pots and pans. They were going from house to house to beg for pennies and treats. Amongst them was a sprightly little girl dressed in a long black cloak and a tall pointed hat. Running up to Cleo, she gave the dog a pat on the head. "Hello," she said.

Beatrice grinned at the little witch.

With a twirl and a wave she danced away. "Goodbye!"

The witches all laughed.

It was nearly dark when they reached their destination, but before they went inside, Adelaide stole behind Eleanor and covered her eyes with her hands.

"Stop that," Eleanor protested. "What are you up to?"

Beatrice giggled. "That's for us to know and you to find out."

"Unhand me. I insist."

Adelaide whispered in her ear, "That's not how this works."

Running ahead of them up the steps to the building adjacent to the house—the place where Tobias Brody once sold a fine array of philosophical instruments—Beatrice knocked on the door and shouted, "We're here."

With that, a great tarp came down from where Dr. Brody had hung it across the windows, and a beautiful new storefront was revealed. The windows were clean and sparkling with candlelight, the door bore a fresh coat of blue paint. The sign over the door read: THE HERMITAGE.

"What's this?" Eleanor asked, hardly believing her eyes.

"You'll see," Adelaide said, leading her to the door.

Taking Madame St. Clair's key from around her neck, Beatrice handed it to Eleanor and said, "You'll be needing this."

Slipping the key in the door's lock, Eleanor opened it to discover a room that looked for all the world like her mother's kitchen. A long, sturdy table ran down the length of it, set with cups and saucers, pitchers of honey and a plate heaped with teacakes. A fire crackled in a hearth in the back of the room, a cauldron hanging over it, filled with stew. The clock from St. Clair and Thom's graced the mantel. Row upon row of shelves and cupboards lined the walls, filled with the shop's jars and tins, teapots and kettles. Dr. Brody tended the fire as Judith Dashley stood on a stepladder with Alden holding her steady so she could finish stringing tin lanterns and garlands of forget-me-nots from the rafters.

Eleanor shook her head in disbelief. "How did you ever manage it?"

"You're not the only witch around here," Adelaide teased.

Beatrice bit her lip. "Do you like it?"

"Yes," Eleanor said, taking the girl's hand. "It feels like home."

Cleo trotted past her and promptly curled herself up on a rug in front of the fire.

Perdu, who'd been watching from his newly installed perch, flapped to the centre of the table, fished a cake from the top of the pile and gobbled it down.

"What a terrible thief you are," Beatrice teased. "What a silly bird." The raven let out a long, stubborn chortle. Eyeing the girl, he declared, "I am no bird."

That night they celebrated with mulled cider and soul cakes. Alden Dashley brought out a fiddle and much to everyone's delight, Dr. Brody sang while Mr. Dashley played. They laughed and told stories and entertained themselves with the games that witches enjoy most on Hallowe'en: paring apples to find their fortunes, dropping egg whites in hot water, playing round after round of three saucers and book and key.

When the night was over and the Dashleys had gone, and

Dr. Brody went off to his bed, the three women stood together in front of the fire.

"It's almost midnight," Eleanor said, looking at the clock.

"I'm ready," Adelaide replied, taking Eleanor's hand.

"So am I," Beatrice said, holding fast to her sister witches.

As the clock struck twelve they recited a special spell they'd crafted to mark their first All Hallows' Eve together.

> *By new moon and twinkling stars,*
> *Bless this night and make it ours.*
> *To those who dare to wish us harm,*
> *We cast on them a wicked charm.*
> *To those who aid us in our powers,*
> *We grace their lives with happy hours.*
> *And to ourselves one wish remains,*
> *That we might ne'er be lost again.*
> *Hecate dear, we ask of thee.*
> *So may it be, so may it be, so may it be.*

January 21, 1881.

Half Moon.

THE GREAT OBELISK TO BE ERECTED

The Egyptian obelisk known as Cleopatra's Needle will be erected on its pedestal tomorrow at noon, on Greywacke Knoll in Central Park. If the attendance during October's dedication of the site is any indication of the public's interest, it should prove to be a crowded and festive affair.

After its arduous months-long journey through the city, the obelisk now waits at the ready atop a great turning structure that in itself is a tribute to man's perseverance and ingenuity. Lt. Commander Gorringe recently remarked, "If all goes accordingly, it will move as easily and deliberately as if it were the minute hand on a lady's watch."

We wish good luck and Godspeed to Gorringe and the good men under his direction.

Cleopatra's Needle.

THE THREE WITCHES spent Christmas with Aunt Lydia in Stony Point. They filled their bellies with crown roast and plum pudding. They admired Lydia's stamp collection. They played many hands of whist. Every night during the week before the New Year, they took turns reading stories to each other in the parlour. One night, after Beatrice had given a particularly lively rendition of *The Cricket on the Hearth*, Lydia, having had one too many glasses of sherry, announced, "I wanted to tell you that I've seen a ghost."

"You have?" Eleanor asked.

"Do tell," Adelaide urged.

Beatrice looked at her aunt with great concern, wondering if perhaps it wasn't good for her to live alone. She still hadn't told Lydia of any of the strange (or terrible) happenings that'd gone on since she'd moved to New York. The time had never seemed right. "It was in October," Lydia said. "Just past mid-month. I remember because it was a full moon. I went out to the porch to sit a spell, and a woman came walking up the road. She was dressed in a long wool cloak with a pointed hood. She came right up to me and asked if I knew a girl with long red hair who wore a wren's feather on her lapel."

Beatrice's eyes went wide.

"Worried some ill might've befallen you, I told her the girl she'd described sounded much like my niece and if she had any news of you she should tell it. With a calm smile and tranquil face she said, 'Beatrice is safe.' Thinking it very queer, I told her I had no reason to think otherwise, then I asked her to leave. In a blink she was gone, no trace of her left. No sign of her in the yard or on the street. If she wasn't a ghost, then what do you suppose she was? And what do you suppose it meant?"

"Who knows . . ." Eleanor said, shaking her head.

"Sounds like a ghost to me," said Adelaide.

Beatrice sat thinking what the other two witches suspected, that Lydia's ghost was Madame St. Clair.

"Well, whatever she was," Lydia said, "I'm sure I never saw the likes of her before, and I suppose I'll never see the likes of her again. What a funny thing to happen, especially in Stony Point. Can you imagine what the ladies at the First United Presbyterian would say if I told them?"

"I wouldn't," Beatrice said.

"Nor would I," added Eleanor.

Shaking her head, Adelaide said, "Better not."

The year got off to a cold and snowy start, one of the worst winters on record. The work on the Dashleys' house got delayed, and then delayed again, so Judith spent much of her time at the Hermitage complaining about the house she couldn't live in and sharing gossip from the hotel. "Marietta's been asking after all of you. She'd like you to know she harbours no hard feelings and that you're welcome any time at the Fifth."

Miss Davis was also a frequent visitor, stopping in to chat with Eleanor, and to invite all three witches to attend the weekly gatherings of the NWSA. When the suffragists lost their regular meeting place, Eleanor had suggested they gather there, any evening except Saturday. (That night was reserved for Dr. Brody and the Unknown Philosophers, many of whom had taken a great liking to Eleanor's tea.) Despite the cold weather, business at the shop was brisk, due in no small part to the ladies of Sisters' Row discovering Eleanor's affinity for making teas, tinctures and powders that met their "specific needs." On any given day the place was full of customers engaged in conversations concerning everything from fortunes to fertility, from tinkering to theosophy.

By day, Beatrice resumed her role as Eleanor's apprentice—helping in the teashop and learning all she could about herbs, potions and the magic of Eleanor's people, the cunning folk. By night, she pored over newspapers and weeklies searching for reports of strange happenings around the city. She'd abandoned the idea of giving public demonstrations in favour of investigating individual sightings of ghosts instead. She'd even wheedled Adelaide and Dr. Brody into visiting several sites around the city, with a few of them turning out to be the real thing. In light of their recent investigations, Beatrice had informed Dr. Brody that she intended to write a book that was akin to Mr. Pratchett's *Compendium*. "But with miracles of the modern age," she'd said. "*A Census of Astonishments*." With that, Adelaide had promptly taken Beatrice to the stationer to have her first calling cards made. After going round and round about what it should say, she'd finally settled on this:

Miss Beatrice Dunn

AGENT OF THE OBSCURE.

The Hermitage
New York, New York

"A far cry from the 'Egyptian Sybil,'" Adelaide had teased.

"I suppose it is," Beatrice had said. "But far nearer to me."

On the evening of January 21, Dr. Brody announced over dinner that he'd arranged for them to take a nighttime sleigh ride through Central Park.

The wind was bitterly cold, but the sleigh driver provided them with blankets, fur pelts and a jug of warm cider. The sound of the sleigh's runners slicing through the snow along with the rhythmic jangle of the bells on the horses' necks cast a charming, happy spell over the cheerful quartet. A few other sleighing parties were out enjoying the evening, and jovial shouts and cheers were often exchanged between them.

It wasn't long before they came to Greywacke Knoll and the site where the obelisk was set to be righted on the morrow. To everyone's surprise except Dr. Brody's, two great bonfires had been lit on either side of the turning mechanism on which the obelisk sat. A small band of men stood between them.

"What's going on?" Eleanor asked, taking hold of Beatrice's hand, worried the sight of the fires might upset her.

"Yes, tell us," Adelaide said, sure that Quinn was keeping something from them. He'd had a terrible twitch in his eyebrow all evening. An endearing tell if she ever saw one.

Dr. Brody asked the driver to stop and to wait for them. Then he leapt from his seat and assisted each of the women down from the sleigh. "Trust me," he said. "You'll want to see this."

As the four of them stood watching, four men went about executing history prematurely. Gorringe, not wanting to leave anything to chance, had called for a dress rehearsal of the obelisk's shining moment. In the glare of the firelight, he stood on a platform and gave the order for the men on the tackles to "haul down, slack away!" Their motions seemed almost inconsequential in comparison with the graceful, effortless movement of the obelisk. Everyone who'd stopped to witness it went silent, struck dumb by the Needle's spell.

When the monument was nearly vertical, Gorringe, satisfied that the contraption could do its job, gave the order to reverse the process. Shouts and cheers rose up when it came to rest, people waving their hats or rising in their sleighs to celebrate the momentous occasion.

Walking to the bonfire that was closest to them, Adelaide, Eleanor, Beatrice and Dr. Brody stood to warm their hands.

"How did you know this was going to happen?" Adelaide asked, in awe of what they'd seen.

"I have my ways," Dr. Brody said with a wink.

"What a sight," Eleanor said, staring up at the Needle. "It truly is magnificent."

Beatrice stood in silence, letting the moment stand.

Before long, her reverie was interrupted by someone tapping her on the shoulder. "Miss," a gentleman's voice said, "remember me?" It was the person who'd bid her to touch the obelisk on her first day in New York.

"Yes," she said, turning to look after the rest of her party, who were making their way back to the sleigh.

"I'm leaving tomorrow," he said, gold tooth glinting in the firelight. "But I've something to give you before I go."

"My friends are leaving."

"I won't let them go without you," he promised. Then reaching his hand into the fire, he pulled out a glowing ember. "Trust me," he said. "Take it."

Closing her eyes, she let him place it in her palm. She felt no burning, no pain.

"Hold it tight," he ordered. "Don't be afraid."

Clutching the ember in her grasp, she felt it turn cold.

When she opened her eyes and her hand, the man was gone. All that remained was a stone scarab sitting in her palm, smooth and sparkling like the granite of the obelisk. She put it in her pocket and ran for the sleigh, planning to keep it to herself for now, or perhaps forever.

That night after everyone had gone to bed, Beatrice sat at her desk staring at the stone scarab. Tomorrow she was to go with Dr. Brody to visit a young telegraph operator who'd reportedly been receiving strange messages after getting a shock from a faulty machine. The *Evening Star* had teasingly asked, "Is she a new witch?" Beatrice wondered what she might say to the girl that would be of any use. Looking through her notes and journals, she searched for a helpful spell Eleanor might've given her, or a bit of worldly wisdom from Adelaide, or some thoughtful saying of Madame St. Clair's. In the end, she chose to pick up her pen.

ADVICE *for* NEW WITCHES.

It starts with an inkling, a twist in the heart. A sigh, a voice without flesh—announcing somewhere between slumber and waking, "Careful what you wish for, lest you receive it."

Next comes the beholding of inexplicable things. A door, shut and locked, opened by forces unseen. A ball of yarn, unravelled in a heap, rolls itself up again. Take note of mysterious happenings—make lists, keep track. See how wonders multiply when magic is not dismissed.

One needn't carry the blood of ancients to be chosen by Fate. No witch's mark, no gap-toothed smile, no dimple in the chin. Only a sense of longing, a restlessness within.

For the time has come, the day has arrived, as the Spinner of Tales once said, when witches the wide world over are no longer born, but made.

By mystery, magic, hopes and dreams. By communing with ghosts in the dark. By ambition, desire, curiosity and need. By tying knots around the wishes of your heart. By charms, enchantments, incantations and schemes. By mixing blood with graveyard dust. By scratching the names of angels on your skin. By struggle, pain, heartbreak and loss.

To all young women who read by foxfire or dance in the crossroads at night—you, darling ladies, are well on your way, nearly ready to take flight. The path lies ahead, daunting and long, so travel it while you are able. Believe in dreams, ghosts and spectres—ignore them at your peril.

And now, you may ask, how will you know when your making's done?

The answer is quite simple, my dear—by the pricking of your thumbs.

The
END

Acknowledgements

My thanks go out to those who kindly lent their expertise and knowledge during both the research and writing phases of this book: the amazing librarians and archivists at both the New York Historical Society and the NYPL; Angie Oriana Jenkins (belly dancing herbalist extraordinaire); and Bree Hyland of BARRE Studio (whose marvellous dream tea kept my imagination flowing).

Of the many books consulted for this work, the following became companions and guides along the way: *Madison Square: The Park and Its Celebrated Landmarks* by Miriam Berman; *America Bewitched: The Story of Witchcraft After Salem* by Owen Davies; *Wonders of the Invisible World* by Cotton Mather; *More Wonders of the Invisible World* by Robert Calef; *Flowers and Flower Lore* by Hilderic Friend; *Ten Days in a Mad-House* by Nellie Bly; *Opium Fiend* by Steven Martin; *Experimental Investigations of the Spirit Manifestations* by Robert Hare; *The History of Last Night's Dream* by Rodger Kamenetz; *Narratives of the Witchcraft Cases: 1648–1706* by George Lincoln Burr; *Egyptian Obelisks* by Henry Honeychurch Gorringe; and *Woman, Church and State* by Matilda Joslyn Gage; as well as the many writings on folk magic, traditions and witchlore by Gerina Dunwich and the late, great Scott Cunningham.

Many thanks go to the Canada Council for the Arts for their generous and vital support during the writing process.

Much gratitude and appreciation goes to the amazing team at Knopf Canada for their enduring dedication to the written word, especially my editor, Anne Collins, whose sublime intuition for finding truth in language always feels like magic.

Thanks also to Claire Wachtel for lunch at Saks, for quoting Frost and for pointing the way; and to Genevieve Pegg at Orion, who saw the heart of the story from the start.

Special thanks to my agent, Helen Heller, for championing my work, and for her archaeological encouragement "to always dig deeper."

Thank you to my friends and family, far and near who have given me such incredible support and love over the years—Skip, Doug and Lori, for cheering me on through scraped knees and spilt milk; Chris O'Neill and Ken Schwartz at the Ross Creek Centre for the Arts and Two Planks and Passion Theatre for your friendship and for building an artistic haven on the mountain; Marta Pelrine-Bacon, Dawn Jones-Graham and Jon Hyneman for late night conversations, cups of tea and witchy consultations.

As always, the most thanks and all my love go to my nearest and dearest: my sons, Ian and Jonah, who have brought more laughter, joy and wonder to my life than I ever imagined possible; and to my beloved husband, Ian, who is my guiding star, my heart and my "yes and" to everything.

Author's Note

While writing this book I stumbled upon a startling fact—
my nine times great-aunt Mary Ayer Parker was executed for
witchcraft. In the midst of the turmoil that was the Salem
witch trials, she and her daughter Sarah were accused and
imprisoned. Mary, a fifty-five-year-old widow, was later tried
and convicted, and on September 22, 1692, she was hanged at
Gallows Hill. Thanks to an edict that put a stop to subse-
quent hangings, Sarah's life was spared.

As you might imagine, discovering this tragic bit of my
family history inevitably shaped the narrative of *The Witches
of New York*. So many questions now came to my mind as I
wrote—What does the word "witch" truly mean? Had any
vestiges of folk magic survived the witch trials? What had
happened between the witch hunts (of both Europe and
North America) and the constraining, patronizing view of
womanhood held in the Victorian era? Surely there were con-
nections to be made.

As a child who loved to play make-believe, I always preferred to pretend to be a witch rather than a princess—spe-
cifically, Glinda, the good sorceress of Oz. Not the glitzy film
version of Glinda, but the mighty witch that L. Frank Baum
originally created for his wonderful series of Oz books. That
Glinda was wise and savvy, kind yet firm, and always erred
on the side of letting Dorothy find her own way. In hindsight,
I suppose I loved her because she reminded me a lot of my
own mother, a woman who never failed to encourage me to
find magic in the world whenever and wherever I could. My

mother, like Glinda, believed in the powers of intellect, tenacity and intuition ("you've always had the power my dear . . . you just had to learn it for yourself"), and taught me that no girl or woman should ever apologize for such gifts.

L. Frank Baum's vision of Glinda (as well as Ozma, the fairy-touched girl who was the rightful ruler of Oz) was inspired by conversations he had with his mother-in-law, Matilda Joslyn Gage, a woman who was a staunch abolitionist, an unapologetic suffragist and a leading voice in the fight for aboriginal rights in the United States. Also a prolific writer, she encouraged her son-in-law to inhabit his Land of Oz with strong female characters so that his four sons might grow up with role models in their fairy tales that would prepare them for a new, enlightened age. In her seminal work, *Women, Church and State*, published in 1893, Matilda boldly addressed the history of witchcraft and the persecution of women accused of it, drawing many parallels to her own time.

The church degraded woman by destroying her self-respect and teaching her to feel consciousness of guilt in the very fact of her existence.

To this day, an open, confident look upon a woman's face is deprecated as evil.

Death by torture was the method of the church for the repression of woman's intellect, knowledge being held as evil and dangerous in her hands.

The witch was in reality the profoundest thinker, the most advanced scientist of those ages.

The testimony of the ages entirely destroys the assertion sometimes made that witchcraft was merely a species of hysteria.

The treatise was a call to action, a rallying cry to women to reclaim the word "witch." She was tired of female voices being silenced (for being too intelligent, too wise, too feminine, too different). She was tired of seeing women get cast aside—dismissed, ostracized or sent off to asylums. This was the era of Charlotte Perkins Gilman's "The Yellow Wallpaper," and Jean-Martin Charcot's weekly lectures at the Salpêtrière where he paraded his "hysterical" female subjects before the general public. It seemed the hunts hadn't ended, they'd just taken on a more subversive, sinister form.

Sadly, Matilda's work was met with sneers and skepticism, even among a few of her sister suffragists. "Too radical," they said, "too divisive." Yet she persisted, speaking out for the suffragist cause until her death in 1898. I wonder what she'd make of the women's movement today.

I'm guessing she'd say there's still plenty of work to be done. How many times are women still told that their stories, their testimonies, their ideas don't matter? Or that they're only meant for our own gender? How many girls are scolded each day for not smiling? Or shamed for the clothes she chose to wear? Or teased for being too smart? Or refused admittance to school?

Ray Bradbury once wrote, "A witch is born out of the true hungers of her time."

I believe that's true for the witches in this book, for their time as well as mine.

Get ready world, something witchy this way comes.

May 16, 2016,
Scots Bay, NS

A MI M CK AY's debut novel, *The Birth House*, was a #1 best-seller in Canada, winner of three CBA Libris Awards, nominated for the International IMPAC Dublin Literary Award, a finalist for Canada Reads and a book-club favourite around the world. Her second novel, *The Virgin Cure*, also a national bestseller and a Best Book pick across numerous lists, was inspired by the life of her great-great-grandmother, Dr. Sarah Fonda Mackintosh, a female physician in nineteenth-century New York. Born and raised in Indiana, McKay now lives in Nova Scotia.